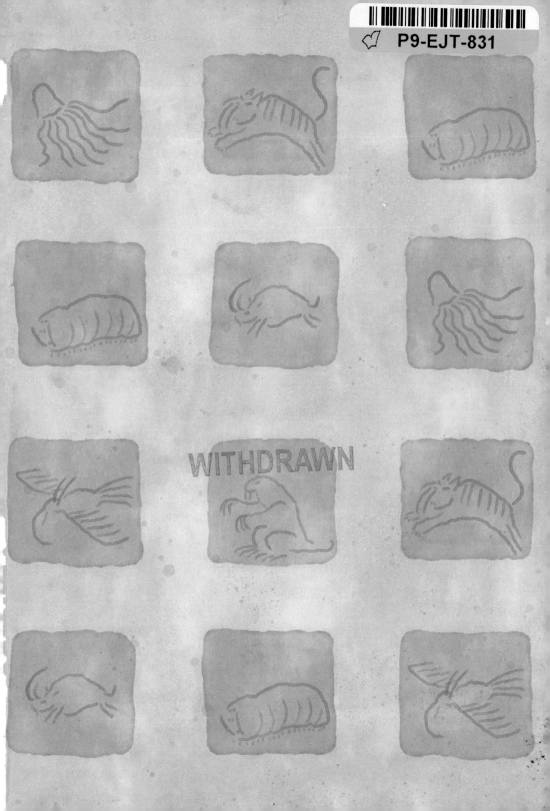

CAVEBOY DAVE

MORE SCRAWNY THAN BRAWNY

by Aaron Reynolds

illustrated by Phil McAndrew

VIKING

VIKING
An imprint of Penguin Random House LLC
375 Hudson Street
New York, New York 10014

First published in the United States of America by Viking,
an imprint of Penguin Random House LLC, 2016

Text copyright © 2016 by Aaron Reynolds
Illustrations copyright © 2016 by Phil McAndrew

LIBRARY OF CONGRESS CATALOGING-IN-PUBLICATION DATA
Names: Reynolds, Aaron, 1970–author. | McAndrew, Phil, illustrator.
Title: Caveboy Dave : more scrawny than brawny / Aaron Reynolds ; illustrated
by Phil McAndrew.
Other titles: More scrawny than brawny
Description: New York : Viking Books for Young Readers, 2016. | Series:
Caveboy Dave ; 1 | Summary: "A young caveman named Dave must complete a
dangerous rite of passage with his peers"—Provided by publisher.
Identifiers: LCCN 2016003728| ISBN 9780147516589 (paperback)
ISBN 9780451475473 (hardcover)
Subjects: LCSH: Graphic novels. | CYAC: Graphic novels. | Prehistoric
peoples—Fiction. | Humorous stories. | BISAC: JUVENILE FICTION / Comics &
Graphic Novels / General. | JUVENILE FICTION / Animals / Dinosaurs &
Prehistoric Creatures. | JUVENILE FICTION / Humorous Stories.
Classification: LCC PZ7.7.R49 Cav 2016 | DDC 741.5/973—dc23 LC record available at
https://lccn.loc.gov/2016003728

Manufactured in China

1   3   5   7   9   10   8   6   4   2

To Lori Kilkelly, cool chick, great friend,
and more brawny than scrawny. - A. R.

For my mother, Joelle, and my father, Mike,
who taught me to hunt and invent. - P. M.

CAVEBOY DAVE

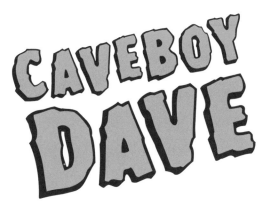

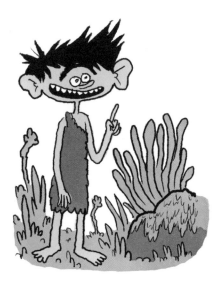

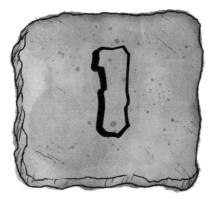

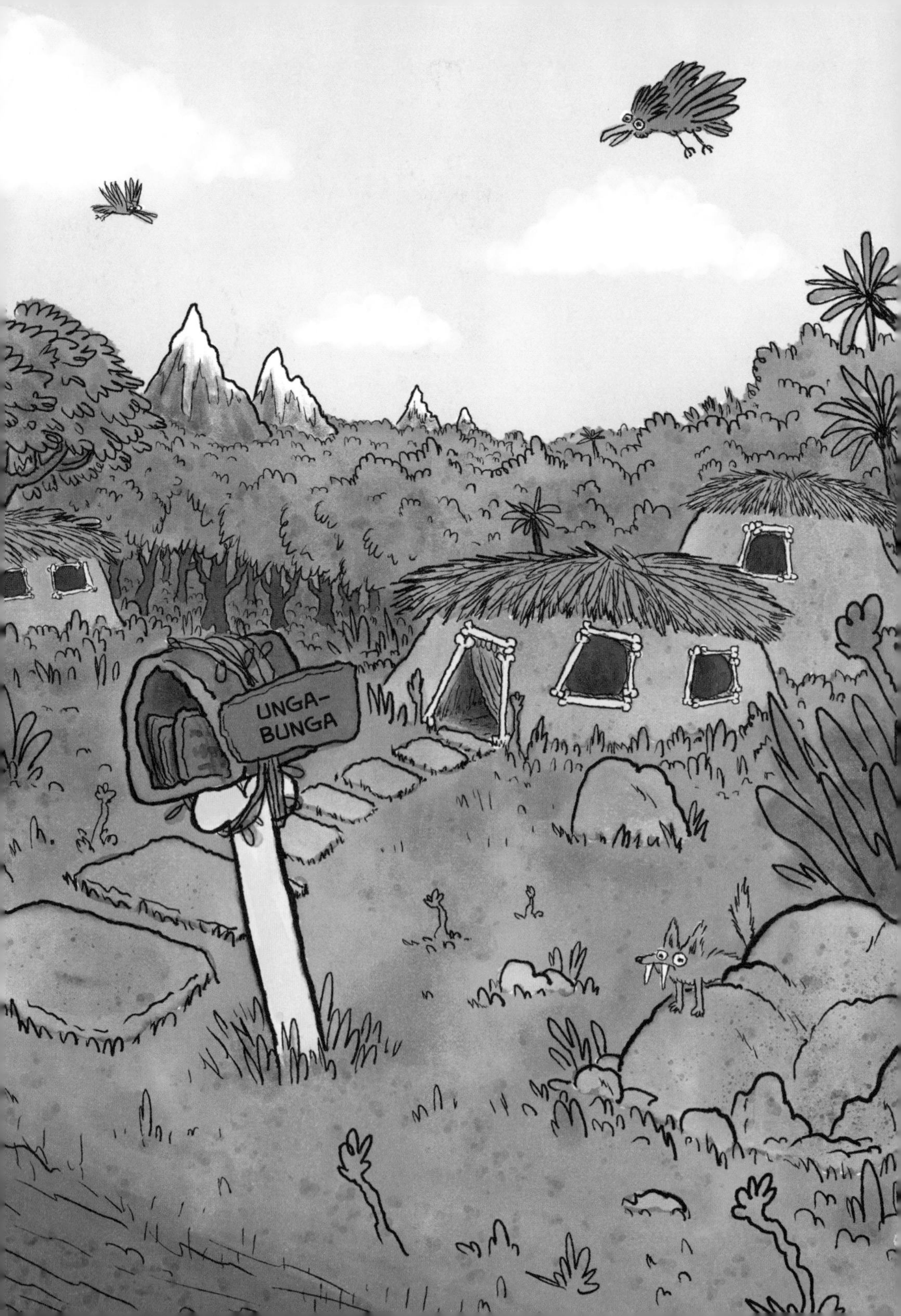
UNGA-
BUNGA

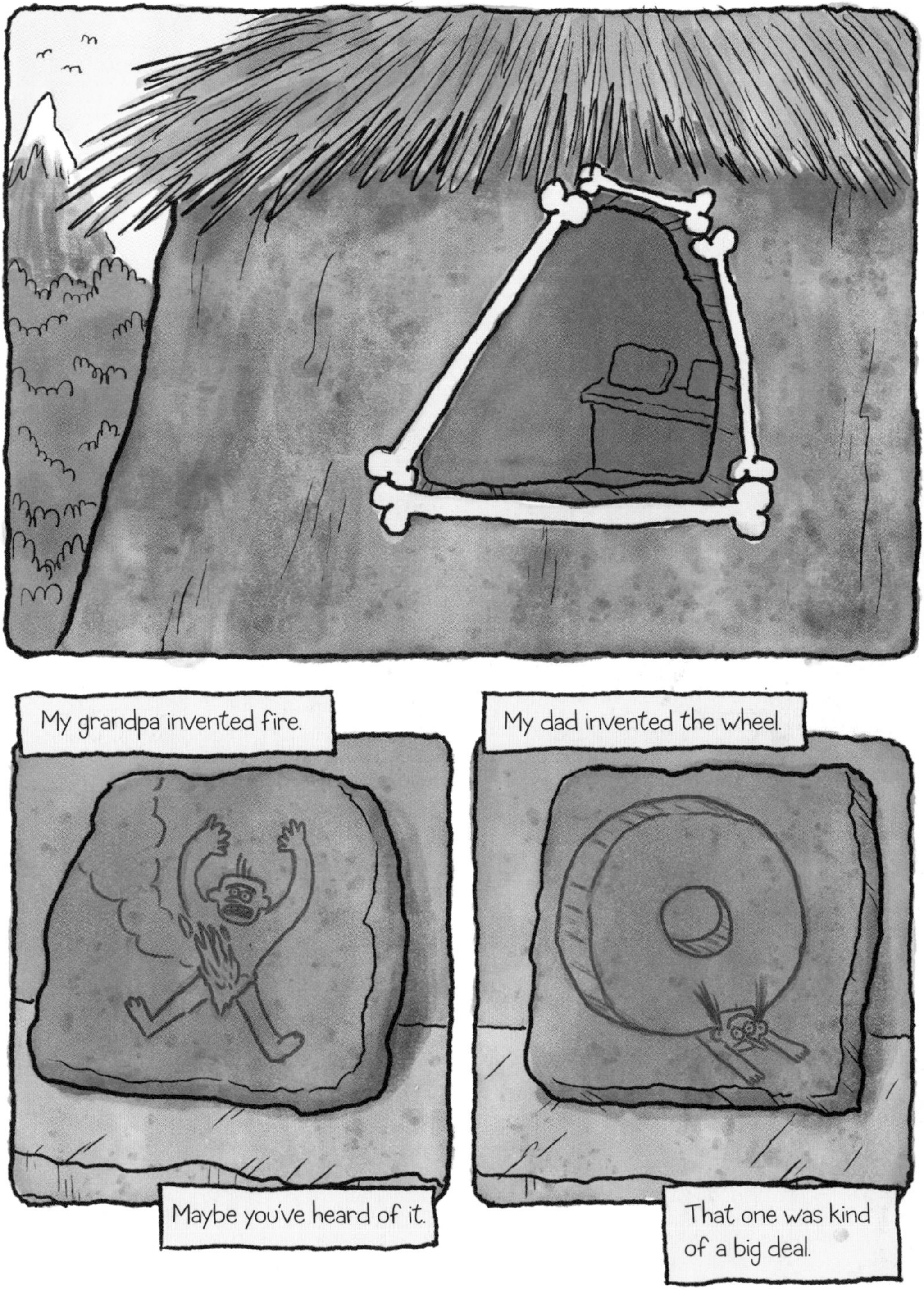
My grandpa invented fire.
Maybe you've heard of it.
My dad invented the wheel.
That one was kind of a big deal.

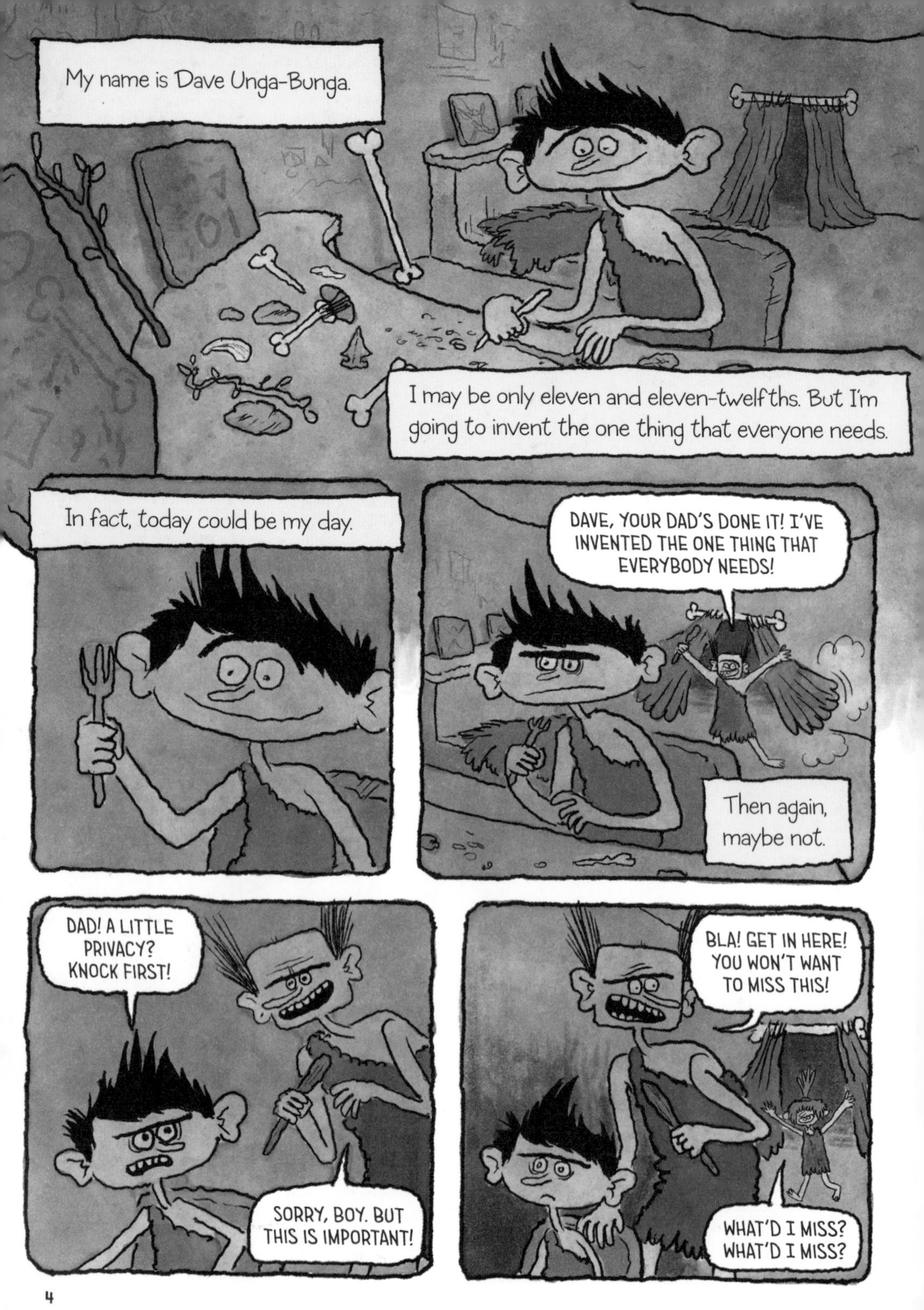

My name is Dave Unga-Bunga.
I may be only eleven and eleven-twelfths. But I'm going to invent the one thing that everyone needs.
In fact, today could be my day.
DAVE, YOUR DAD'S DONE IT! I'VE INVENTED THE ONE THING THAT EVERYBODY NEEDS!
Then again, maybe not.
DAD! A LITTLE PRIVACY? KNOCK FIRST!
SORRY, BOY. BUT THIS IS IMPORTANT!
BLA! GET IN HERE! YOU WON'T WANT TO MISS THIS!
WHAT'D I MISS? WHAT'D I MISS?

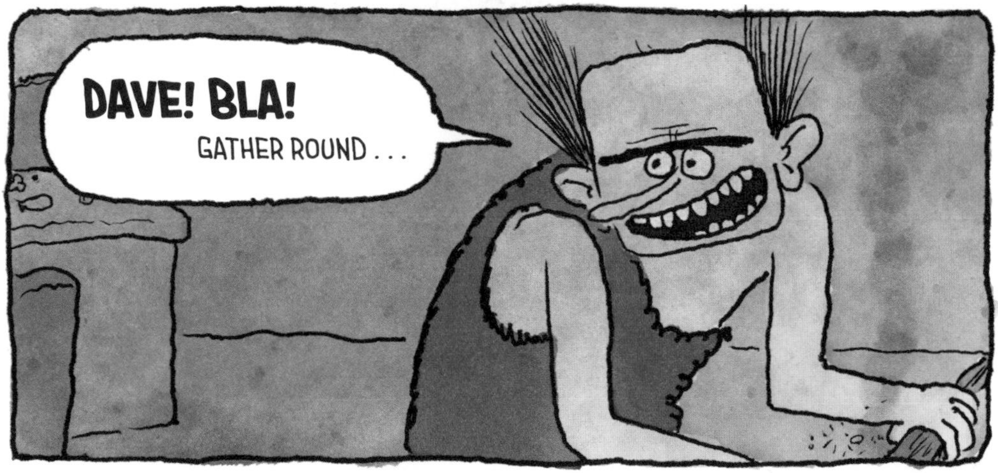
DAVE! BLA!
GATHER ROUND . . .

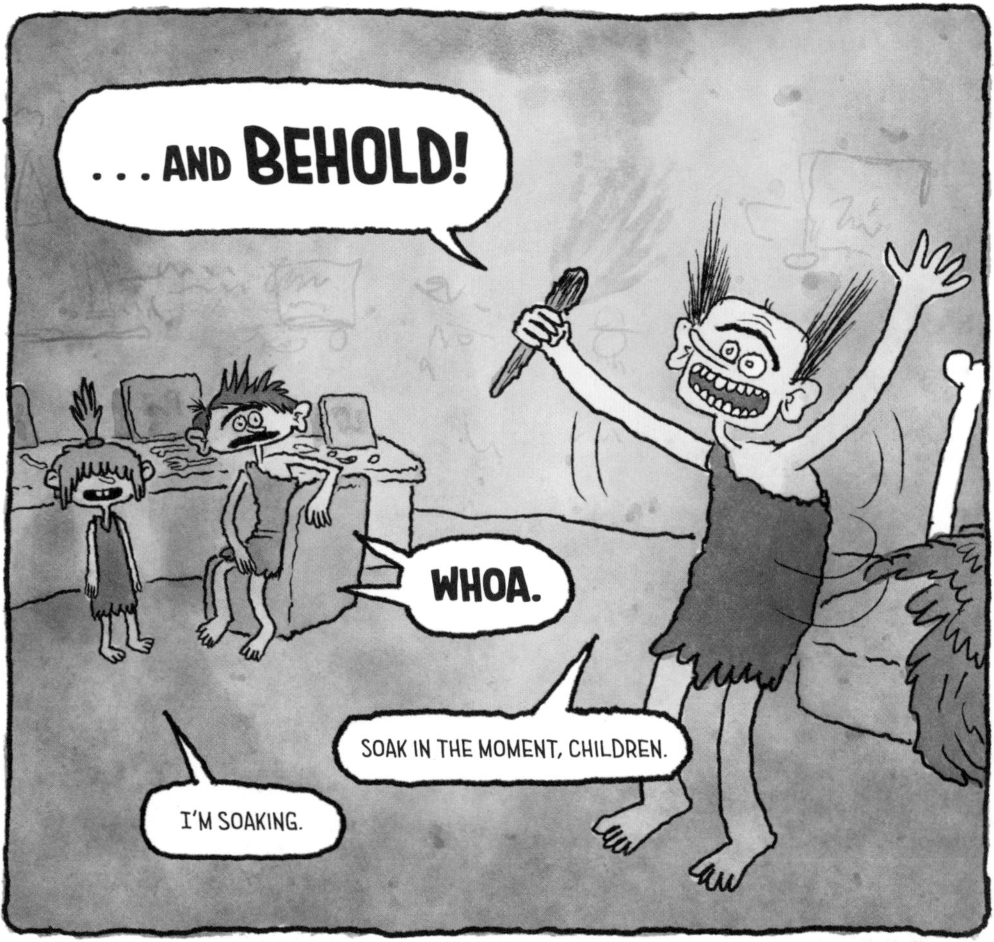
. . . AND BEHOLD!
WHOA.
SOAK IN THE MOMENT, CHILDREN.
I'M SOAKING.

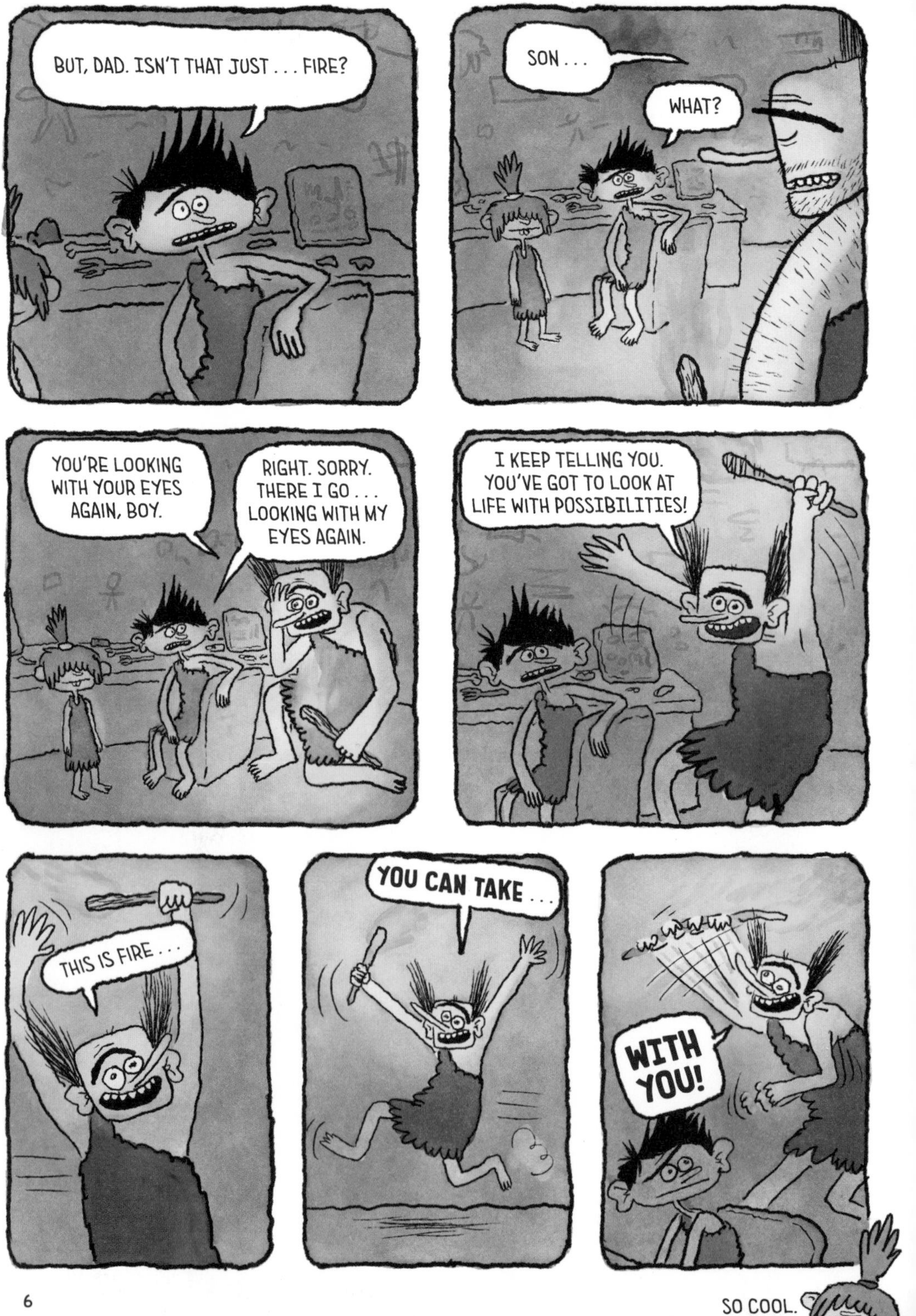
BUT, DAD. ISN'T THAT JUST . . . FIRE?
SON . . .
WHAT?
YOU'RE LOOKING WITH YOUR EYES AGAIN, BOY.
RIGHT. SORRY. THERE I GO . . . LOOKING WITH MY EYES AGAIN.
I KEEP TELLING YOU. YOU'VE GOT TO LOOK AT LIFE WITH POSSIBILITIES!
THIS IS FIRE . . .
YOU CAN TAKE . . .
WITH YOU!
SO COOL.

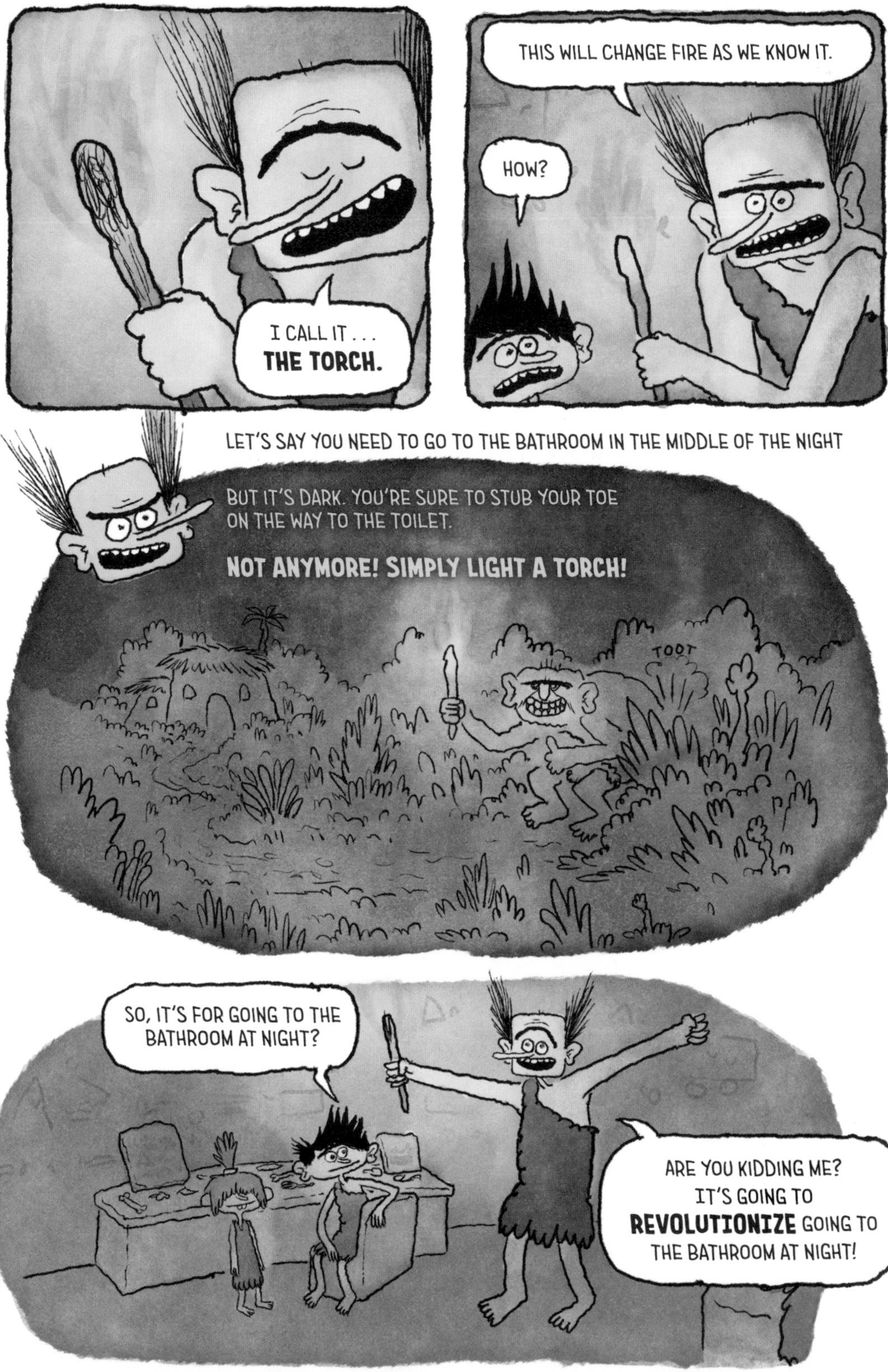
I CALL IT . . .
THE TORCH.
THIS WILL CHANGE FIRE AS WE KNOW IT.
HOW?
LET'S SAY YOU NEED TO GO TO THE BATHROOM IN THE MIDDLE OF THE NIGHT
BUT IT'S DARK. YOU'RE SURE TO STUB YOUR TOE ON THE WAY TO THE TOILET.
NOT ANYMORE! SIMPLY LIGHT A TORCH!
TOOT
SO, IT'S FOR GOING TO THE BATHROOM AT NIGHT?
ARE YOU KIDDING ME? IT'S GOING TO REVOLUTIONIZE GOING TO THE BATHROOM AT NIGHT!

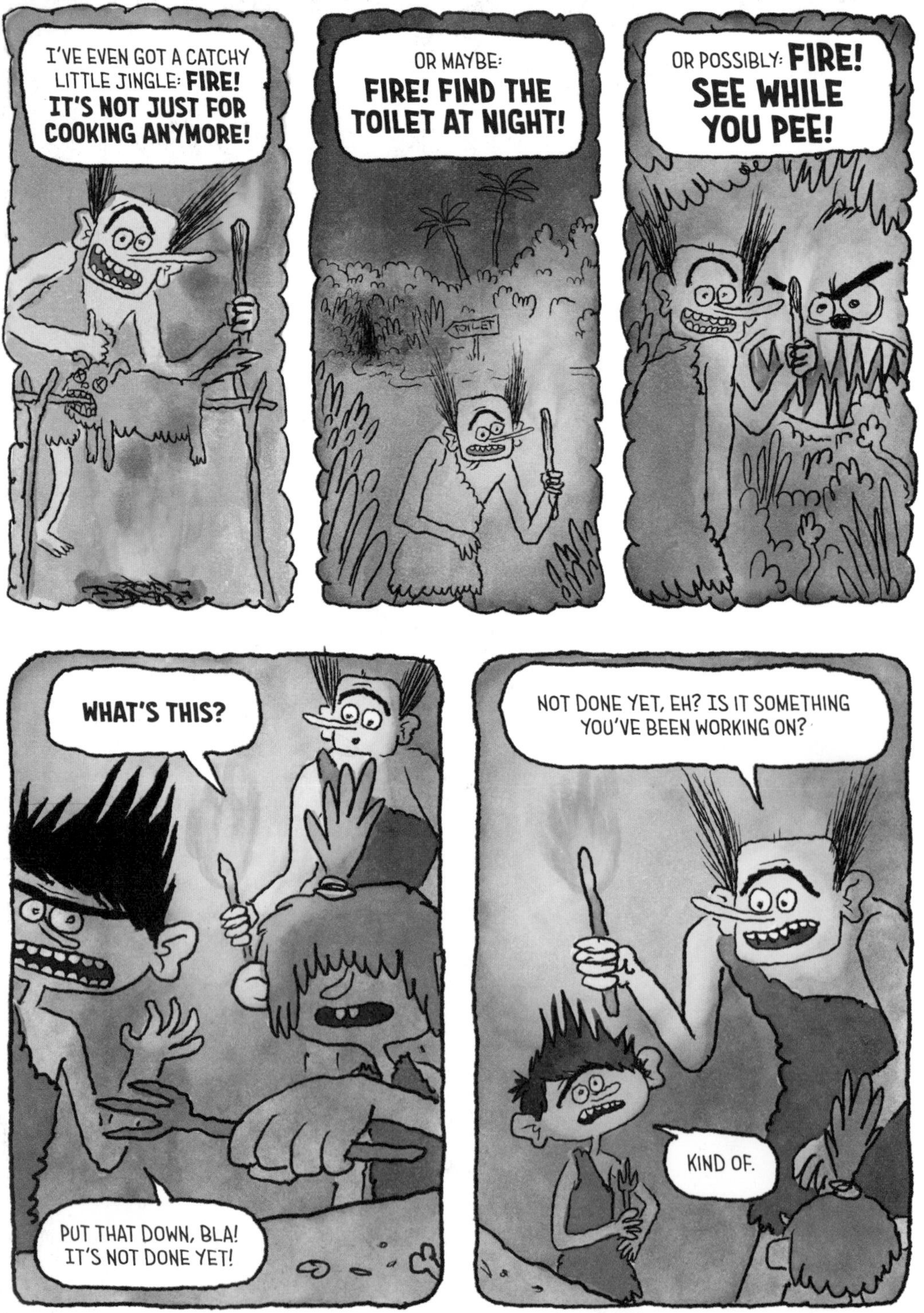
I'VE EVEN GOT A CATCHY LITTLE JINGLE: **FIRE! IT'S NOT JUST FOR COOKING ANYMORE!**
OR MAYBE: **FIRE! FIND THE TOILET AT NIGHT!**
TOILET
OR POSSIBLY: **FIRE! SEE WHILE YOU PEE!**
WHAT'S THIS?
PUT THAT DOWN, BLA! IT'S NOT DONE YET!
NOT DONE YET, EH? IS IT SOMETHING YOU'VE BEEN WORKING ON?
KIND OF.

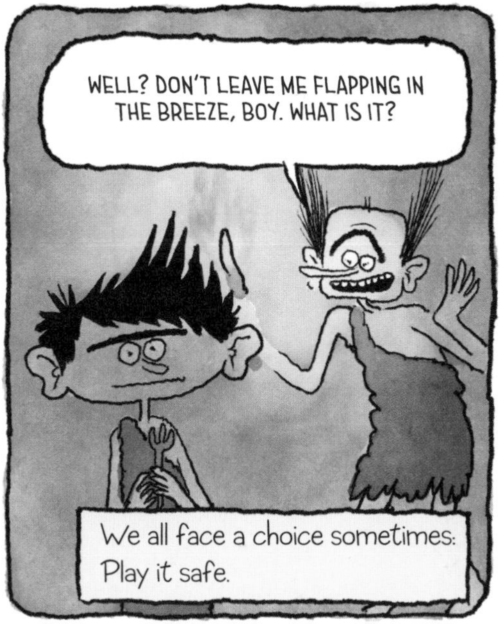

WELL? DON'T LEAVE ME FLAPPING IN THE BREEZE, BOY. WHAT IS IT?
We all face a choice sometimes:
Play it safe.

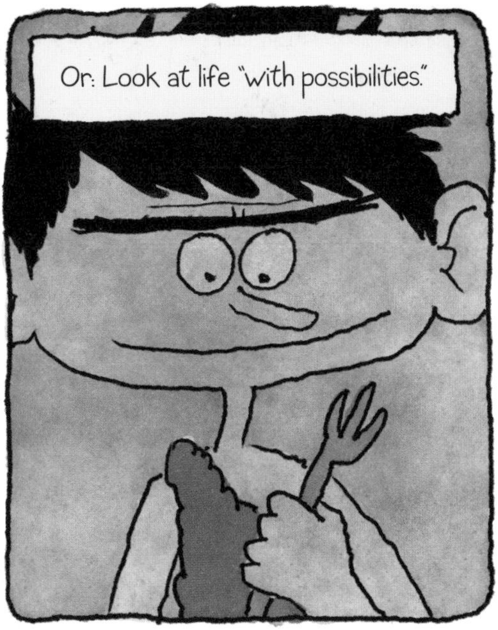

Or: Look at life "with possibilities."

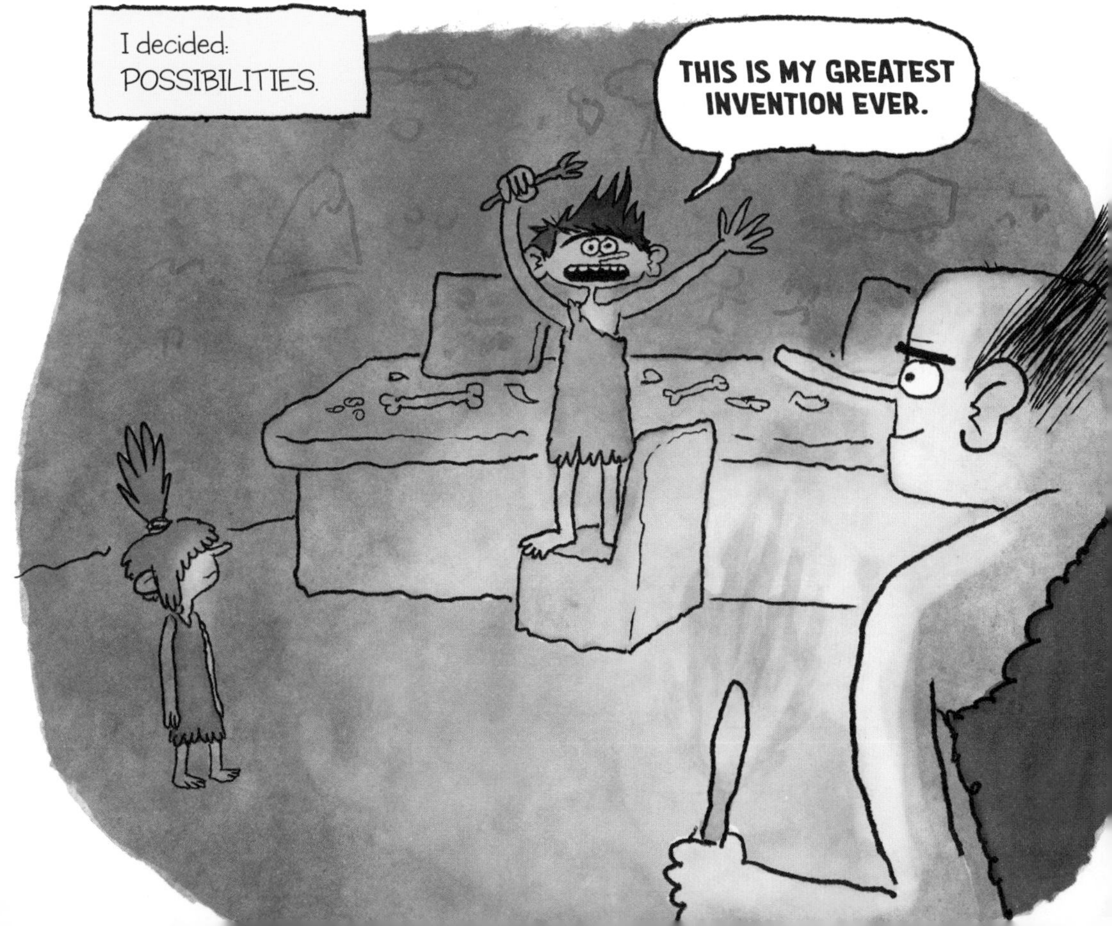

I decided:
POSSIBILITIES.
THIS IS MY GREATEST INVENTION EVER.

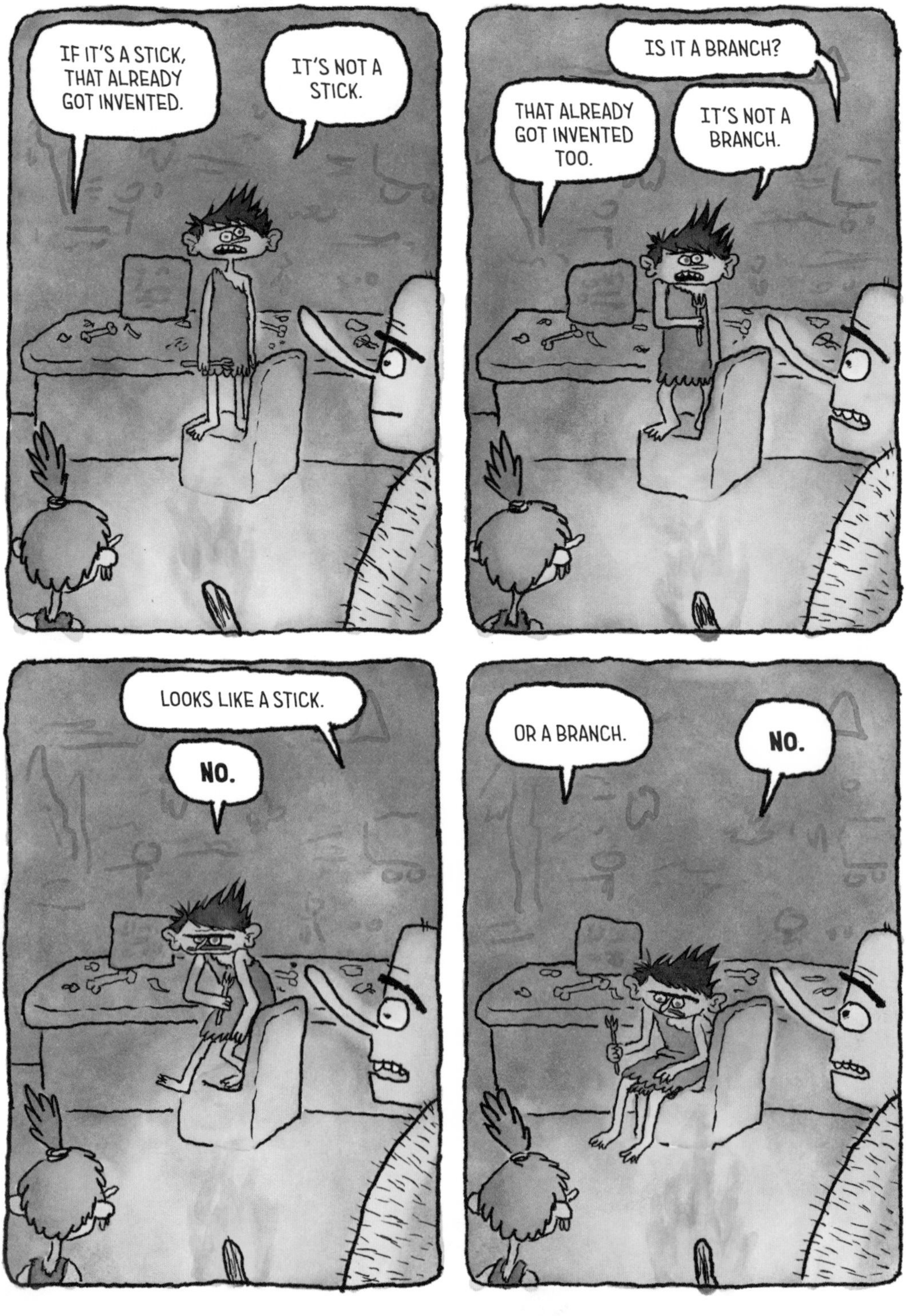

IF IT'S A STICK, THAT ALREADY GOT INVENTED.
IT'S NOT A STICK.
IS IT A BRANCH?
THAT ALREADY GOT INVENTED TOO.
IT'S NOT A BRANCH.
LOOKS LIKE A STICK.
NO.
OR A BRANCH.
NO.

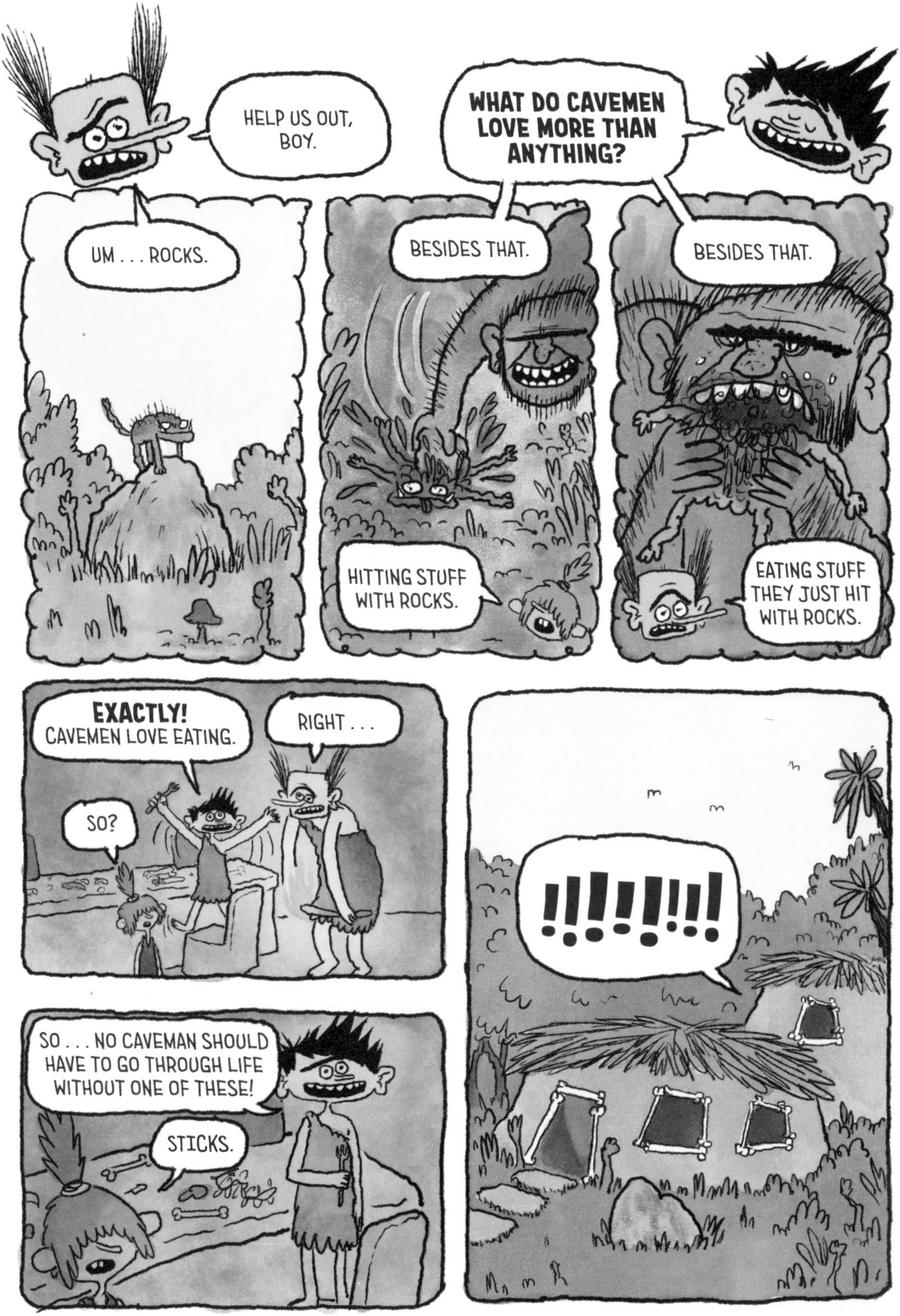
HELP US OUT, BOY.
WHAT DO CAVEMEN LOVE MORE THAN ANYTHING?
UM . . . ROCKS.
BESIDES THAT.
HITTING STUFF WITH ROCKS.
BESIDES THAT.
EATING STUFF THEY JUST HIT WITH ROCKS.
EXACTLY! CAVEMEN LOVE EATING.
RIGHT . . .
SO?
SO . . . NO CAVEMAN SHOULD HAVE TO GO THROUGH LIFE WITHOUT ONE OF THESE!
STICKS.
!!!!!!!!

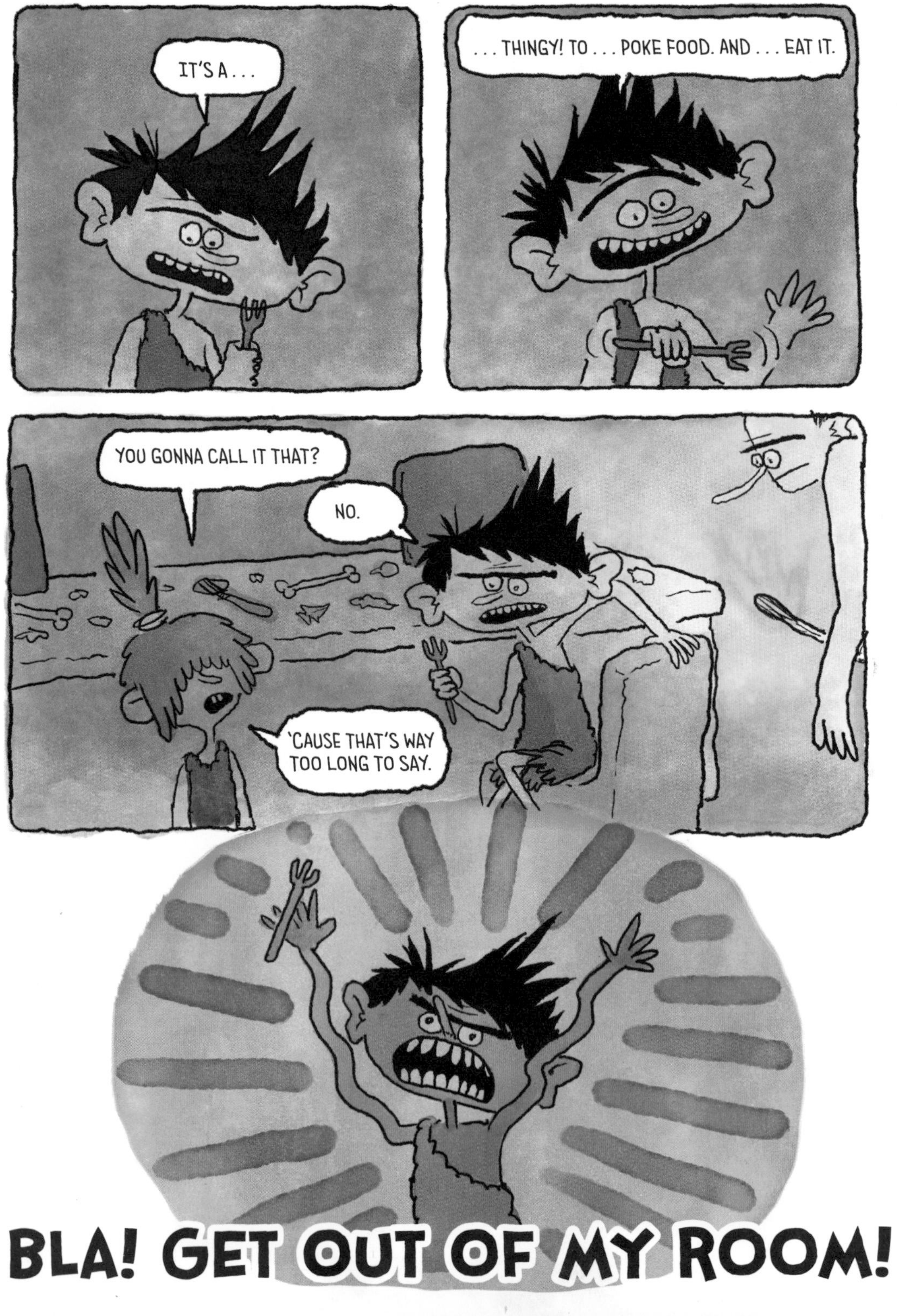
IT'S A . . .
. . . THINGY! TO . . . POKE FOOD. AND . . . EAT IT.
YOU GONNA CALL IT THAT?
NO.
'CAUSE THAT'S WAY TOO LONG TO SAY.
BLA! GET OUT OF MY ROOM!

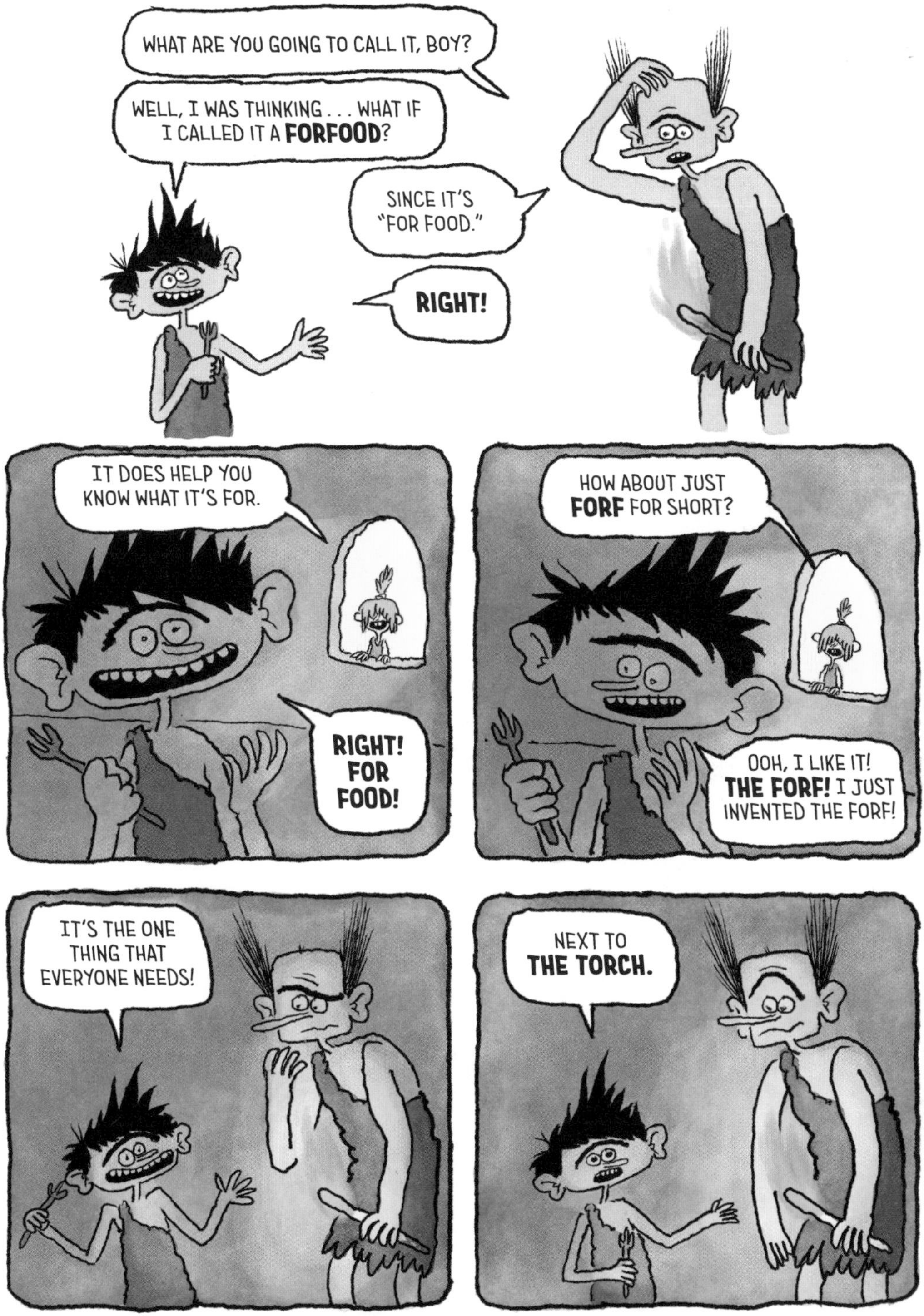
WHAT ARE YOU GOING TO CALL IT, BOY?
WELL, I WAS THINKING . . . WHAT IF I CALLED IT A **FORFOOD**?
SINCE IT'S "FOR FOOD."
RIGHT!
IT DOES HELP YOU KNOW WHAT IT'S FOR.
RIGHT! FOR FOOD!
HOW ABOUT JUST **FORF** FOR SHORT?
OOH, I LIKE IT! **THE FORF!** I JUST INVENTED THE FORF!
IT'S THE ONE THING THAT EVERYONE NEEDS!
NEXT TO **THE TORCH.**

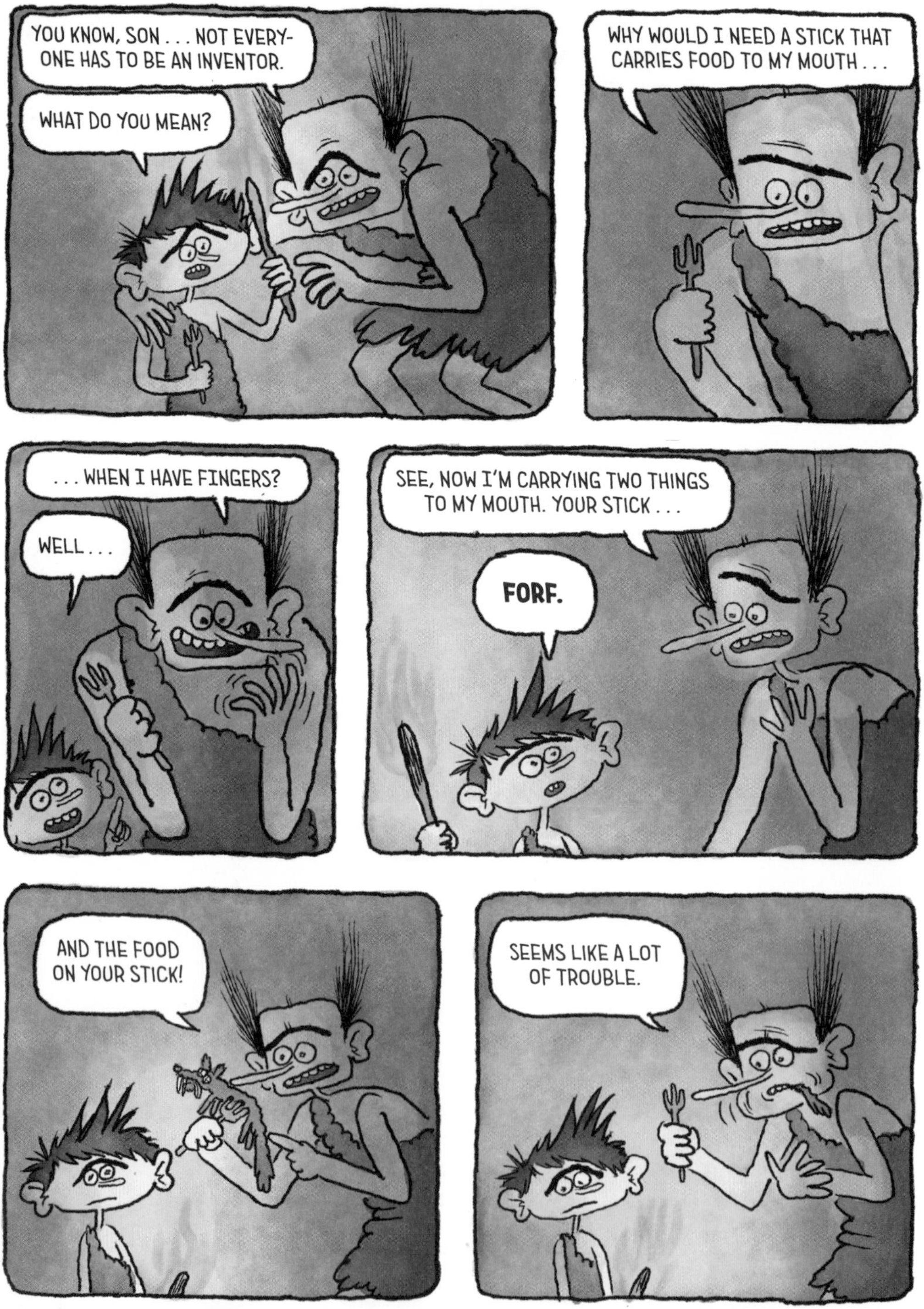
YOU KNOW, SON . . . NOT EVERY-ONE HAS TO BE AN INVENTOR.
WHAT DO YOU MEAN?
WHY WOULD I NEED A STICK THAT CARRIES FOOD TO MY MOUTH . . .
. . . WHEN I HAVE FINGERS?
WELL . . .
SEE, NOW I'M CARRYING TWO THINGS TO MY MOUTH. YOUR STICK . . .
FORF.
AND THE FOOD ON YOUR STICK!
SEEMS LIKE A LOT OF TROUBLE.

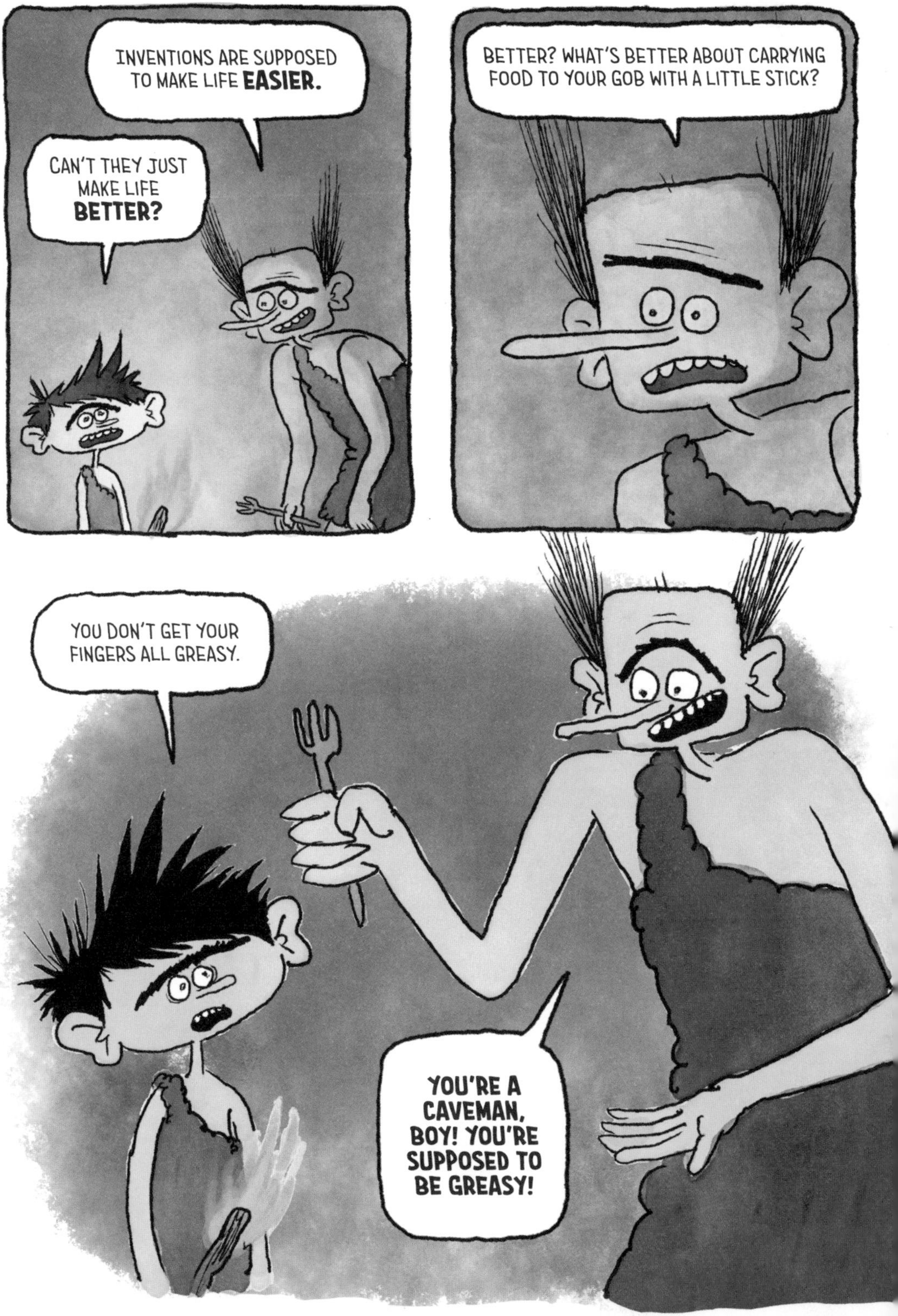
INVENTIONS ARE SUPPOSED TO MAKE LIFE **EASIER.**
CAN'T THEY JUST MAKE LIFE **BETTER?**
BETTER? WHAT'S BETTER ABOUT CARRYING FOOD TO YOUR GOB WITH A LITTLE STICK?
YOU DON'T GET YOUR FINGERS ALL GREASY.
YOU'RE A CAVEMAN, BOY! YOU'RE SUPPOSED TO BE GREASY!

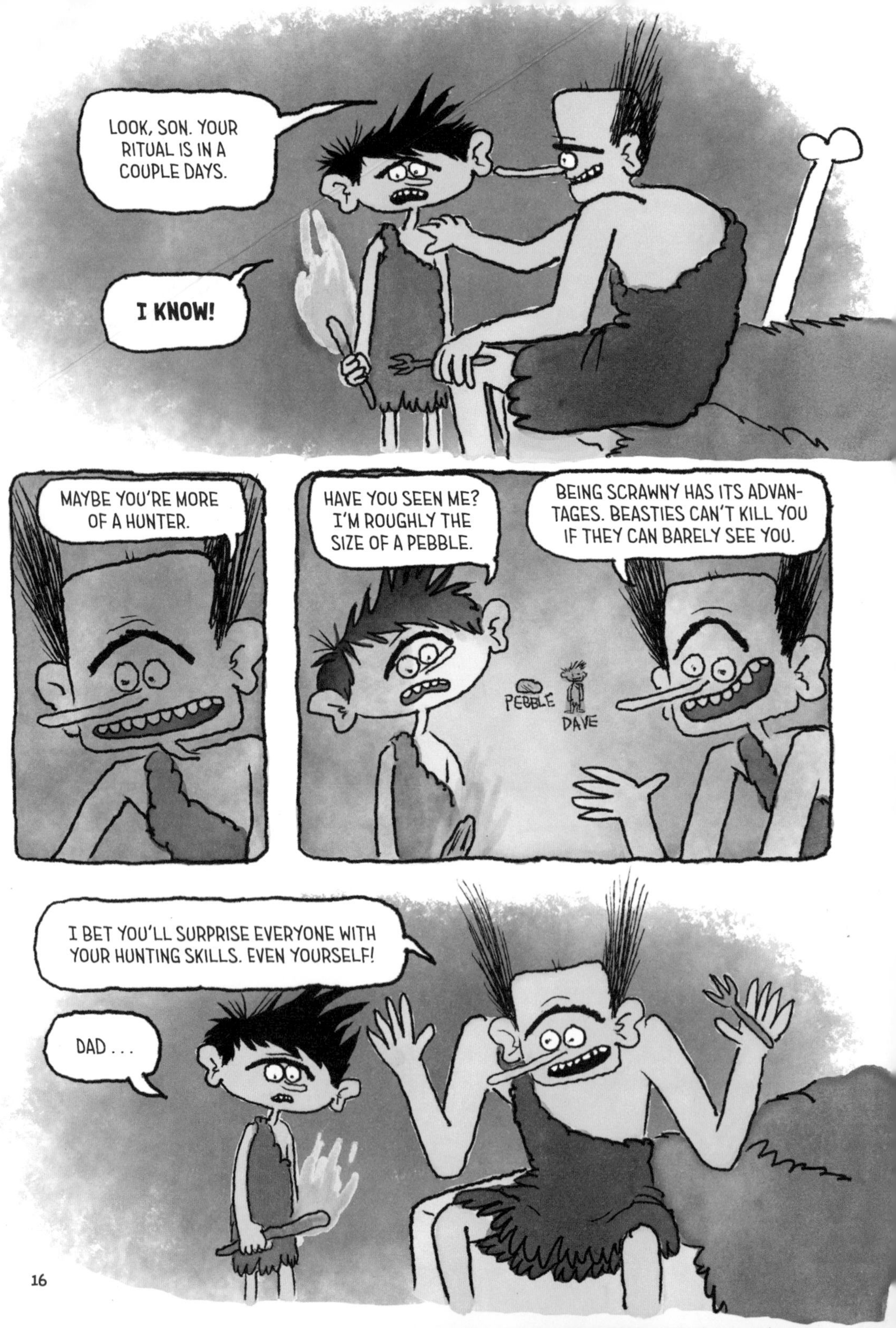
LOOK, SON. YOUR RITUAL IS IN A COUPLE DAYS.
I KNOW!
MAYBE YOU'RE MORE OF A HUNTER.
HAVE YOU SEEN ME? I'M ROUGHLY THE SIZE OF A PEBBLE.
PEBBLE
DAVE
BEING SCRAWNY HAS ITS ADVANTAGES. BEASTIES CAN'T KILL YOU IF THEY CAN BARELY SEE YOU.
I BET YOU'LL SURPRISE EVERYONE WITH YOUR HUNTING SKILLS. EVEN YOURSELF!
DAD . . .

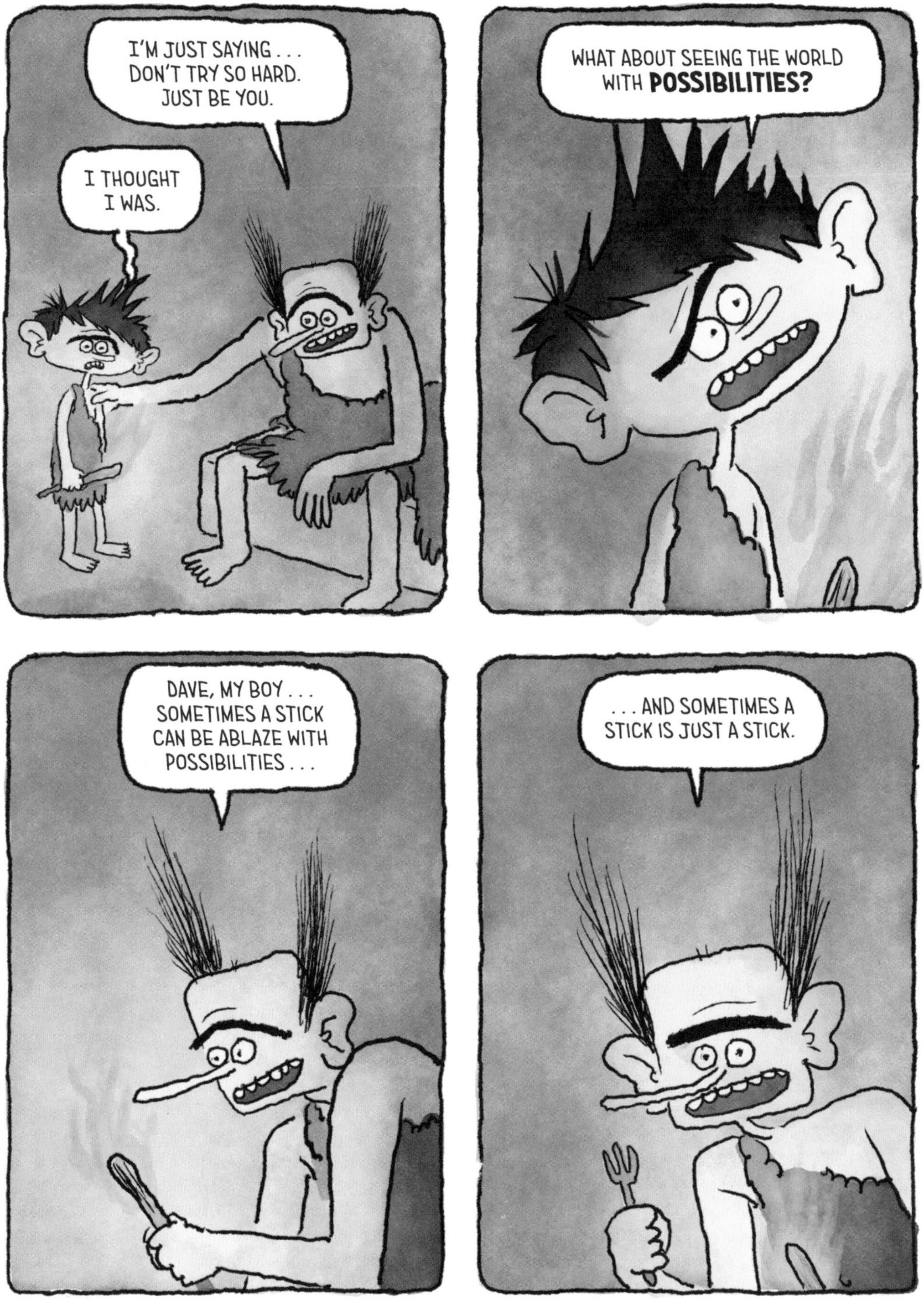
I'M JUST SAYING . . . DON'T TRY SO HARD. JUST BE YOU.
I THOUGHT I WAS.
WHAT ABOUT SEEING THE WORLD WITH **POSSIBILITIES?**
DAVE, MY BOY . . . SOMETIMES A STICK CAN BE ABLAZE WITH POSSIBILITIES . . .
. . . AND SOMETIMES A STICK IS JUST A STICK.

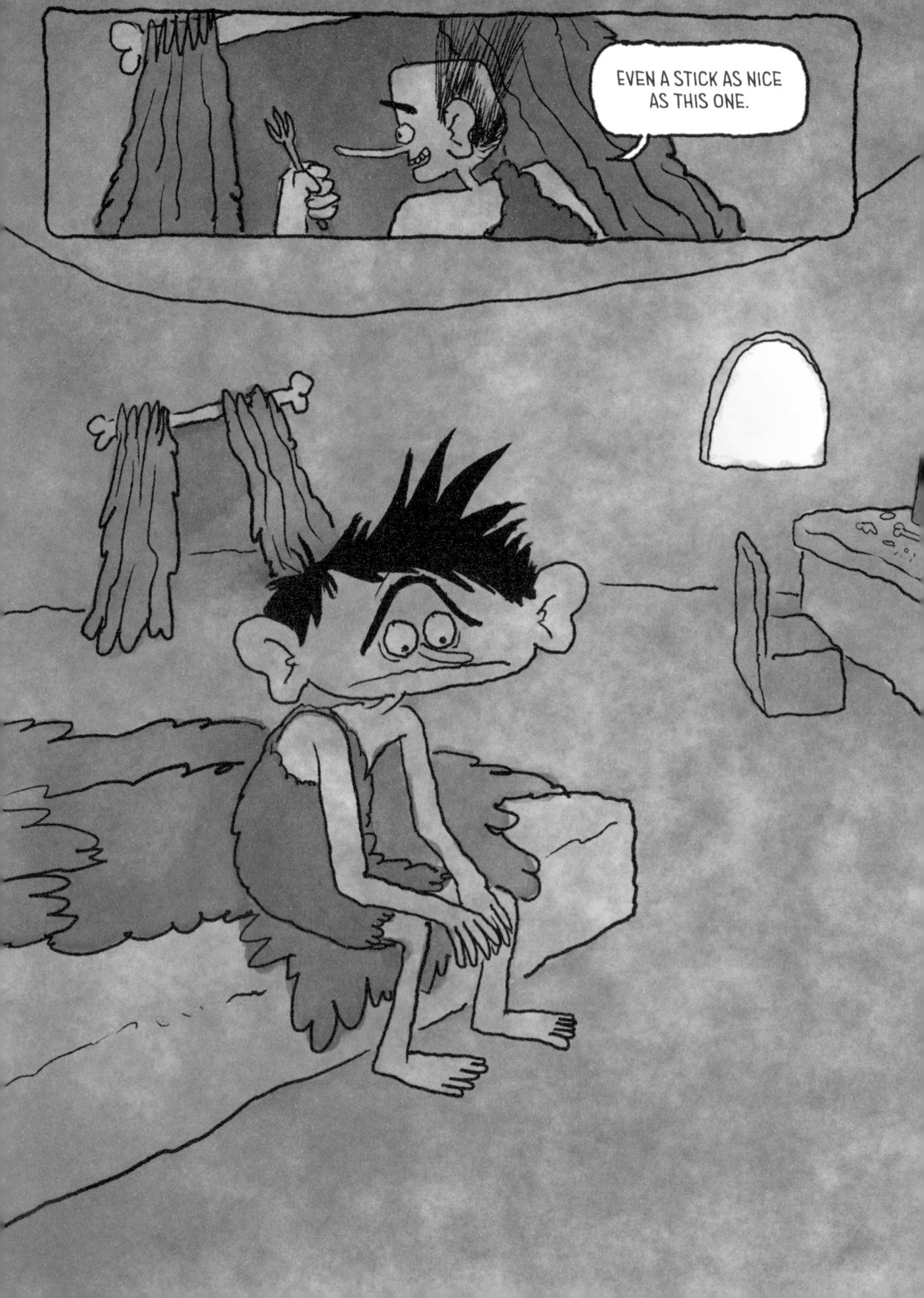
EVEN A STICK AS NICE AS THIS ONE.

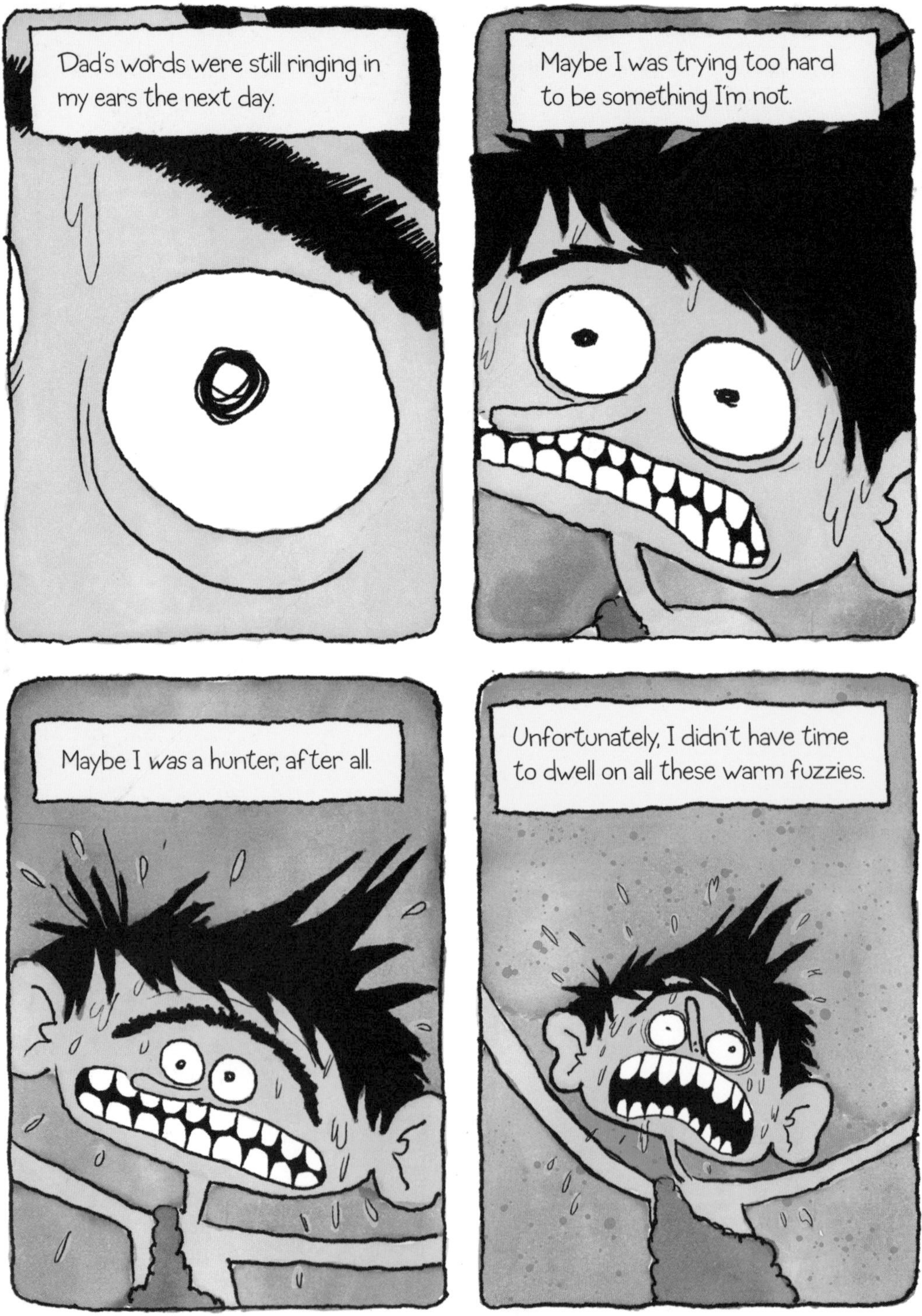
Dad's words were still ringing in my ears the next day.
Maybe I was trying too hard to be something I'm not.
Maybe I *was* a hunter, after all.
Unfortunately, I didn't have time to dwell on all these warm fuzzies.

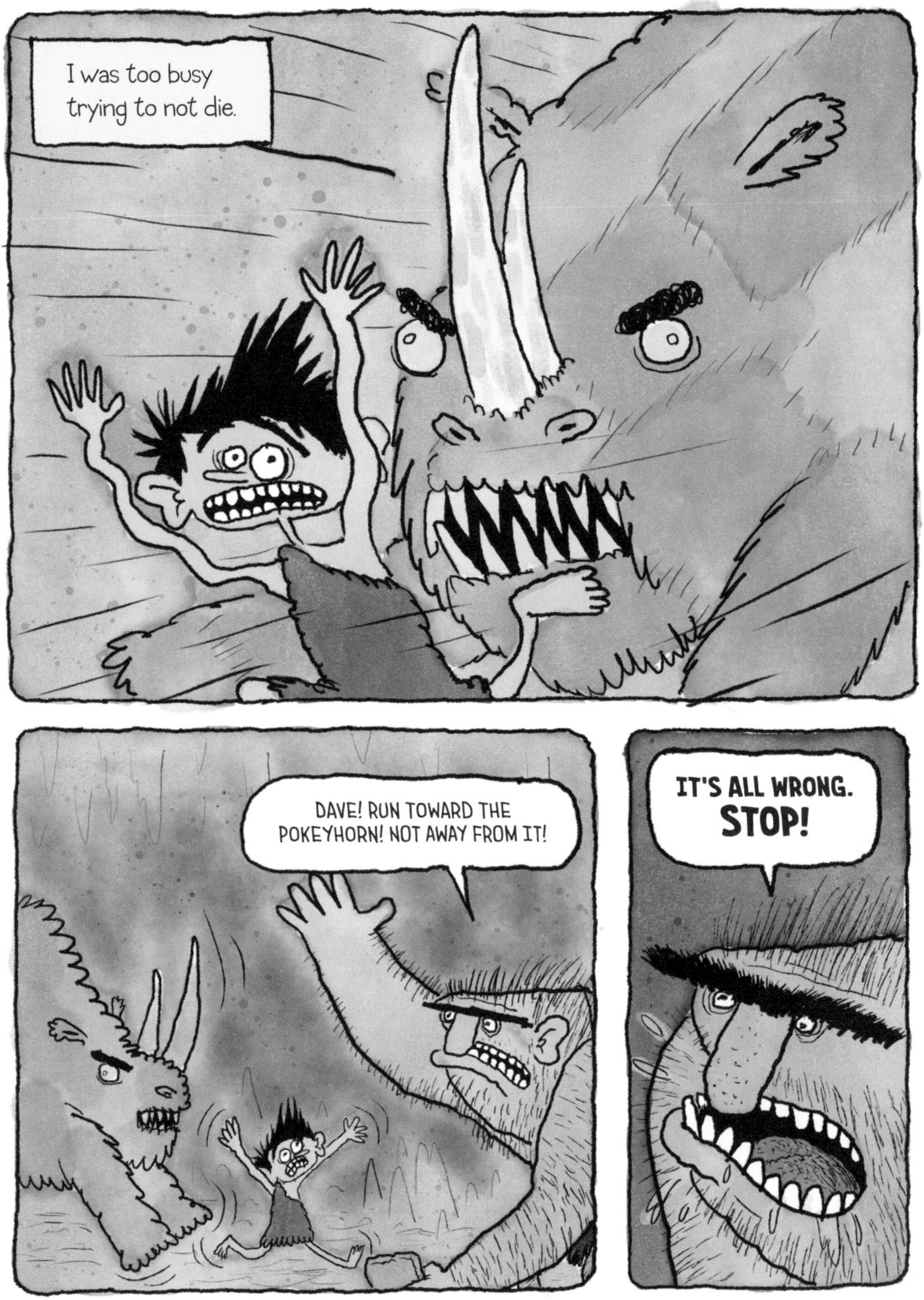
I was too busy trying to not die.
DAVE! RUN TOWARD THE POKEYHORN! NOT AWAY FROM IT!
IT'S ALL WRONG. STOP!

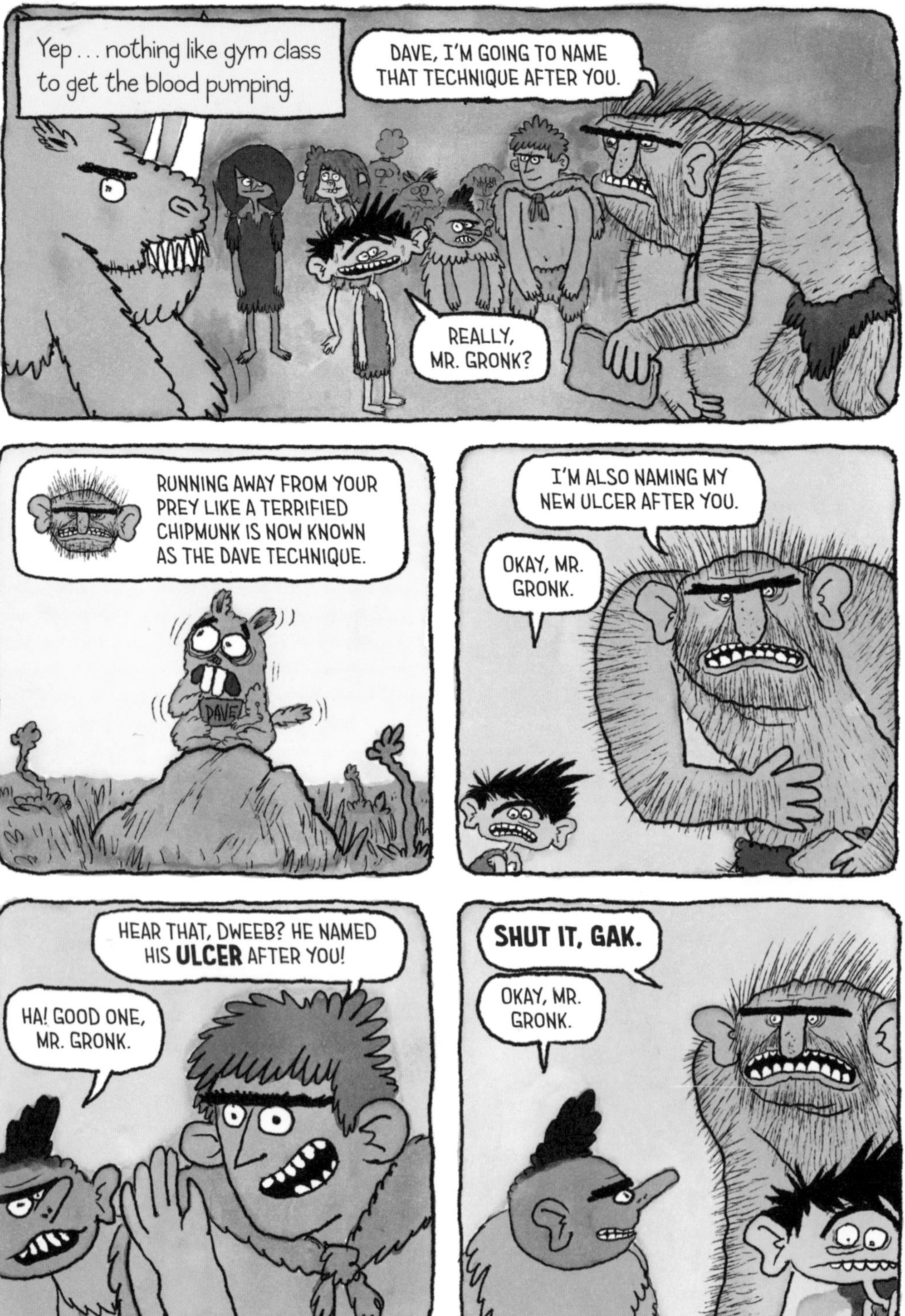

Yep . . . nothing like gym class to get the blood pumping.
DAVE, I'M GOING TO NAME THAT TECHNIQUE AFTER YOU.
REALLY, MR. GRONK?
RUNNING AWAY FROM YOUR PREY LIKE A TERRIFIED CHIPMUNK IS NOW KNOWN AS THE DAVE TECHNIQUE.
DAVE
I'M ALSO NAMING MY NEW ULCER AFTER YOU.
OKAY, MR. GRONK.
HEAR THAT, DWEEB? HE NAMED HIS **ULCER** AFTER YOU!
HA! GOOD ONE, MR. GRONK.
SHUT IT, GAK.
OKAY, MR. GRONK.

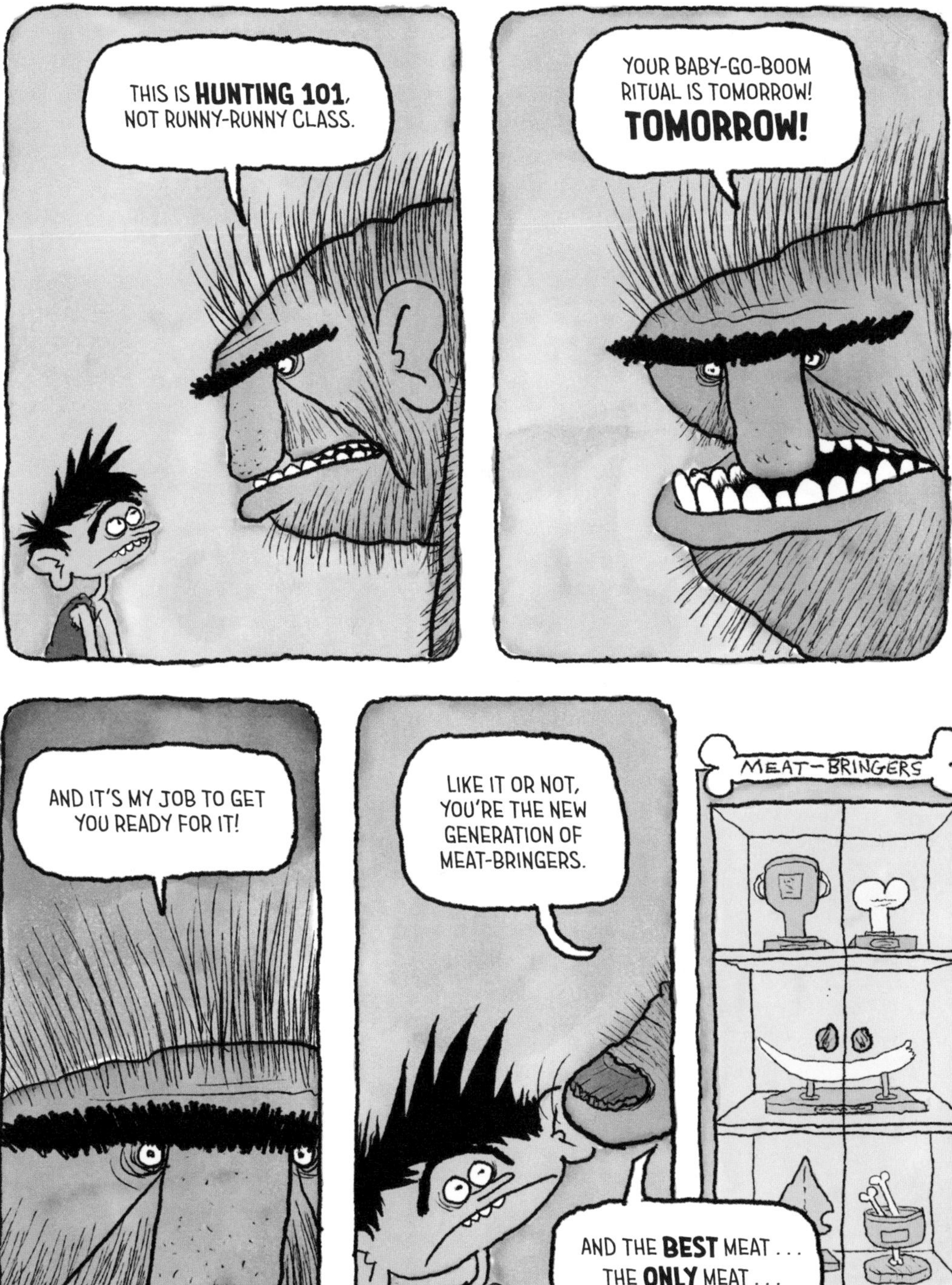
THIS IS **HUNTING 101**, NOT RUNNY-RUNNY CLASS.
YOUR BABY-GO-BOOM RITUAL IS TOMORROW! **TOMORROW!**
AND IT'S MY JOB TO GET YOU READY FOR IT!
LIKE IT OR NOT, YOU'RE THE NEW GENERATION OF MEAT-BRINGERS.
MEAT–BRINGERS
AND THE **BEST** MEAT . . . THE **ONLY** MEAT . . . COMES FROM THE **BIG SIX**.

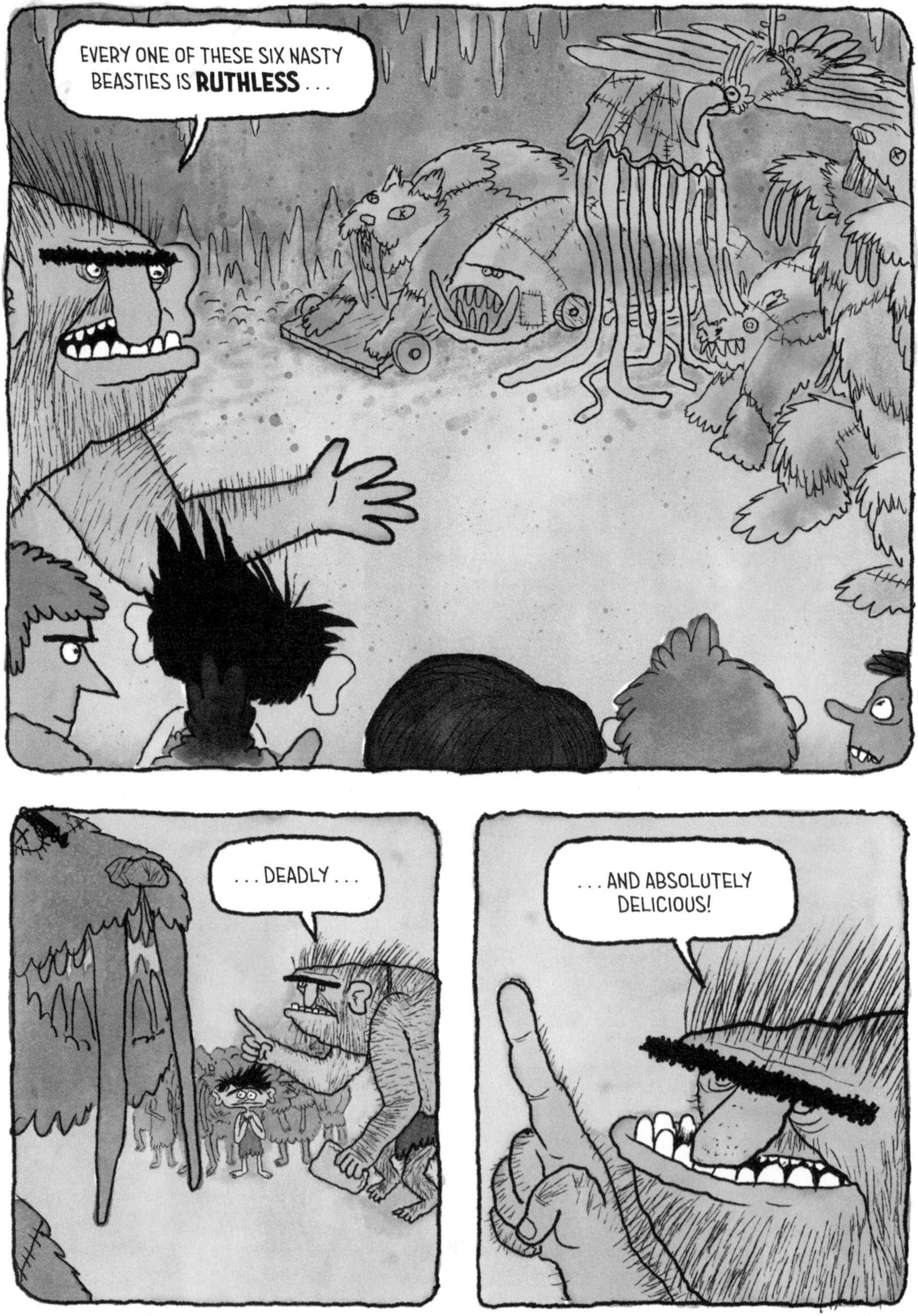
EVERY ONE OF THESE SIX NASTY BEASTIES IS **RUTHLESS** . . .
. . . DEADLY . . .
. . . AND ABSOLUTELY DELICIOUS!

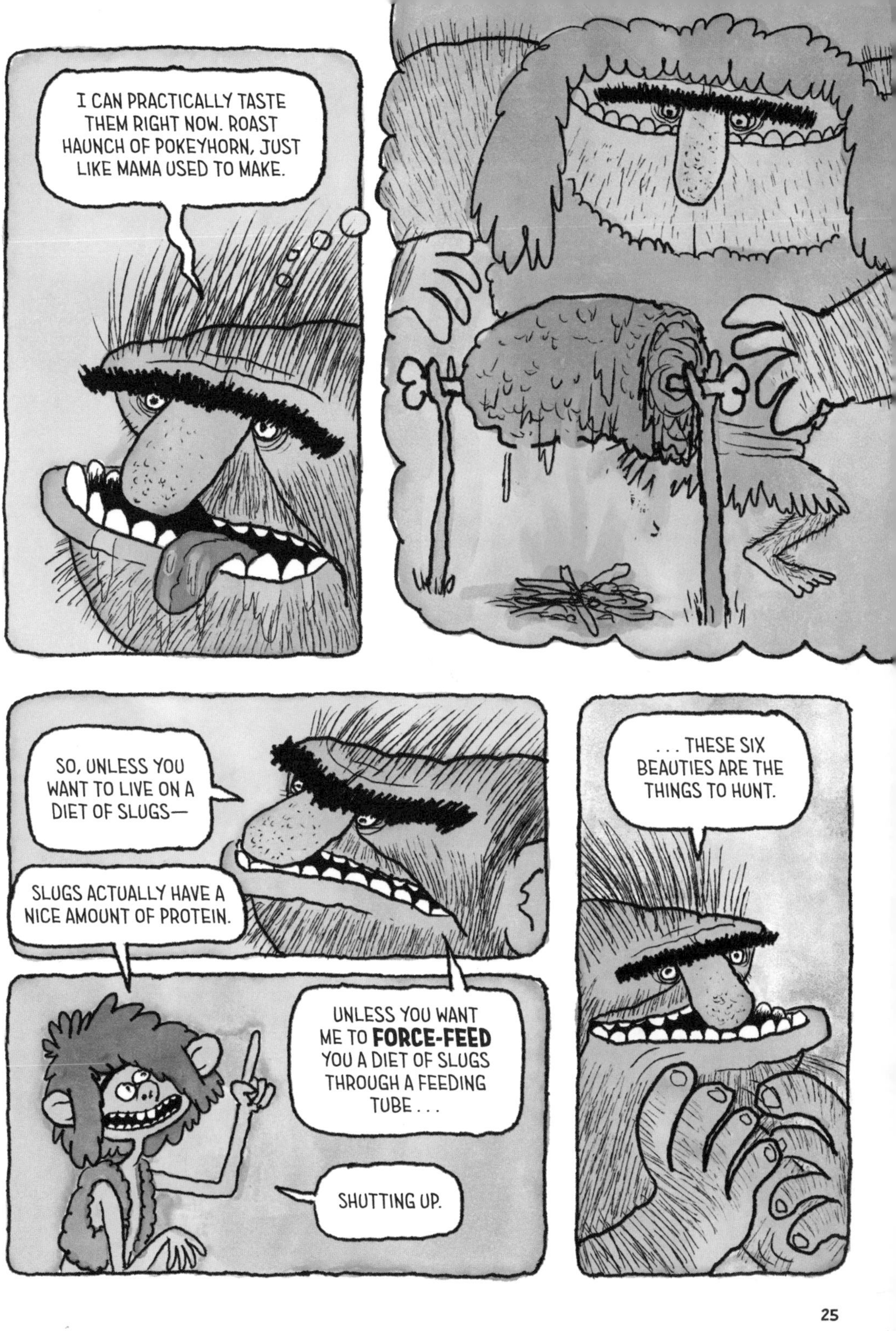

I CAN PRACTICALLY TASTE THEM RIGHT NOW. ROAST HAUNCH OF POKEYHORN, JUST LIKE MAMA USED TO MAKE.
SO, UNLESS YOU WANT TO LIVE ON A DIET OF SLUGS—
SLUGS ACTUALLY HAVE A NICE AMOUNT OF PROTEIN.
UNLESS YOU WANT ME TO **FORCE-FEED** YOU A DIET OF SLUGS THROUGH A FEEDING TUBE . . .
SHUTTING UP.
. . . THESE SIX BEAUTIES ARE THE THINGS TO HUNT.

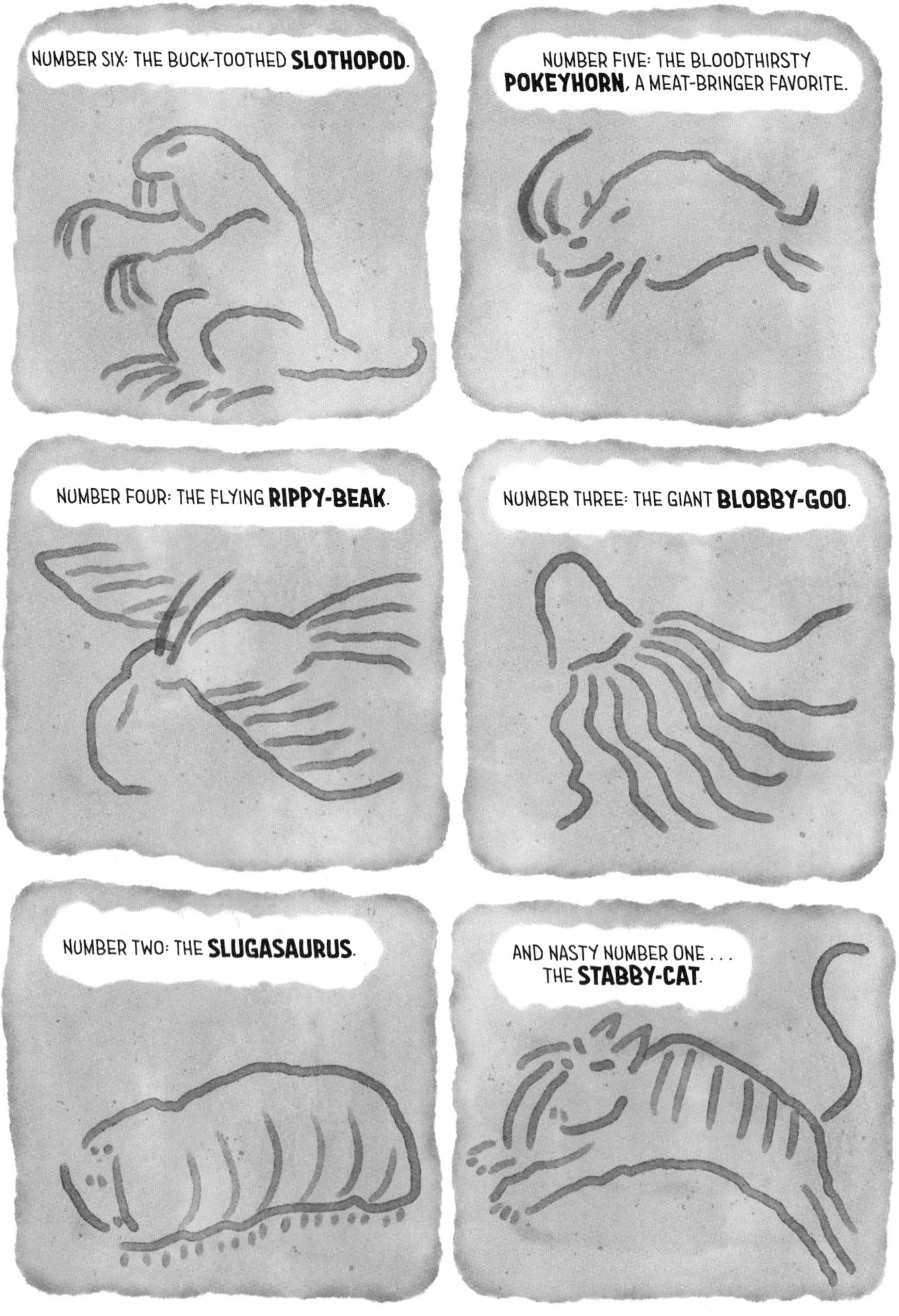
NUMBER SIX: THE BUCK-TOOTHED **SLOTHOPOD**.
NUMBER FIVE: THE BLOODTHIRSTY **POKEYHORN**, A MEAT-BRINGER FAVORITE.
NUMBER FOUR: THE FLYING **RIPPY-BEAK**.
NUMBER THREE: THE GIANT **BLOBBY-GOO**.
NUMBER TWO: THE **SLUGASAURUS**.
AND NASTY NUMBER ONE . . . THE **STABBY-CAT**.

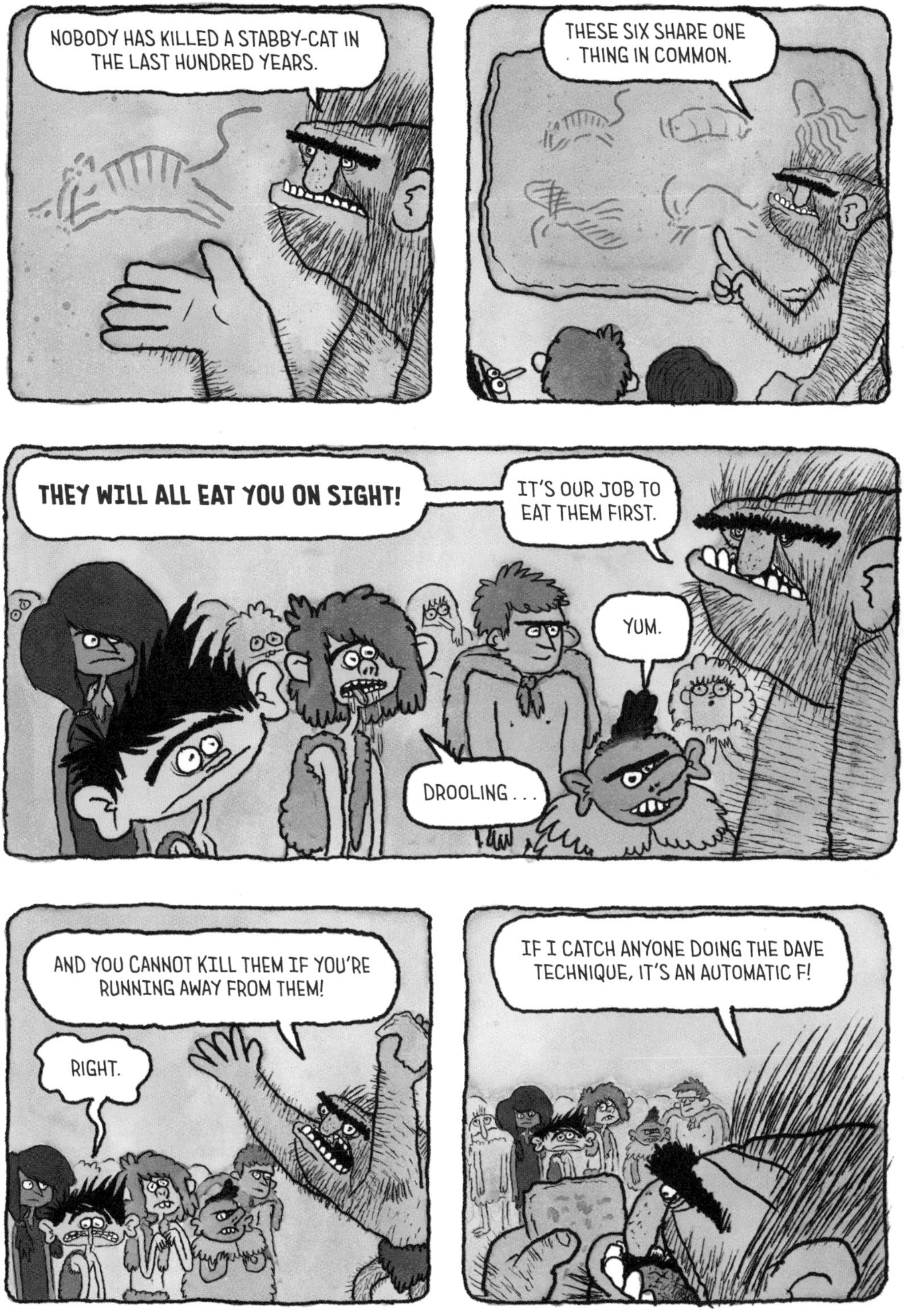
NOBODY HAS KILLED A STABBY-CAT IN THE LAST HUNDRED YEARS.
THESE SIX SHARE ONE THING IN COMMON.
THEY WILL ALL EAT YOU ON SIGHT!
IT'S OUR JOB TO EAT THEM FIRST.
YUM.
DROOLING . . .
AND YOU CANNOT KILL THEM IF YOU'RE RUNNING AWAY FROM THEM!
RIGHT.
IF I CATCH ANYONE DOING THE DAVE TECHNIQUE, IT'S AN AUTOMATIC F!

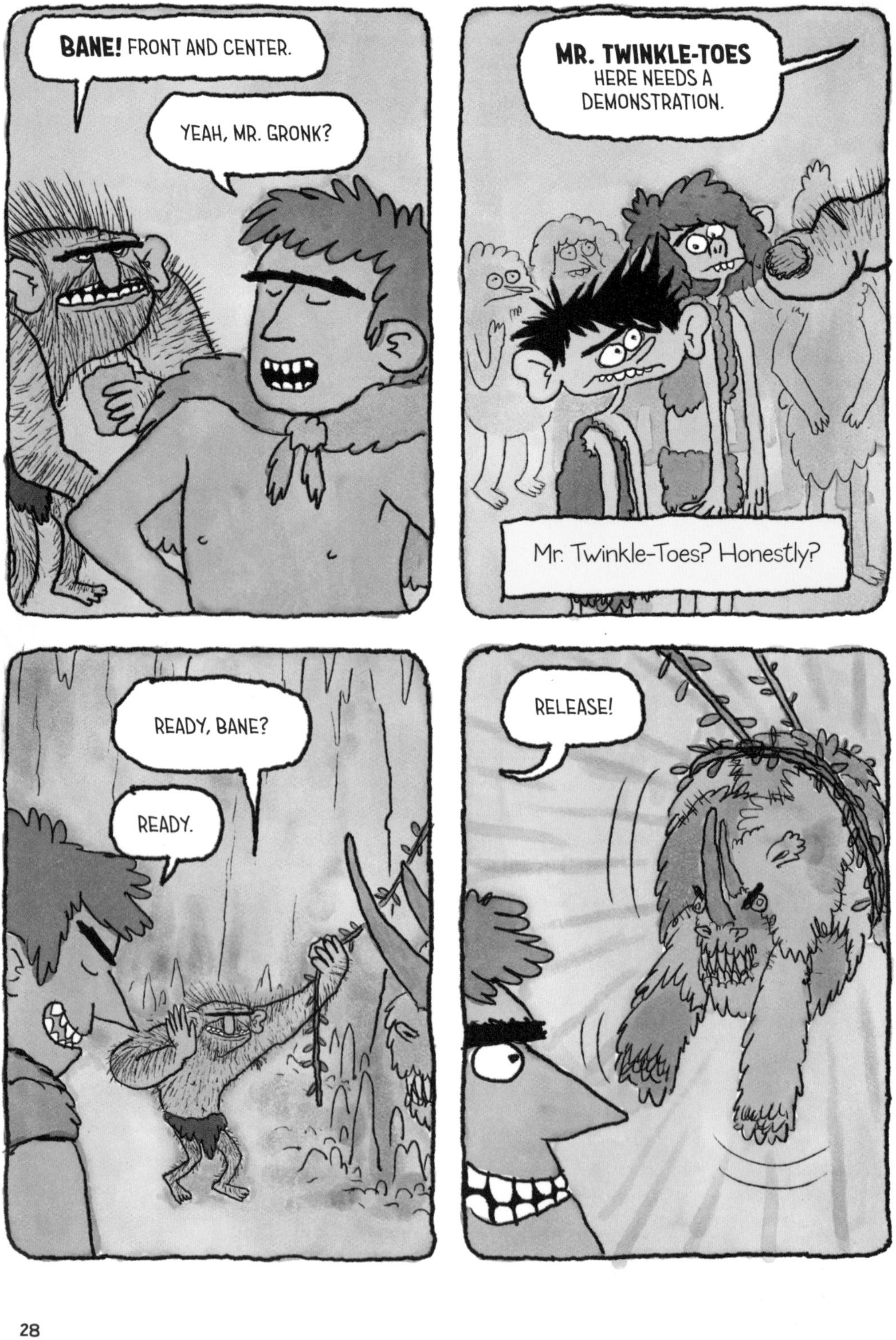

BANE! FRONT AND CENTER.
YEAH, MR. GRONK?
MR. TWINKLE-TOES HERE NEEDS A DEMONSTRATION.
Mr. Twinkle-Toes? Honestly?
READY, BANE?
READY.
RELEASE!

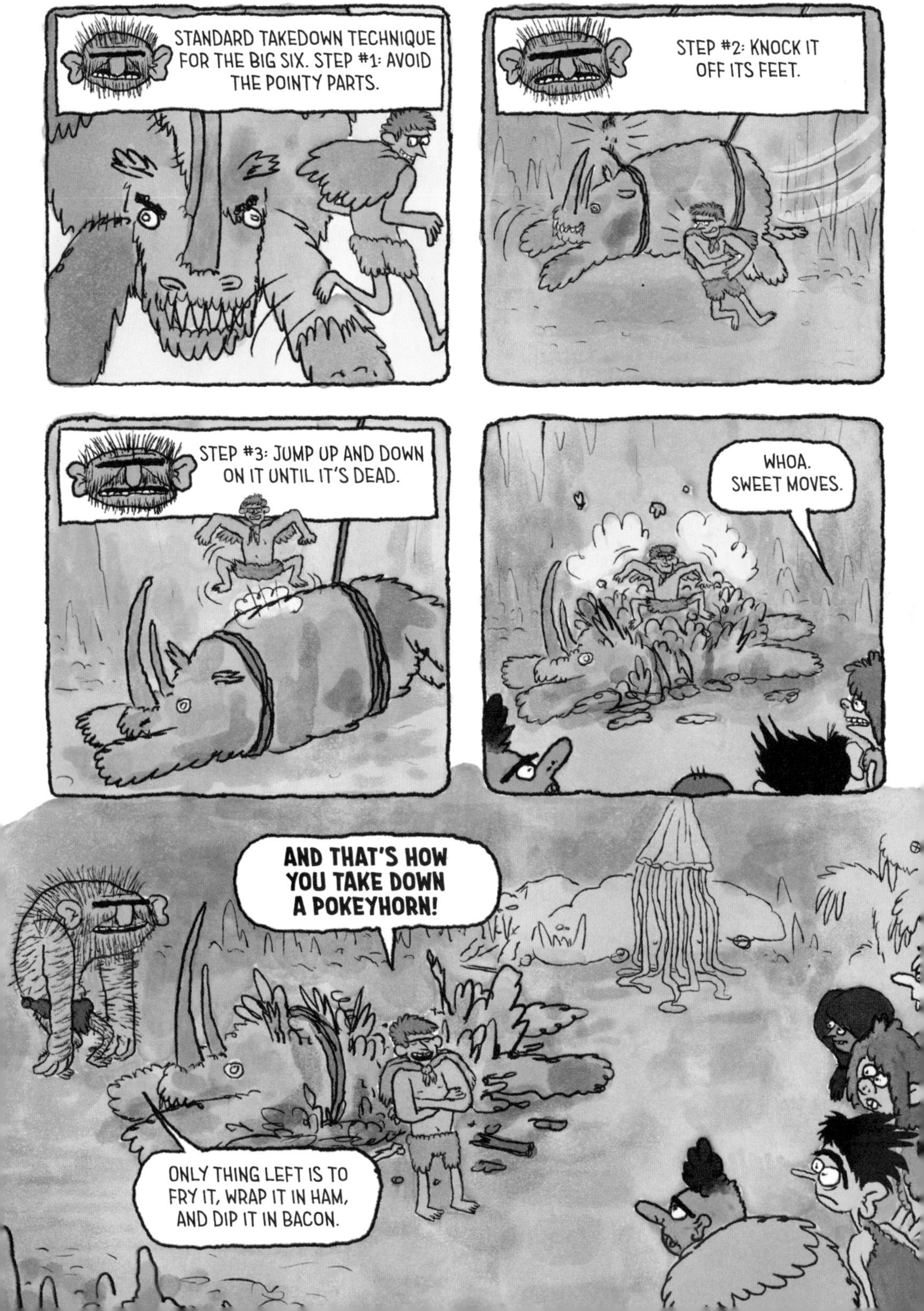

STANDARD TAKEDOWN TECHNIQUE FOR THE BIG SIX. STEP #1: AVOID THE POINTY PARTS.
STEP #2: KNOCK IT OFF ITS FEET.
STEP #3: JUMP UP AND DOWN ON IT UNTIL IT'S DEAD.
WHOA. SWEET MOVES.
AND THAT'S HOW YOU TAKE DOWN A POKEYHORN!
ONLY THING LEFT IS TO FRY IT, WRAP IT IN HAM, AND DIP IT IN BACON.

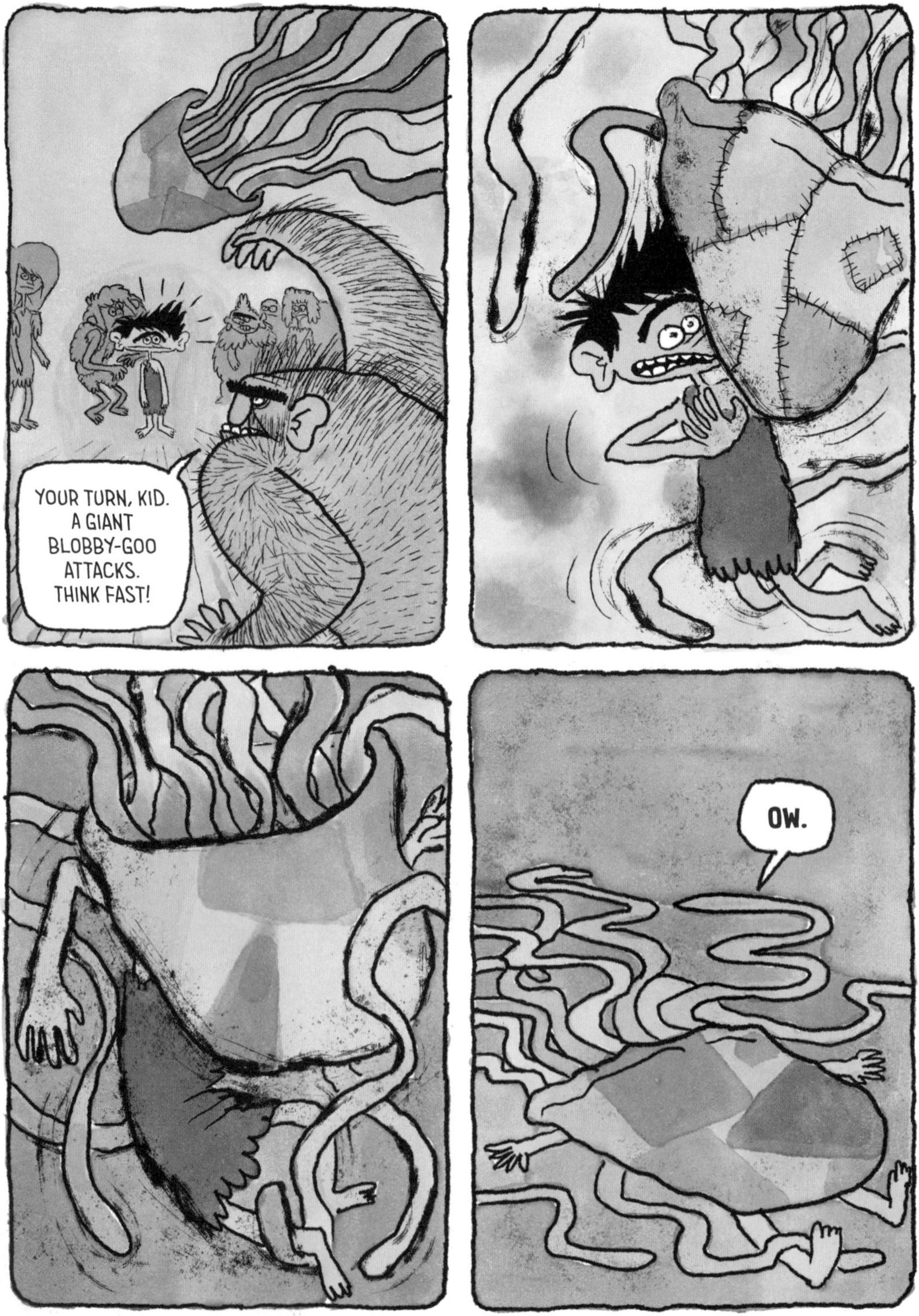
YOUR TURN, KID. A GIANT BLOBBY-GOO ATTACKS. THINK FAST!
OW.

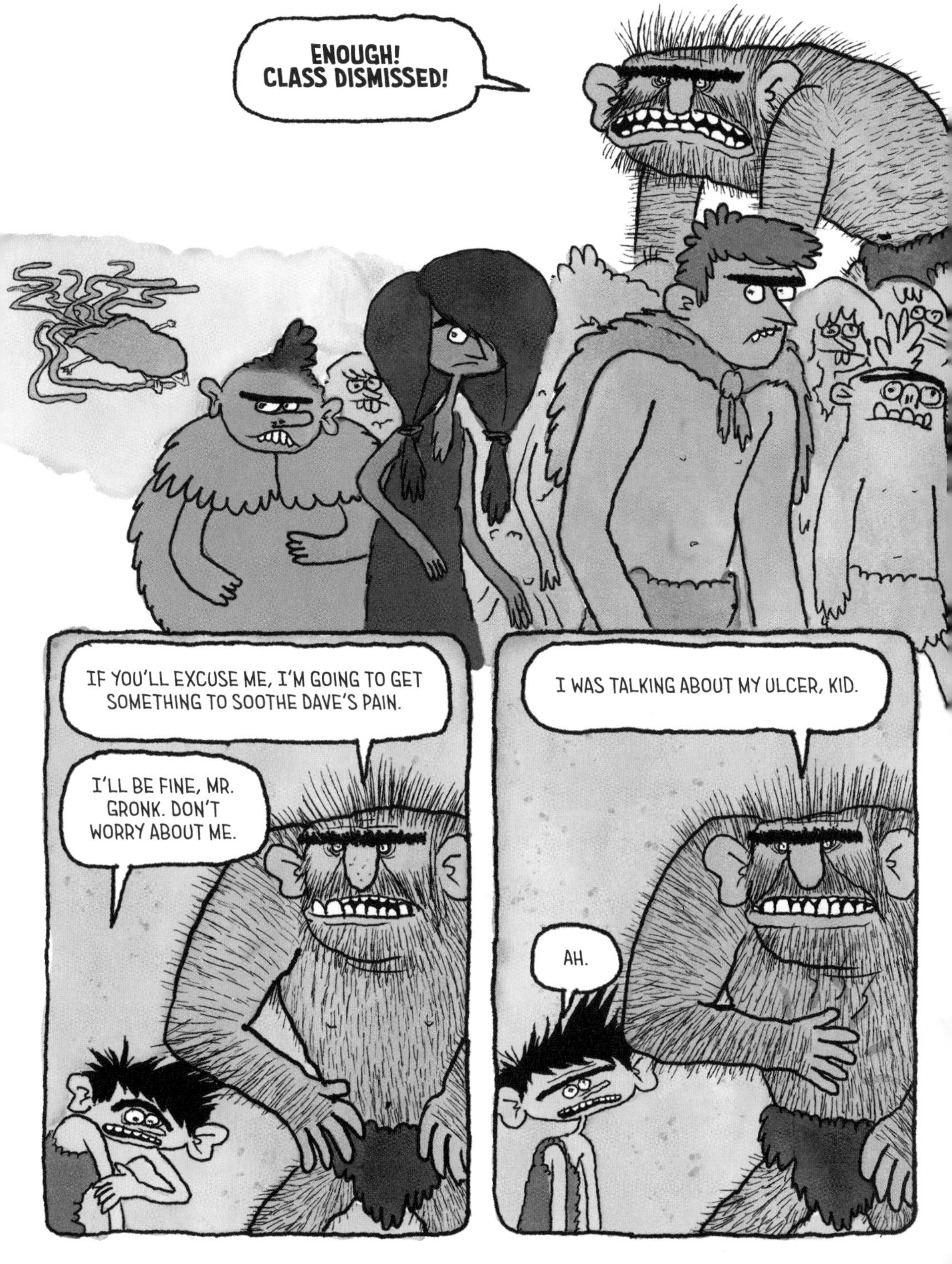
ENOUGH! CLASS DISMISSED!
IF YOU'LL EXCUSE ME, I'M GOING TO GET SOMETHING TO SOOTHE DAVE'S PAIN.
I'LL BE FINE, MR. GRONK. DON'T WORRY ABOUT ME.
I WAS TALKING ABOUT MY ULCER, KID.
AH.

ROAST POKEYHORN

(JUST LIKE MAMA USED TO MAKE)

STEP ONE: MAKE FIRE. FIRE GOOD.

STEP TWO: TIE UP POKEYHORN WITH VINES. ROLL IN BUGS FOR EXTRA CRUNCH.

STEP THREE: FIND BIG STICK. HANG POKEYHORN ON STICK.

STEP FOUR: REMEMBER FIRE? FIRE GOOD. PUT POKEYHORN OVER THE FIRE.

STEP FIVE (OPTIONAL): ATTACH BACON TO POKEYHORN FROM WARTHOG YOU CAUGHT. (YOU REAL GOOD HUNTER!)

STEP SIX: COOK POKEYHORN UNTIL BROWN AND SIZZLY. BE PATIENT. MAYBE GO DO SOMETHING ELSE TO TAKE MIND OFF TENDER, SUCCULENT POKEYHORN YOU NOT EATING. TRY A GAME OF HIT ROCK WITH STICK. ALWAYS FUN.

STEP SEVEN: EAT POKEYHORN. GET GREASY. BURP LOTS. YOU CAVEMAN, AFTER ALL.

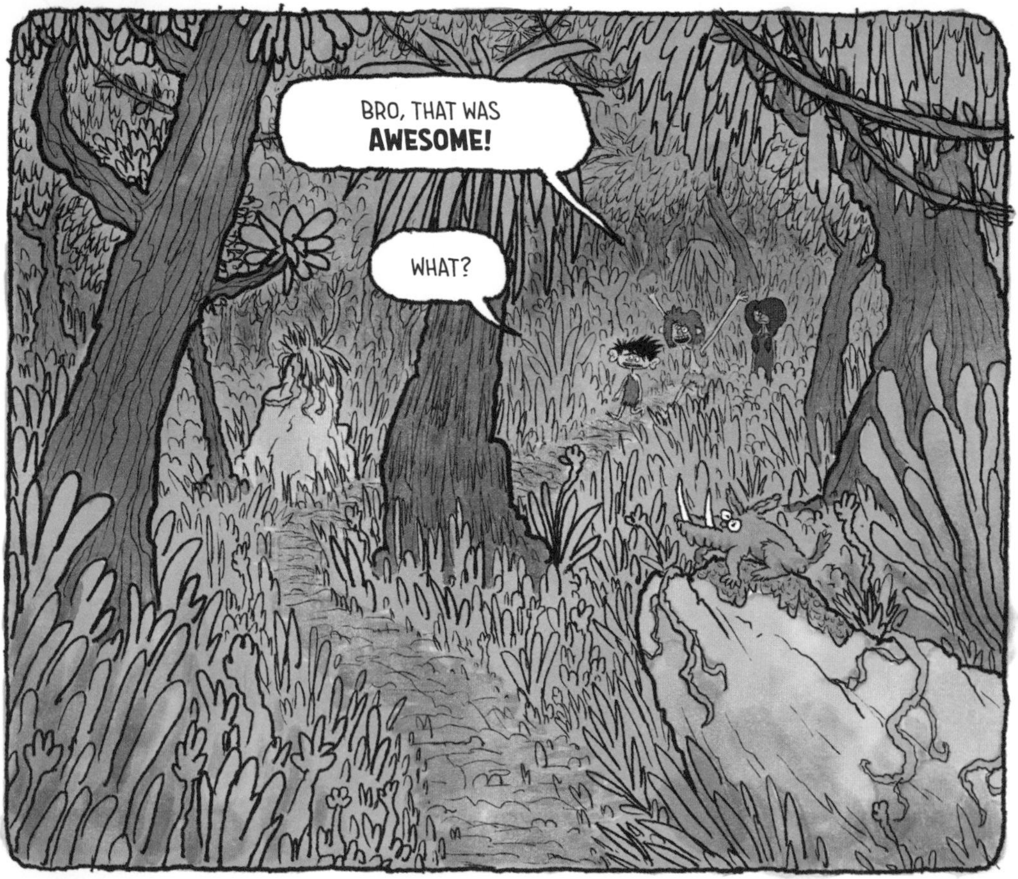
BRO, THAT WAS **AWESOME!**
WHAT?

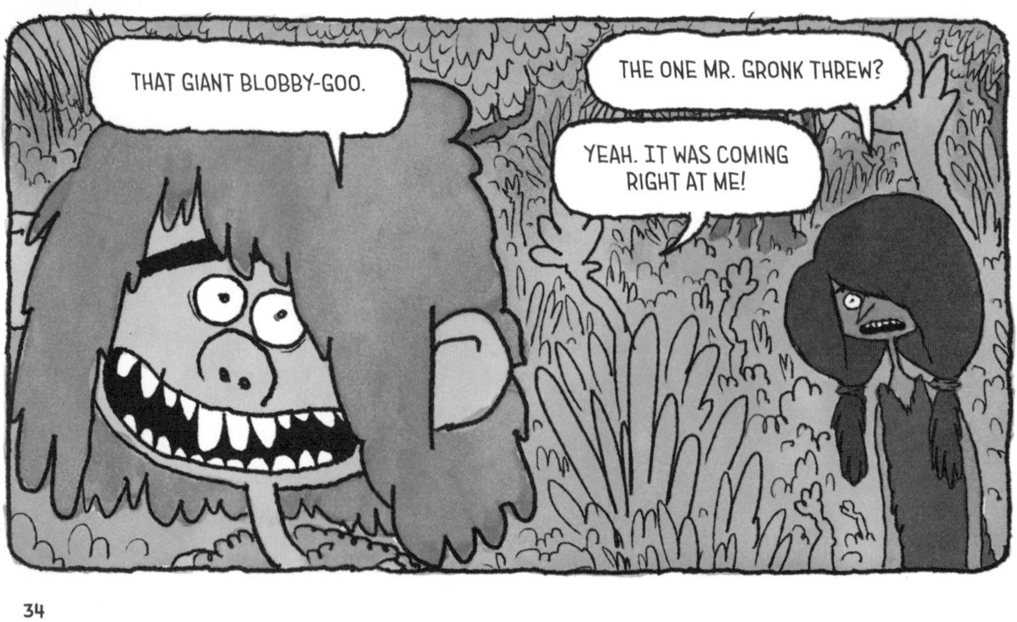
THAT GIANT BLOBBY-GOO.
THE ONE MR. GRONK THREW?
YEAH. IT WAS COMING RIGHT AT ME!

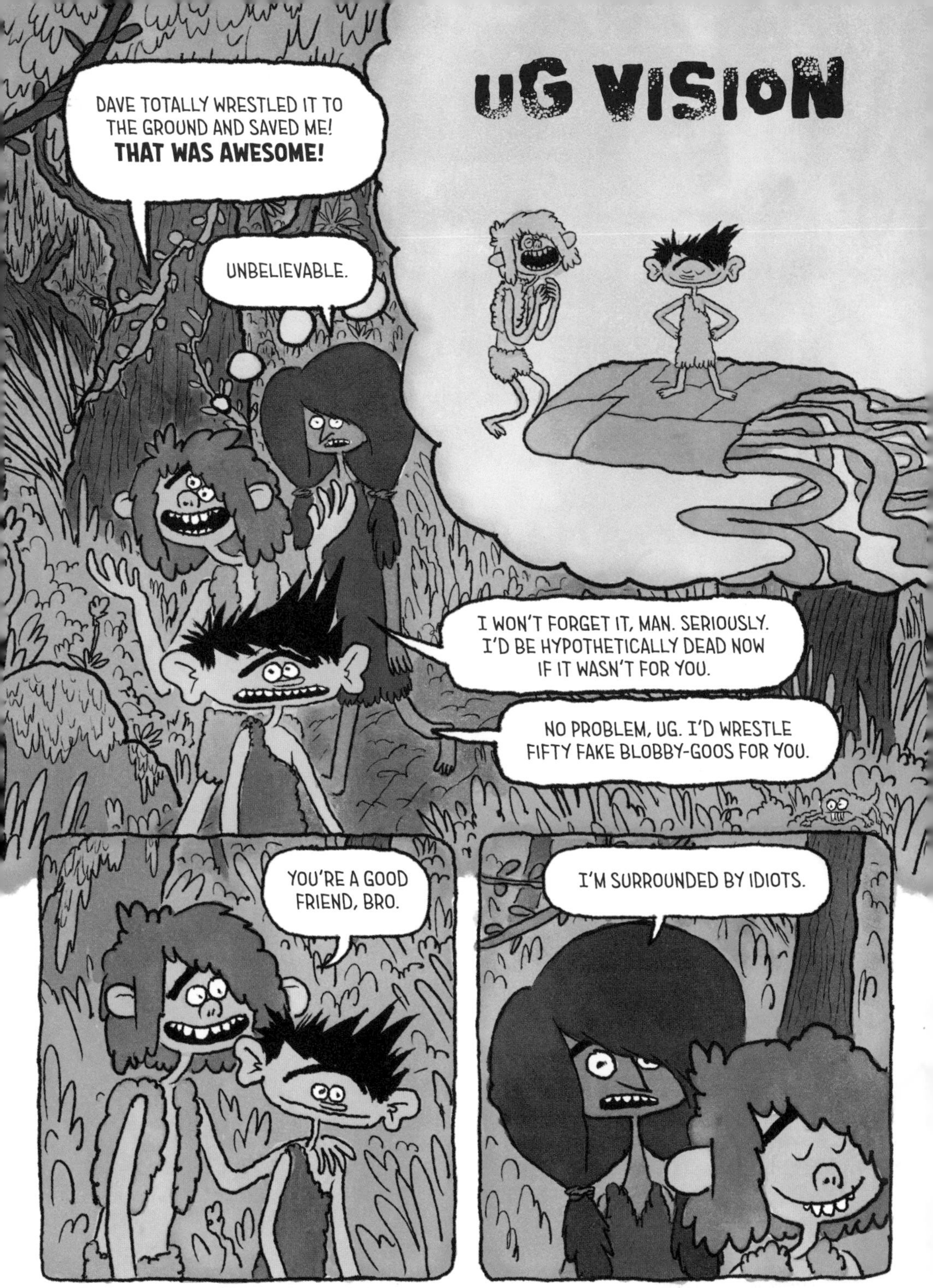
UG VISION
DAVE TOTALLY WRESTLED IT TO THE GROUND AND SAVED ME! **THAT WAS AWESOME!**
UNBELIEVABLE.
I WON'T FORGET IT, MAN. SERIOUSLY. I'D BE HYPOTHETICALLY DEAD NOW IF IT WASN'T FOR YOU.
NO PROBLEM, UG. I'D WRESTLE FIFTY FAKE BLOBBY-GOOS FOR YOU.
YOU'RE A GOOD FRIEND, BRO.
I'M SURROUNDED BY IDIOTS.

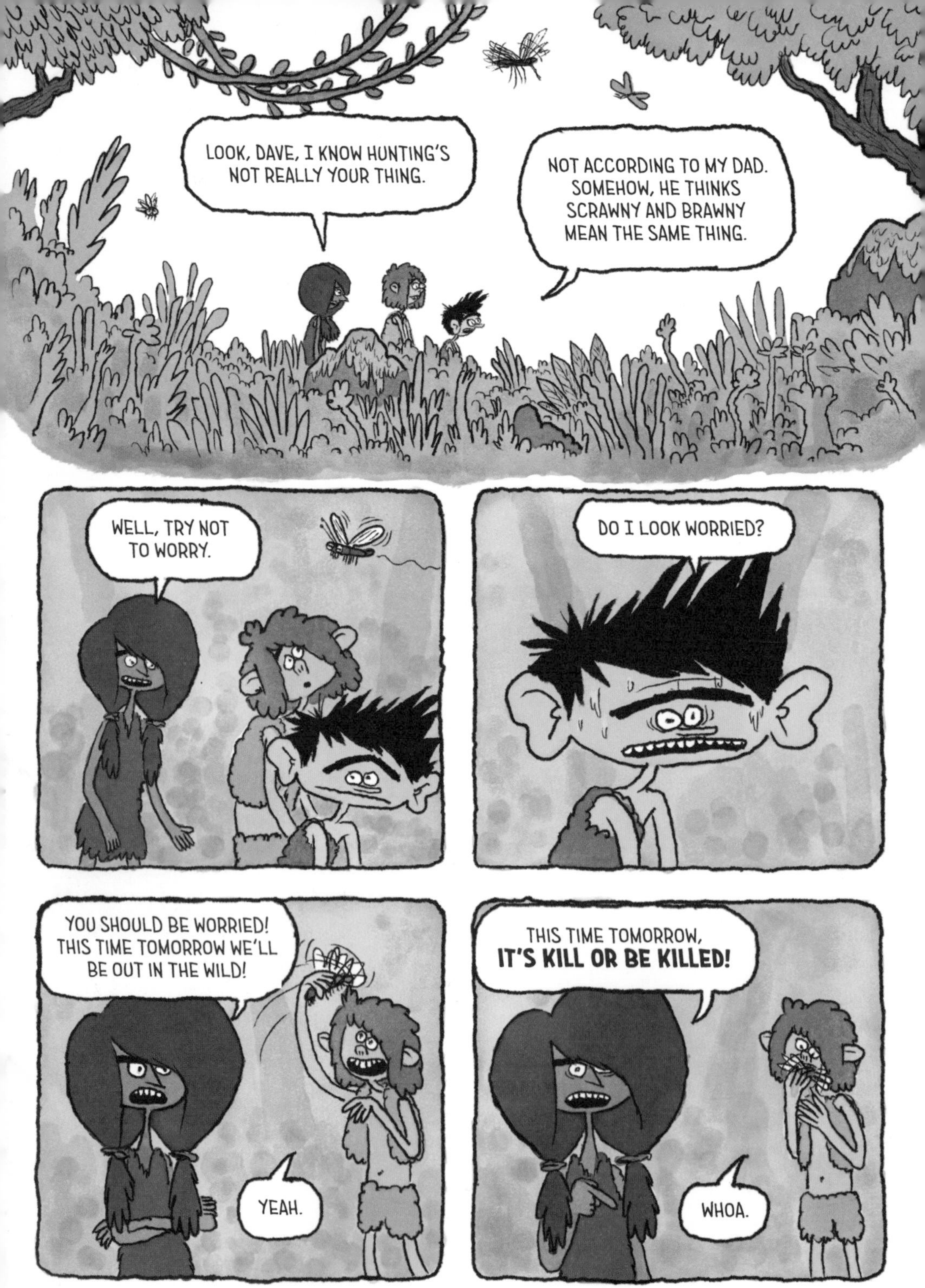
LOOK, DAVE, I KNOW HUNTING'S NOT REALLY YOUR THING.
NOT ACCORDING TO MY DAD. SOMEHOW, HE THINKS SCRAWNY AND BRAWNY MEAN THE SAME THING.
WELL, TRY NOT TO WORRY.
DO I LOOK WORRIED?
YOU SHOULD BE WORRIED! THIS TIME TOMORROW WE'LL BE OUT IN THE WILD!
YEAH.
THIS TIME TOMORROW, **IT'S KILL OR BE KILLED!**
WHOA.

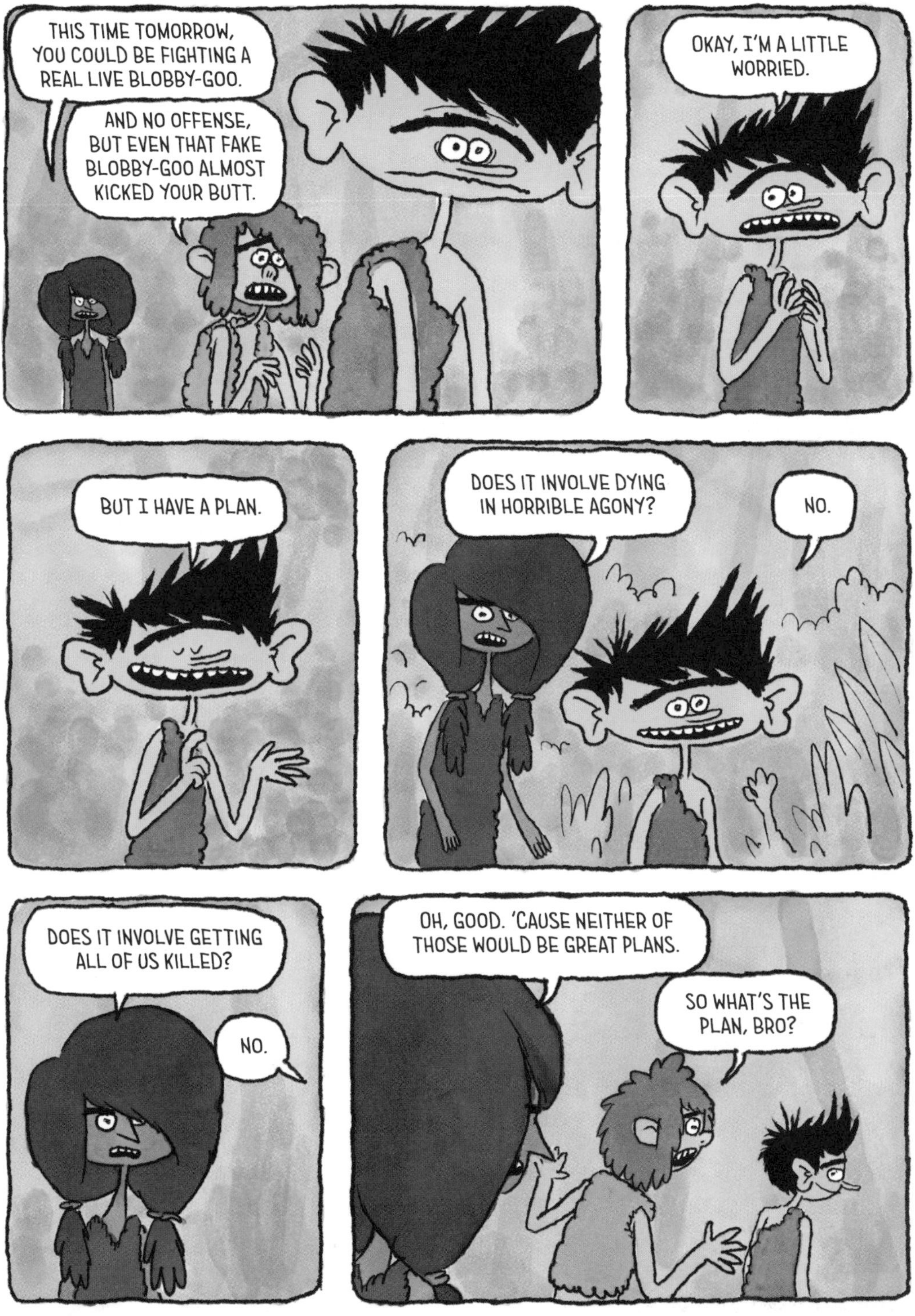
THIS TIME TOMORROW, YOU COULD BE FIGHTING A REAL LIVE BLOBBY-GOO.
AND NO OFFENSE, BUT EVEN THAT FAKE BLOBBY-GOO ALMOST KICKED YOUR BUTT.
OKAY, I'M A LITTLE WORRIED.
BUT I HAVE A PLAN.
DOES IT INVOLVE DYING IN HORRIBLE AGONY?
NO.
DOES IT INVOLVE GETTING ALL OF US KILLED?
NO.
OH, GOOD. 'CAUSE NEITHER OF THOSE WOULD BE GREAT PLANS.
SO WHAT'S THE PLAN, BRO?

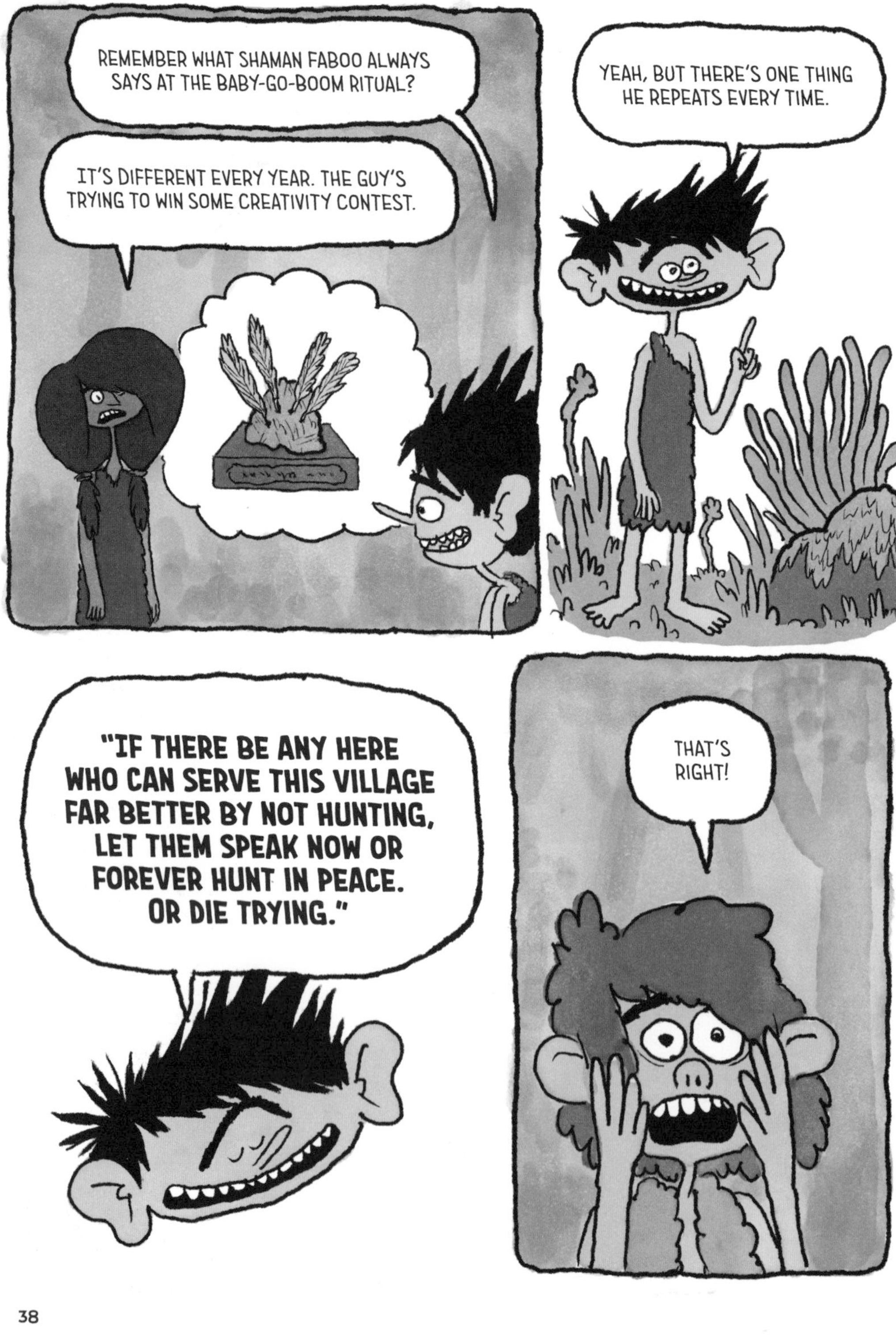
REMEMBER WHAT SHAMAN FABOO ALWAYS SAYS AT THE BABY-GO-BOOM RITUAL?
IT'S DIFFERENT EVERY YEAR. THE GUY'S TRYING TO WIN SOME CREATIVITY CONTEST.
YEAH, BUT THERE'S ONE THING HE REPEATS EVERY TIME.
"IF THERE BE ANY HERE WHO CAN SERVE THIS VILLAGE FAR BETTER BY NOT HUNTING, LET THEM SPEAK NOW OR FOREVER HUNT IN PEACE. OR DIE TRYING."
THAT'S RIGHT!

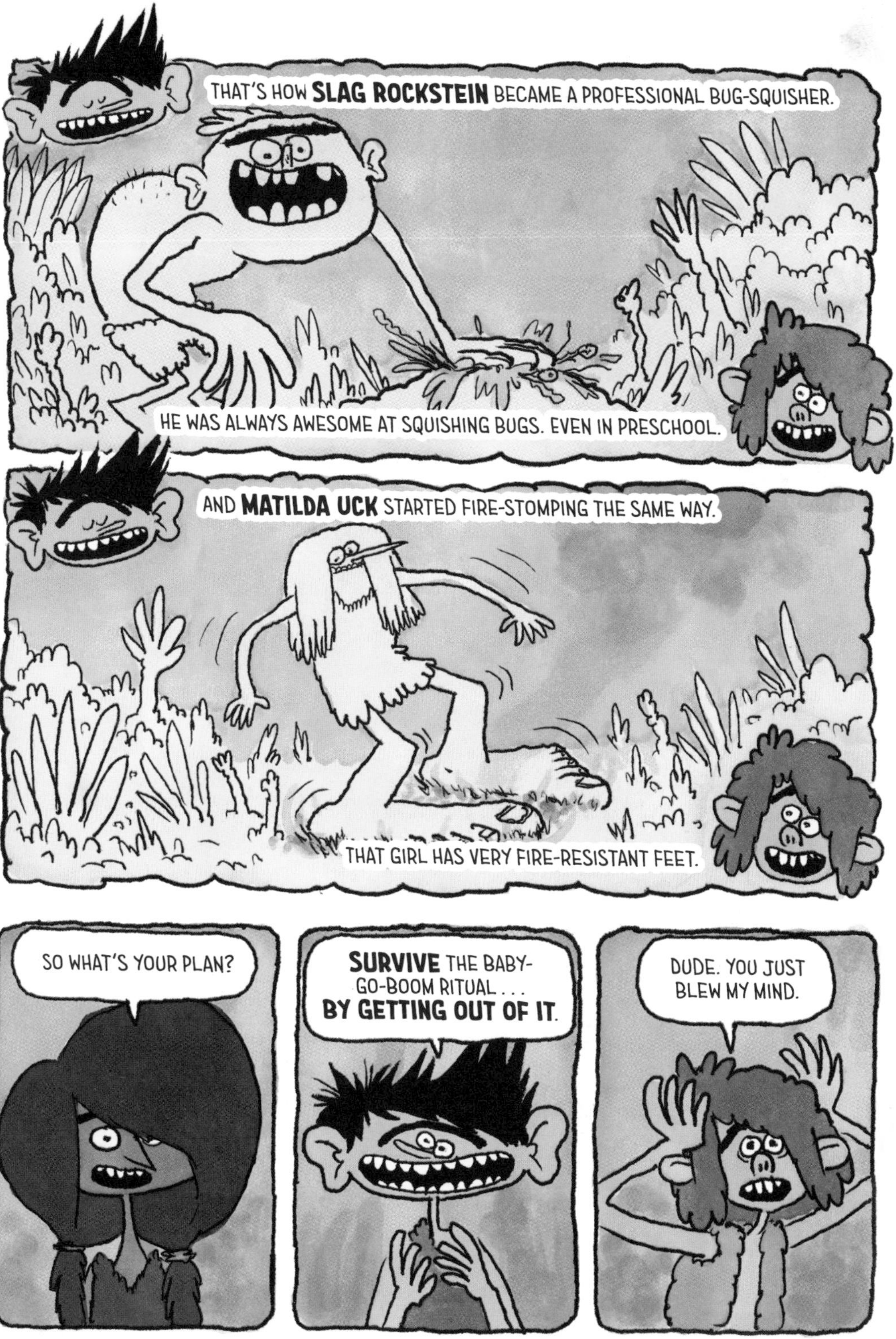
THAT'S HOW **SLAG ROCKSTEIN** BECAME A PROFESSIONAL BUG-SQUISHER.
HE WAS ALWAYS AWESOME AT SQUISHING BUGS. EVEN IN PRESCHOOL.
AND **MATILDA UCK** STARTED FIRE-STOMPING THE SAME WAY.
THAT GIRL HAS VERY FIRE-RESISTANT FEET.
SO WHAT'S YOUR PLAN?
SURVIVE THE BABY-GO-BOOM RITUAL . . . **BY GETTING OUT OF IT**.
DUDE. YOU JUST BLEW MY MIND.

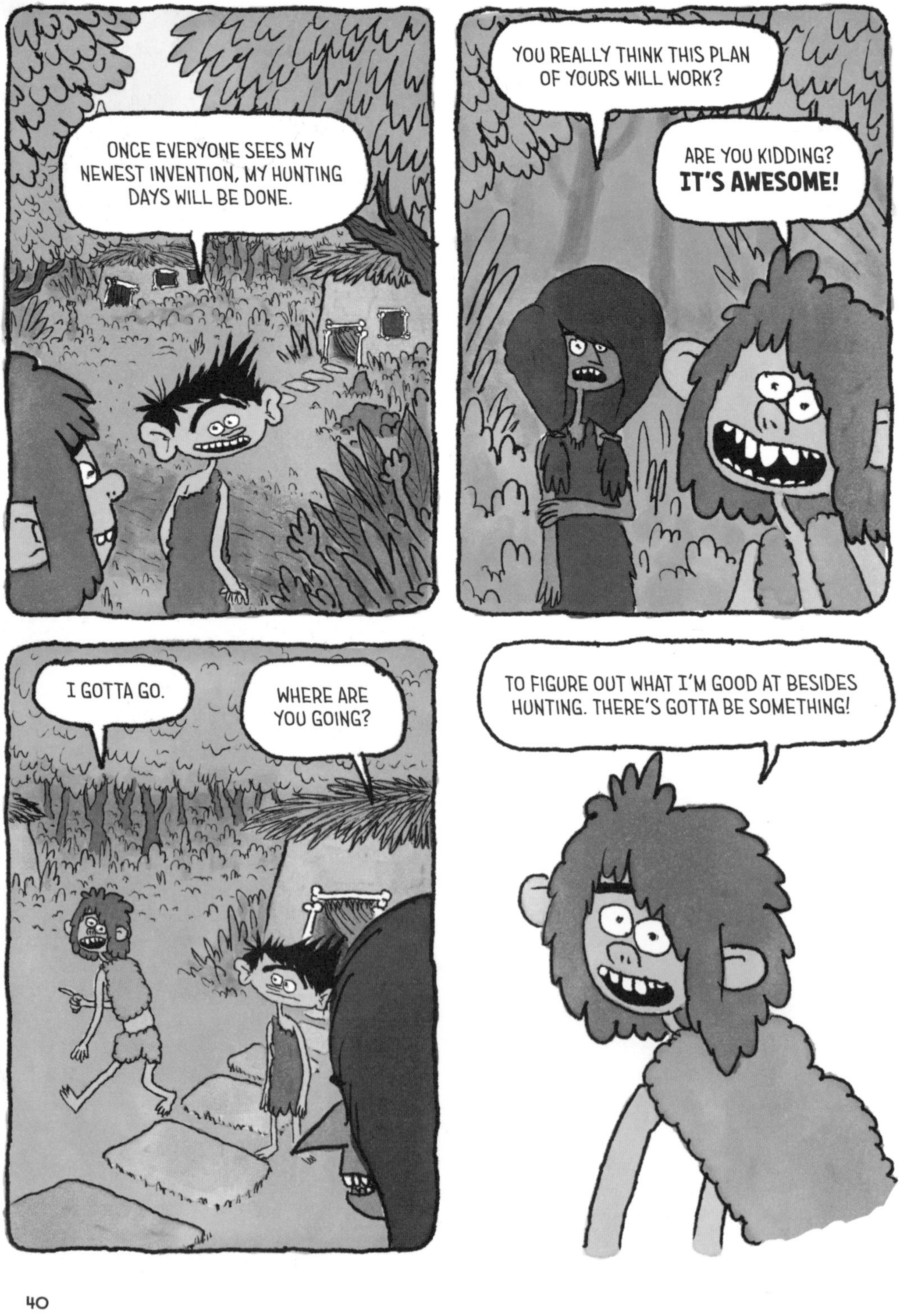
ONCE EVERYONE SEES MY NEWEST INVENTION, MY HUNTING DAYS WILL BE DONE.
YOU REALLY THINK THIS PLAN OF YOURS WILL WORK?
ARE YOU KIDDING? **IT'S AWESOME!**
I GOTTA GO.
WHERE ARE YOU GOING?
TO FIGURE OUT WHAT I'M GOOD AT BESIDES HUNTING. THERE'S GOTTA BE SOMETHING!

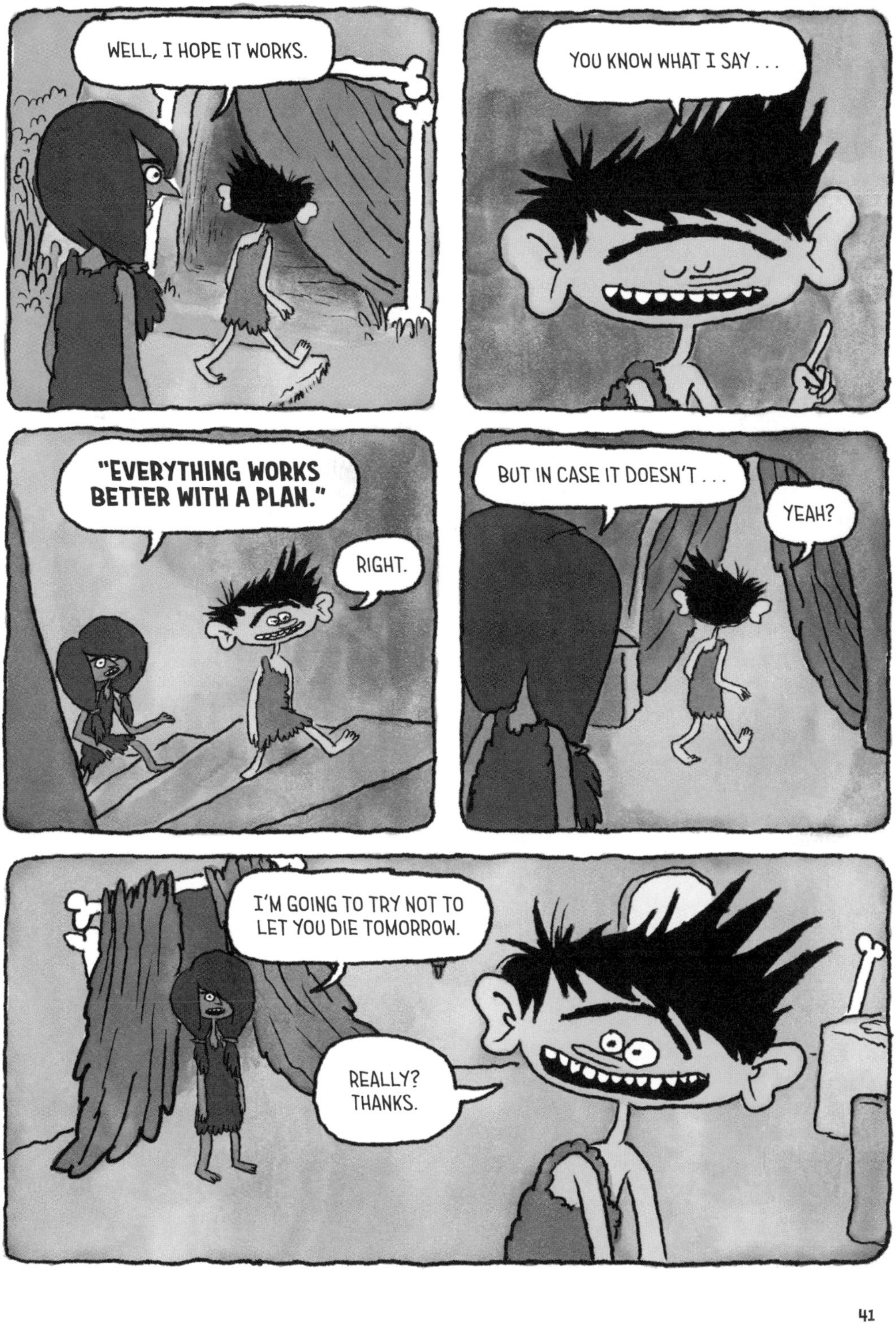

WELL, I HOPE IT WORKS.
YOU KNOW WHAT I SAY . . .
"EVERYTHING WORKS BETTER WITH A PLAN."
RIGHT.
BUT IN CASE IT DOESN'T . . .
YEAH?
I'M GOING TO TRY NOT TO LET YOU DIE TOMORROW.
REALLY? THANKS.

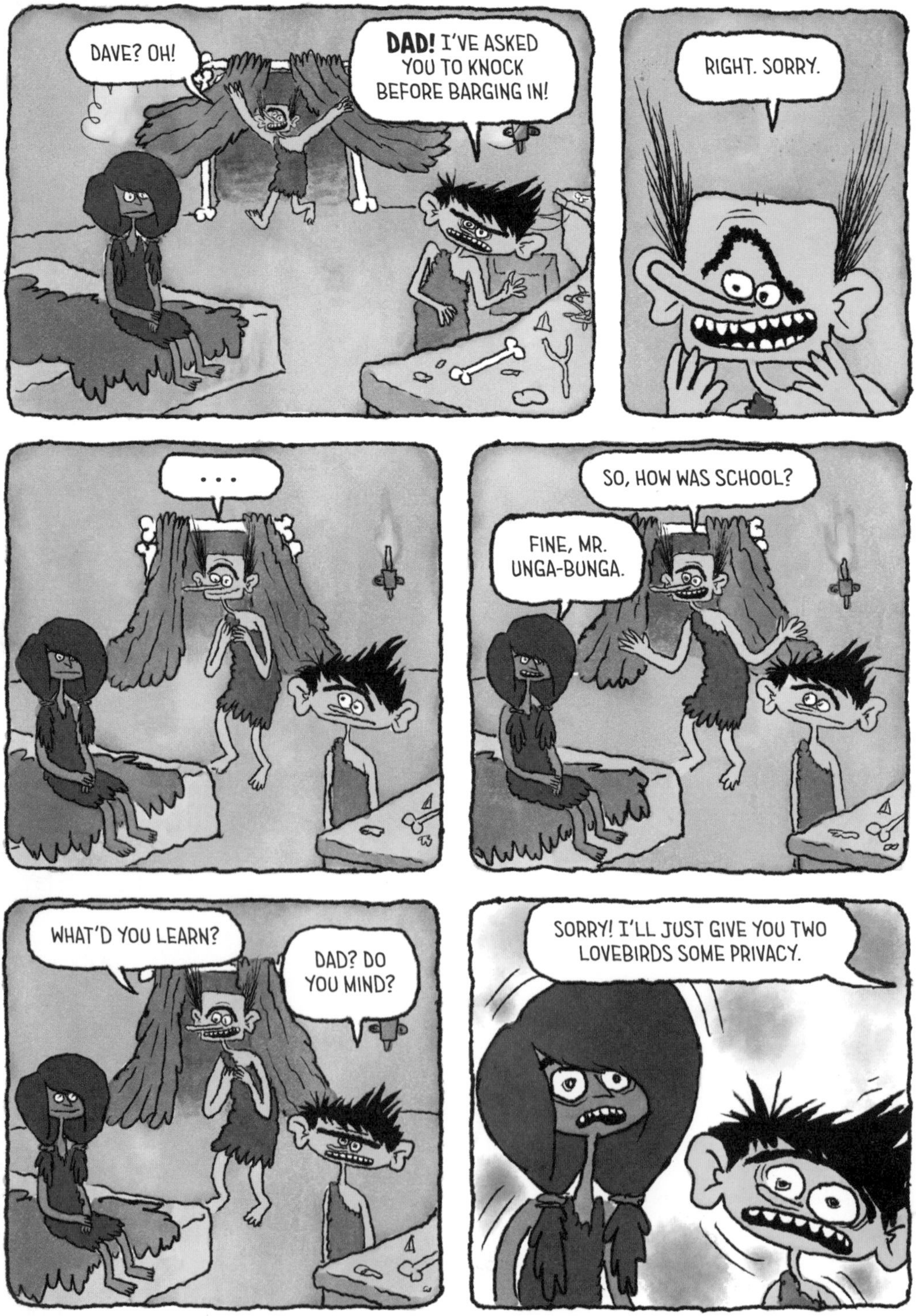
DAVE? OH!
DAD! I'VE ASKED YOU TO KNOCK BEFORE BARGING IN!
RIGHT. SORRY.
. . .
SO, HOW WAS SCHOOL?
FINE, MR. UNGA-BUNGA.
WHAT'D YOU LEARN?
DAD? DO YOU MIND?
SORRY! I'LL JUST GIVE YOU TWO LOVEBIRDS SOME PRIVACY.

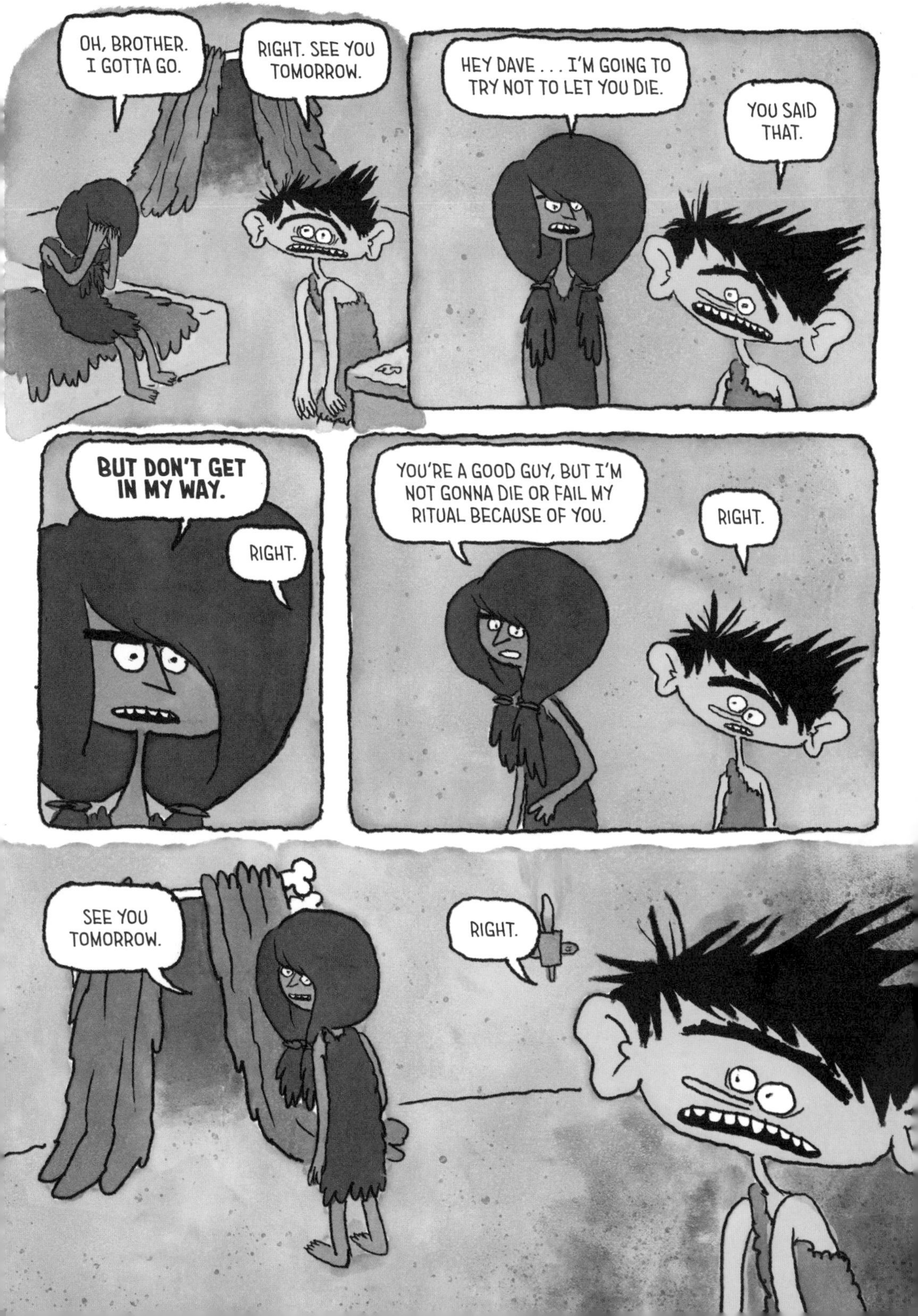

OH, BROTHER. I GOTTA GO.
RIGHT. SEE YOU TOMORROW.
HEY DAVE . . . I'M GOING TO TRY NOT TO LET YOU DIE.
YOU SAID THAT.
BUT DON'T GET IN MY WAY.
RIGHT.
YOU'RE A GOOD GUY, BUT I'M NOT GONNA DIE OR FAIL MY RITUAL BECAUSE OF YOU.
RIGHT.
SEE YOU TOMORROW.
RIGHT.

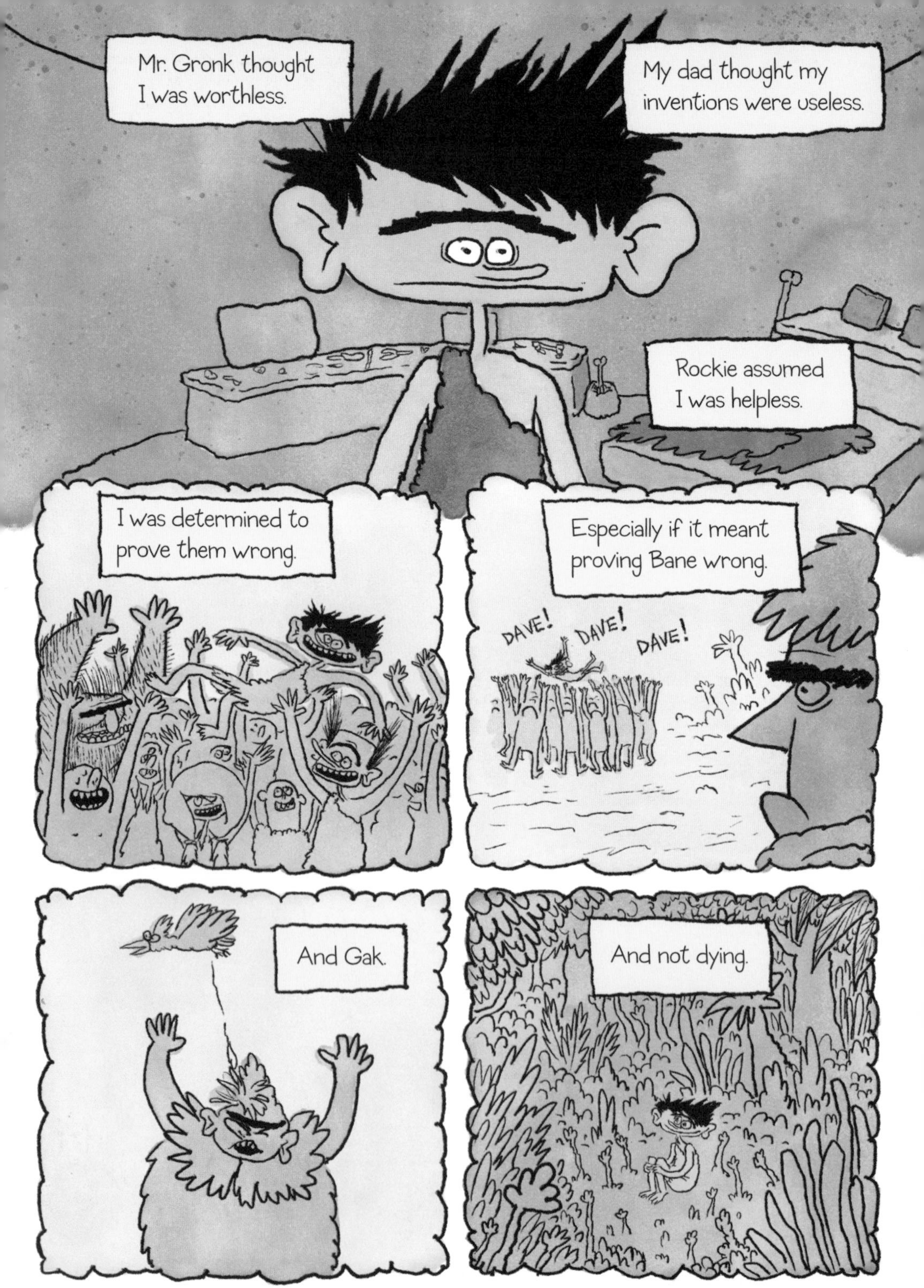
Mr. Gronk thought I was worthless.
My dad thought my inventions were useless.
Rockie assumed I was helpless.
I was determined to prove them wrong.
Especially if it meant proving Bane wrong.
DAVE!
DAVE!
DAVE!
And Gak.
And not dying.

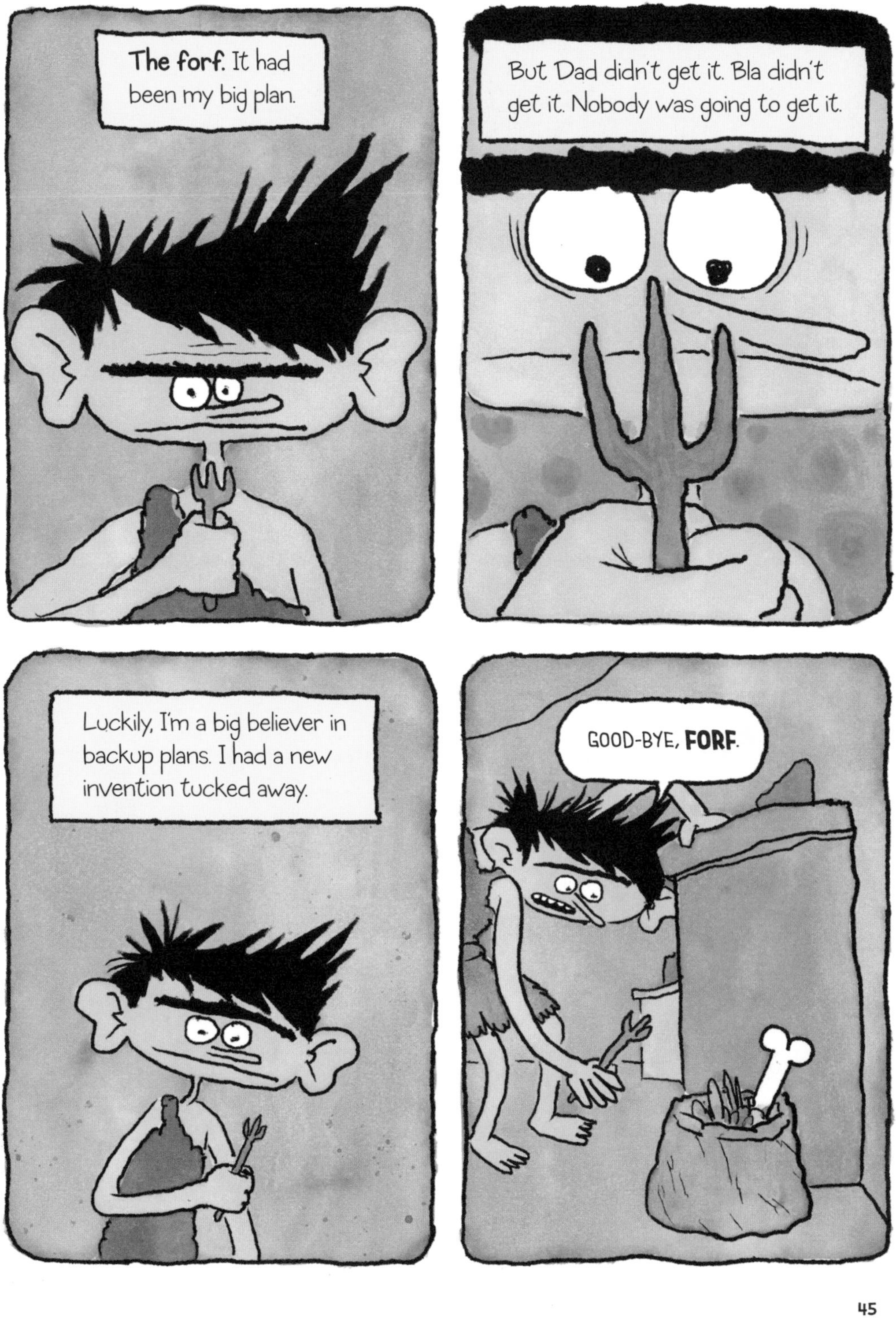
The forf. It had been my big plan.
But Dad didn't get it. Bla didn't get it. Nobody was going to get it.
Luckily, I'm a big believer in backup plans. I had a new invention tucked away.
GOOD-BYE, **FORF**.

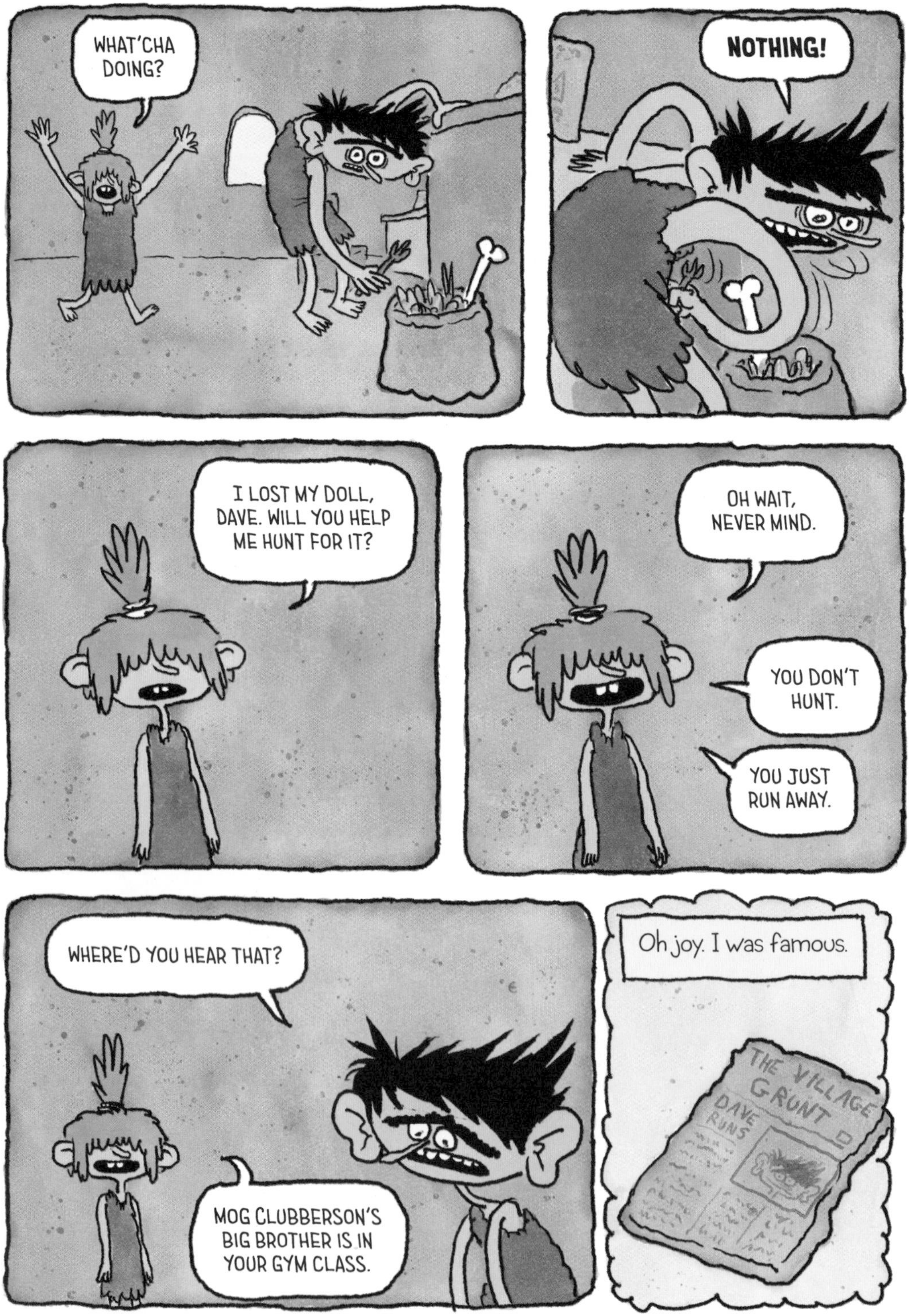
WHAT'CHA DOING?
NOTHING!
I LOST MY DOLL, DAVE. WILL YOU HELP ME HUNT FOR IT?
OH WAIT, NEVER MIND.
YOU DON'T HUNT.
YOU JUST RUN AWAY.
WHERE'D YOU HEAR THAT?
MOG CLUBBERSON'S BIG BROTHER IS IN YOUR GYM CLASS.
Oh joy. I was famous.
THE VILLAGE GRUNT
DAVE RUNS

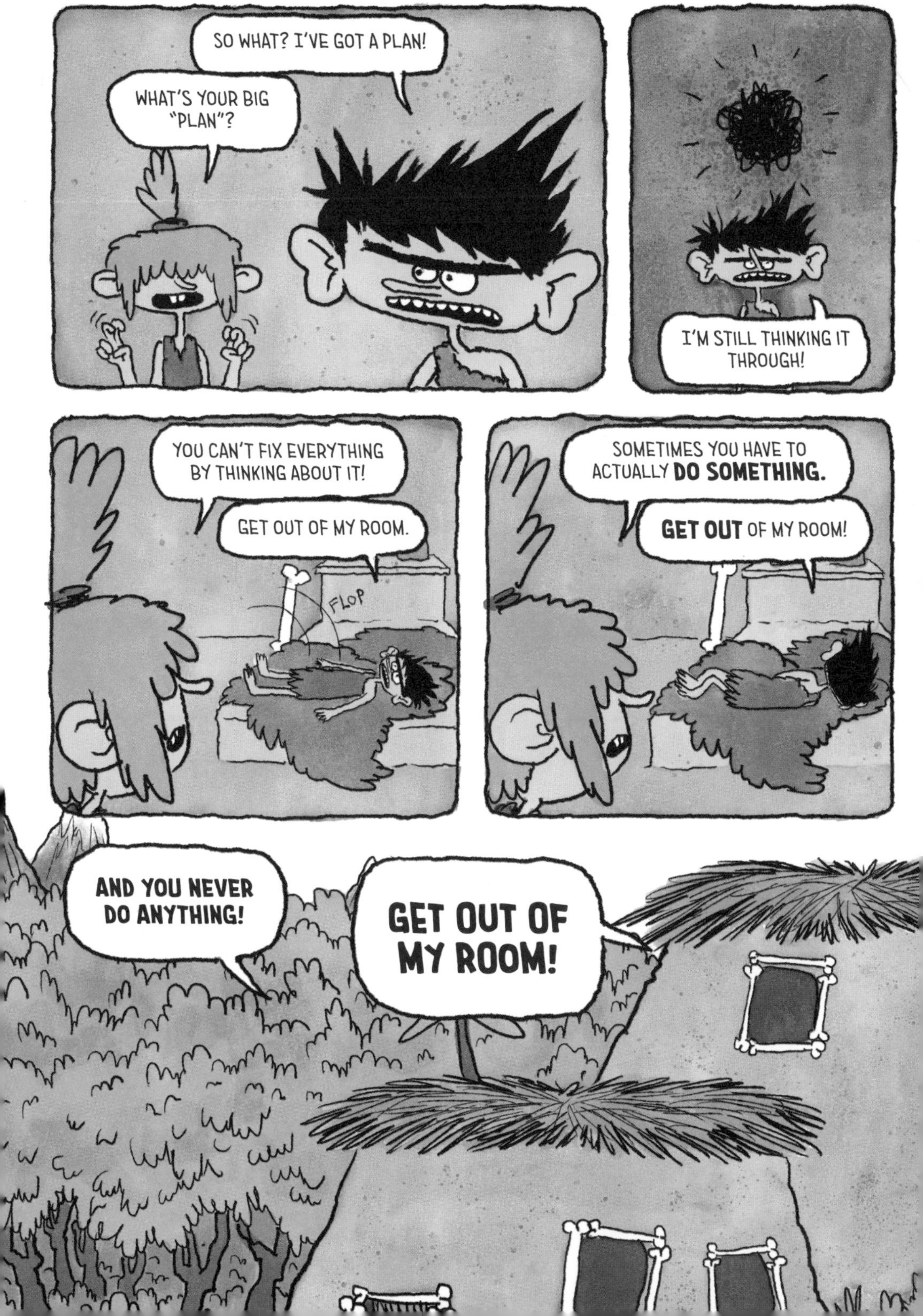

WHAT'S YOUR BIG "PLAN"?
SO WHAT? I'VE GOT A PLAN!
I'M STILL THINKING IT THROUGH!
YOU CAN'T FIX EVERYTHING BY THINKING ABOUT IT!
GET OUT OF MY ROOM.
FLOP
SOMETIMES YOU HAVE TO ACTUALLY **DO SOMETHING.**
GET OUT OF MY ROOM!
AND YOU NEVER DO ANYTHING!
GET OUT OF MY ROOM!

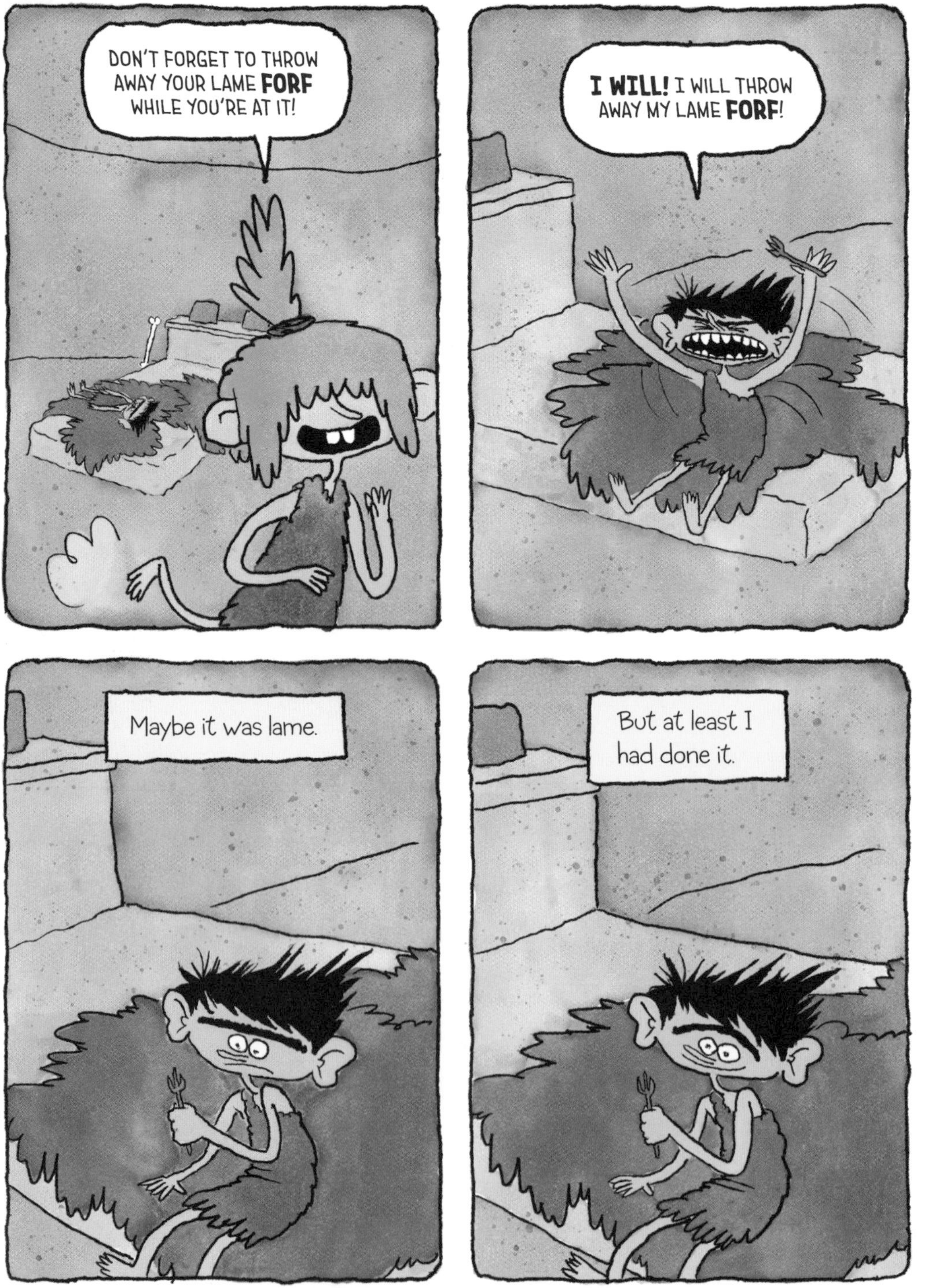
DON'T FORGET TO THROW AWAY YOUR LAME **FORF** WHILE YOU'RE AT IT!
I WILL! I WILL THROW AWAY MY LAME **FORF**!
Maybe it was lame.
But at least I had done it.

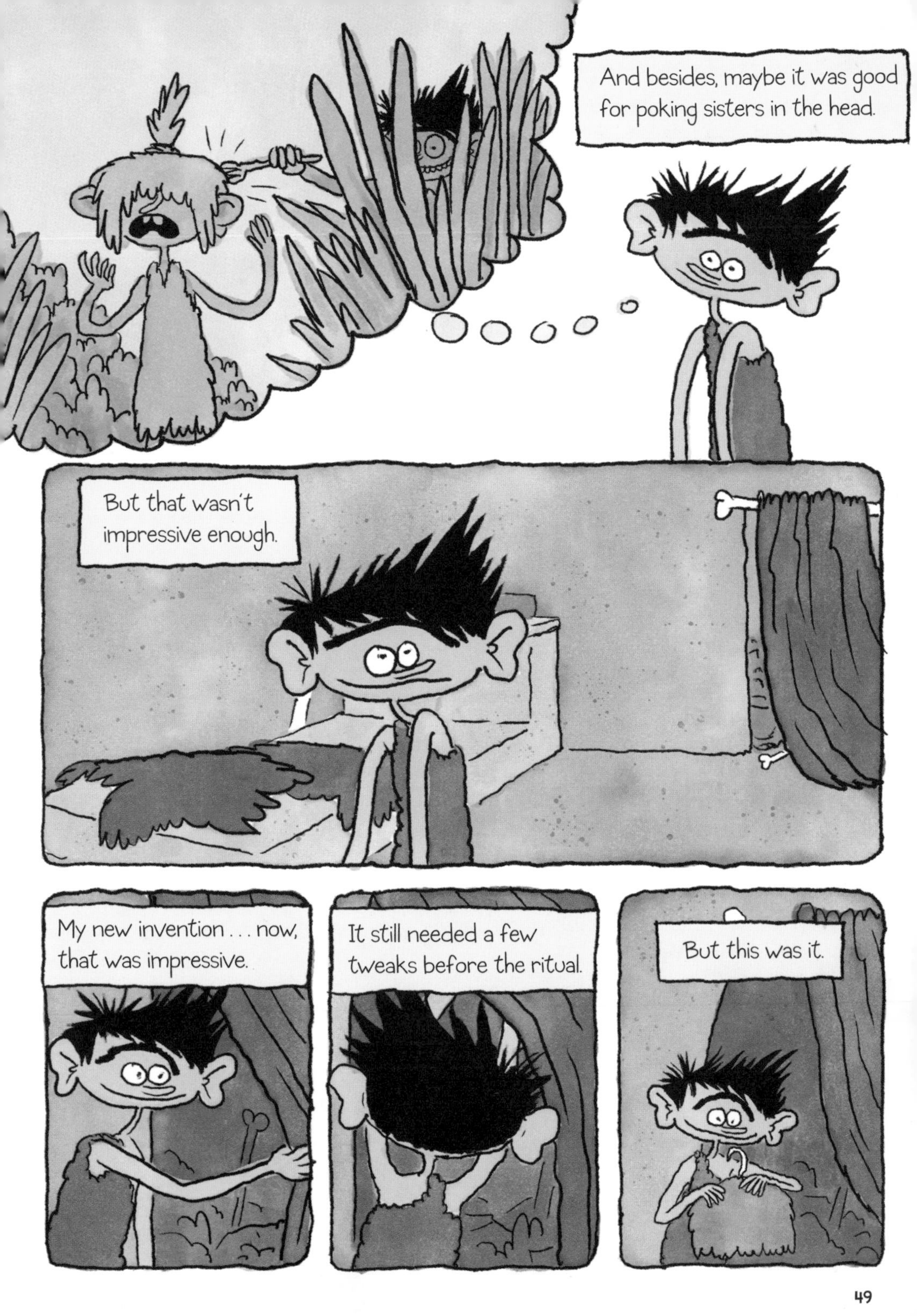

And besides, maybe it was good for poking sisters in the head.
But that wasn't impressive enough.
My new invention . . . now, that was impressive.
It still needed a few tweaks before the ritual.
But this was it.

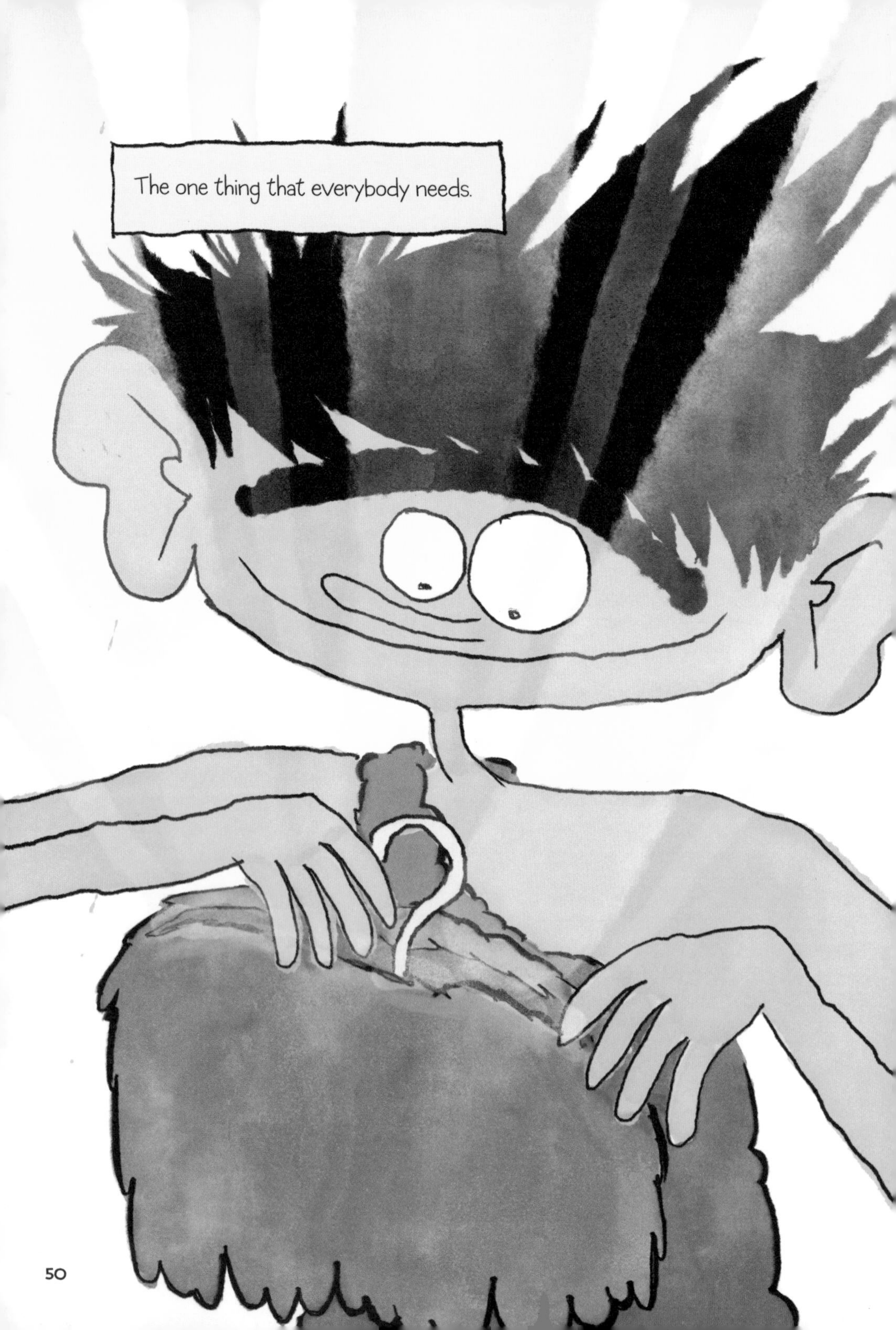
The one thing that everybody needs.

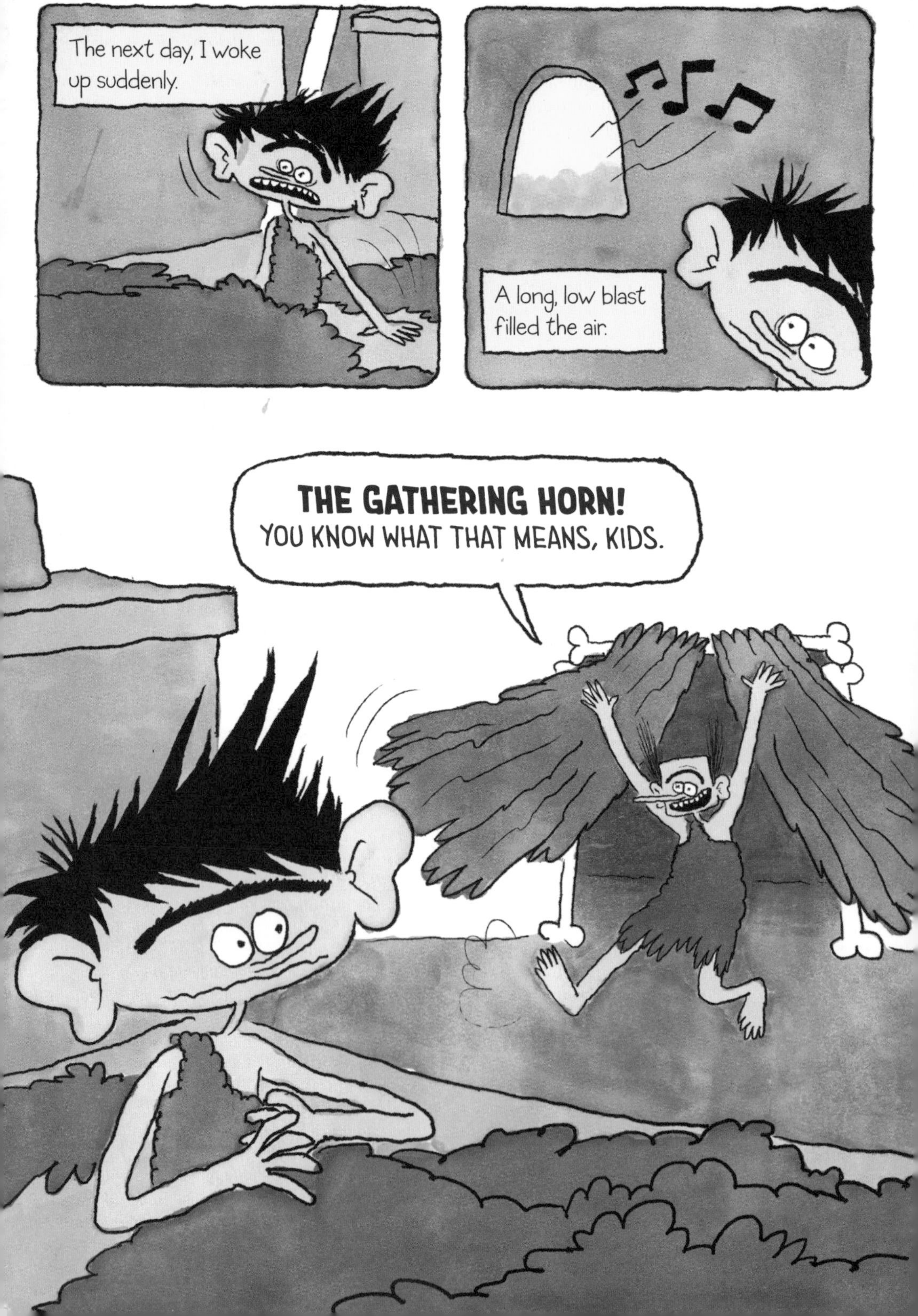

The next day, I woke up suddenly.
A long, low blast filled the air.
THE GATHERING HORN! YOU KNOW WHAT THAT MEANS, KIDS.

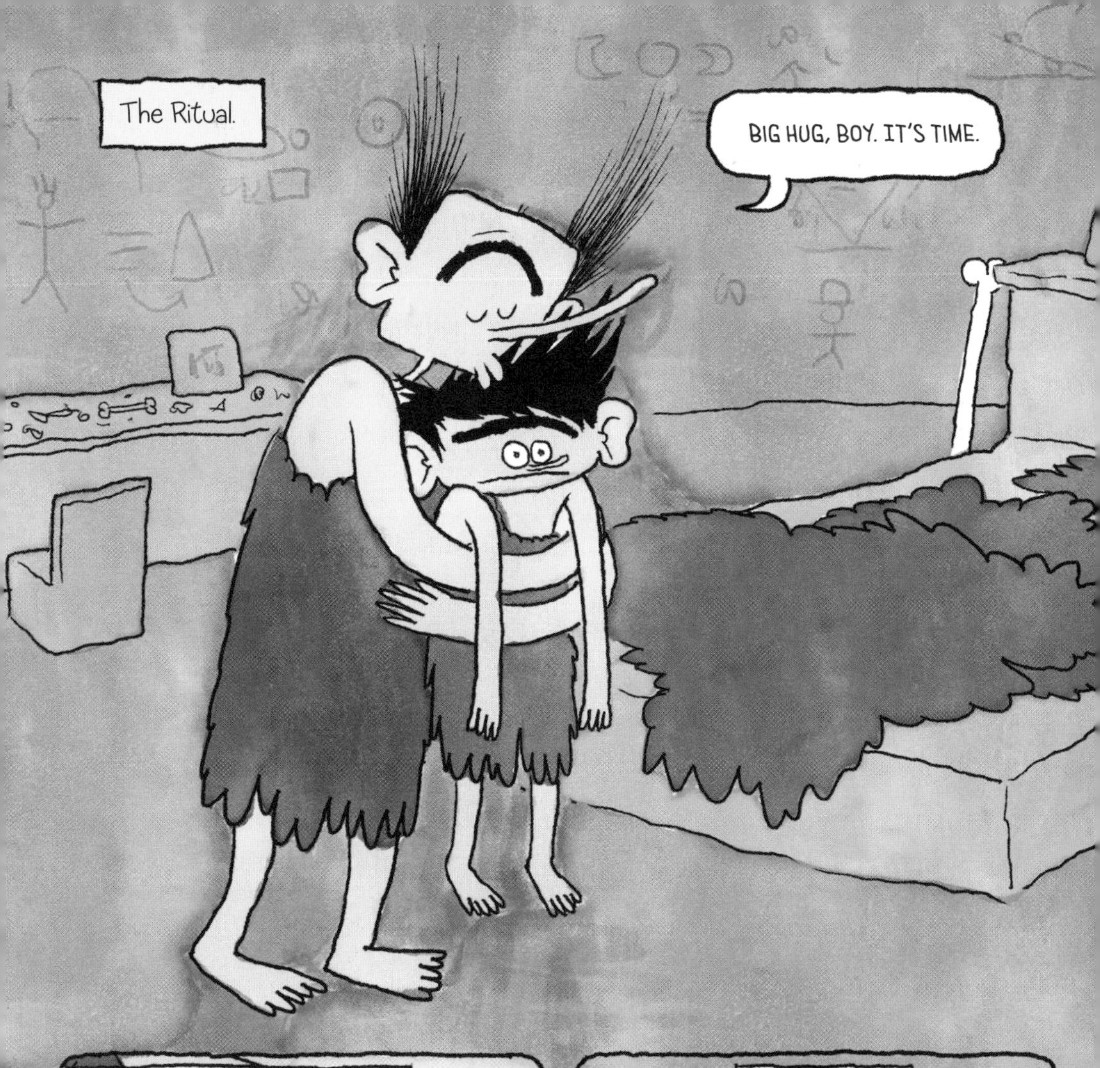
The Ritual.
BIG HUG, BOY. IT'S TIME.

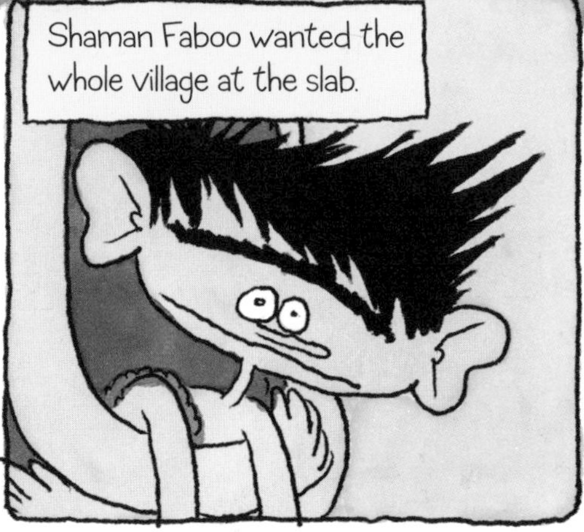
Shaman Faboo wanted the whole village at the slab.

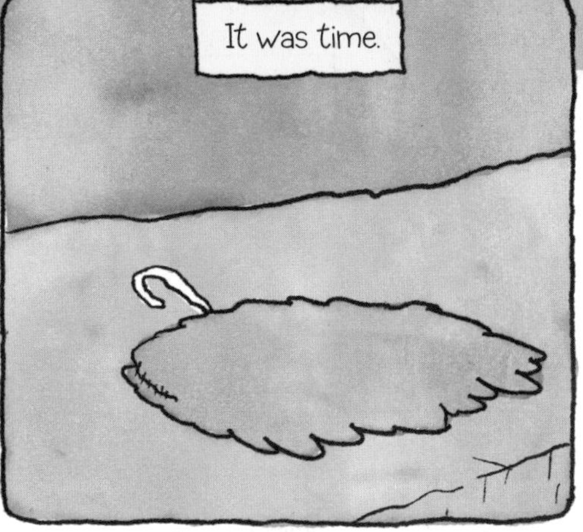
It was time.

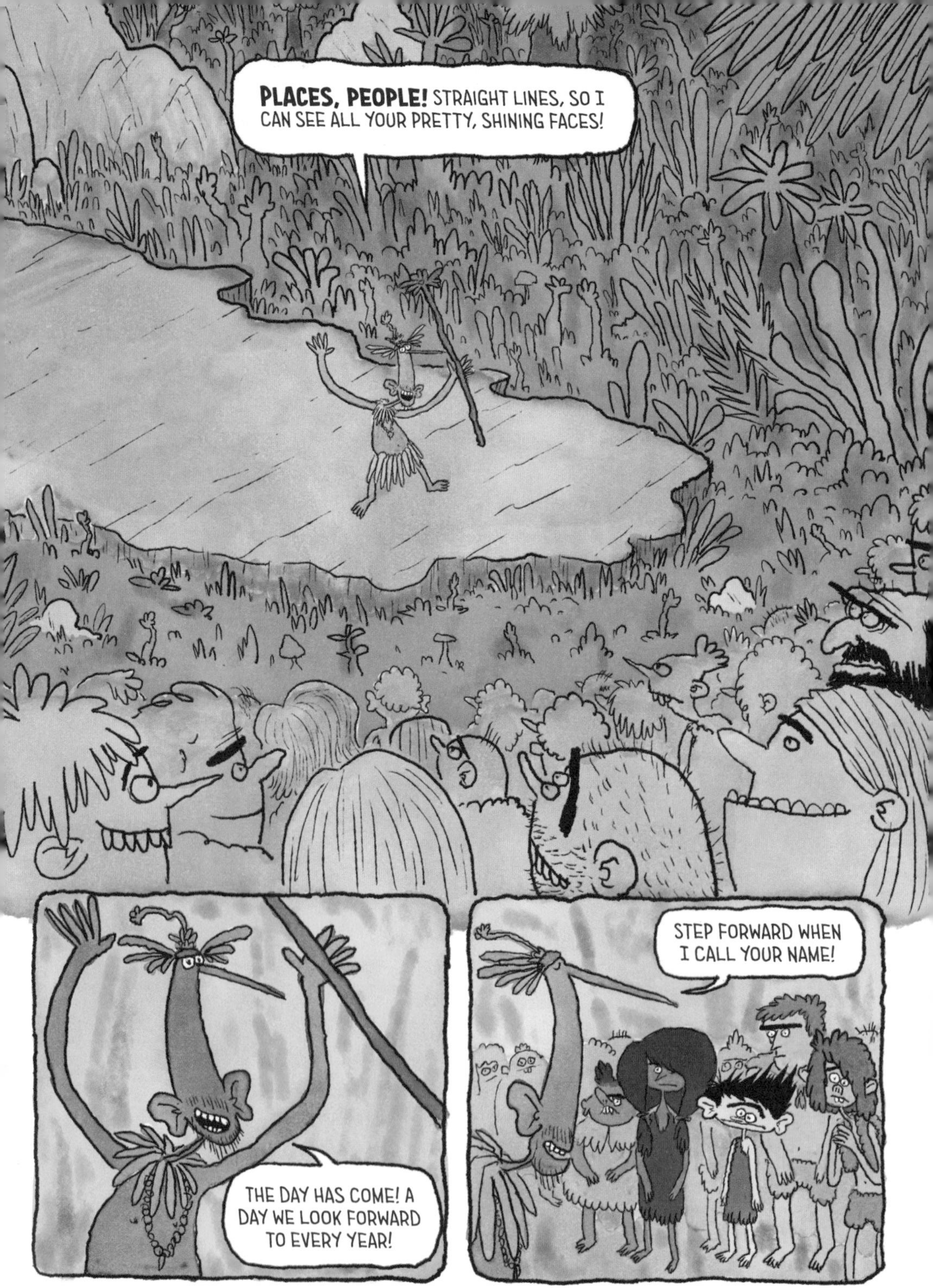
PLACES, PEOPLE! STRAIGHT LINES, SO I CAN SEE ALL YOUR PRETTY, SHINING FACES!
THE DAY HAS COME! A DAY WE LOOK FORWARD TO EVERY YEAR!
STEP FORWARD WHEN I CALL YOUR NAME!

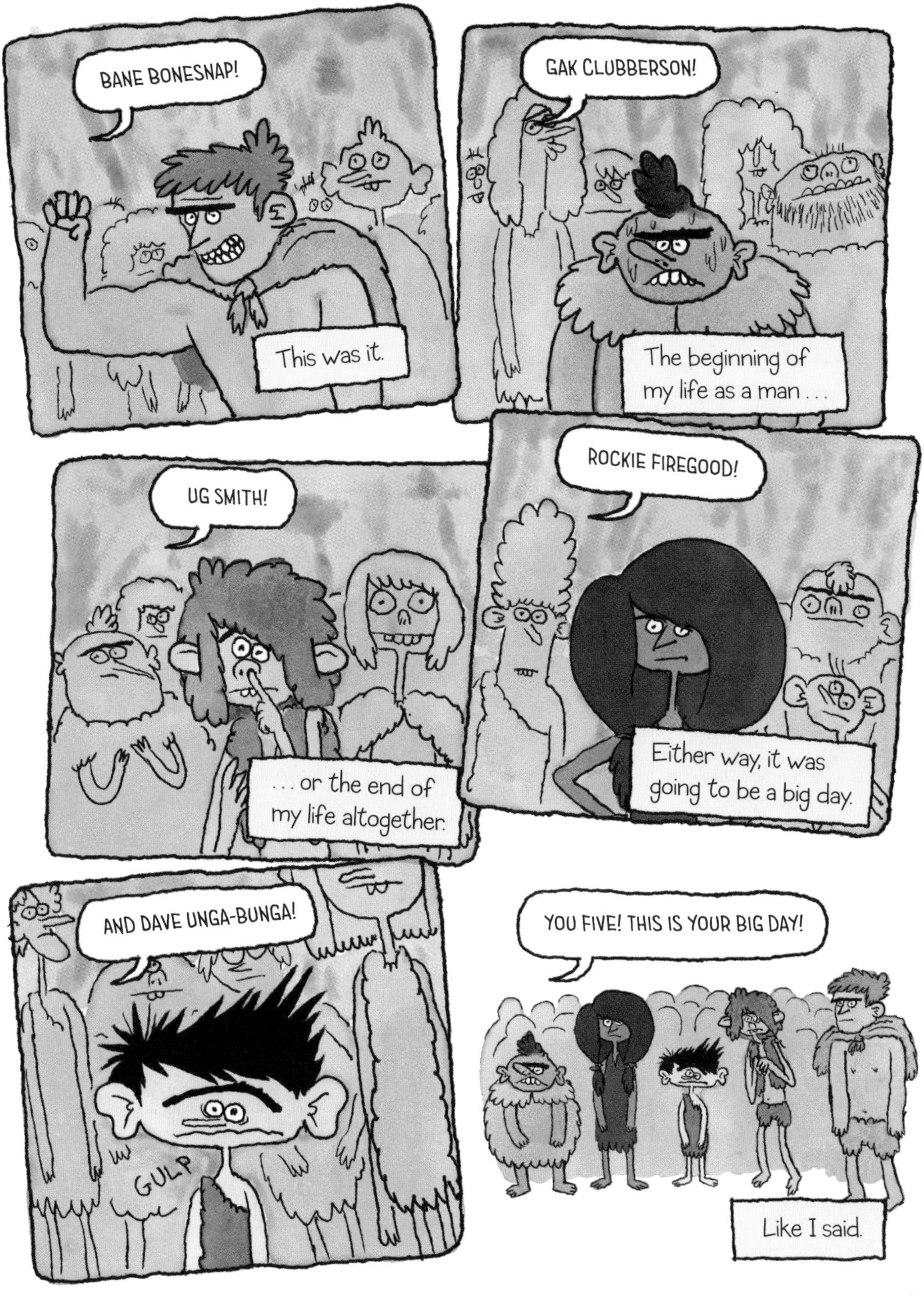
BANE BONESNAP!
This was it.
GAK CLUBBERSON!
The beginning of my life as a man . . .
UG SMITH!
. . . or the end of my life altogether.
ROCKIE FIREGOOD!
Either way, it was going to be a big day.
AND DAVE UNGA-BUNGA!
GULP
YOU FIVE! THIS IS YOUR BIG DAY!
Like I said.

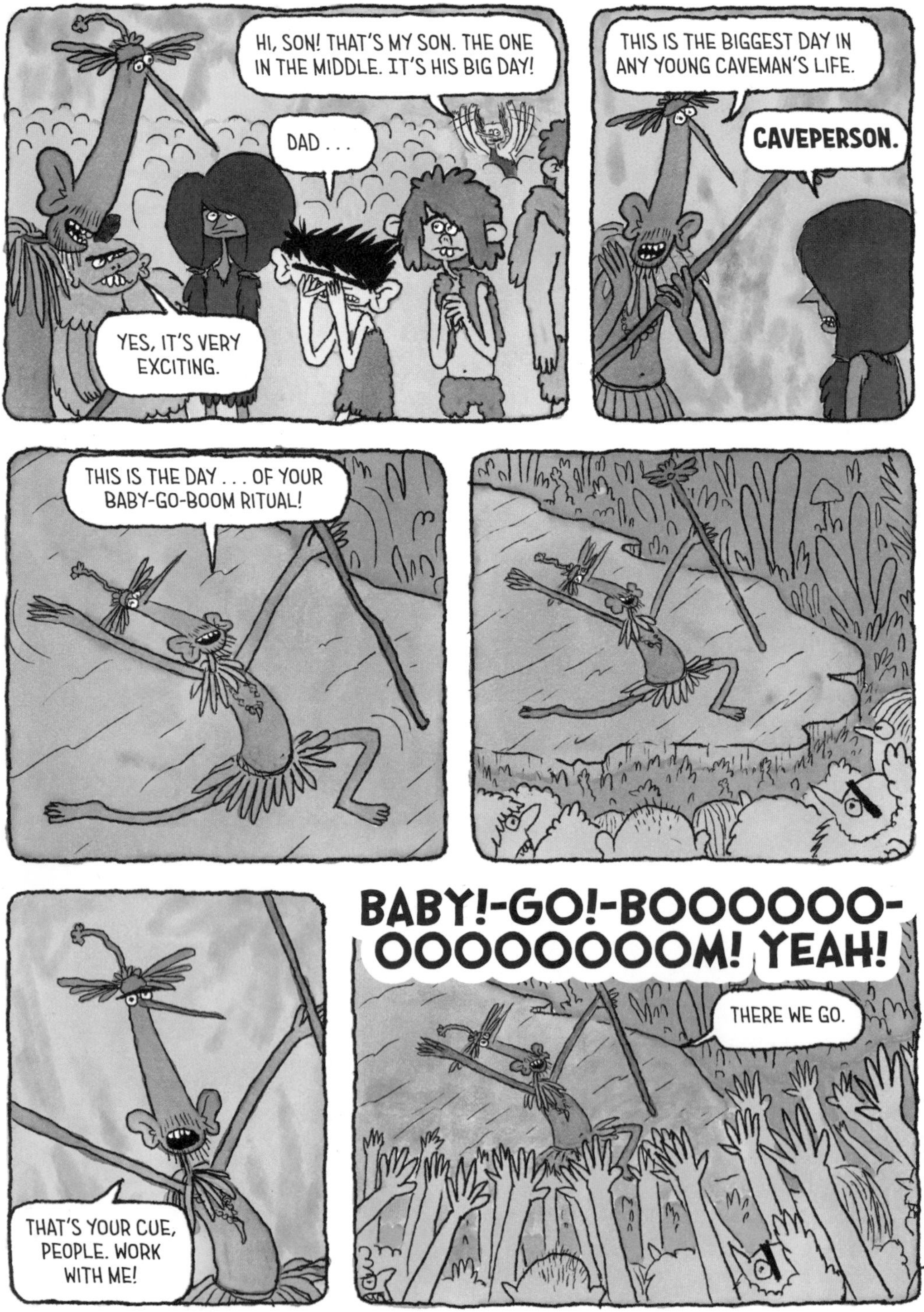
HI, SON! THAT'S MY SON. THE ONE IN THE MIDDLE. IT'S HIS BIG DAY!
DAD . . .
YES, IT'S VERY EXCITING.
THIS IS THE BIGGEST DAY IN ANY YOUNG CAVEMAN'S LIFE.
CAVEPERSON.
THIS IS THE DAY . . . OF YOUR BABY-GO-BOOM RITUAL!
THAT'S YOUR CUE, PEOPLE. WORK WITH ME!
BABY!-GO!-BOOOOOO-OOOOOOOOM! YEAH!
THERE WE GO.

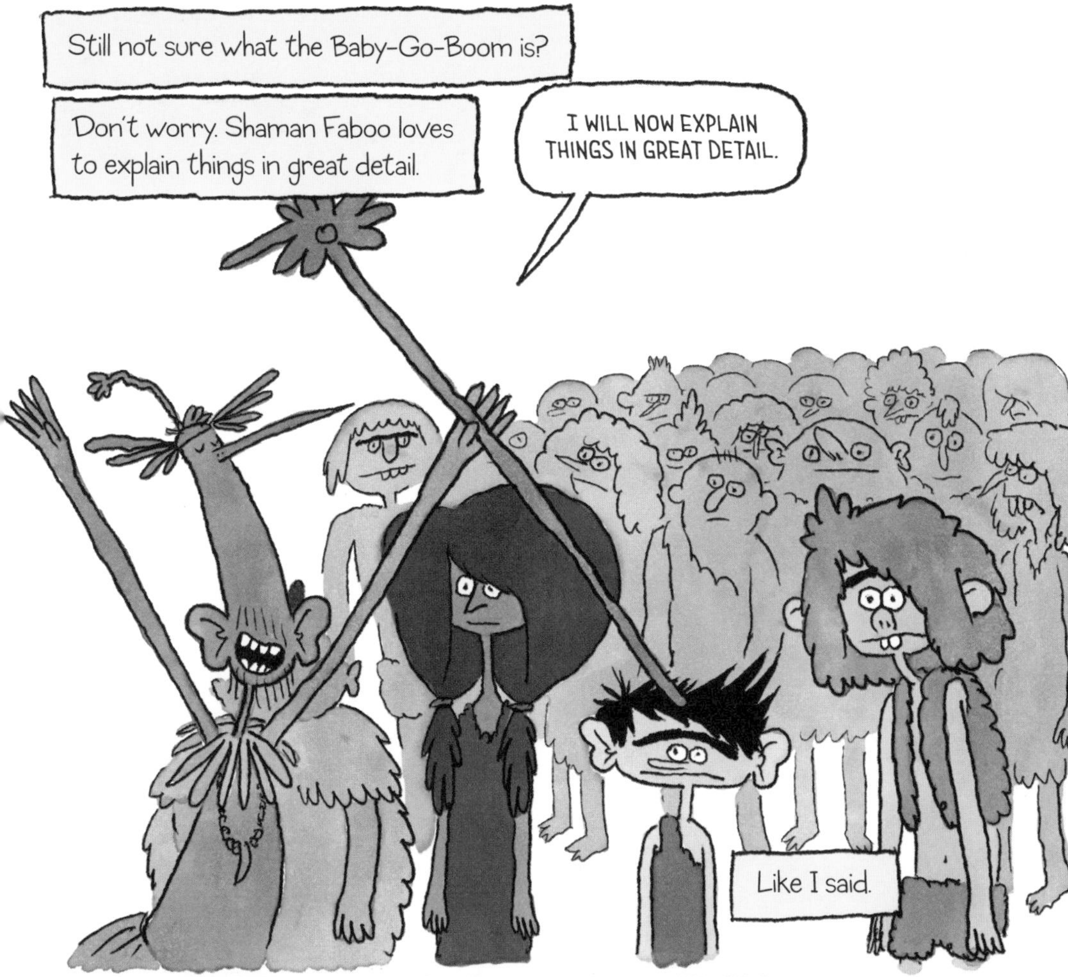
Still not sure what the Baby-Go-Boom is?
Don't worry. Shaman Faboo loves to explain things in great detail.
I WILL NOW EXPLAIN THINGS IN GREAT DETAIL.
Like I said.

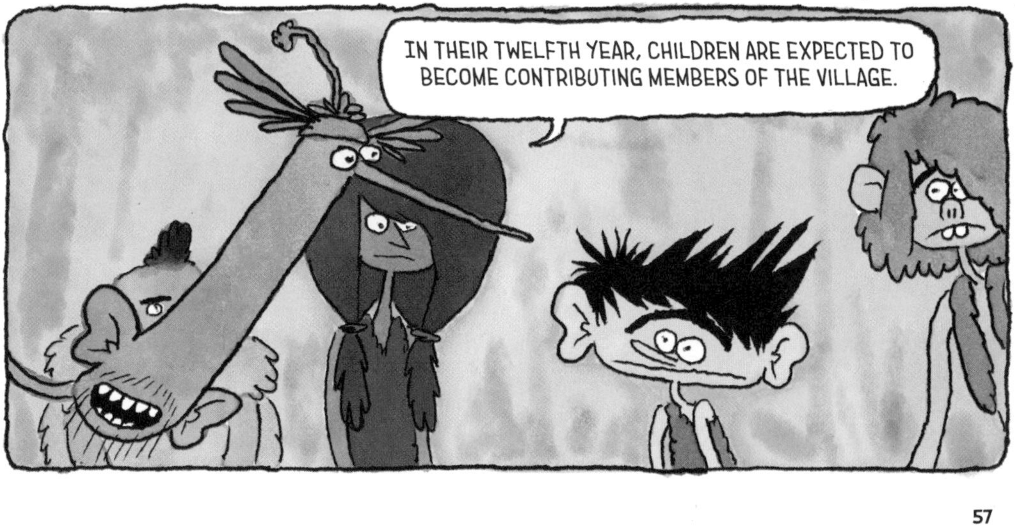
IN THEIR TWELFTH YEAR, CHILDREN ARE EXPECTED TO BECOME CONTRIBUTING MEMBERS OF THE VILLAGE.

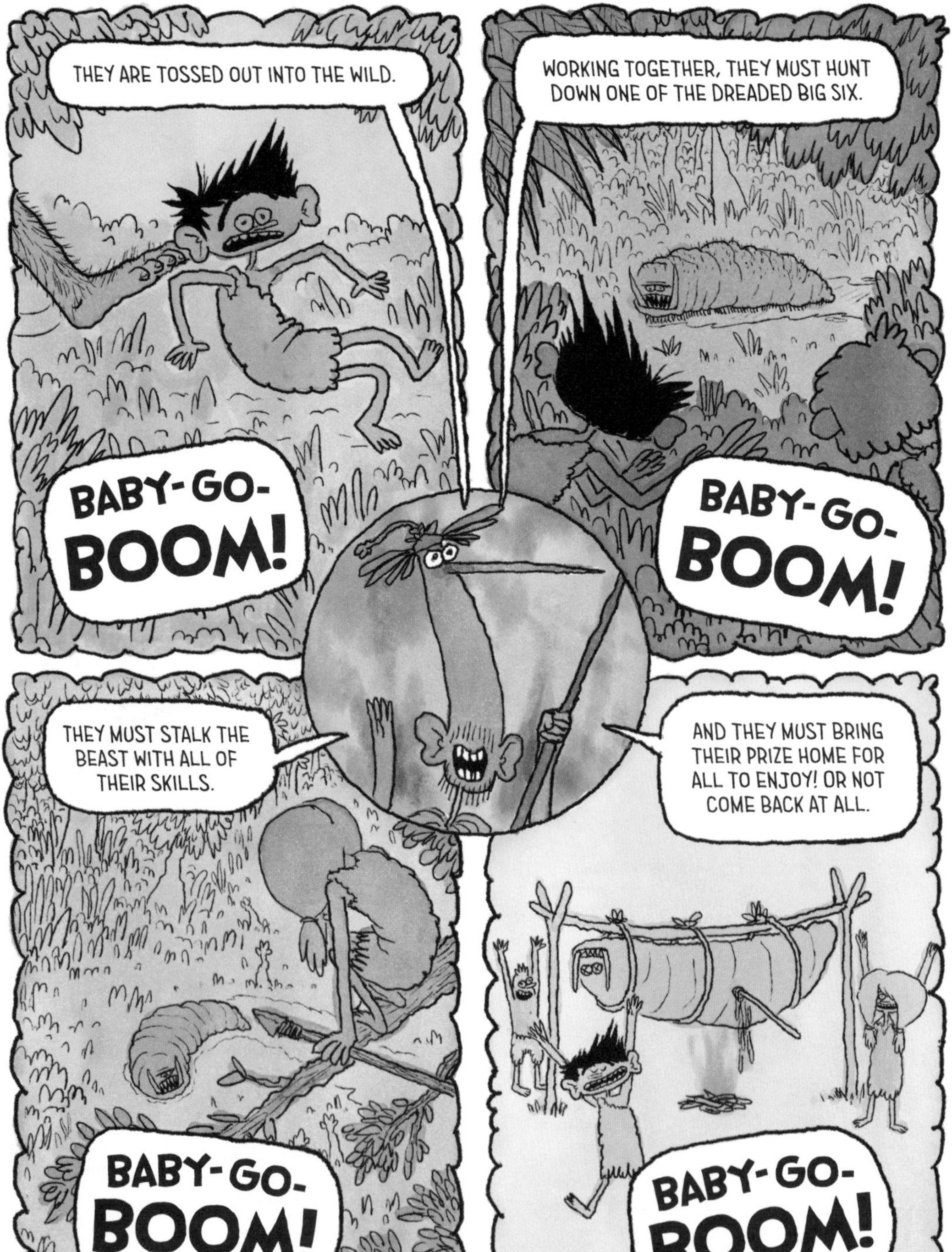
THEY ARE TOSSED OUT INTO THE WILD.
BABY-GO-BOOM!
WORKING TOGETHER, THEY MUST HUNT DOWN ONE OF THE DREADED BIG SIX.
BABY-GO-BOOM!
THEY MUST STALK THE BEAST WITH ALL OF THEIR SKILLS.
BABY-GO-BOOM!
AND THEY MUST BRING THEIR PRIZE HOME FOR ALL TO ENJOY! OR NOT COME BACK AT ALL.
BABY-GO-BOOM!

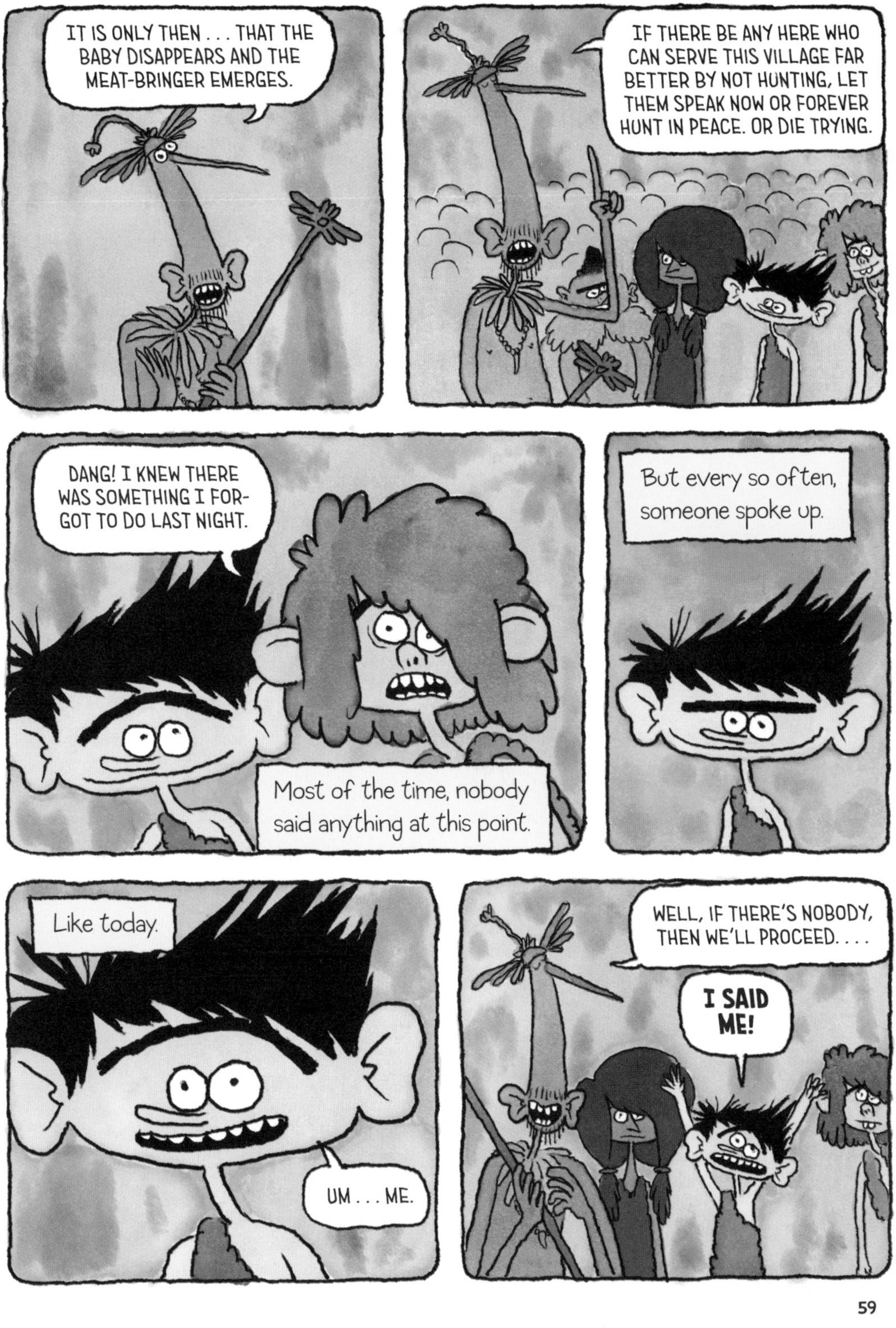
IT IS ONLY THEN . . . THAT THE BABY DISAPPEARS AND THE MEAT-BRINGER EMERGES.
IF THERE BE ANY HERE WHO CAN SERVE THIS VILLAGE FAR BETTER BY NOT HUNTING, LET THEM SPEAK NOW OR FOREVER HUNT IN PEACE. OR DIE TRYING.
DANG! I KNEW THERE WAS SOMETHING I FOR-GOT TO DO LAST NIGHT.
Most of the time, nobody said anything at this point.
But every so often, someone spoke up.
Like today.
UM . . . ME.
WELL, IF THERE'S NOBODY, THEN WE'LL PROCEED. . . .
I SAID ME!

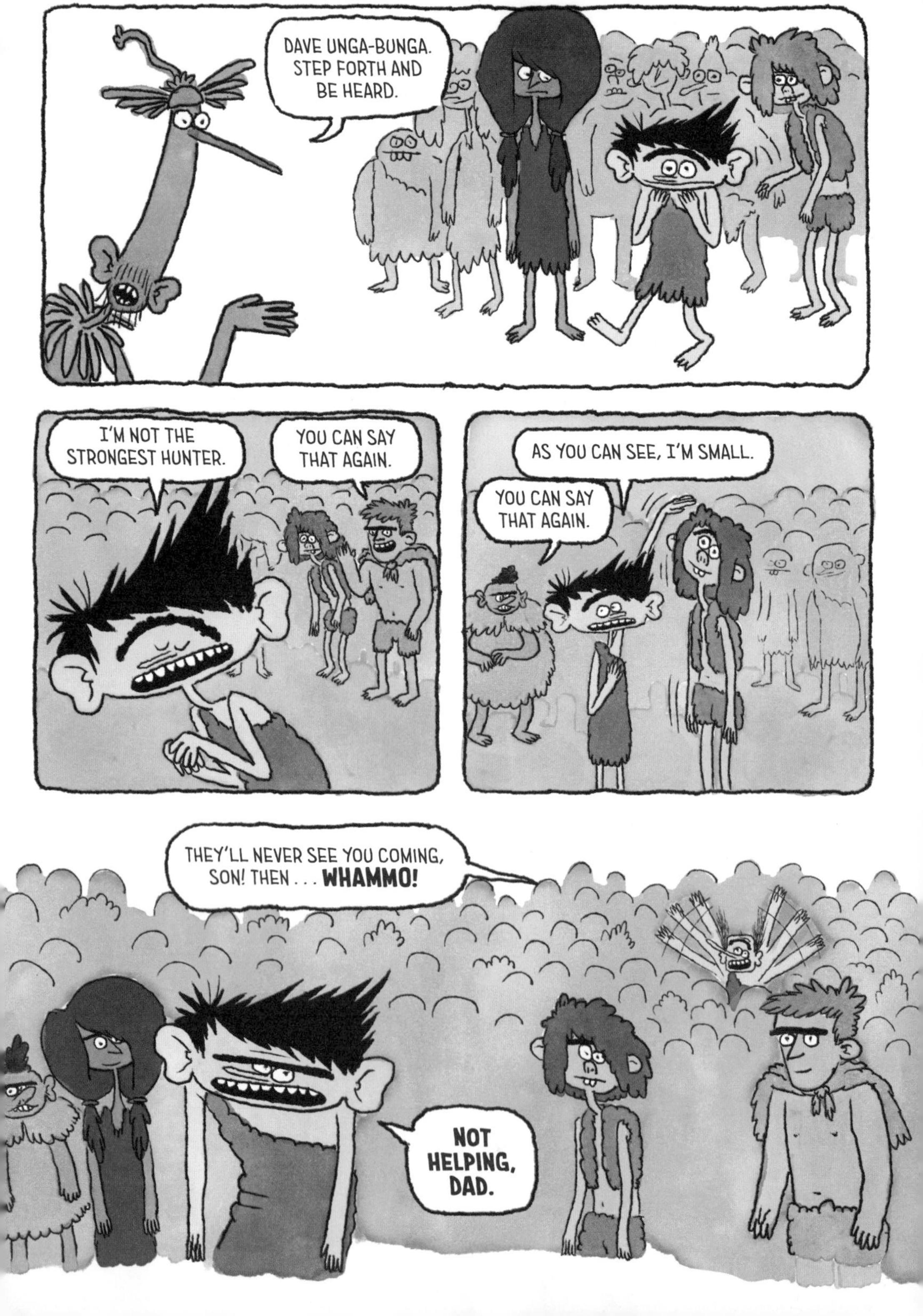
DAVE UNGA-BUNGA. STEP FORTH AND BE HEARD.
I'M NOT THE STRONGEST HUNTER.
YOU CAN SAY THAT AGAIN.
AS YOU CAN SEE, I'M SMALL.
YOU CAN SAY THAT AGAIN.
THEY'LL NEVER SEE YOU COMING, SON! THEN . . . **WHAMMO!**
NOT HELPING, DAD.

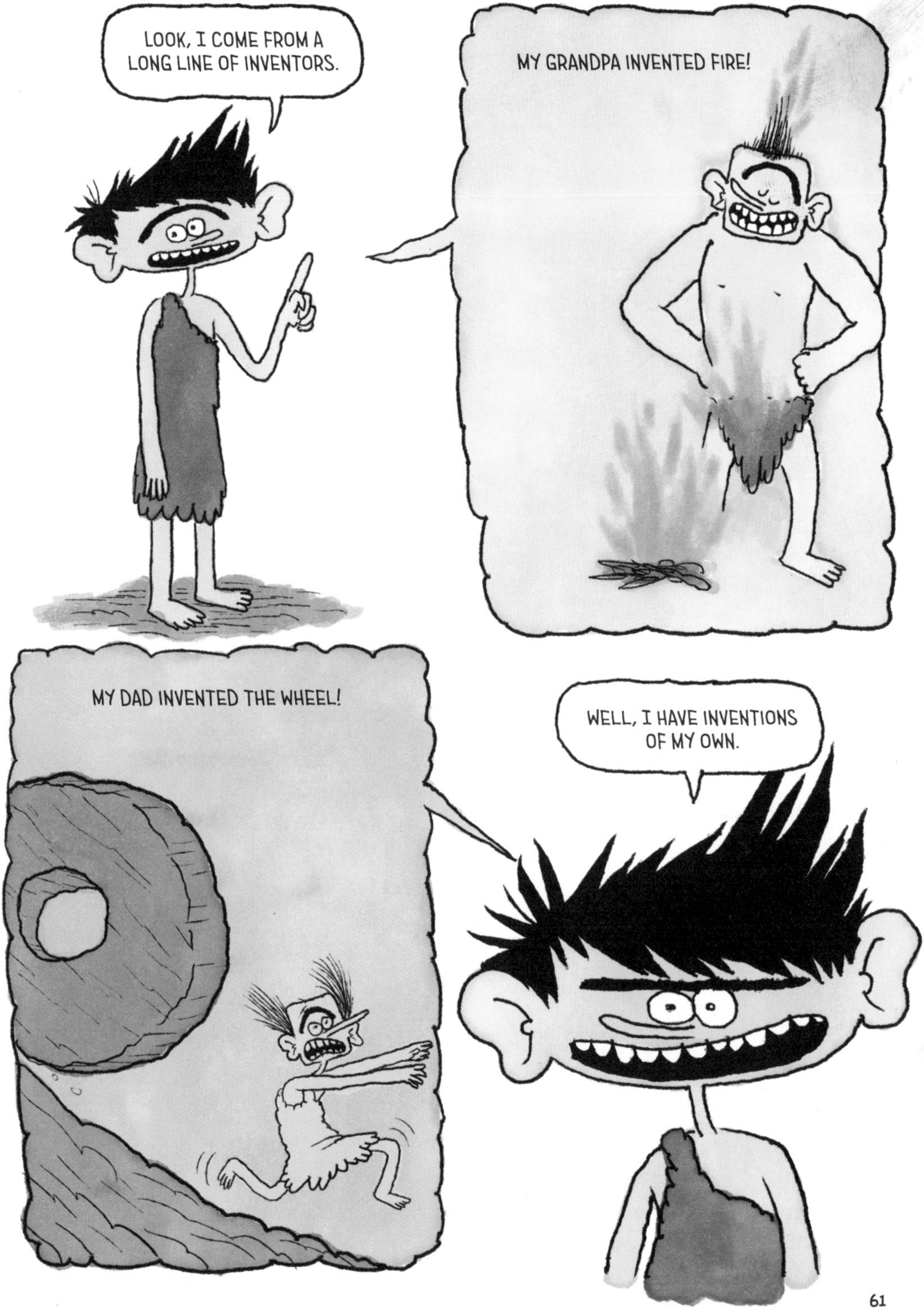

LOOK, I COME FROM A LONG LINE OF INVENTORS.
MY GRANDPA INVENTED FIRE!
MY DAD INVENTED THE WHEEL!
WELL, I HAVE INVENTIONS OF MY OWN.

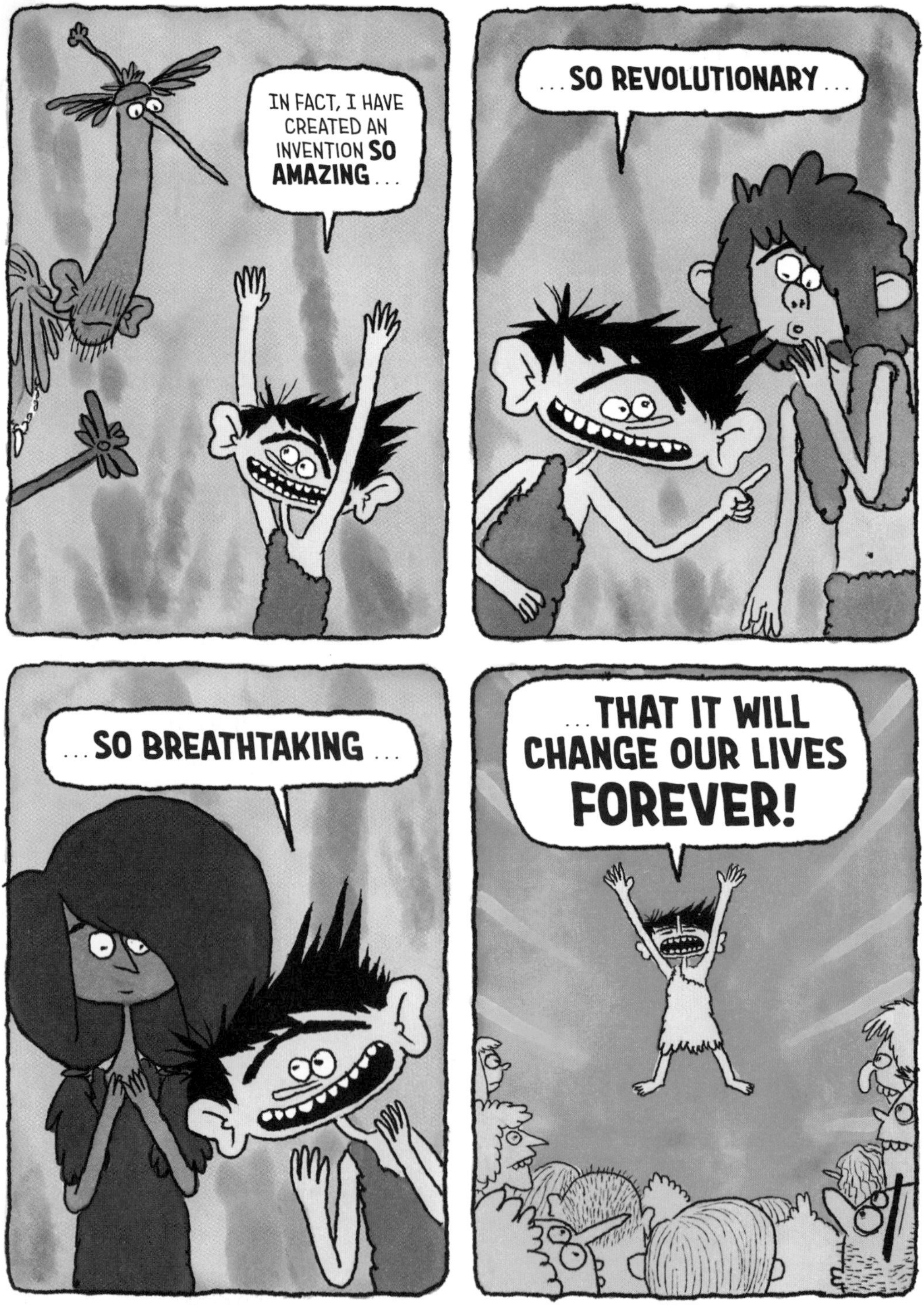
IN FACT, I HAVE CREATED AN INVENTION SO AMAZING . . .
. . . SO REVOLUTIONARY . . .
. . . SO BREATHTAKING . . .
. . . THAT IT WILL CHANGE OUR LIVES FOREVER!

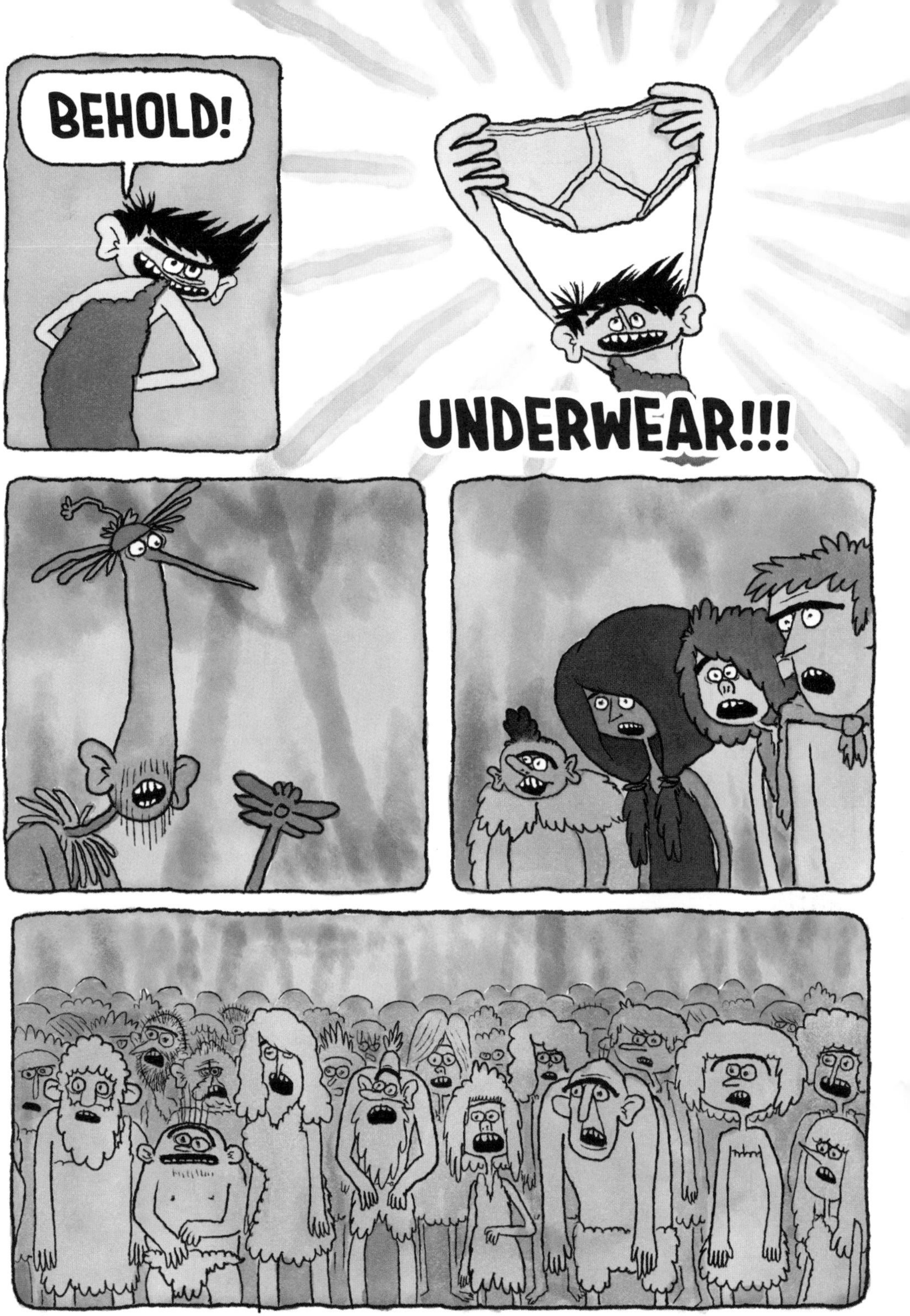
BEHOLD!
UNDERWEAR!!!

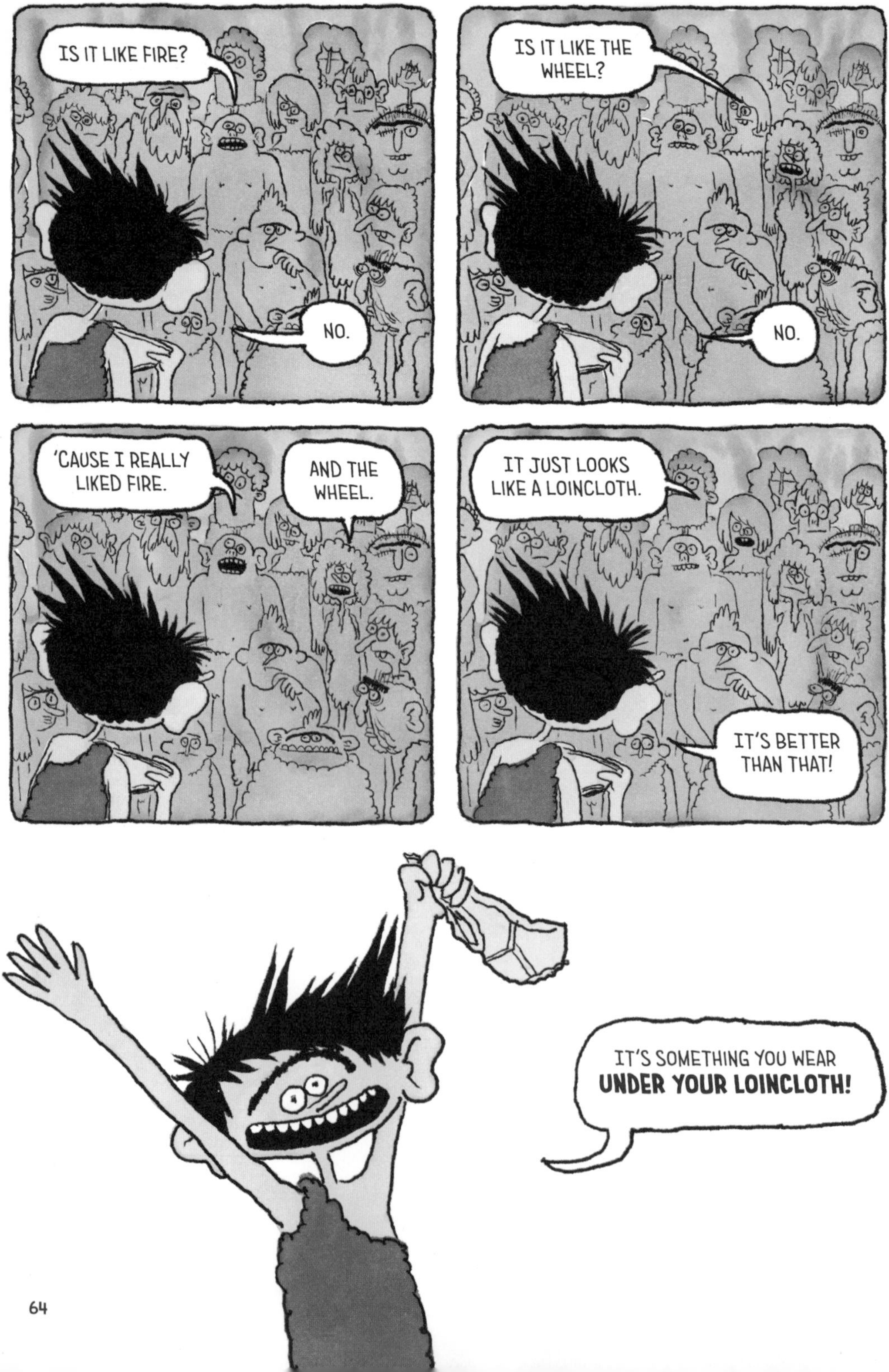
IS IT LIKE FIRE?
NO.
IS IT LIKE THE WHEEL?
NO.
'CAUSE I REALLY LIKED FIRE.
AND THE WHEEL.
IT JUST LOOKS LIKE A LOINCLOTH.
IT'S BETTER THAN THAT!
IT'S SOMETHING YOU WEAR **UNDER YOUR LOINCLOTH!**

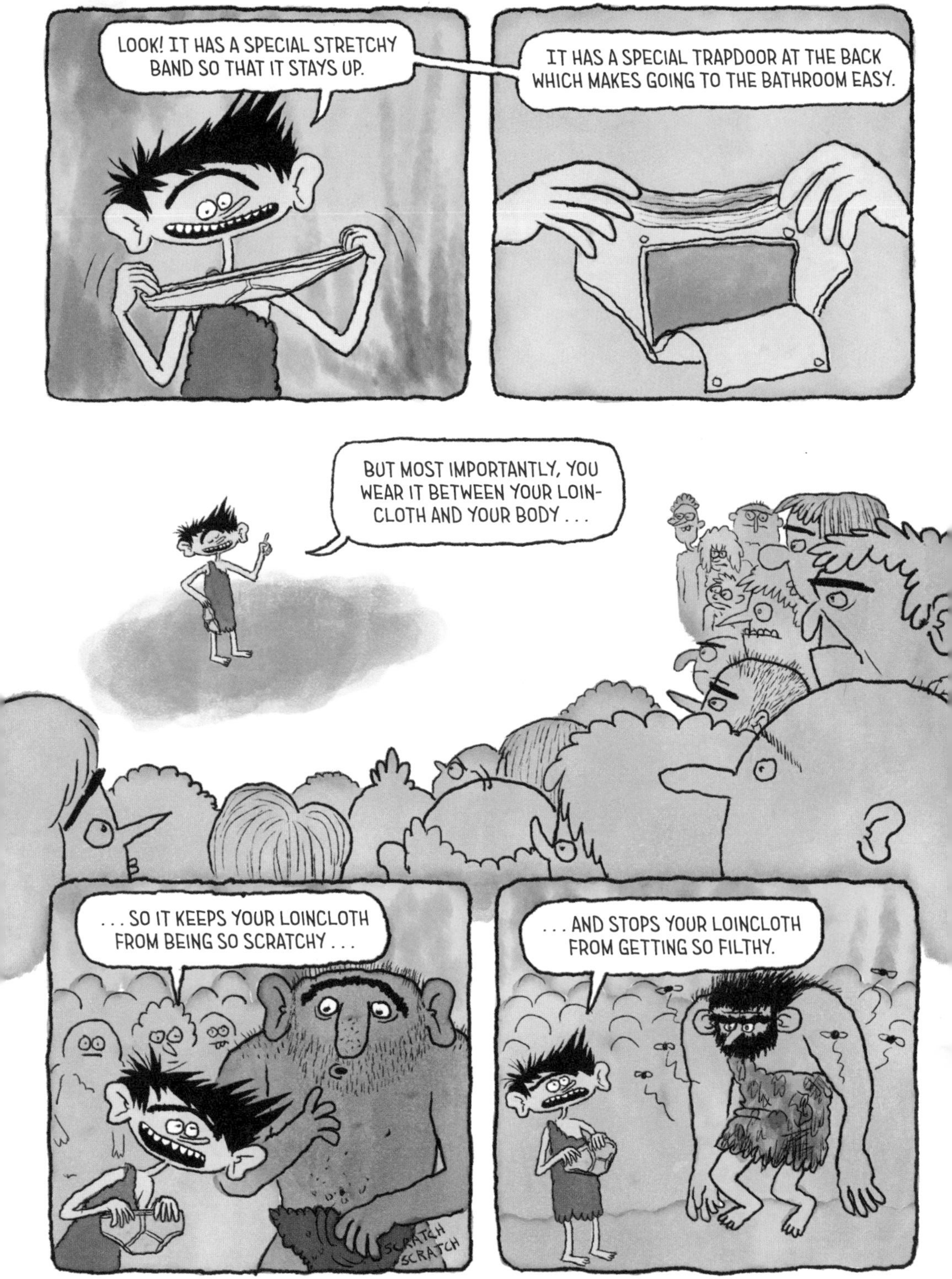
LOOK! IT HAS A SPECIAL STRETCHY BAND SO THAT IT STAYS UP.
IT HAS A SPECIAL TRAPDOOR AT THE BACK WHICH MAKES GOING TO THE BATHROOM EASY.
BUT MOST IMPORTANTLY, YOU WEAR IT BETWEEN YOUR LOIN-CLOTH AND YOUR BODY . . .
. . . SO IT KEEPS YOUR LOINCLOTH FROM BEING SO SCRATCHY . . .
SCRATCH SCRATCH
. . . AND STOPS YOUR LOINCLOTH FROM GETTING SO FILTHY.

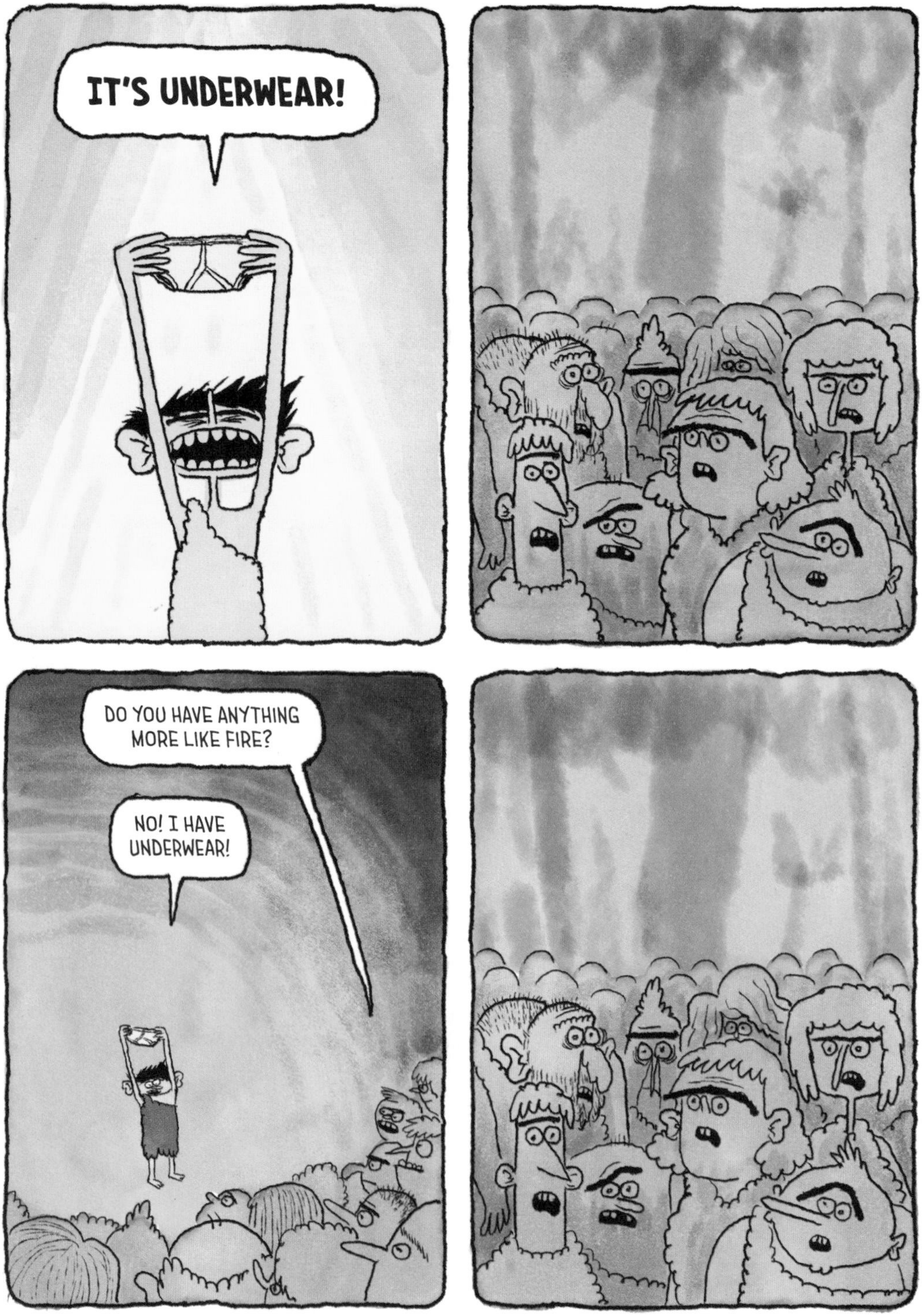
IT'S UNDERWEAR!
DO YOU HAVE ANYTHING MORE LIKE FIRE?
NO! I HAVE UNDERWEAR!

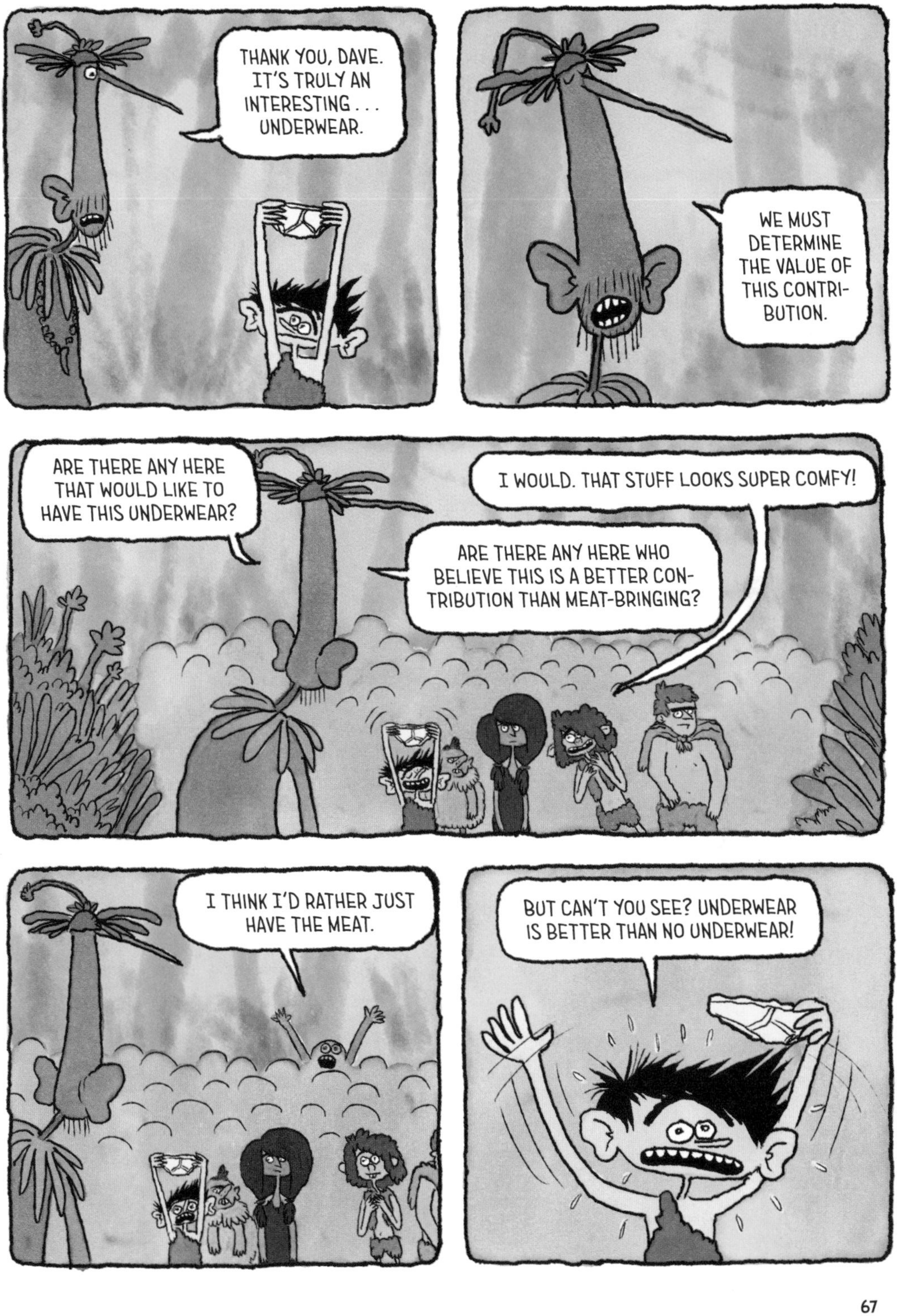
THANK YOU, DAVE. IT'S TRULY AN INTERESTING . . . UNDERWEAR.
WE MUST DETERMINE THE VALUE OF THIS CONTRI-BUTION.
ARE THERE ANY HERE THAT WOULD LIKE TO HAVE THIS UNDERWEAR?
ARE THERE ANY HERE WHO BELIEVE THIS IS A BETTER CON-TRIBUTION THAN MEAT-BRINGING?
I WOULD. THAT STUFF LOOKS SUPER COMFY!
I THINK I'D RATHER JUST HAVE THE MEAT.
BUT CAN'T YOU SEE? UNDERWEAR IS BETTER THAN NO UNDERWEAR!

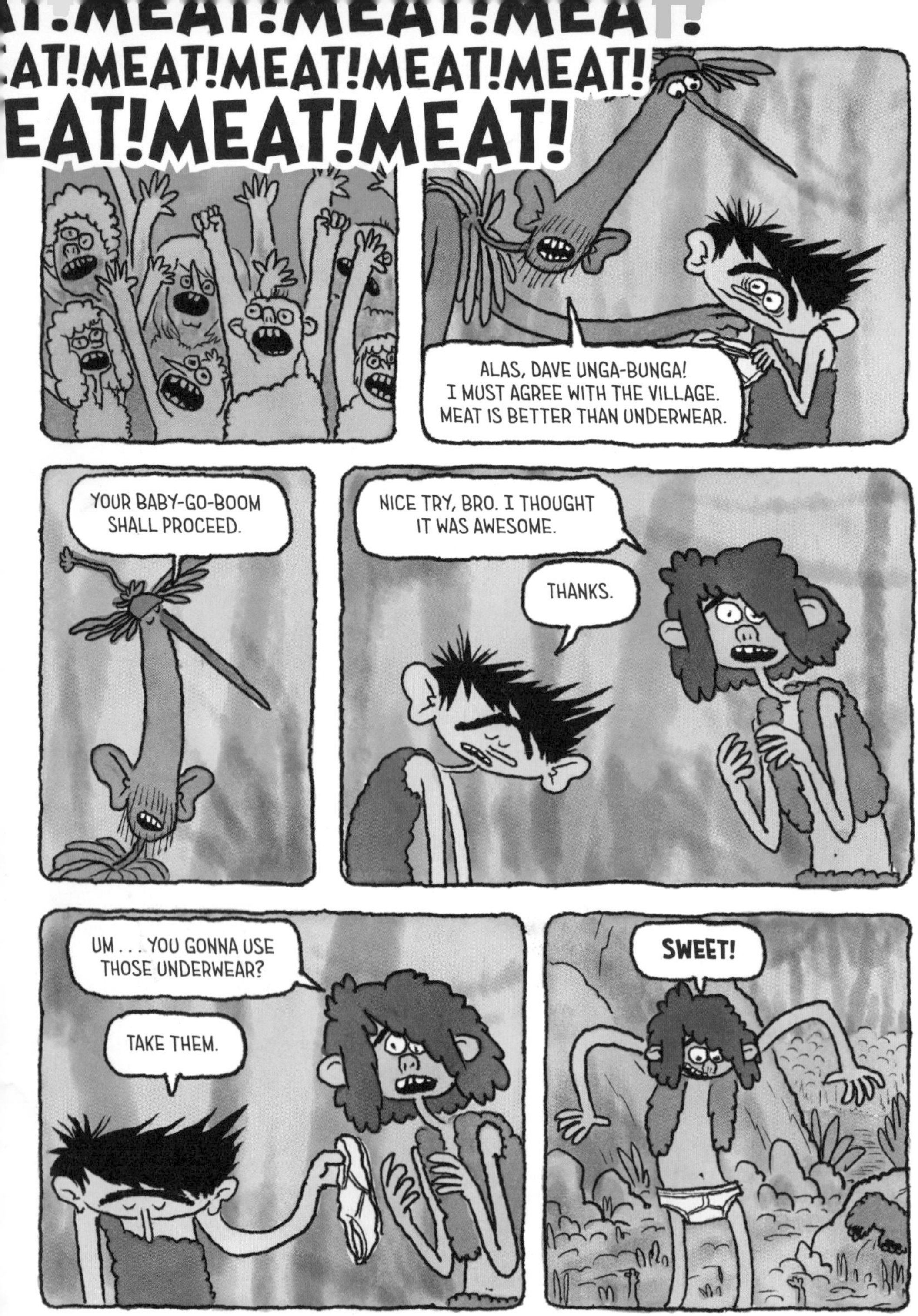
AT!MEAT!MEAT!MEAT!MEAT!
EAT!MEAT!MEAT!
ALAS, DAVE UNGA-BUNGA! I MUST AGREE WITH THE VILLAGE. MEAT IS BETTER THAN UNDERWEAR.
YOUR BABY-GO-BOOM SHALL PROCEED.
NICE TRY, BRO. I THOUGHT IT WAS AWESOME.
THANKS.
UM . . . YOU GONNA USE THOSE UNDERWEAR?
TAKE THEM.
SWEET!

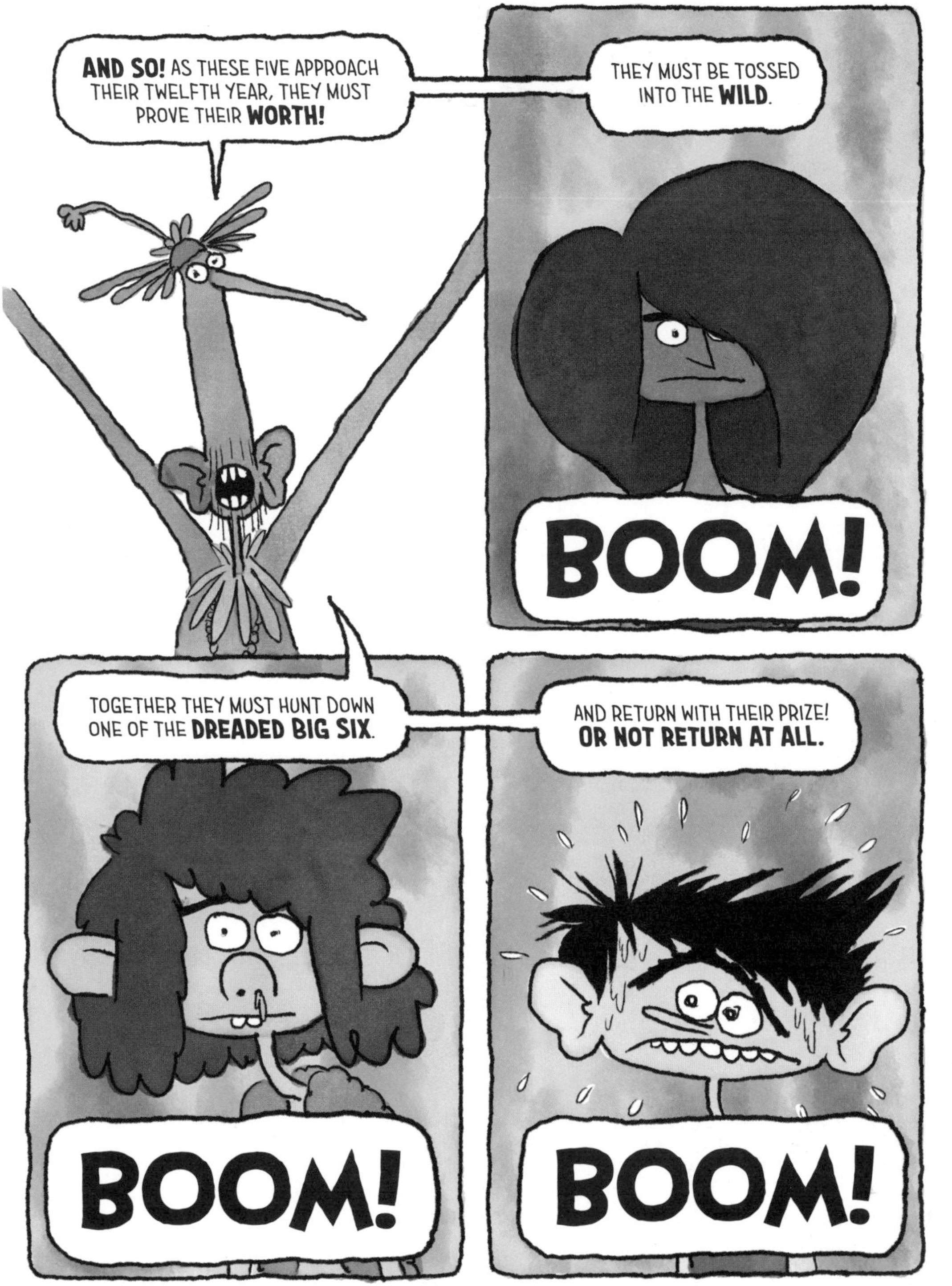
AND SO! AS THESE FIVE APPROACH THEIR TWELFTH YEAR, THEY MUST PROVE THEIR WORTH!
THEY MUST BE TOSSED INTO THE WILD.
BOOM!
TOGETHER THEY MUST HUNT DOWN ONE OF THE DREADED BIG SIX.
AND RETURN WITH THEIR PRIZE! OR NOT RETURN AT ALL.
BOOM!
BOOM!

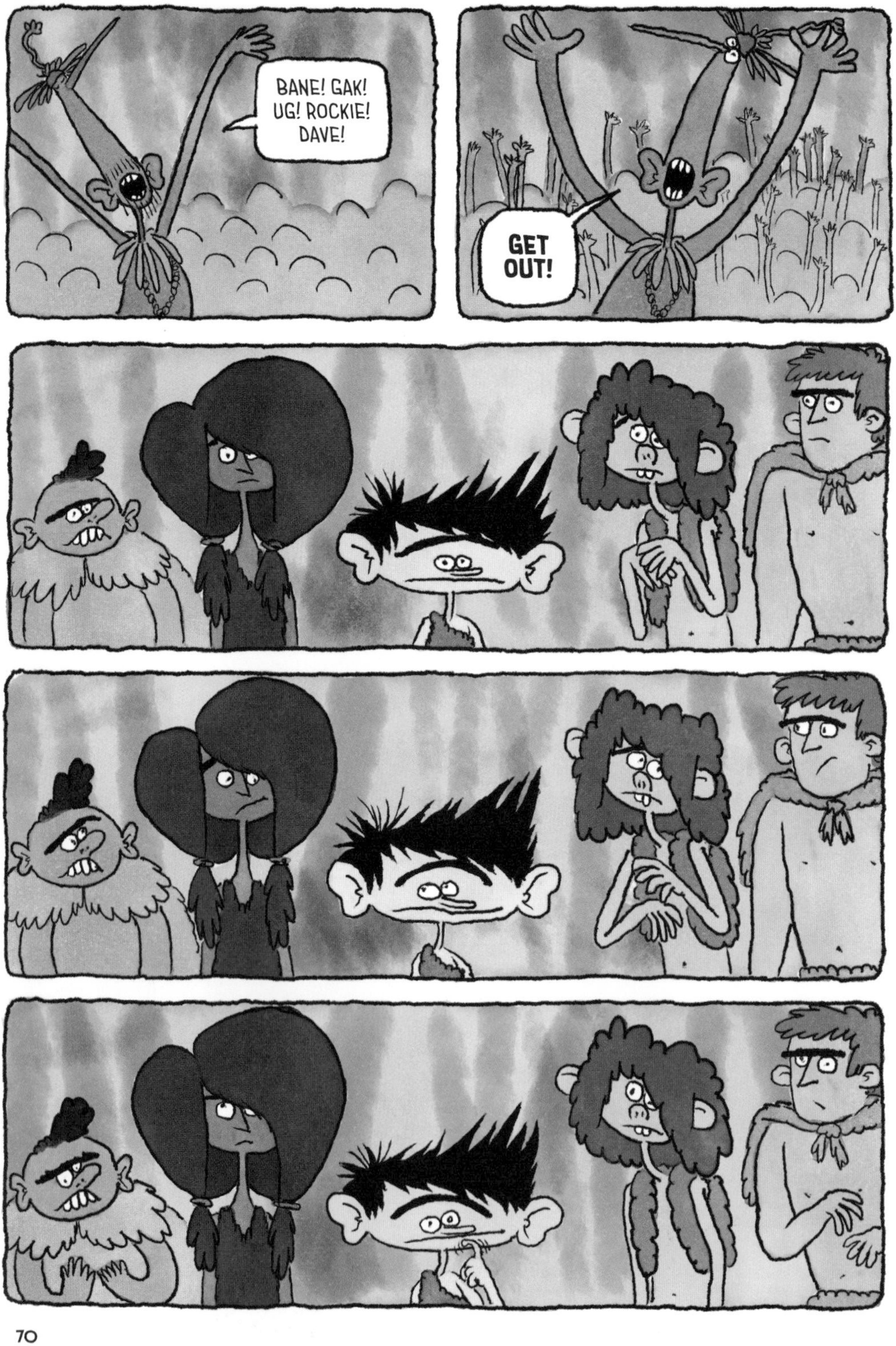

BANE! GAK! UG! ROCKIE! DAVE!
GET OUT!

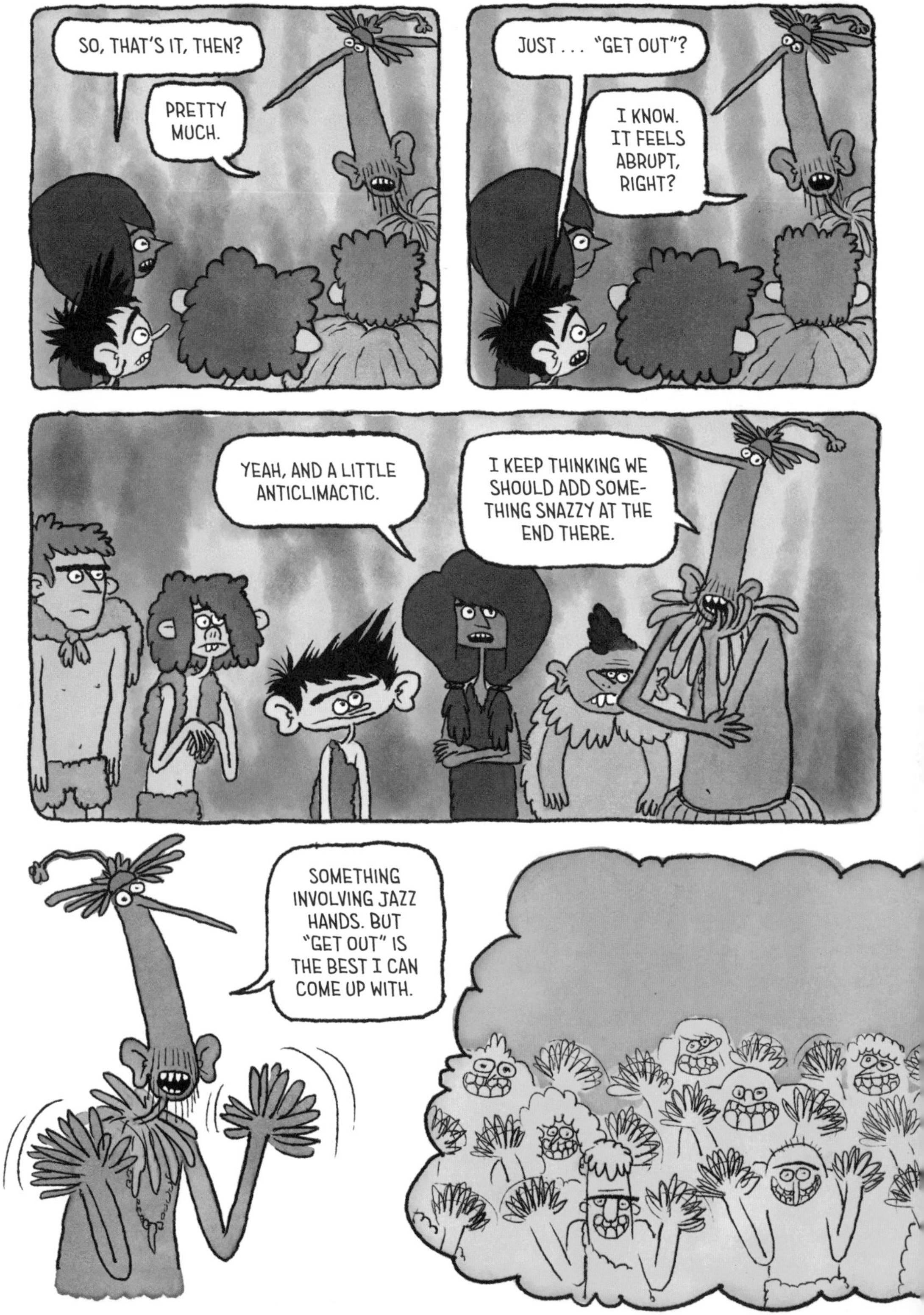
SO, THAT'S IT, THEN?
PRETTY MUCH.
JUST . . . "GET OUT"?
I KNOW. IT FEELS ABRUPT, RIGHT?
YEAH, AND A LITTLE ANTICLIMACTIC.
I KEEP THINKING WE SHOULD ADD SOME-THING SNAZZY AT THE END THERE.
SOMETHING INVOLVING JAZZ HANDS. BUT "GET OUT" IS THE BEST I CAN COME UP WITH.

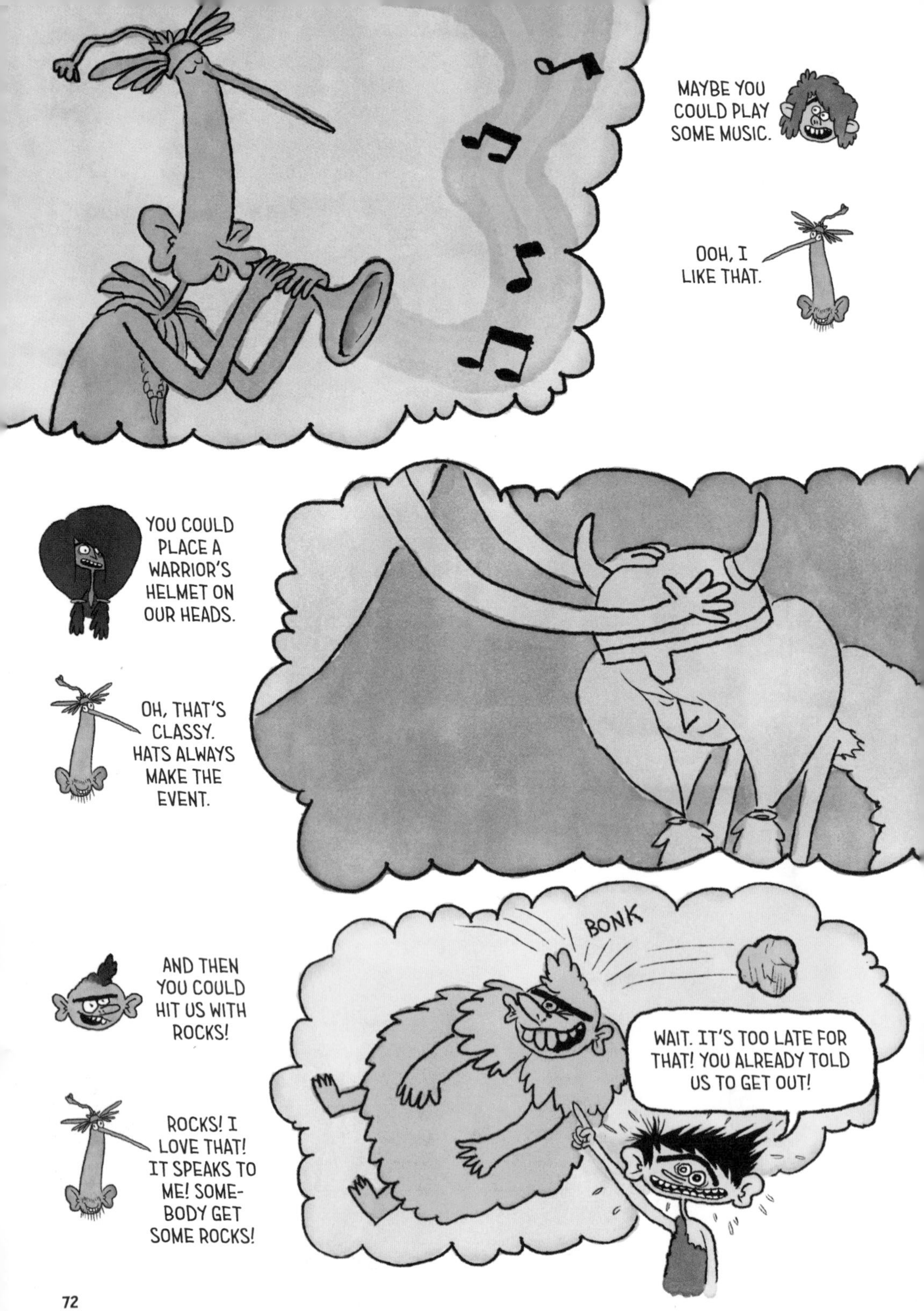
MAYBE YOU COULD PLAY SOME MUSIC.
OOH, I LIKE THAT.
YOU COULD PLACE A WARRIOR'S HELMET ON OUR HEADS.
OH, THAT'S CLASSY. HATS ALWAYS MAKE THE EVENT.
AND THEN YOU COULD HIT US WITH ROCKS!
BONK
ROCKS! I LOVE THAT! IT SPEAKS TO ME! SOME-BODY GET SOME ROCKS!
WAIT. IT'S TOO LATE FOR THAT! YOU ALREADY TOLD US TO GET OUT!

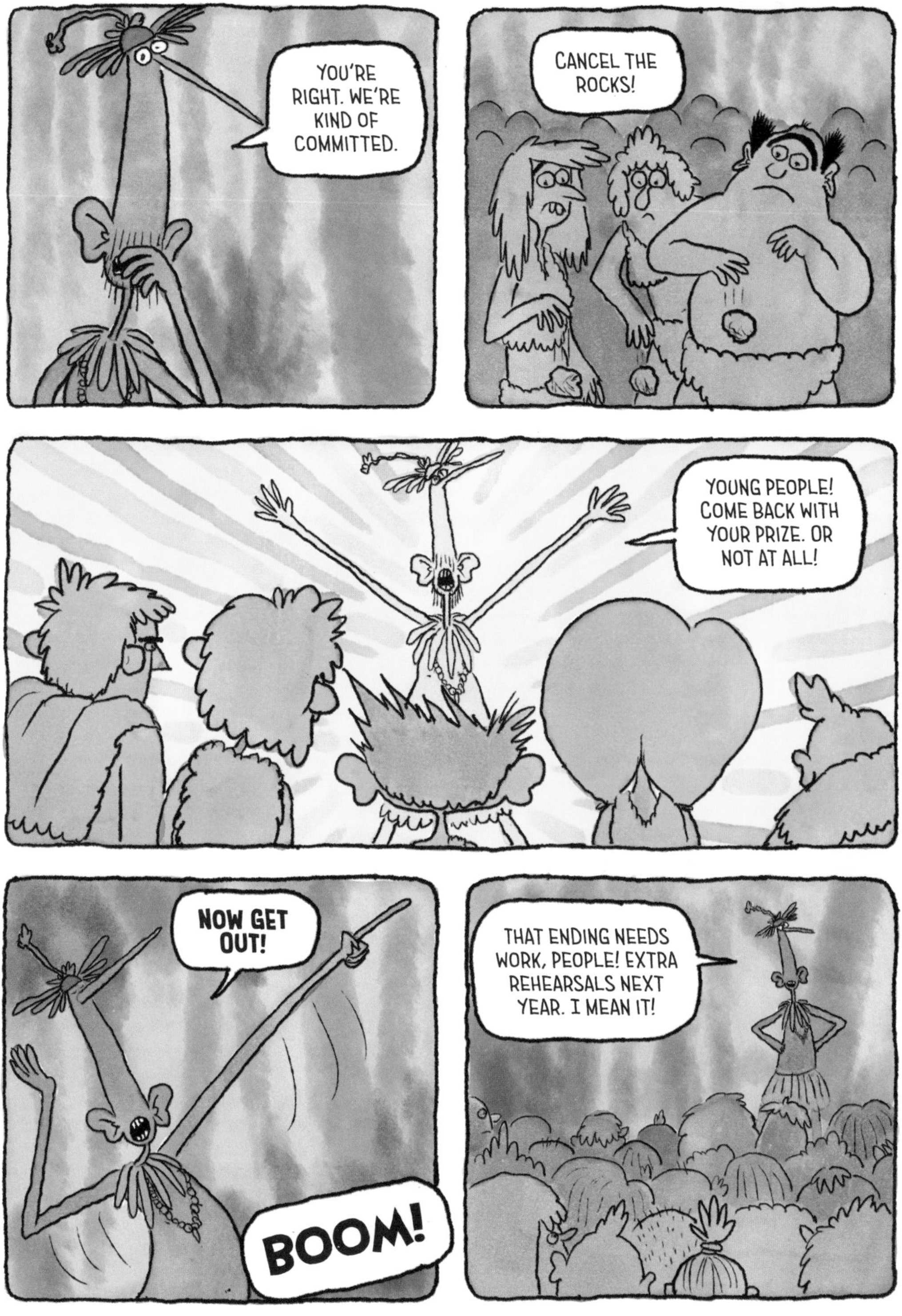
YOU'RE RIGHT. WE'RE KIND OF COMMITTED.
CANCEL THE ROCKS!
YOUNG PEOPLE! COME BACK WITH YOUR PRIZE. OR NOT AT ALL!
NOW GET OUT!
BOOM!
THAT ENDING NEEDS WORK, PEOPLE! EXTRA REHEARSALS NEXT YEAR. I MEAN IT!

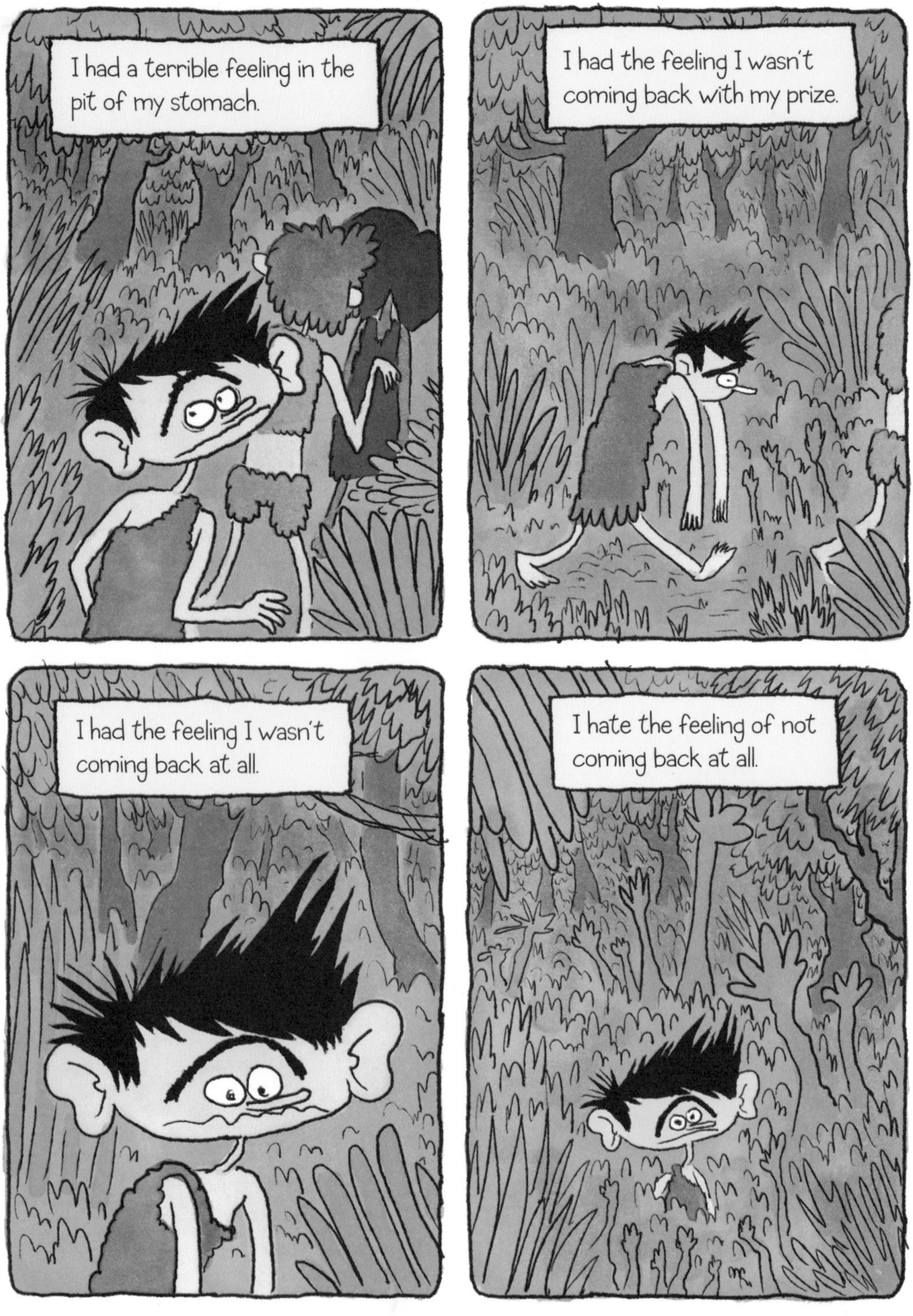
I had a terrible feeling in the pit of my stomach.
I had the feeling I wasn't coming back with my prize.
I had the feeling I wasn't coming back at all.
I hate the feeling of not coming back at all.

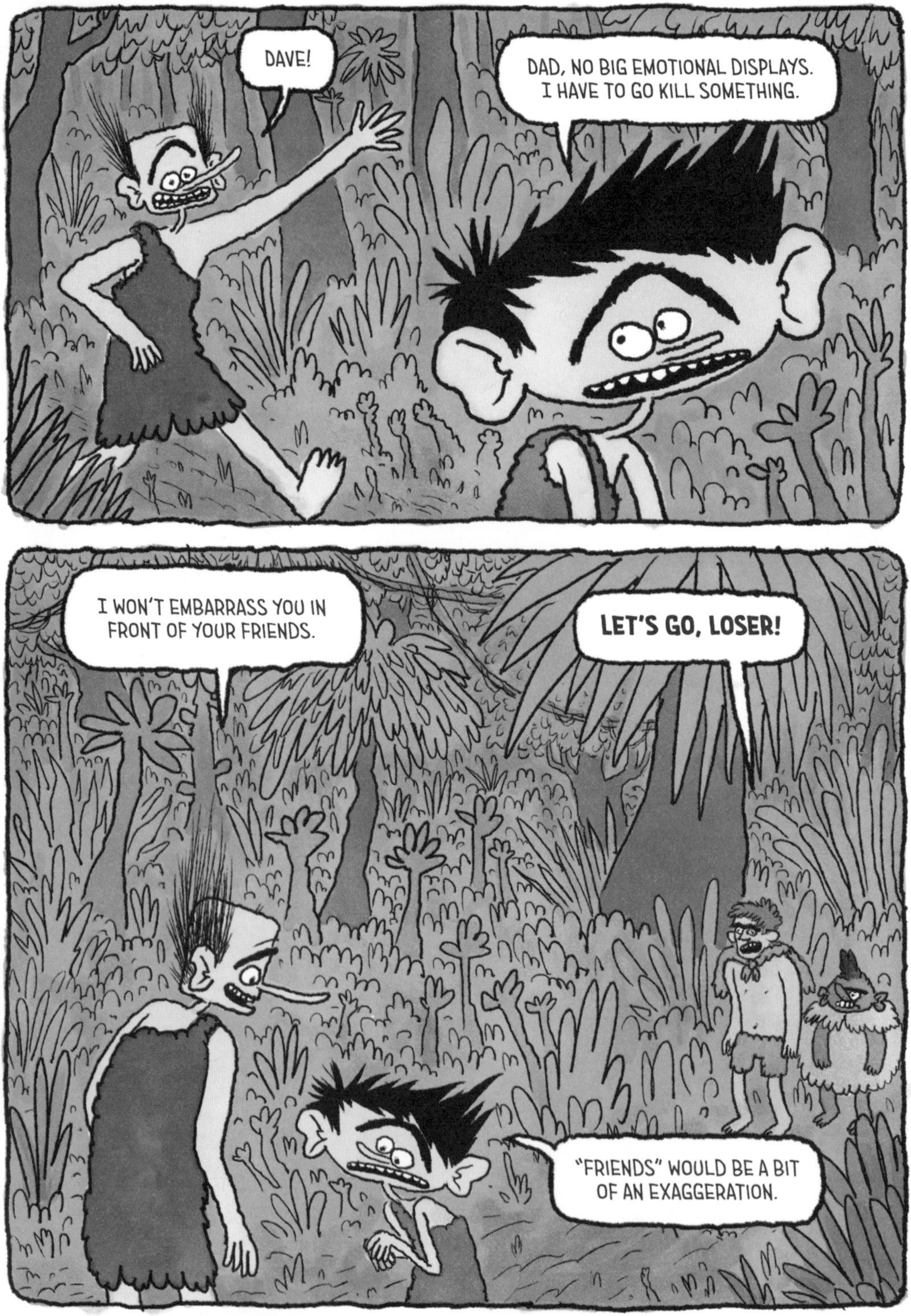
DAVE!
DAD, NO BIG EMOTIONAL DISPLAYS. I HAVE TO GO KILL SOMETHING.
I WON'T EMBARRASS YOU IN FRONT OF YOUR FRIENDS.
LET'S GO, LOSER!
"FRIENDS" WOULD BE A BIT OF AN EXAGGERATION.

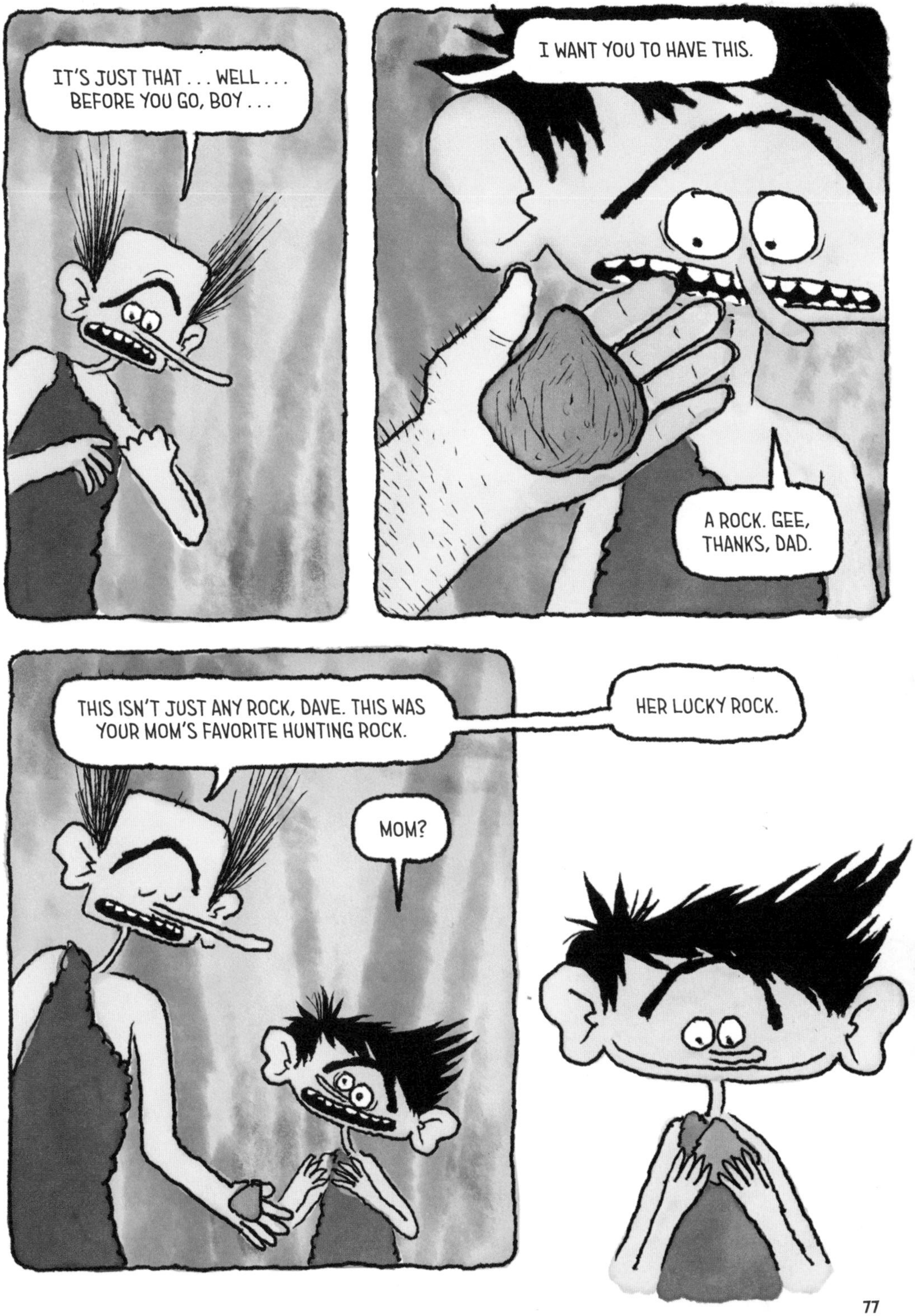
IT'S JUST THAT . . . WELL . . . BEFORE YOU GO, BOY . . .
I WANT YOU TO HAVE THIS.
A ROCK. GEE, THANKS, DAD.
THIS ISN'T JUST ANY ROCK, DAVE. THIS WAS YOUR MOM'S FAVORITE HUNTING ROCK.
HER LUCKY ROCK.
MOM?

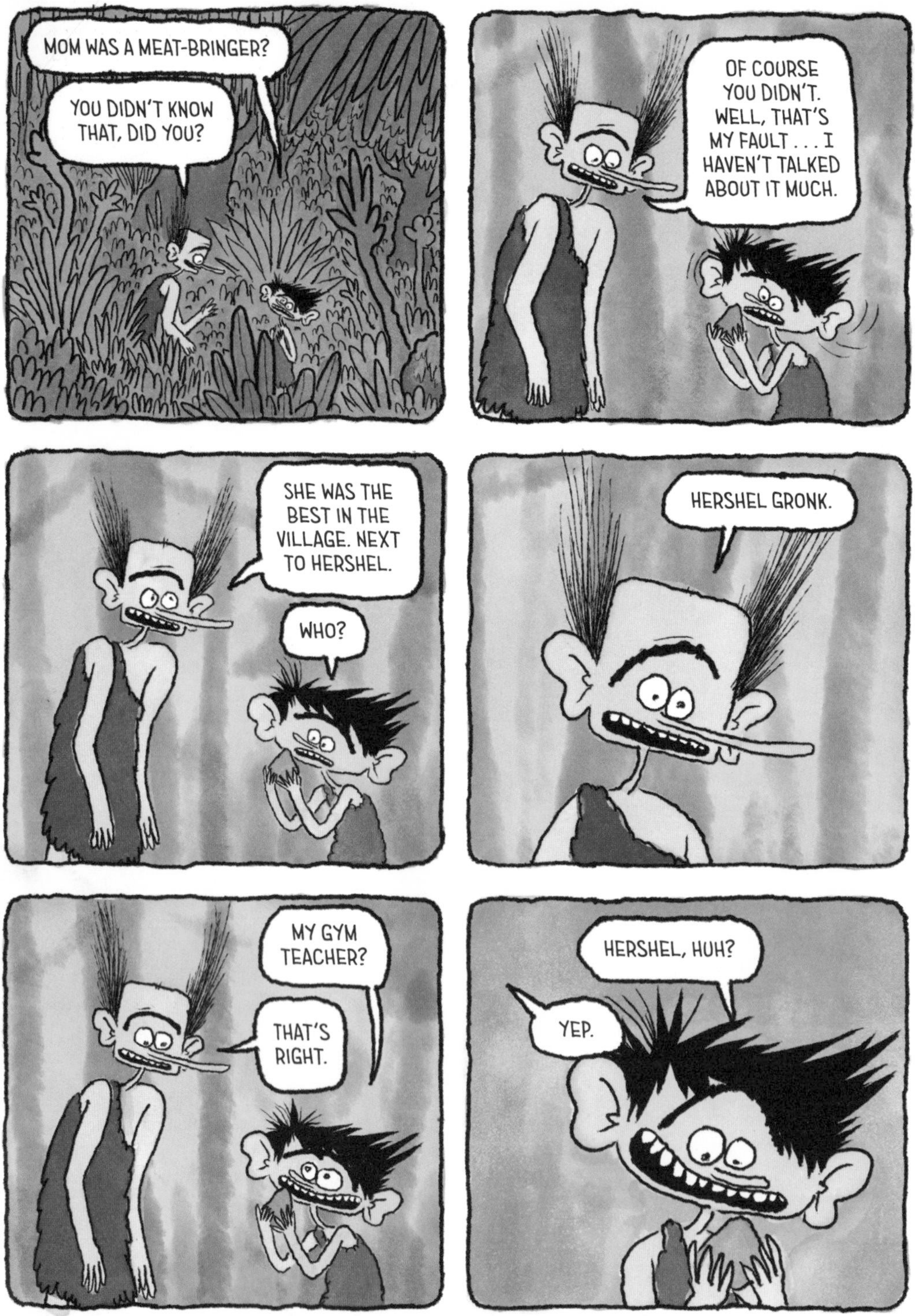
MOM WAS A MEAT-BRINGER?
YOU DIDN'T KNOW THAT, DID YOU?
OF COURSE YOU DIDN'T. WELL, THAT'S MY FAULT . . . I HAVEN'T TALKED ABOUT IT MUCH.
SHE WAS THE BEST IN THE VILLAGE. NEXT TO HERSHEL.
WHO?
HERSHEL GRONK.
MY GYM TEACHER?
THAT'S RIGHT.
HERSHEL, HUH?
YEP.

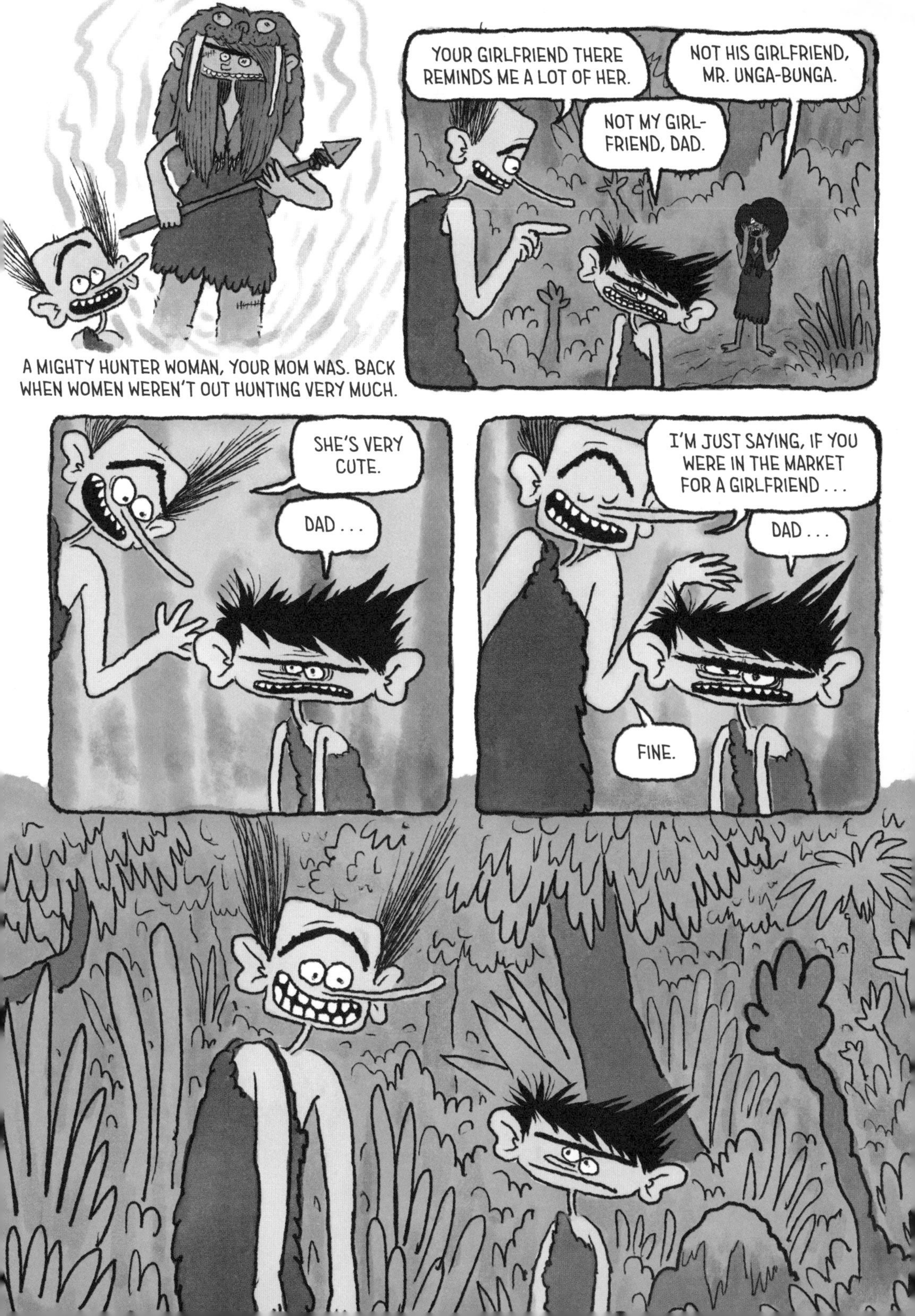
A MIGHTY HUNTER WOMAN, YOUR MOM WAS. BACK WHEN WOMEN WEREN'T OUT HUNTING VERY MUCH.
YOUR GIRLFRIEND THERE REMINDS ME A LOT OF HER.
NOT MY GIRL-FRIEND, DAD.
NOT HIS GIRLFRIEND, MR. UNGA-BUNGA.
SHE'S VERY CUTE.
DAD . . .
I'M JUST SAYING, IF YOU WERE IN THE MARKET FOR A GIRLFRIEND . . .
DAD . . .
FINE.

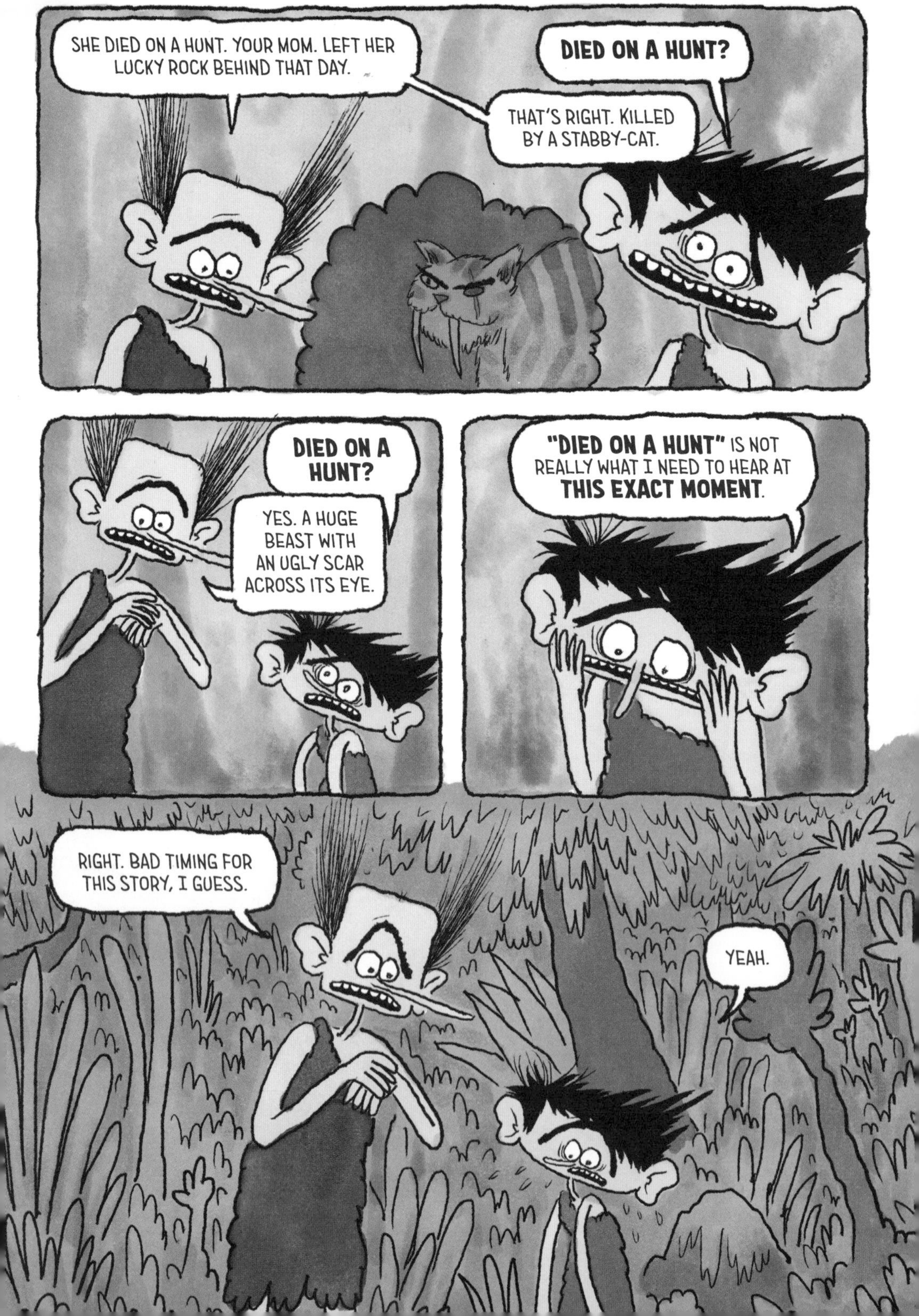
SHE DIED ON A HUNT. YOUR MOM. LEFT HER LUCKY ROCK BEHIND THAT DAY.
DIED ON A HUNT?
THAT'S RIGHT. KILLED BY A STABBY-CAT.
DIED ON A HUNT?
YES. A HUGE BEAST WITH AN UGLY SCAR ACROSS ITS EYE.
"DIED ON A HUNT" IS NOT REALLY WHAT I NEED TO HEAR AT THIS EXACT MOMENT.
RIGHT. BAD TIMING FOR THIS STORY, I GUESS.
YEAH.

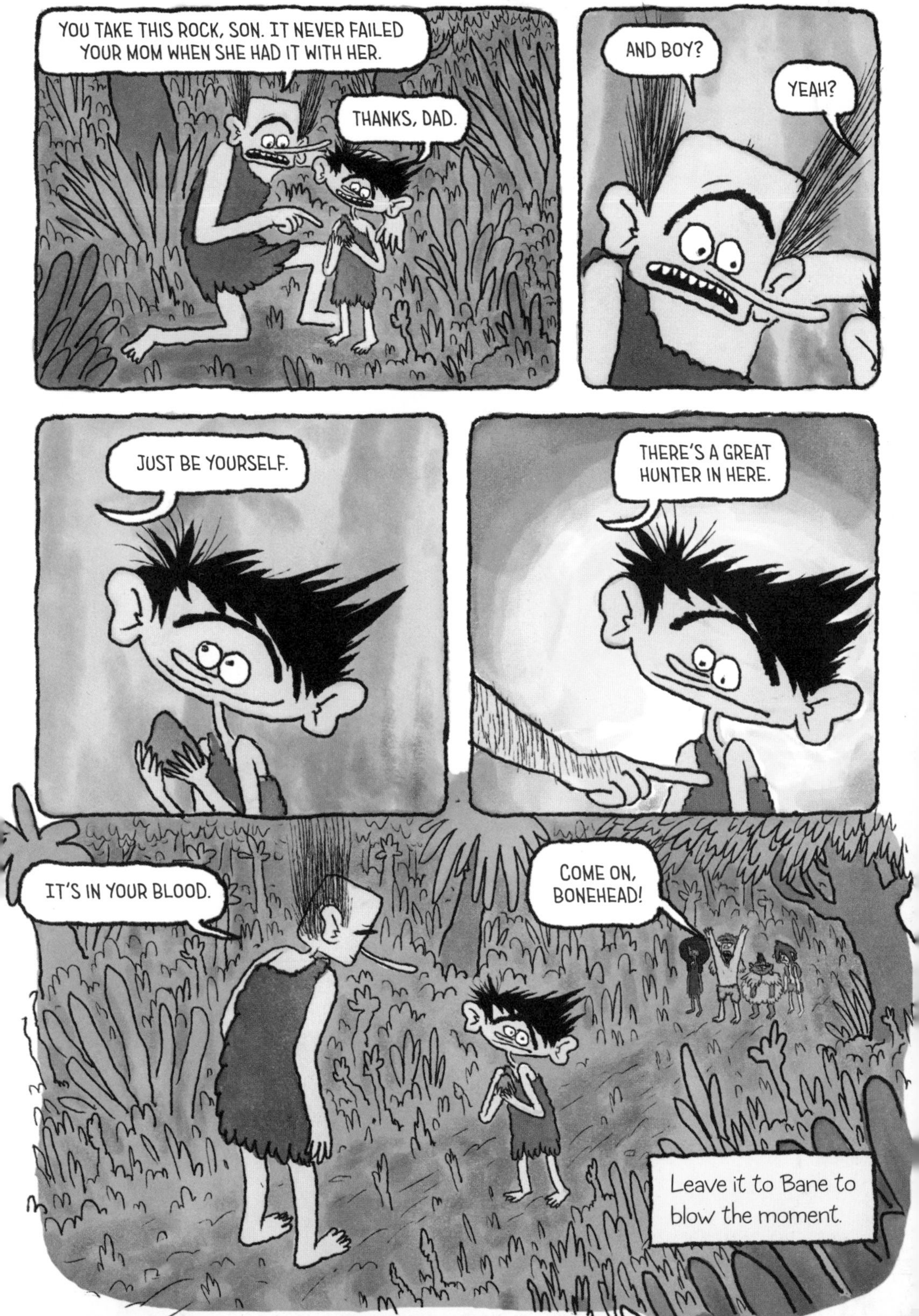

YOU TAKE THIS ROCK, SON. IT NEVER FAILED YOUR MOM WHEN SHE HAD IT WITH HER.
THANKS, DAD.
AND BOY?
YEAH?
JUST BE YOURSELF.
THERE'S A GREAT HUNTER IN HERE.
IT'S IN YOUR BLOOD.
COME ON, BONEHEAD!
Leave it to Bane to blow the moment.

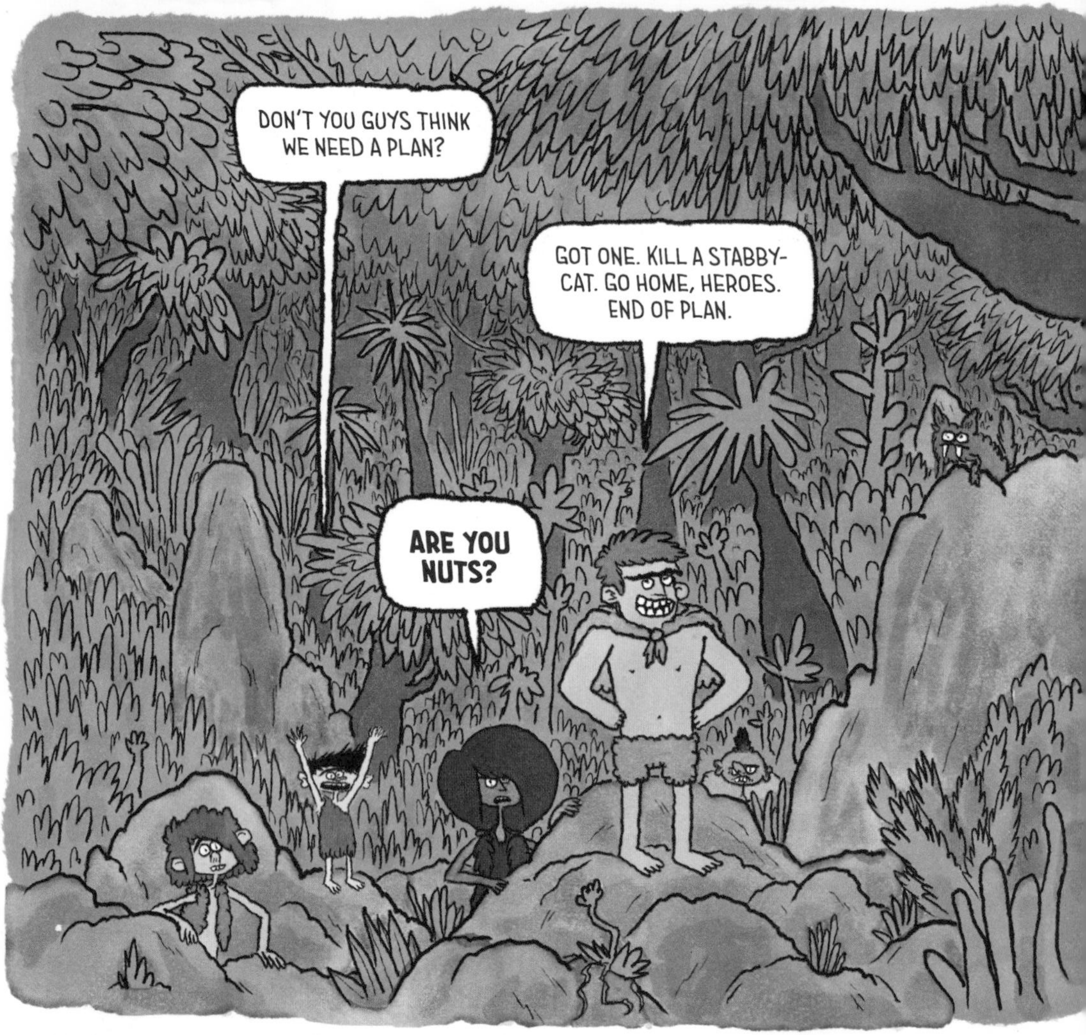
DON'T YOU GUYS THINK WE NEED A PLAN?
GOT ONE. KILL A STABBY-CAT. GO HOME, HEROES. END OF PLAN.
ARE YOU NUTS?

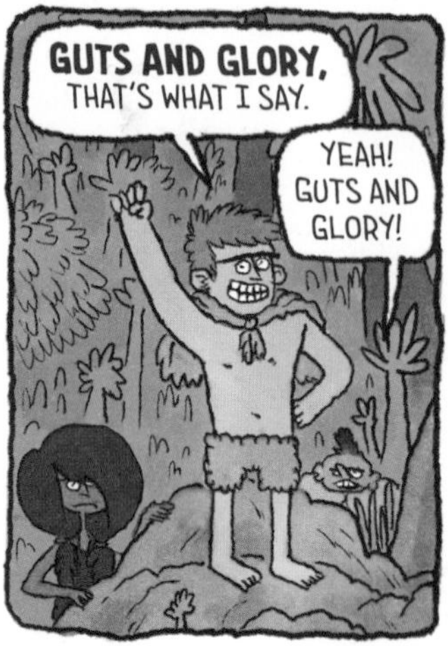
GUTS AND GLORY, THAT'S WHAT I SAY.
YEAH! GUTS AND GLORY!

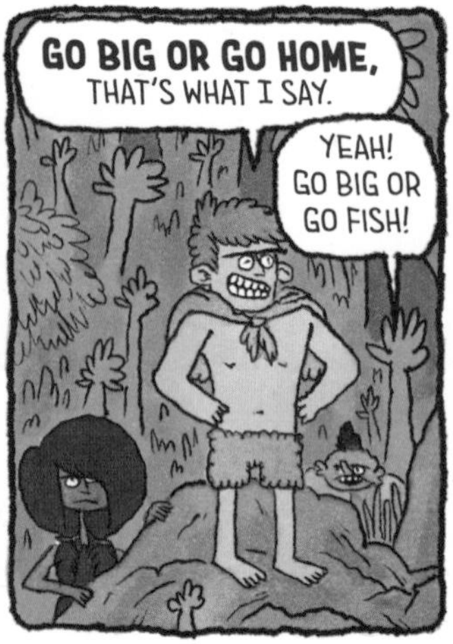
GO BIG OR GO HOME, THAT'S WHAT I SAY.
YEAH! GO BIG OR GO FISH!

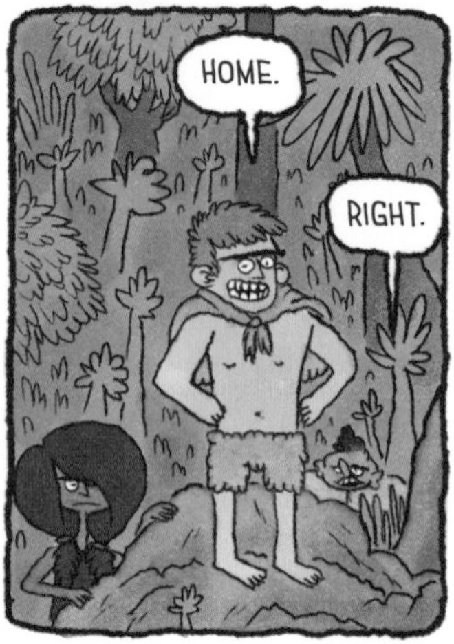
HOME.
RIGHT.

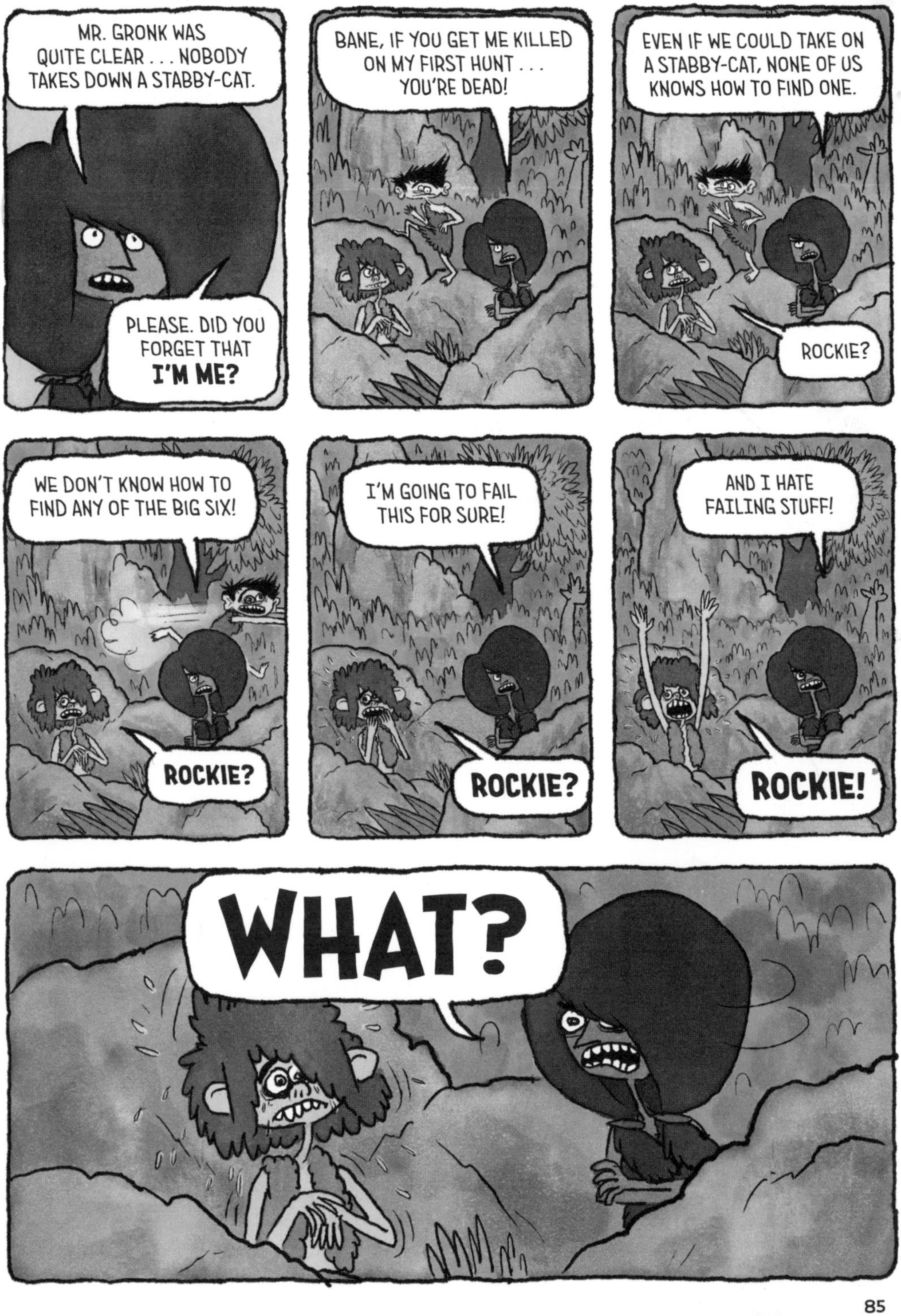
MR. GRONK WAS QUITE CLEAR . . . NOBODY TAKES DOWN A STABBY-CAT.
PLEASE. DID YOU FORGET THAT **I'M ME?**
BANE, IF YOU GET ME KILLED ON MY FIRST HUNT . . . YOU'RE DEAD!
EVEN IF WE COULD TAKE ON A STABBY-CAT, NONE OF US KNOWS HOW TO FIND ONE.
ROCKIE?
WE DON'T KNOW HOW TO FIND ANY OF THE BIG SIX!
ROCKIE?
I'M GOING TO FAIL THIS FOR SURE!
ROCKIE?
AND I HATE FAILING STUFF!
ROCKIE!
WHAT?

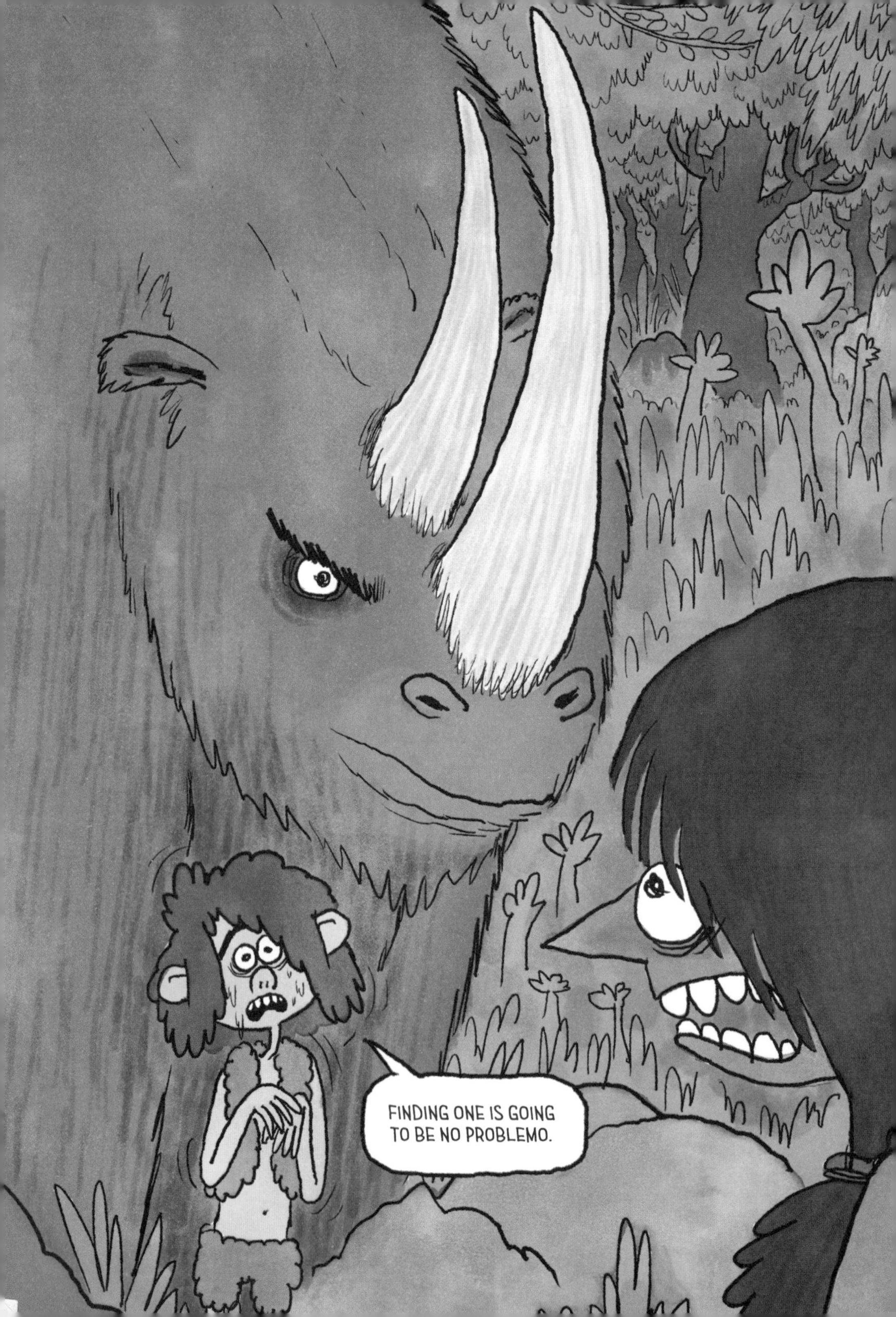
FINDING ONE IS GOING
TO BE NO PROBLEMO.

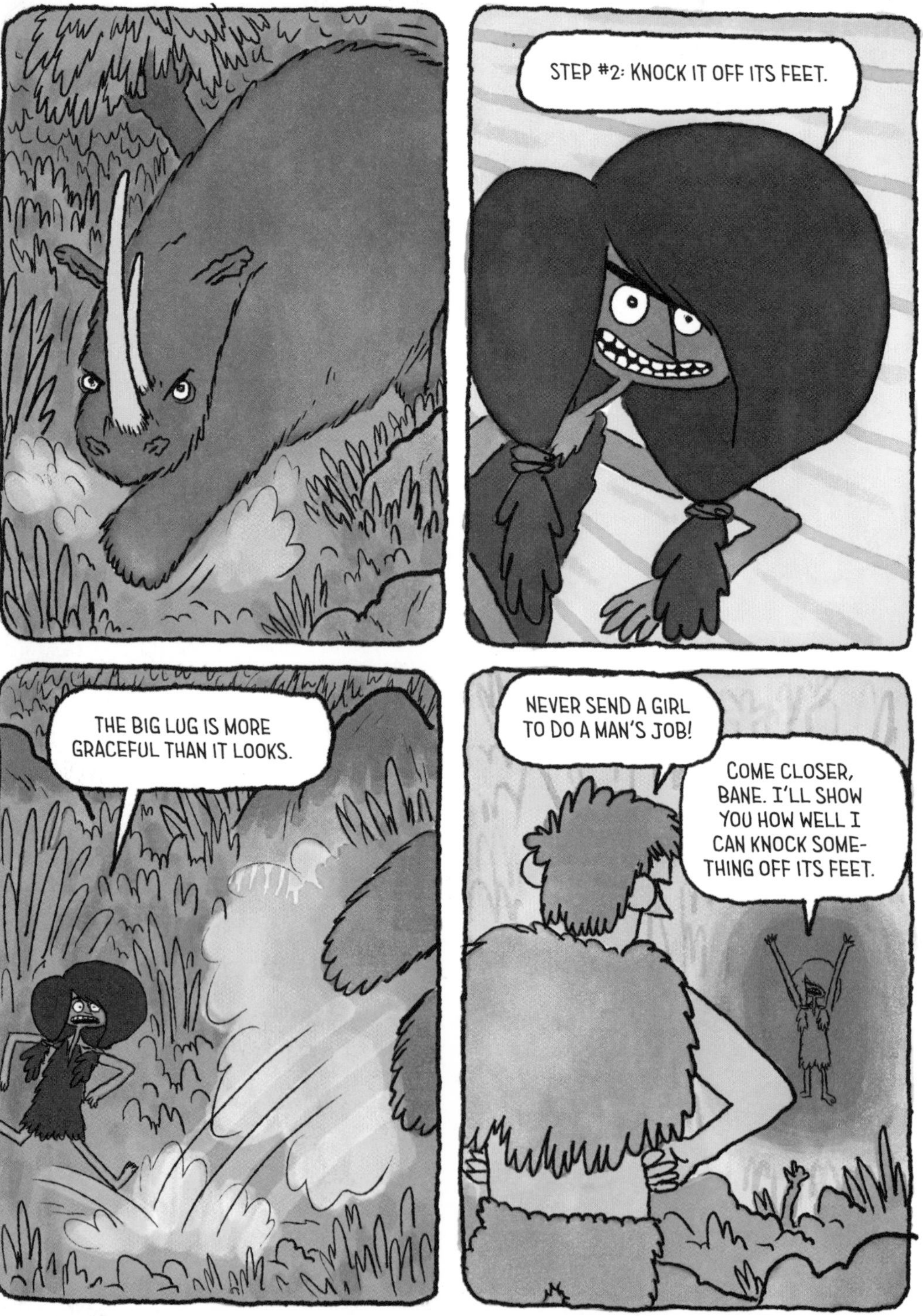
STEP #2: KNOCK IT OFF ITS FEET.
THE BIG LUG IS MORE GRACEFUL THAN IT LOOKS.
NEVER SEND A GIRL TO DO A MAN'S JOB!
COME CLOSER, BANE. I'LL SHOW YOU HOW WELL I CAN KNOCK SOME-THING OFF ITS FEET.

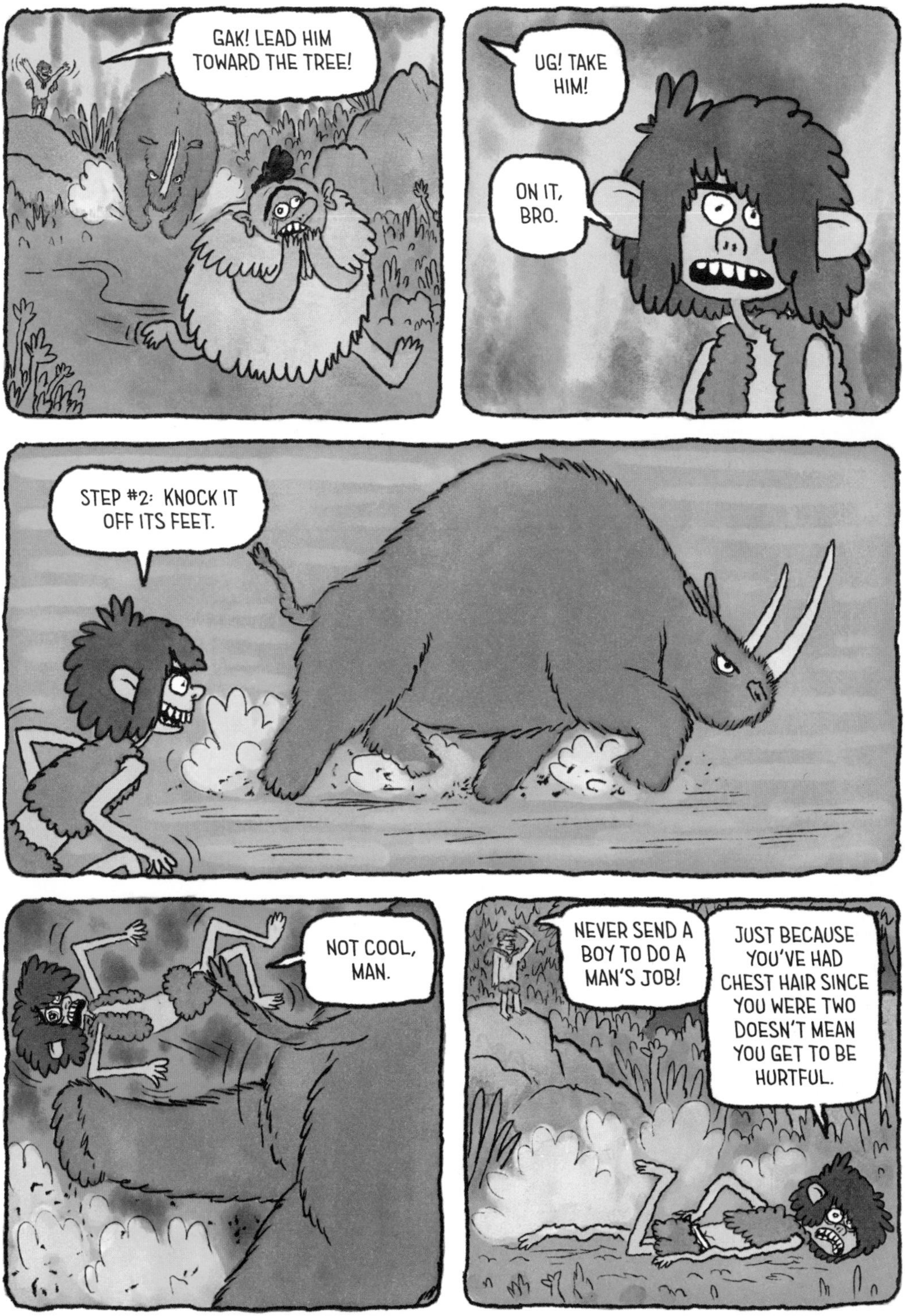
GAK! LEAD HIM TOWARD THE TREE!
UG! TAKE HIM!
ON IT, BRO.
STEP #2: KNOCK IT OFF ITS FEET.
NOT COOL, MAN.
NEVER SEND A BOY TO DO A MAN'S JOB!
JUST BECAUSE YOU'VE HAD CHEST HAIR SINCE YOU WERE TWO DOESN'T MEAN YOU GET TO BE HURTFUL.

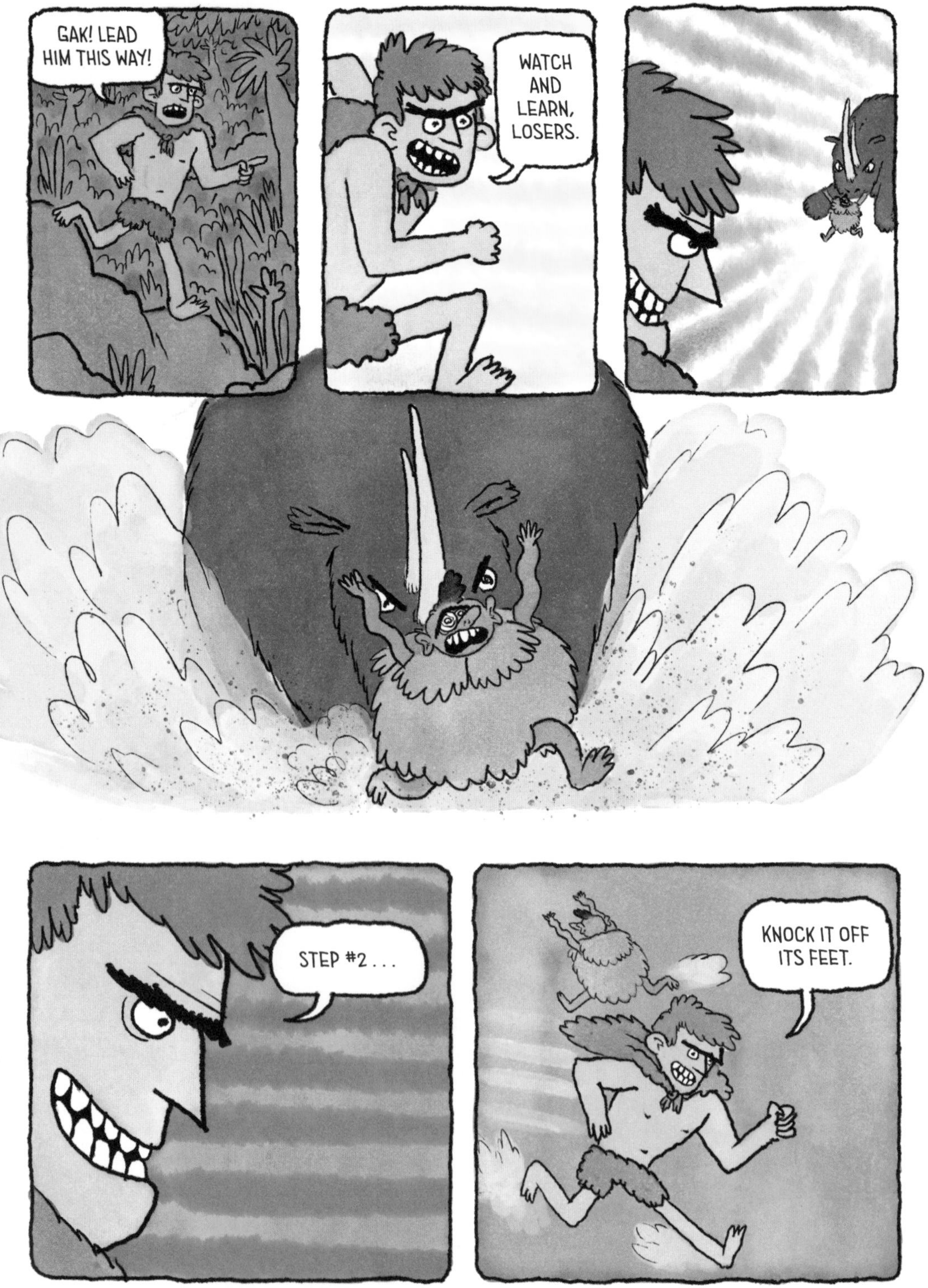
GAK! LEAD HIM THIS WAY!
WATCH AND LEARN, LOSERS.
STEP #2 . . .
KNOCK IT OFF ITS FEET.

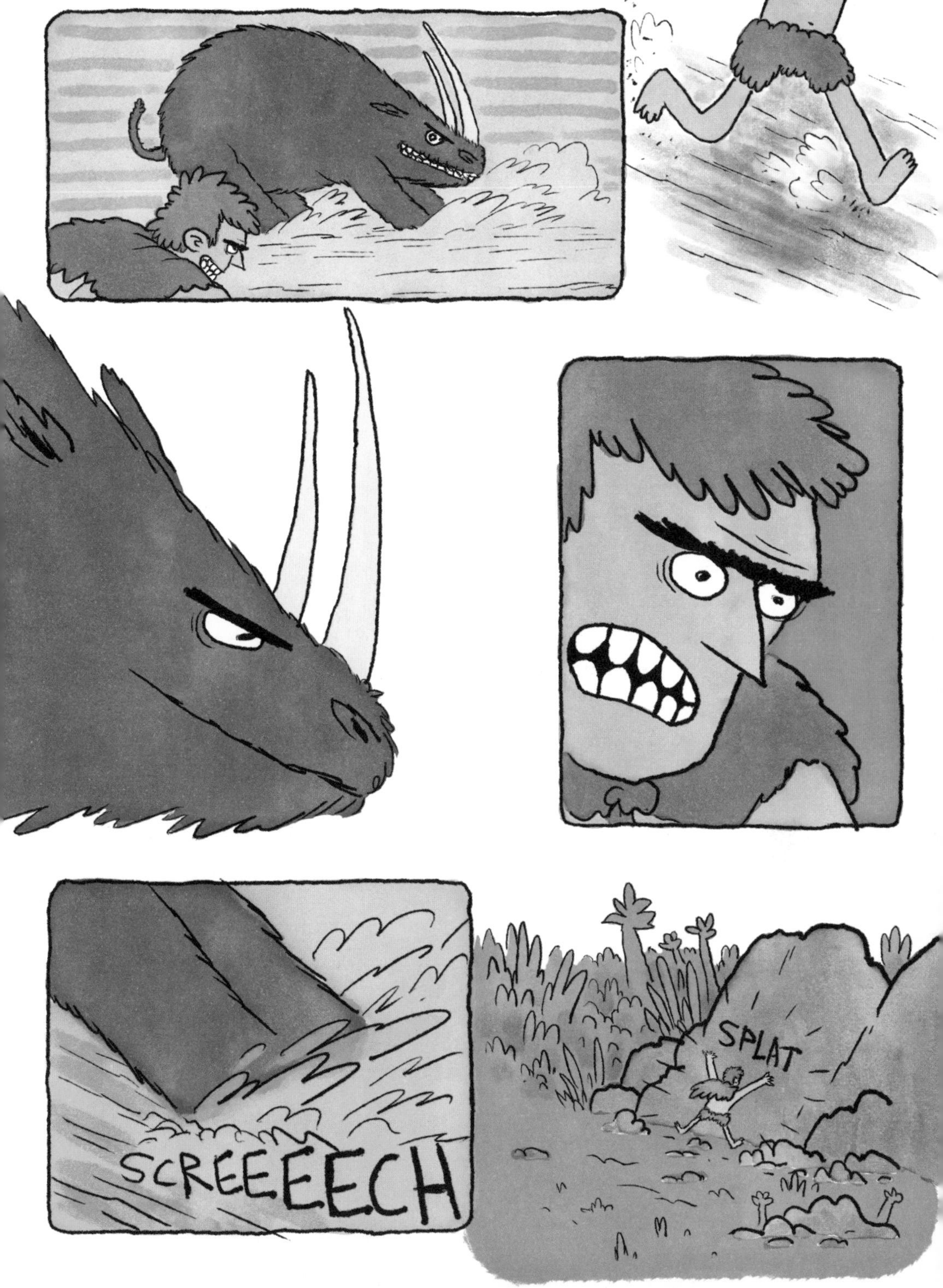
SCREEEEECH
SPLAT

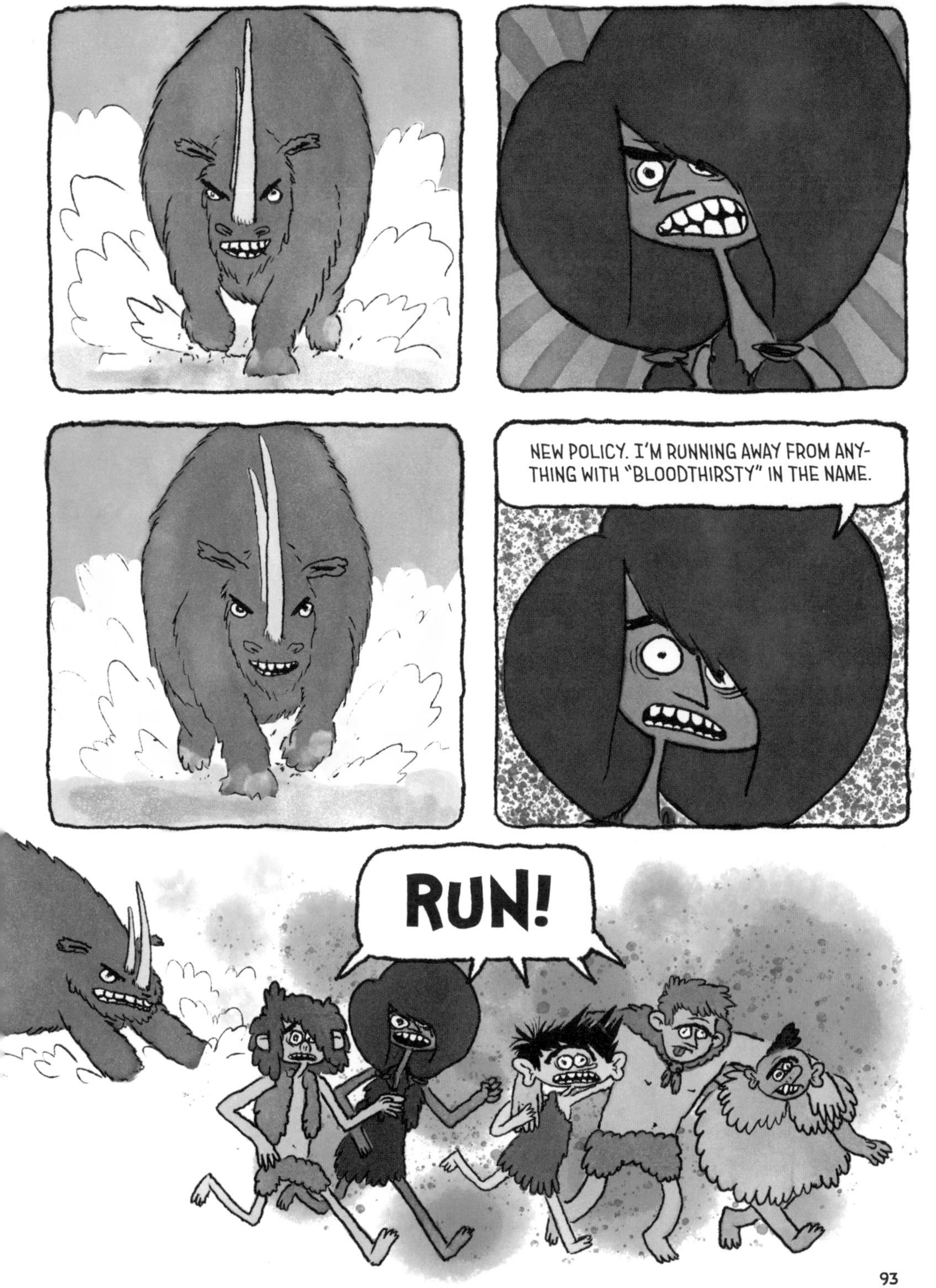
NEW POLICY. I'M RUNNING AWAY FROM ANY-
THING WITH "BLOODTHIRSTY" IN THE NAME.
RUN!

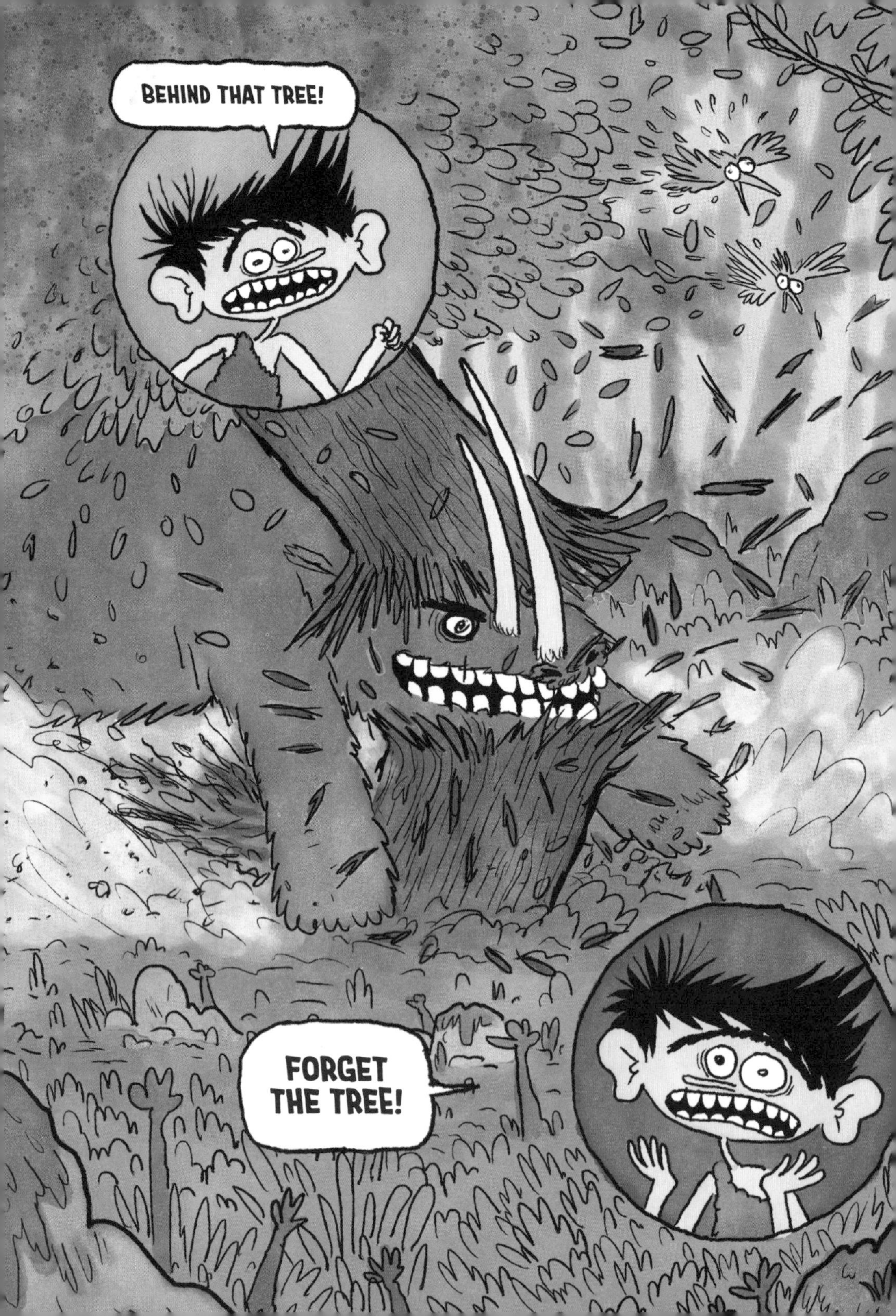
BEHIND THAT TREE!
FORGET THE TREE!

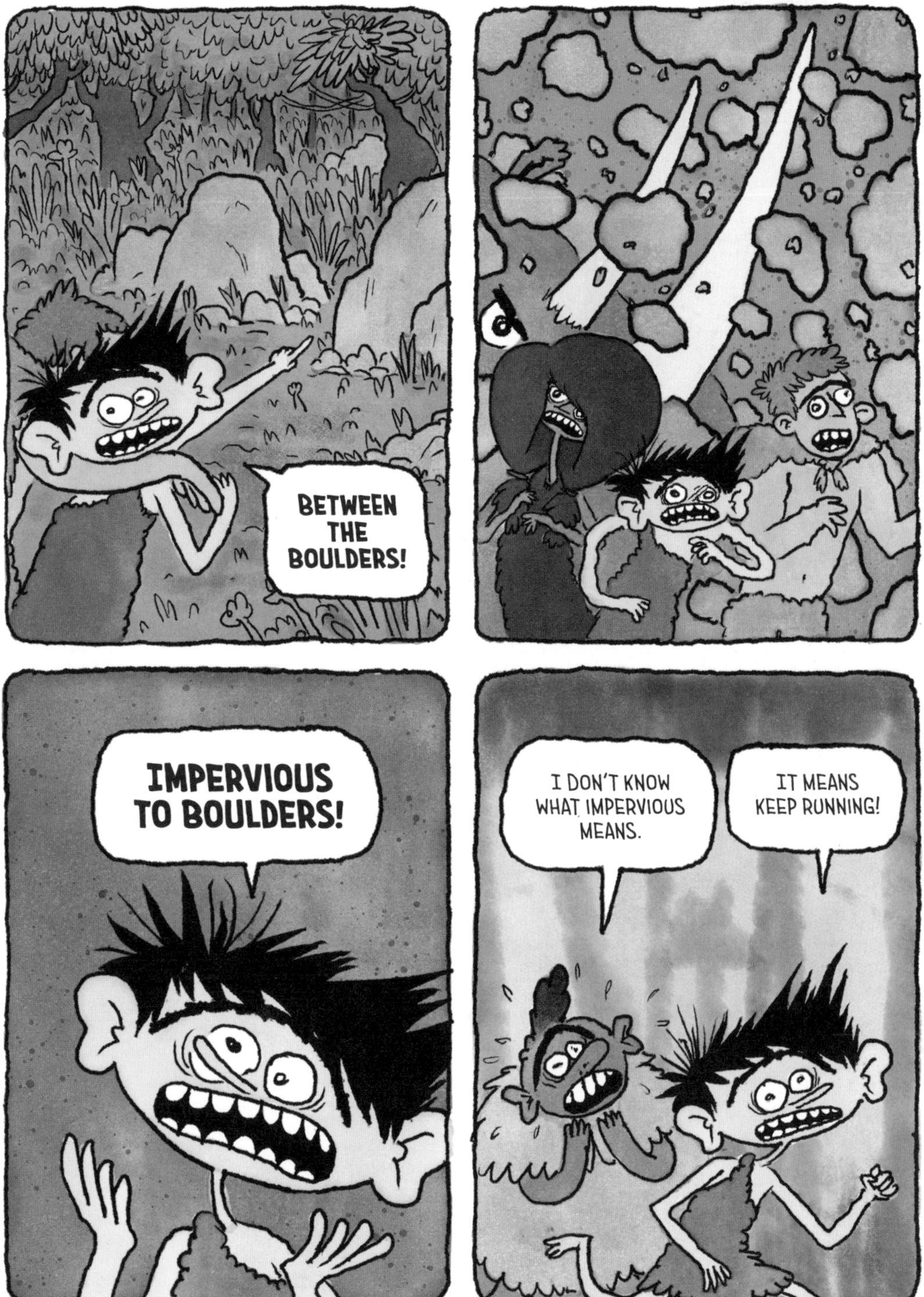

BETWEEN THE BOULDERS!
IMPERVIOUS TO BOULDERS!
I DON'T KNOW WHAT IMPERVIOUS MEANS.
IT MEANS KEEP RUNNING!

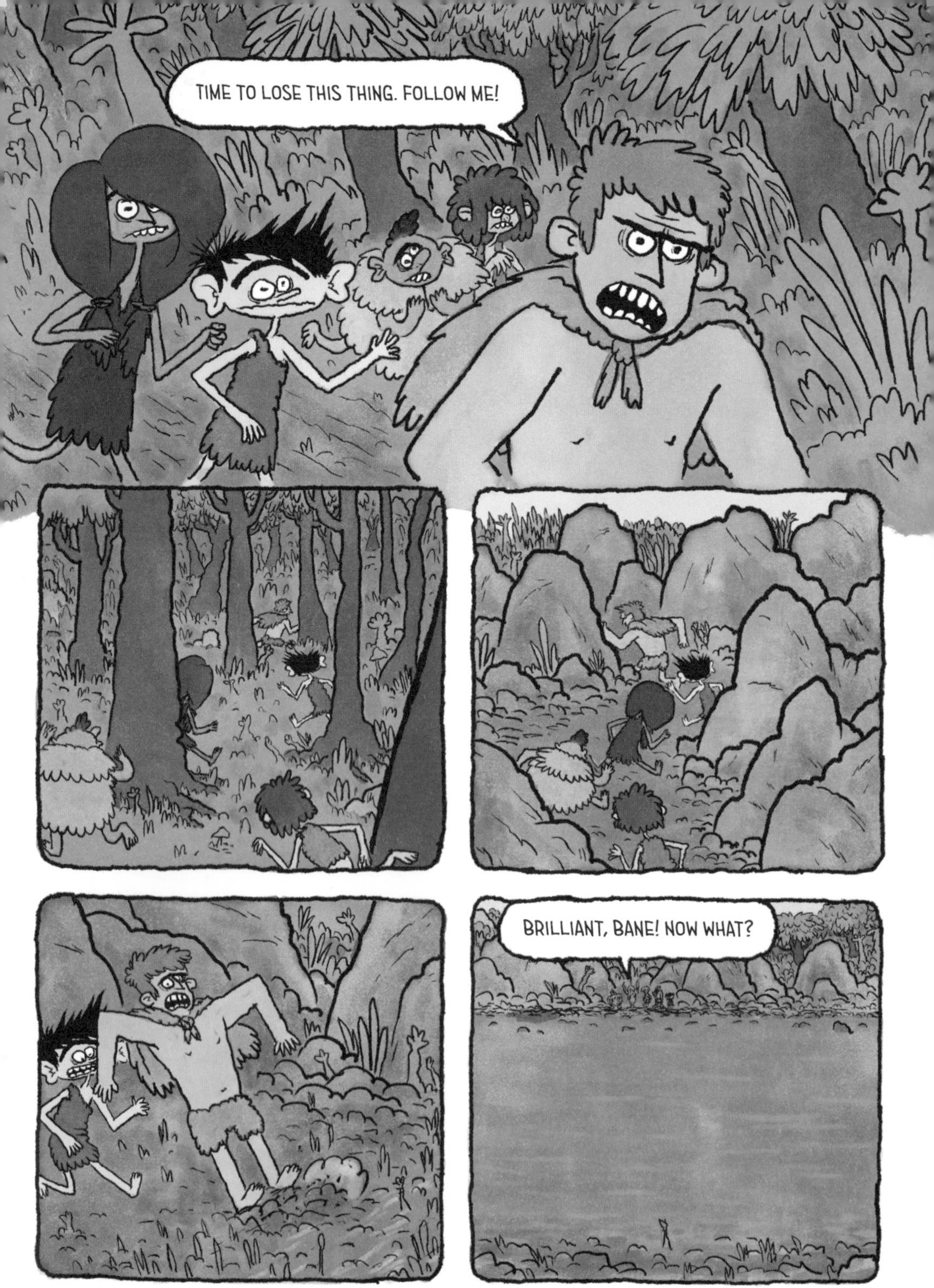
TIME TO LOSE THIS THING. FOLLOW ME!
BRILLIANT, BANE! NOW WHAT?

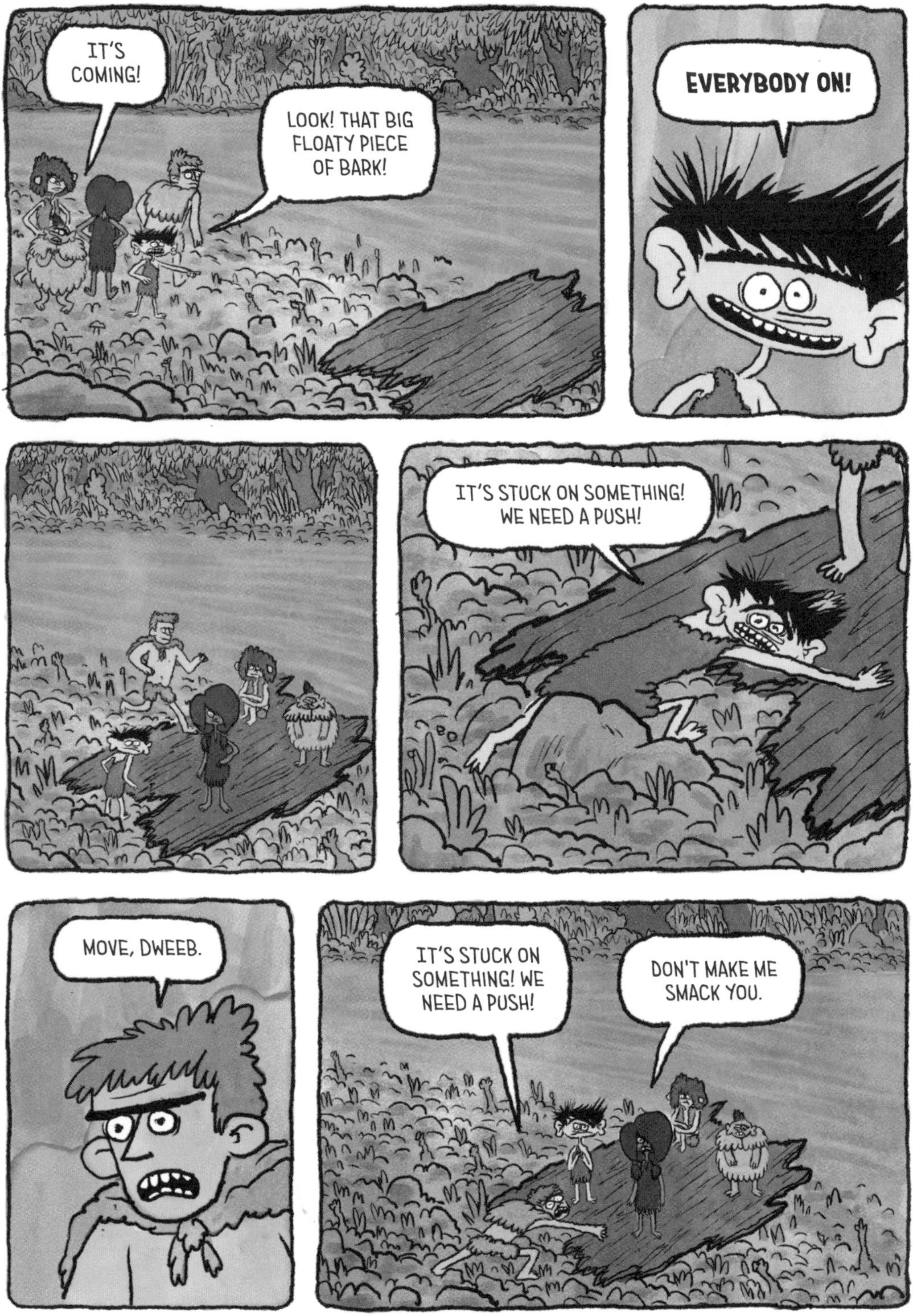
IT'S COMING!
LOOK! THAT BIG FLOATY PIECE OF BARK!
EVERYBODY ON!
IT'S STUCK ON SOMETHING! WE NEED A PUSH!
MOVE, DWEEB.
IT'S STUCK ON SOMETHING! WE NEED A PUSH!
DON'T MAKE ME SMACK YOU.

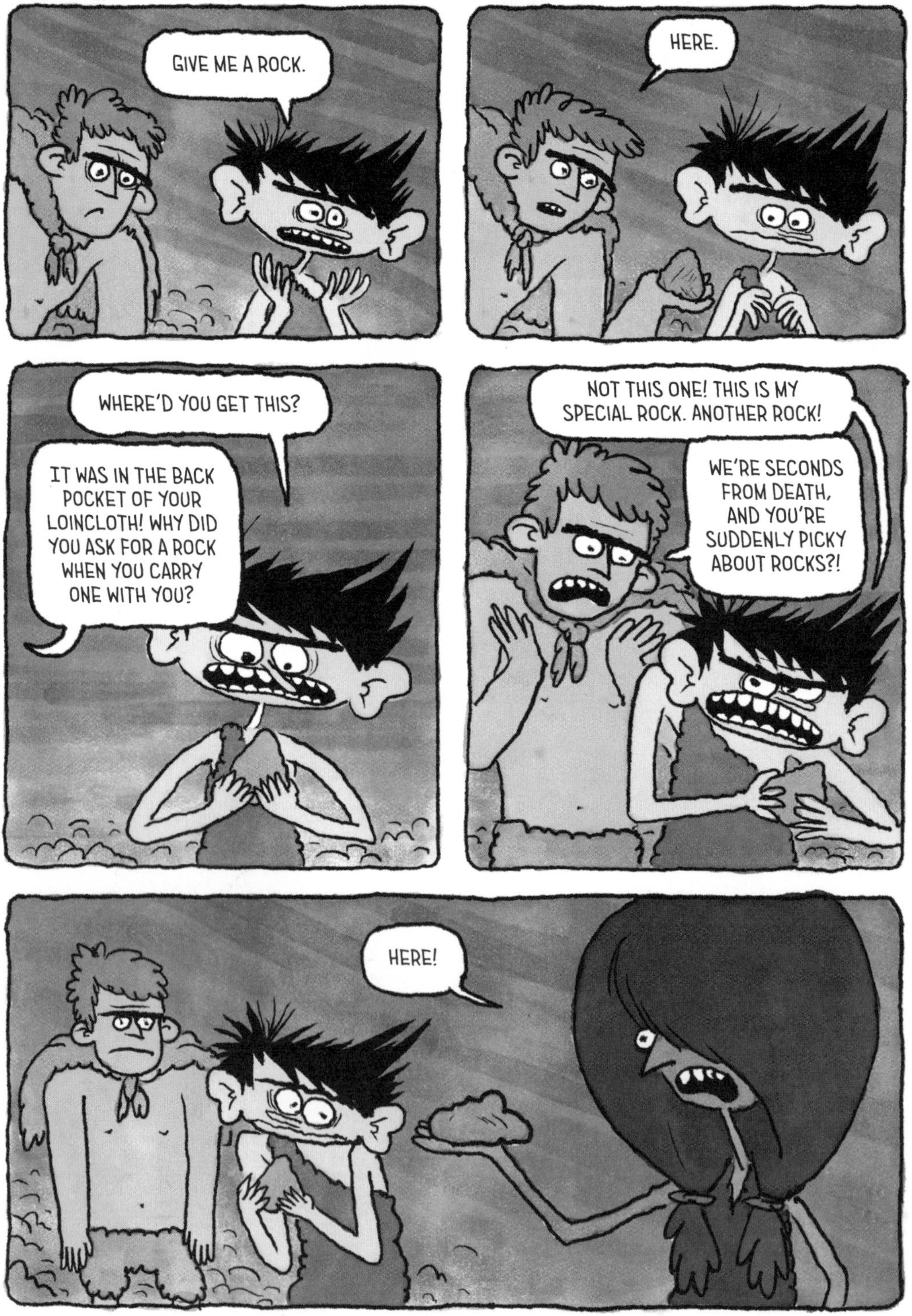
GIVE ME A ROCK.
HERE.
WHERE'D YOU GET THIS?
IT WAS IN THE BACK POCKET OF YOUR LOINCLOTH! WHY DID YOU ASK FOR A ROCK WHEN YOU CARRY ONE WITH YOU?
NOT THIS ONE! THIS IS MY SPECIAL ROCK. ANOTHER ROCK!
WE'RE SECONDS FROM DEATH, AND YOU'RE SUDDENLY PICKY ABOUT ROCKS?!
HERE!

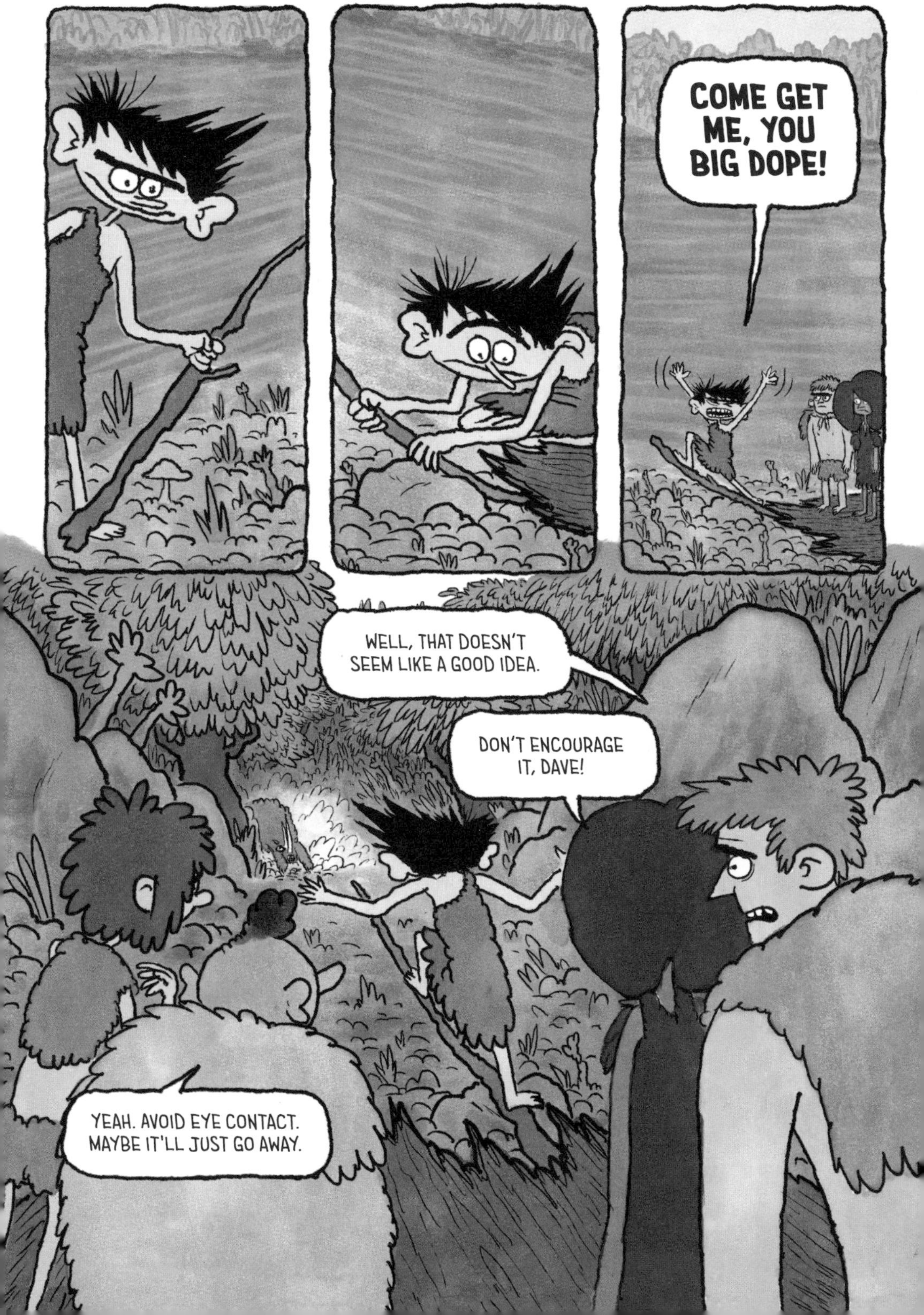
COME GET ME, YOU BIG DOPE!
WELL, THAT DOESN'T SEEM LIKE A GOOD IDEA.
DON'T ENCOURAGE IT, DAVE!
YEAH. AVOID EYE CONTACT. MAYBE IT'LL JUST GO AWAY.

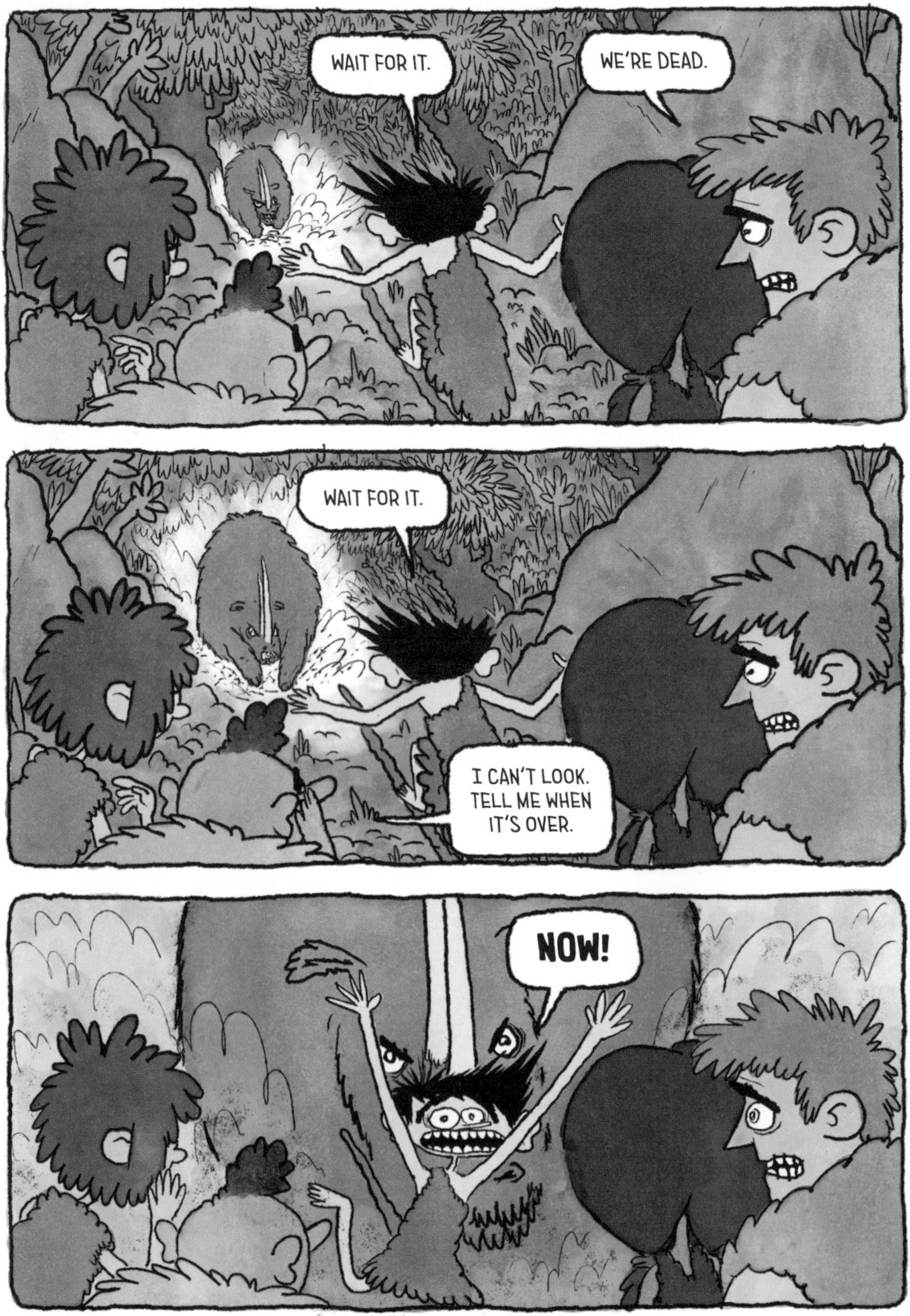
WAIT FOR IT.
WE'RE DEAD.
WAIT FOR IT.
I CAN'T LOOK. TELL ME WHEN IT'S OVER.
NOW!

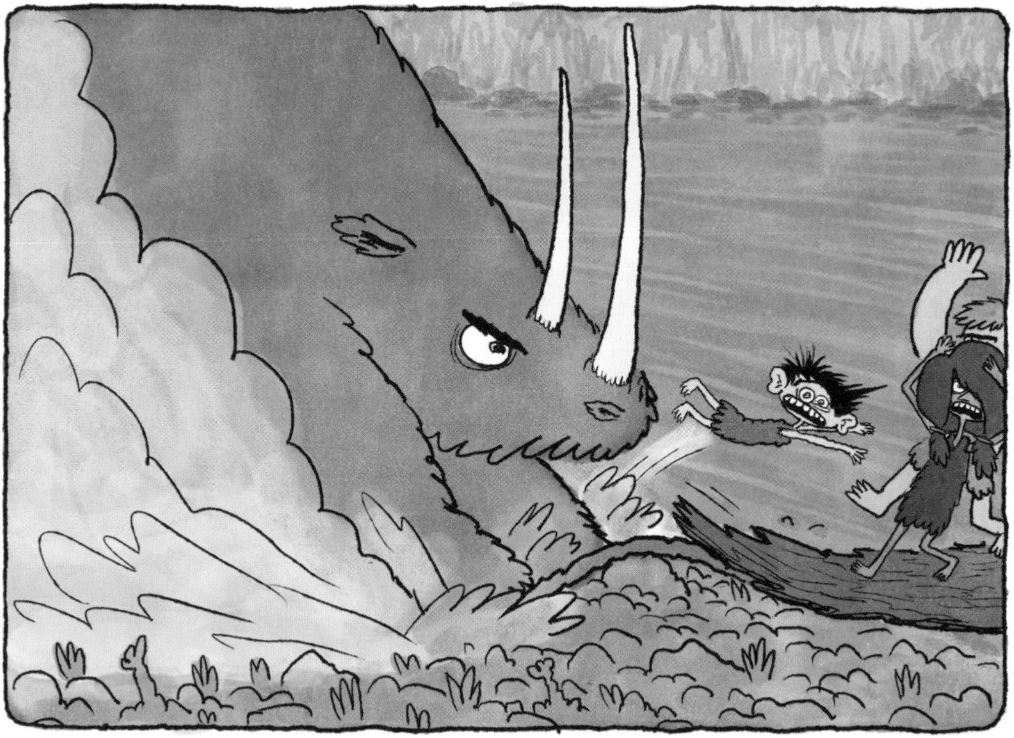

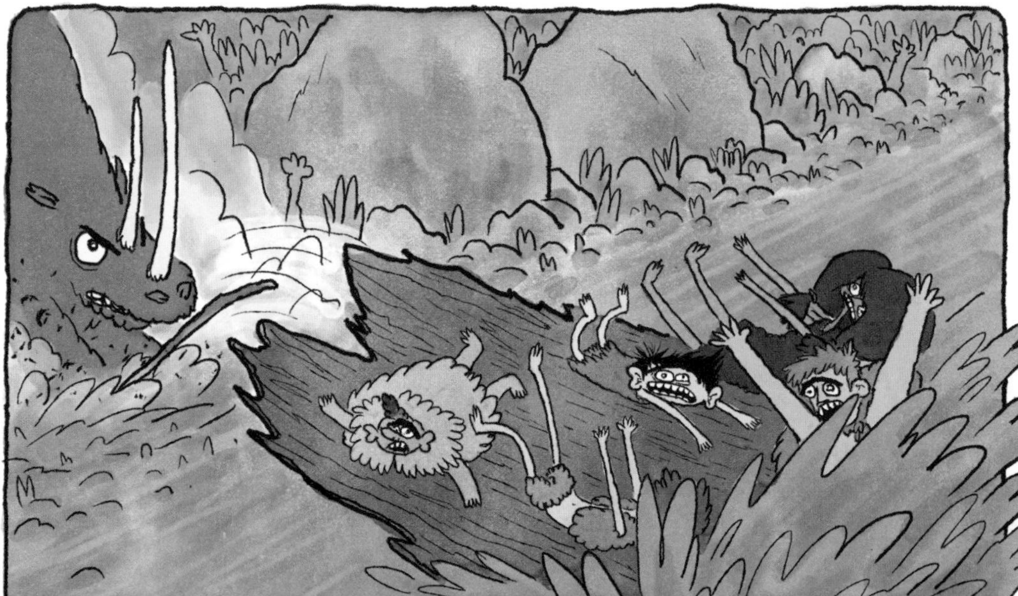

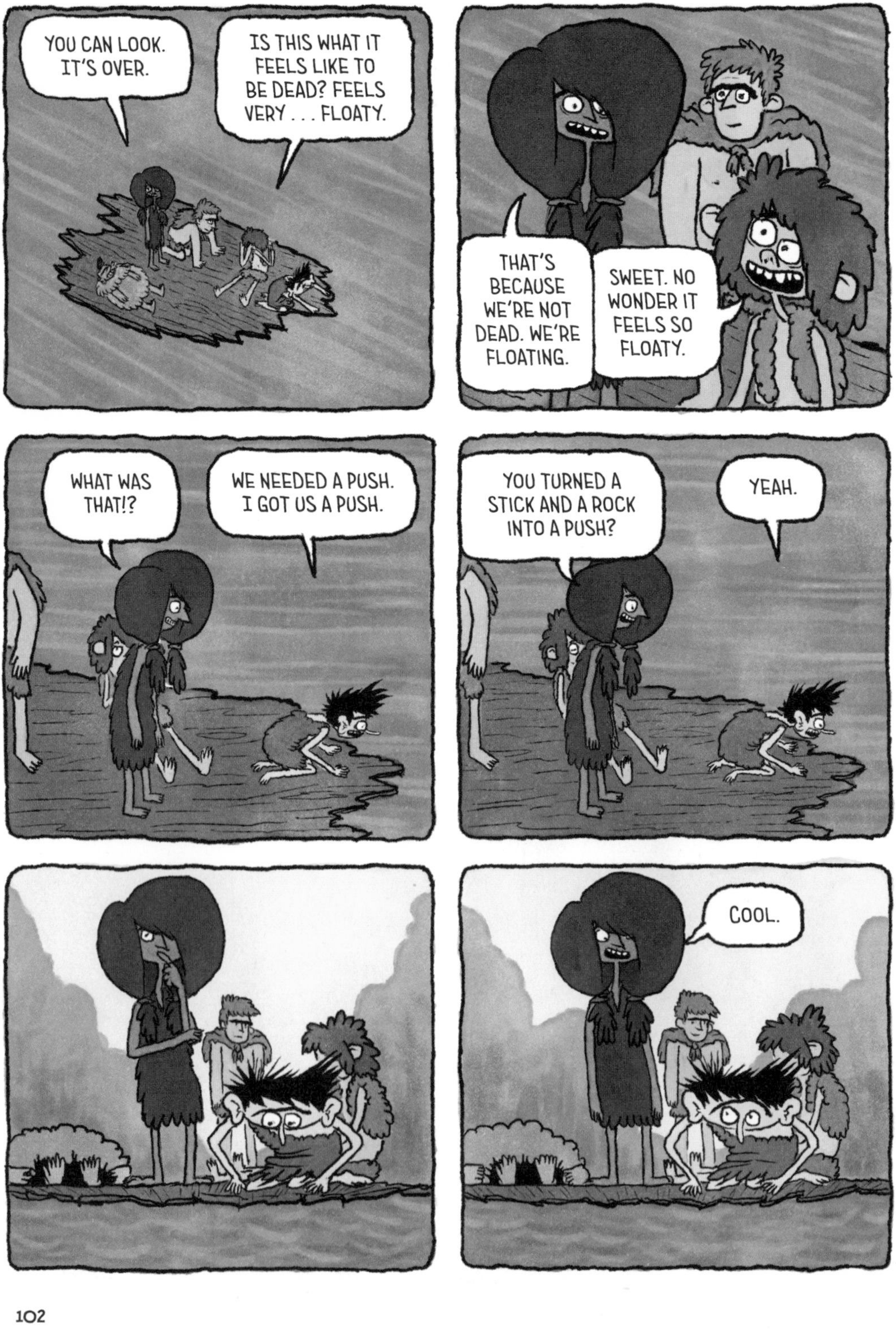
YOU CAN LOOK. IT'S OVER.
IS THIS WHAT IT FEELS LIKE TO BE DEAD? FEELS VERY . . . FLOATY.
THAT'S BECAUSE WE'RE NOT DEAD. WE'RE FLOATING.
SWEET. NO WONDER IT FEELS SO FLOATY.
WHAT WAS THAT!?
WE NEEDED A PUSH. I GOT US A PUSH.
YOU TURNED A STICK AND A ROCK INTO A PUSH?
YEAH.
COOL.

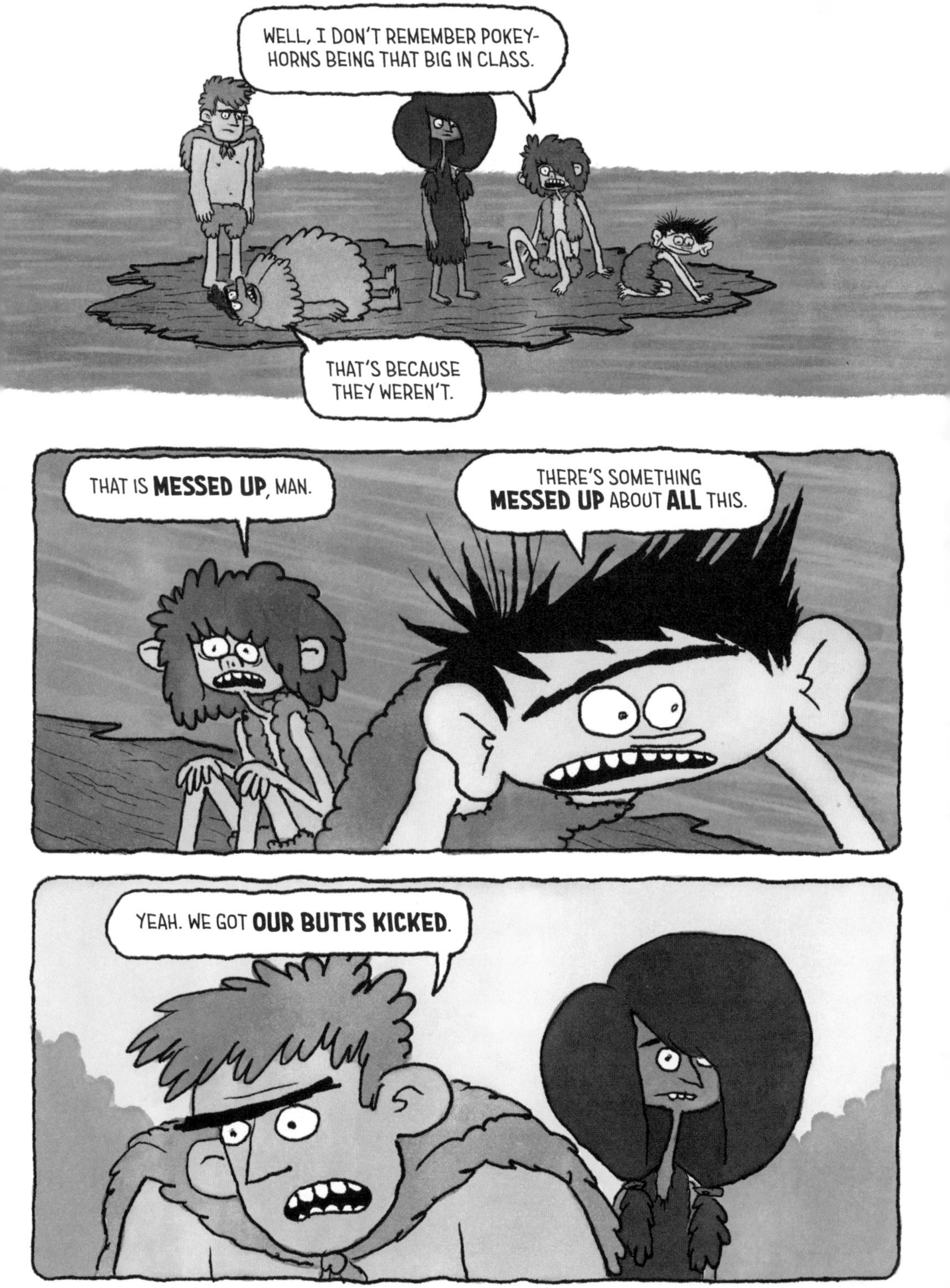
WELL, I DON'T REMEMBER POKEY-HORNS BEING THAT BIG IN CLASS.
THAT'S BECAUSE THEY WEREN'T.
THAT IS **MESSED UP**, MAN.
THERE'S SOMETHING **MESSED UP** ABOUT **ALL** THIS.
YEAH. WE GOT **OUR BUTTS KICKED**.

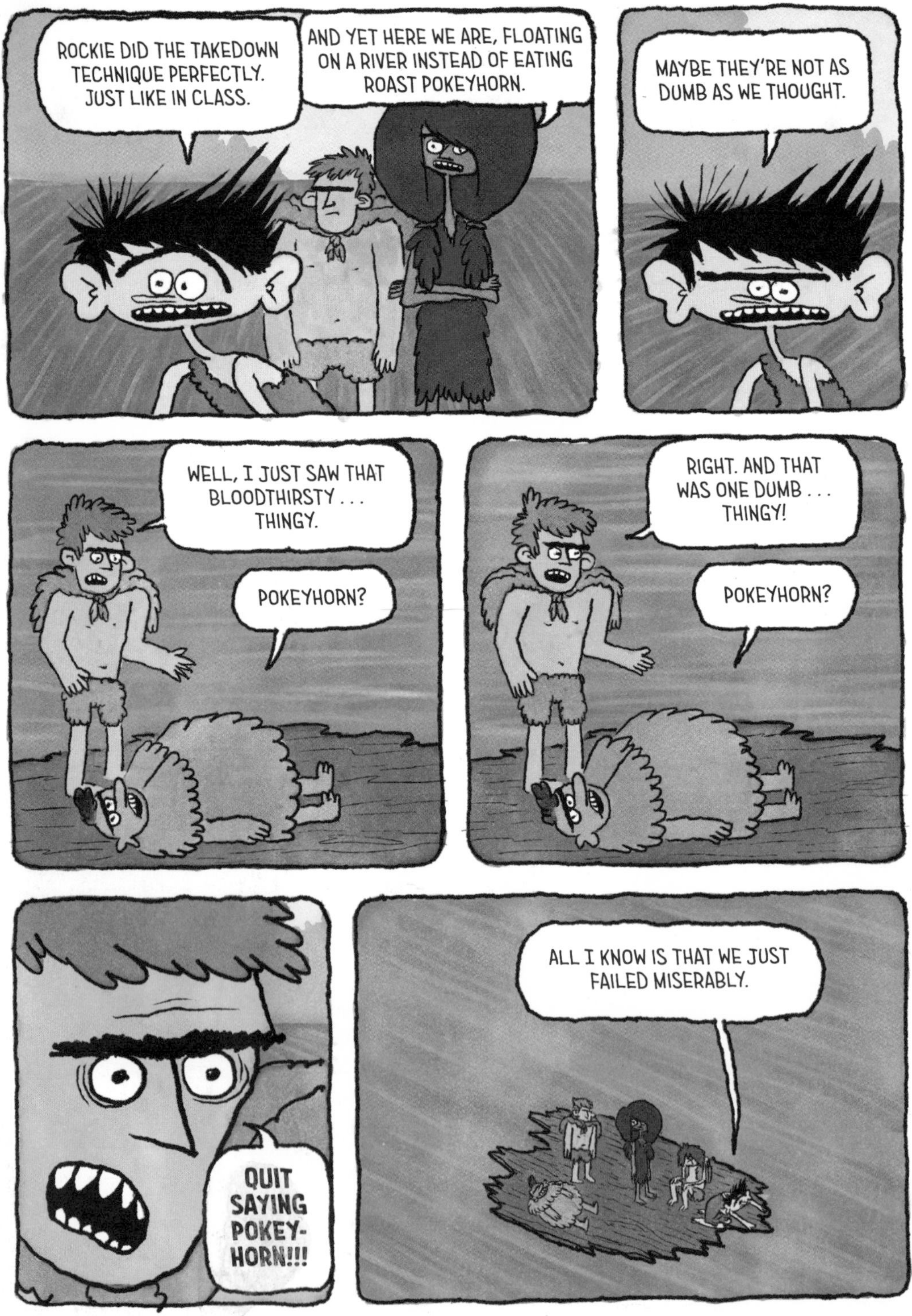

ROCKIE DID THE TAKEDOWN TECHNIQUE PERFECTLY. JUST LIKE IN CLASS.
AND YET HERE WE ARE, FLOATING ON A RIVER INSTEAD OF EATING ROAST POKEYHORN.
MAYBE THEY'RE NOT AS DUMB AS WE THOUGHT.
WELL, I JUST SAW THAT BLOODTHIRSTY . . . THINGY.
POKEYHORN?
RIGHT. AND THAT WAS ONE DUMB . . . THINGY!
POKEYHORN?
QUIT SAYING POKEY-HORN!!!
ALL I KNOW IS THAT WE JUST FAILED MISERABLY.

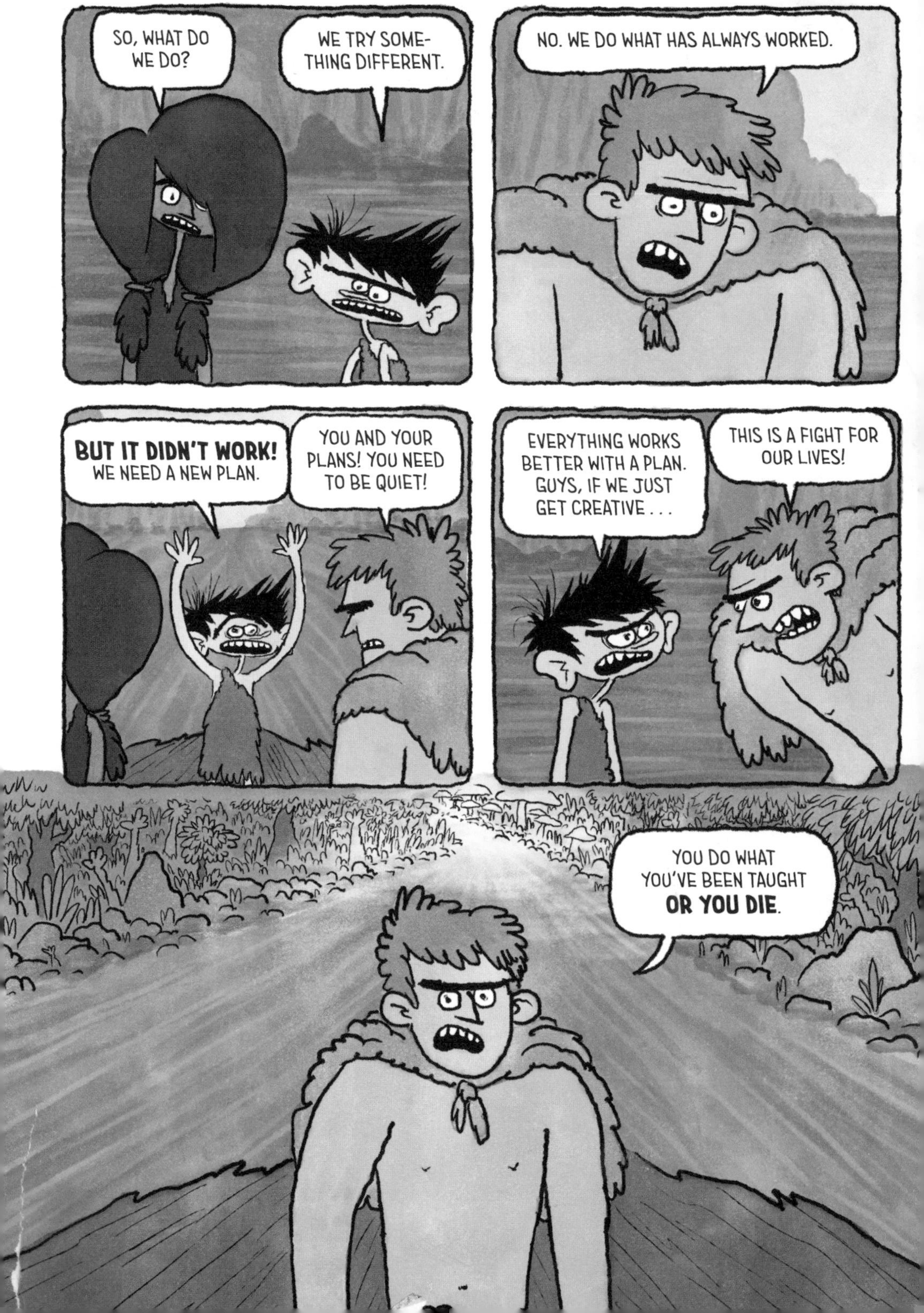

SO, WHAT DO WE DO?
WE TRY SOMETHING DIFFERENT.
NO. WE DO WHAT HAS ALWAYS WORKED.
BUT IT DIDN'T WORK! WE NEED A NEW PLAN.
YOU AND YOUR PLANS! YOU NEED TO BE QUIET!
EVERYTHING WORKS BETTER WITH A PLAN. GUYS, IF WE JUST GET CREATIVE . . .
THIS IS A FIGHT FOR OUR LIVES!
YOU DO WHAT YOU'VE BEEN TAUGHT **OR YOU DIE**.

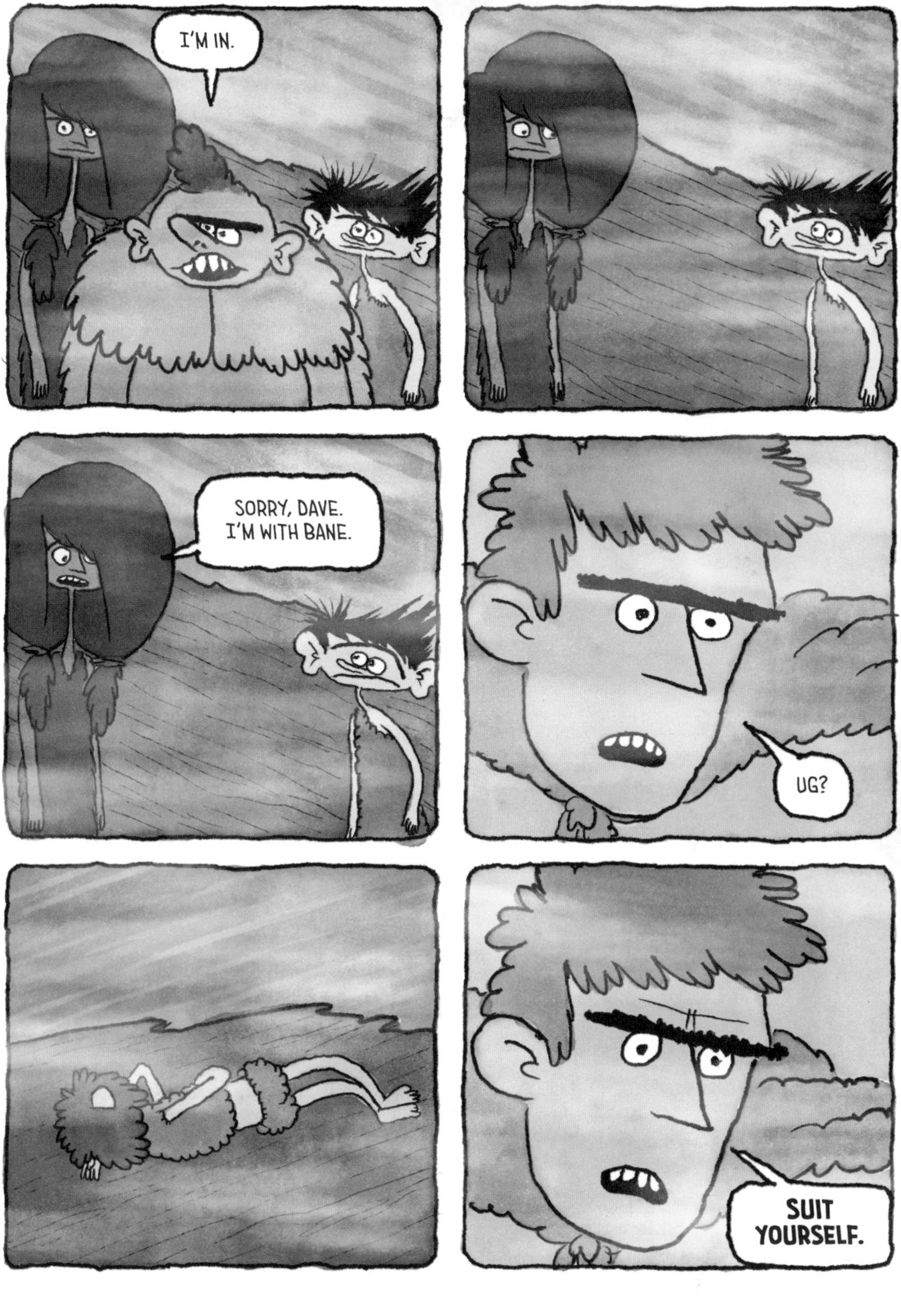
I'M IN.
SORRY, DAVE. I'M WITH BANE.
UG?
SUIT YOURSELF.

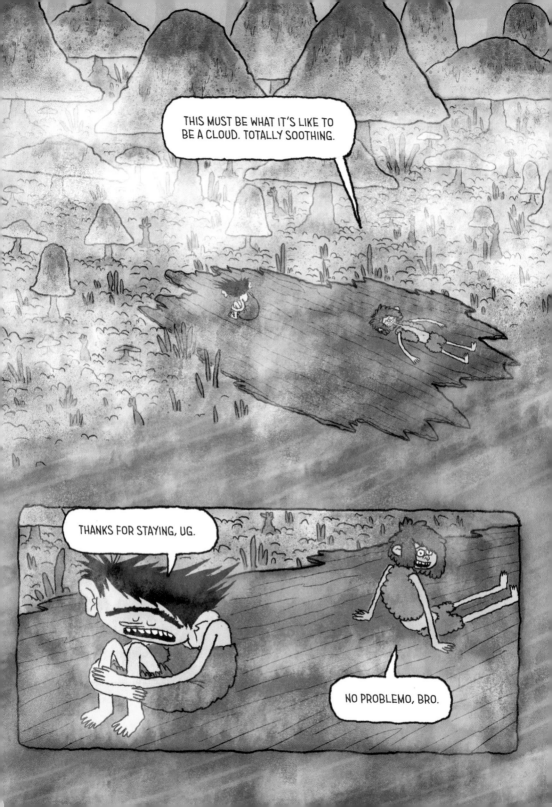

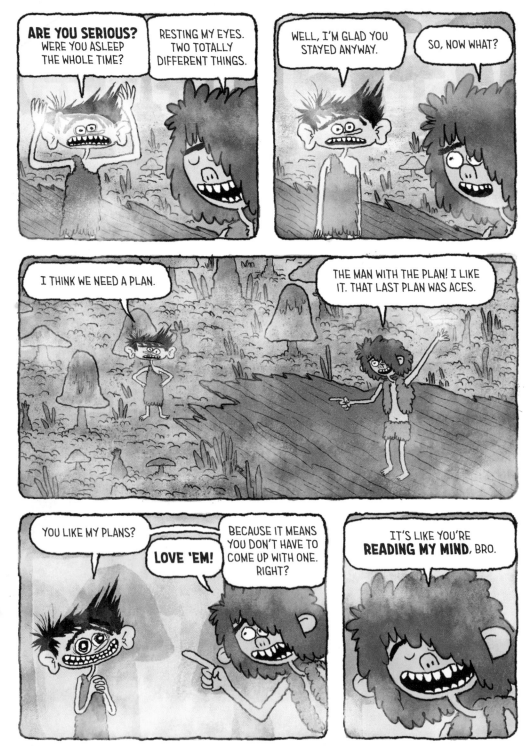

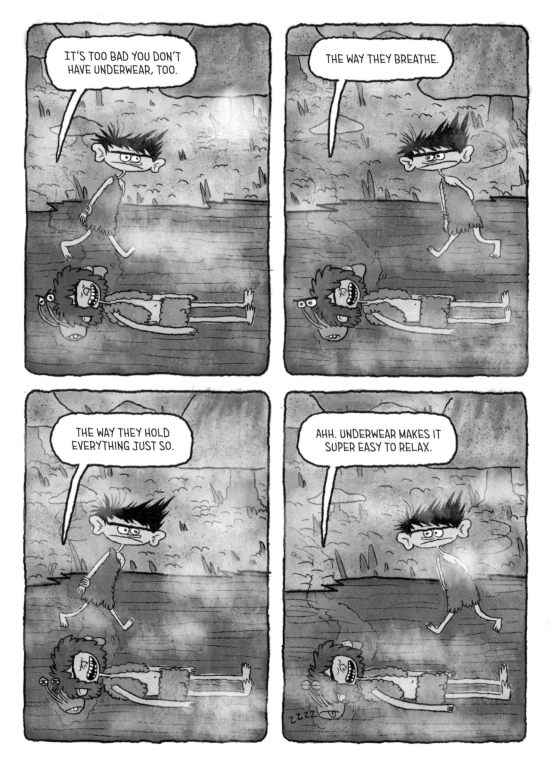

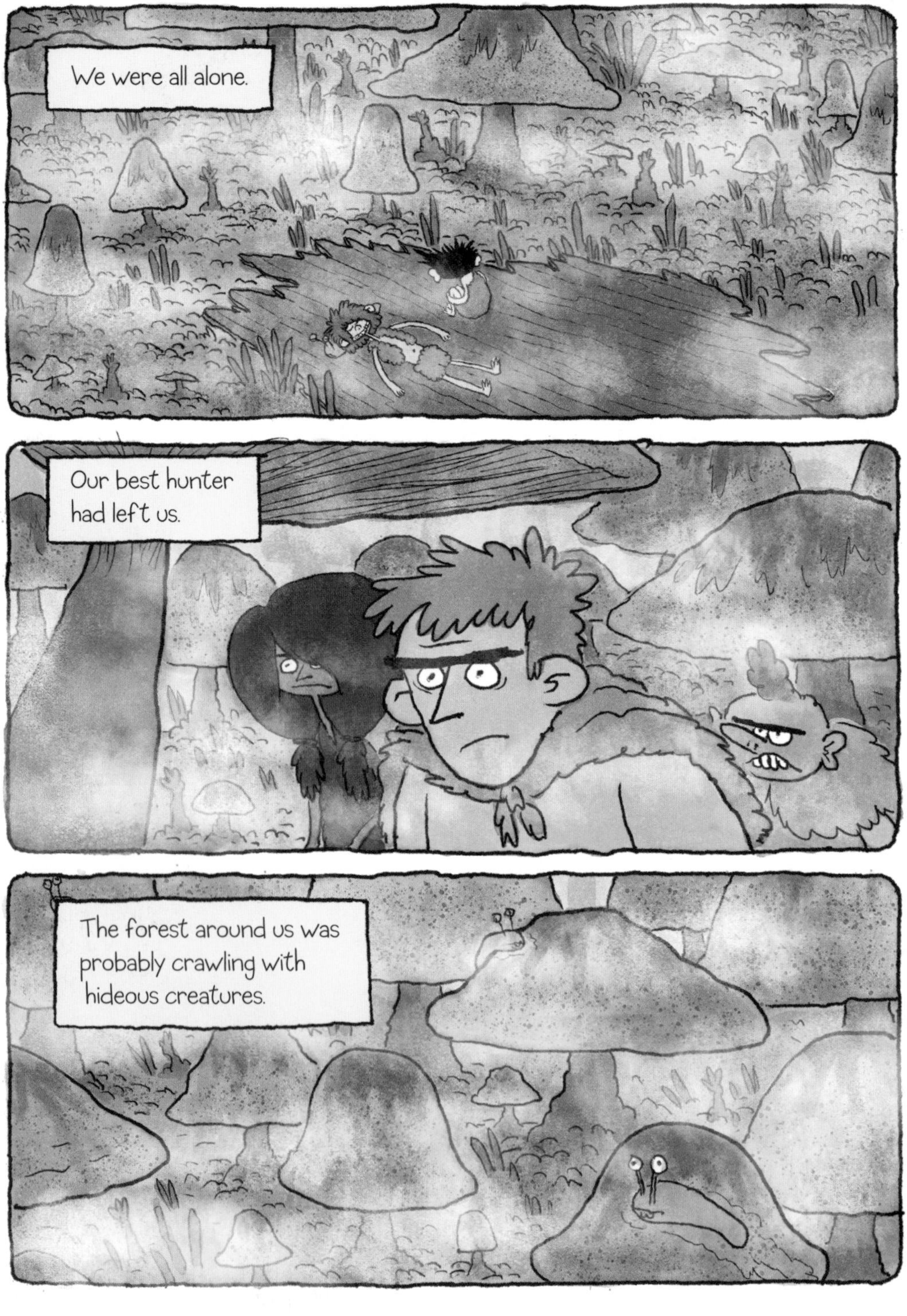
We were all alone.
Our best hunter had left us.
The forest around us was probably crawling with hideous creatures.

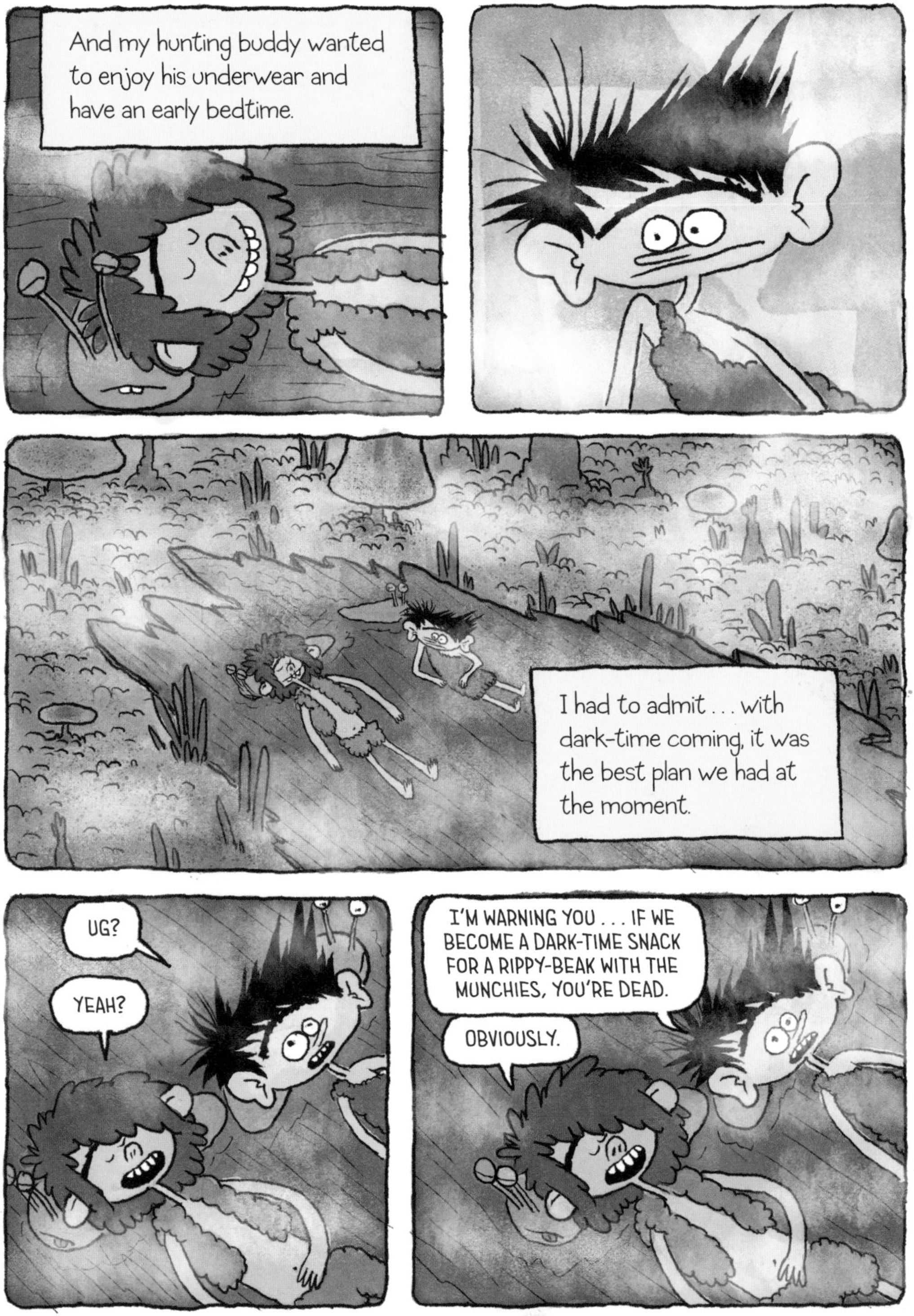

And my hunting buddy wanted to enjoy his underwear and have an early bedtime.
I had to admit . . . with dark-time coming, it was the best plan we had at the moment.
UG?
YEAH?
I'M WARNING YOU . . . IF WE BECOME A DARK-TIME SNACK FOR A RIPPY-BEAK WITH THE MUNCHIES, YOU'RE DEAD.
OBVIOUSLY.

121

125

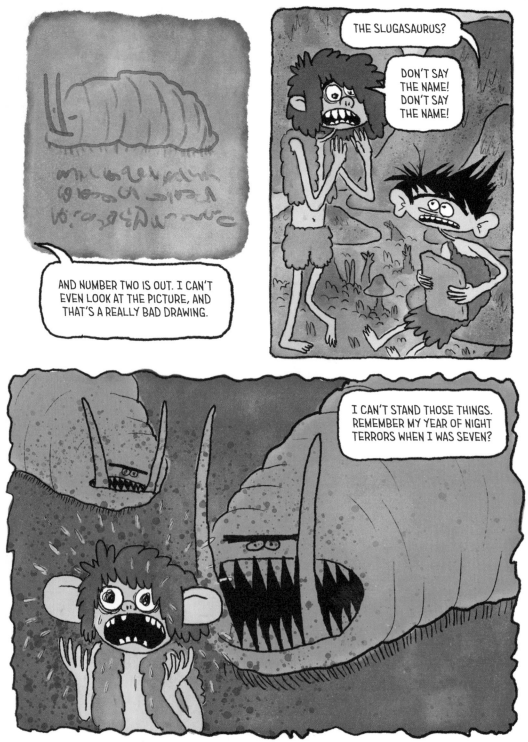

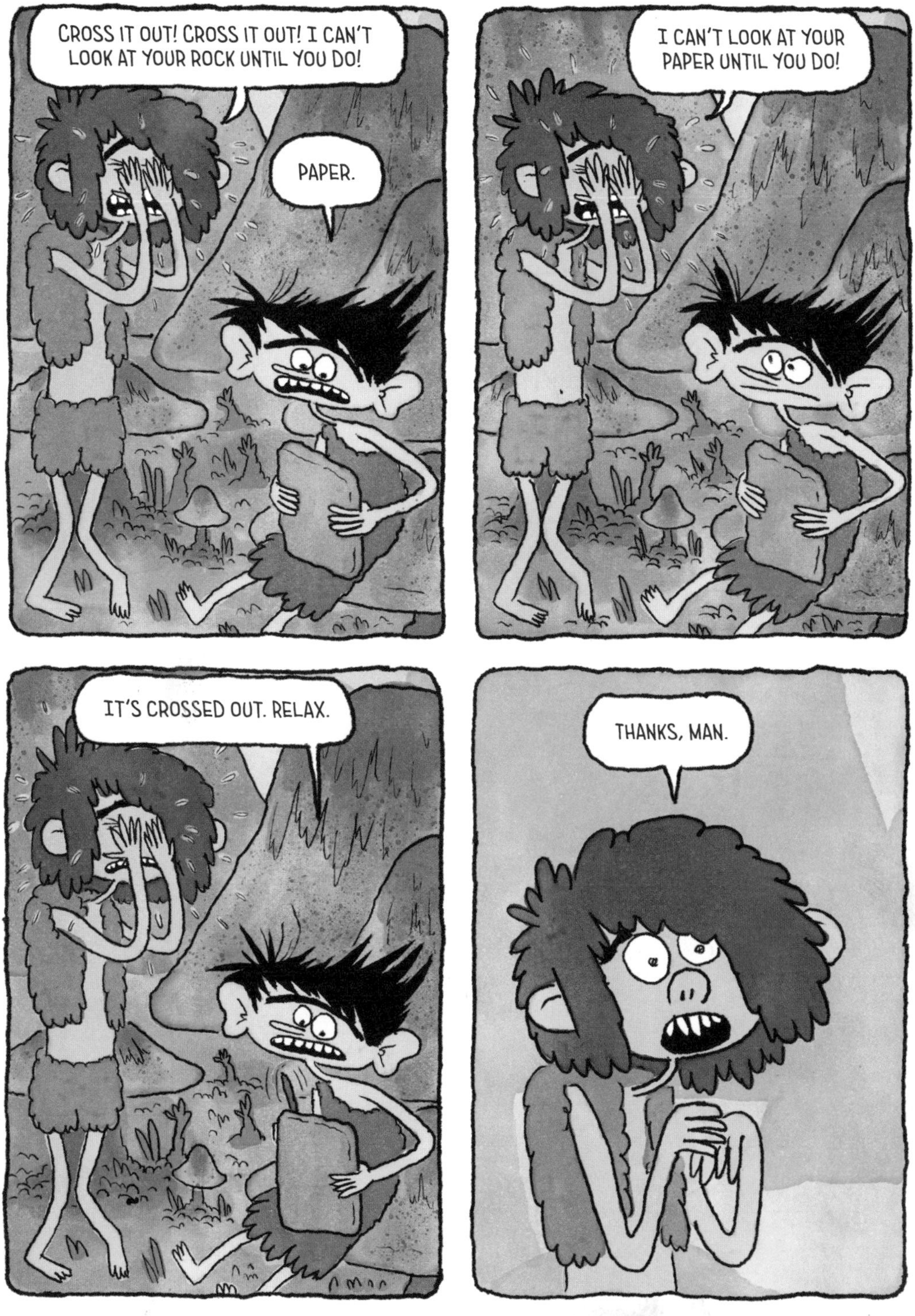
CROSS IT OUT! CROSS IT OUT! I CAN'T LOOK AT YOUR ROCK UNTIL YOU DO!
PAPER.
I CAN'T LOOK AT YOUR PAPER UNTIL YOU DO!
IT'S CROSSED OUT. RELAX.
THANKS, MAN.

136

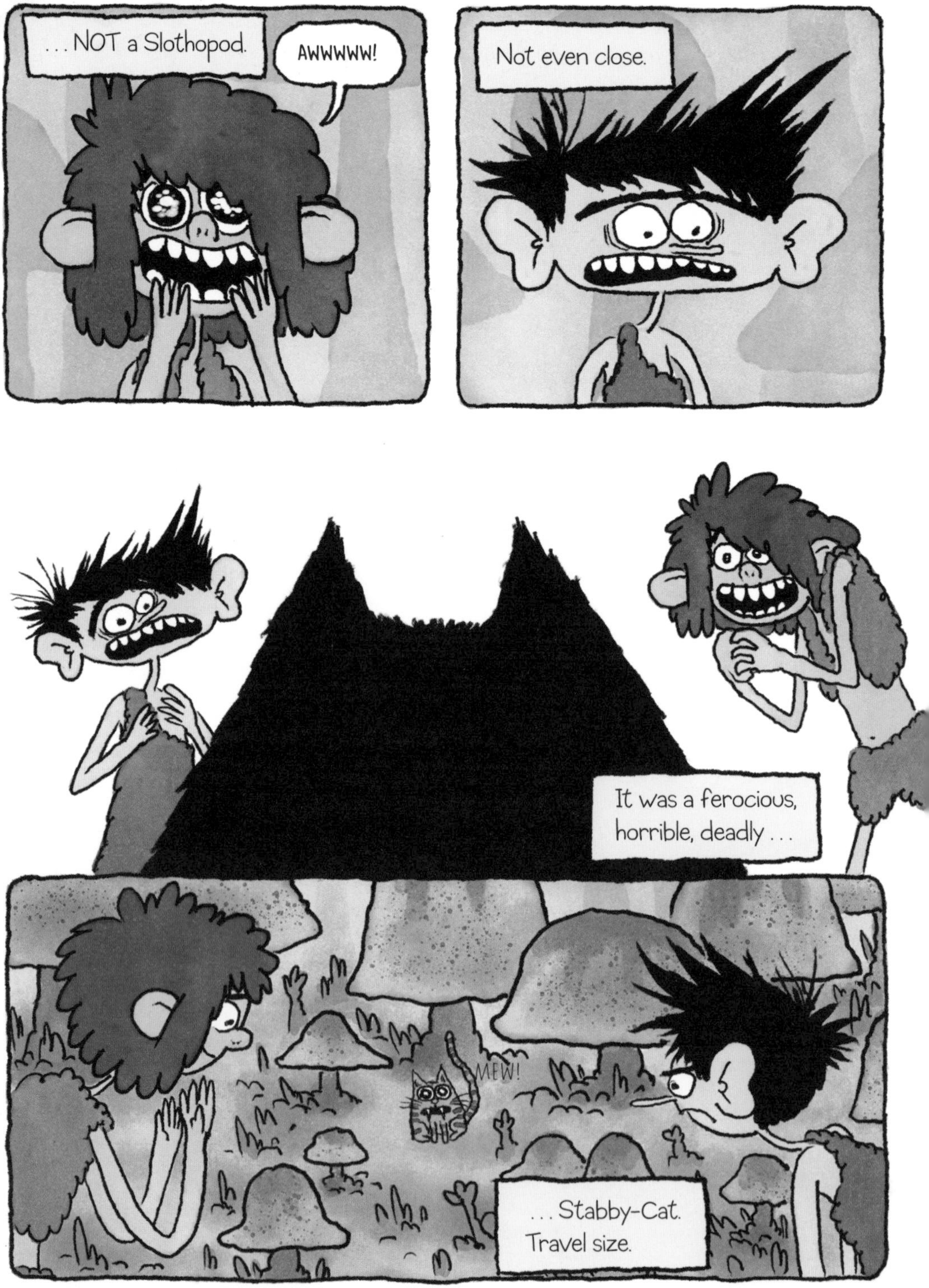
. . . NOT a Slothopod.
AWWWWW!
Not even close.
It was a ferocious, horrible, deadly . . .
MEW!
. . . Stabby-Cat. Travel size.

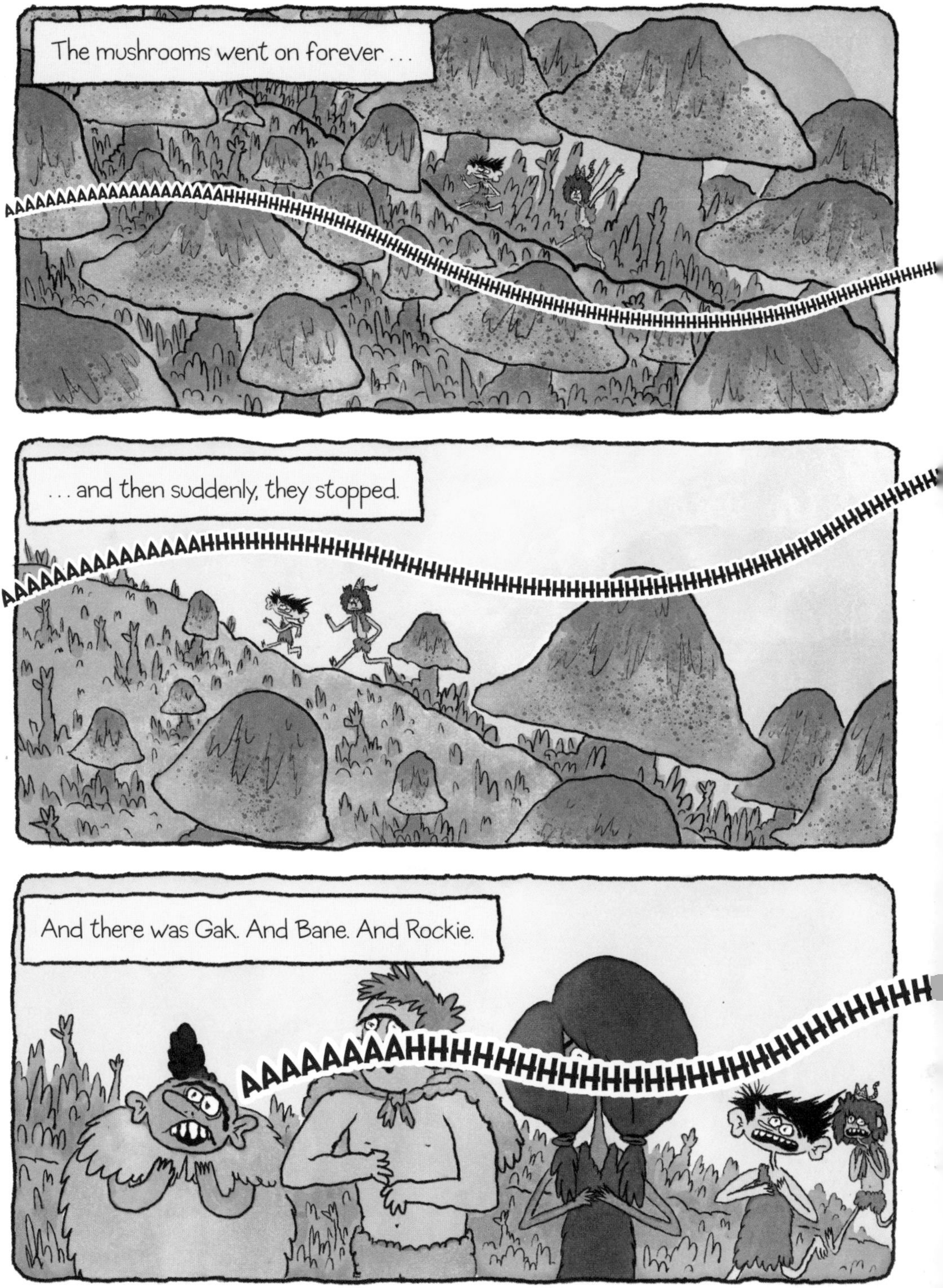
The mushrooms went on forever . . .
AAAAAAAAAAAAAAAAAAAAAAHHHHHHHHHHHHHHHHHHHHHHHHHHHHHHHHHHHHHHHHHHHHHHHHHHHHHHHHHHHHHHHHHHHHHHHHHHHH
. . . and then suddenly, they stopped.
AAAAAAAAAAAAAAAAHHHHHHHHHHHHHHHHHHHHHHHHHHHHHHHHHHHHHHHHHHHHHHHHHHHHHHHHHHHHHHH
And there was Gak. And Bane. And Rockie.
AAAAAAAAHHHHHHHHHHHHHHHHHHHHHHHHHHHHHHHH

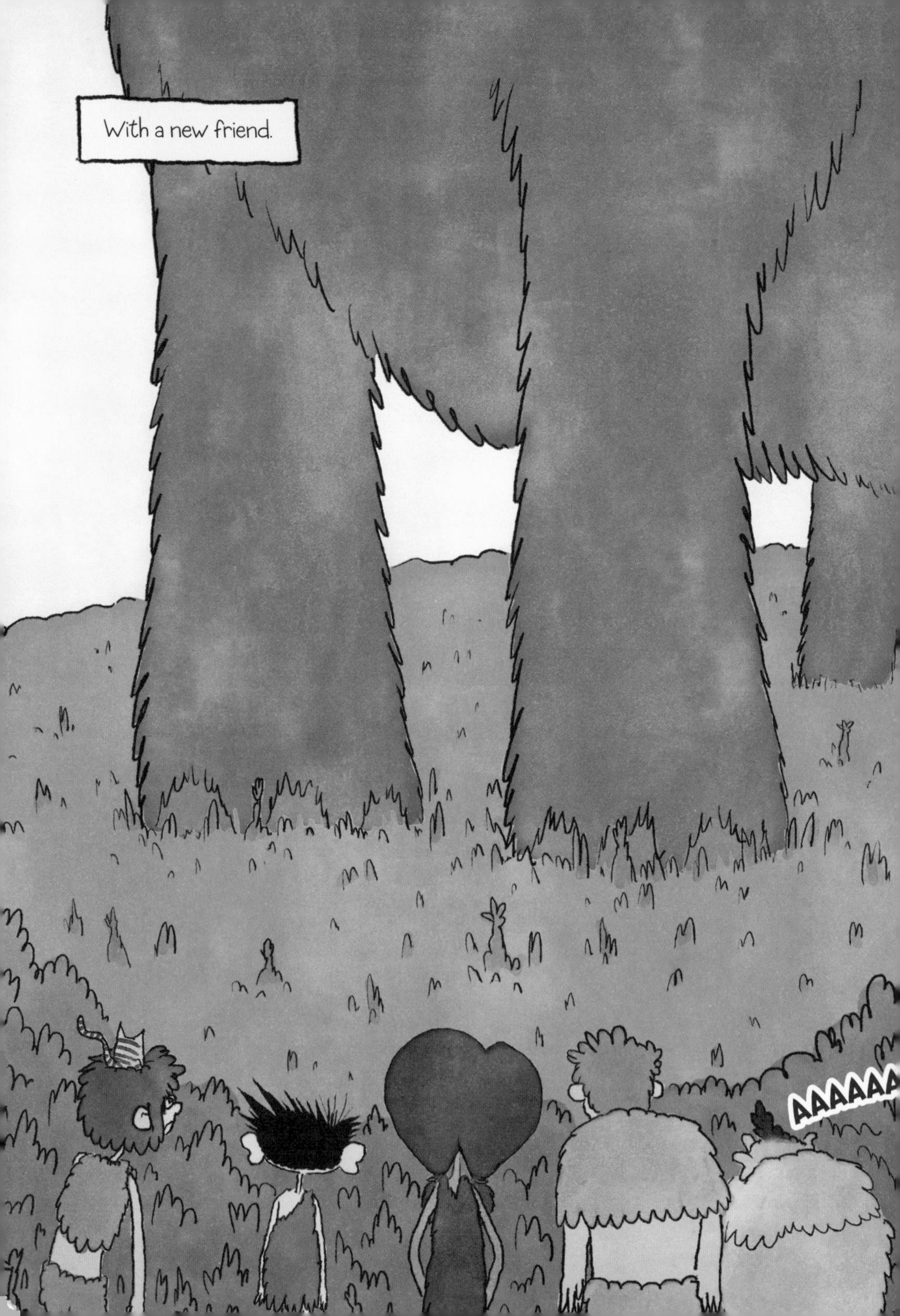
With a new friend.
AAAAA

UNLIKE ANYTHING EVER SEEN

HHHHHHHHHH!!!

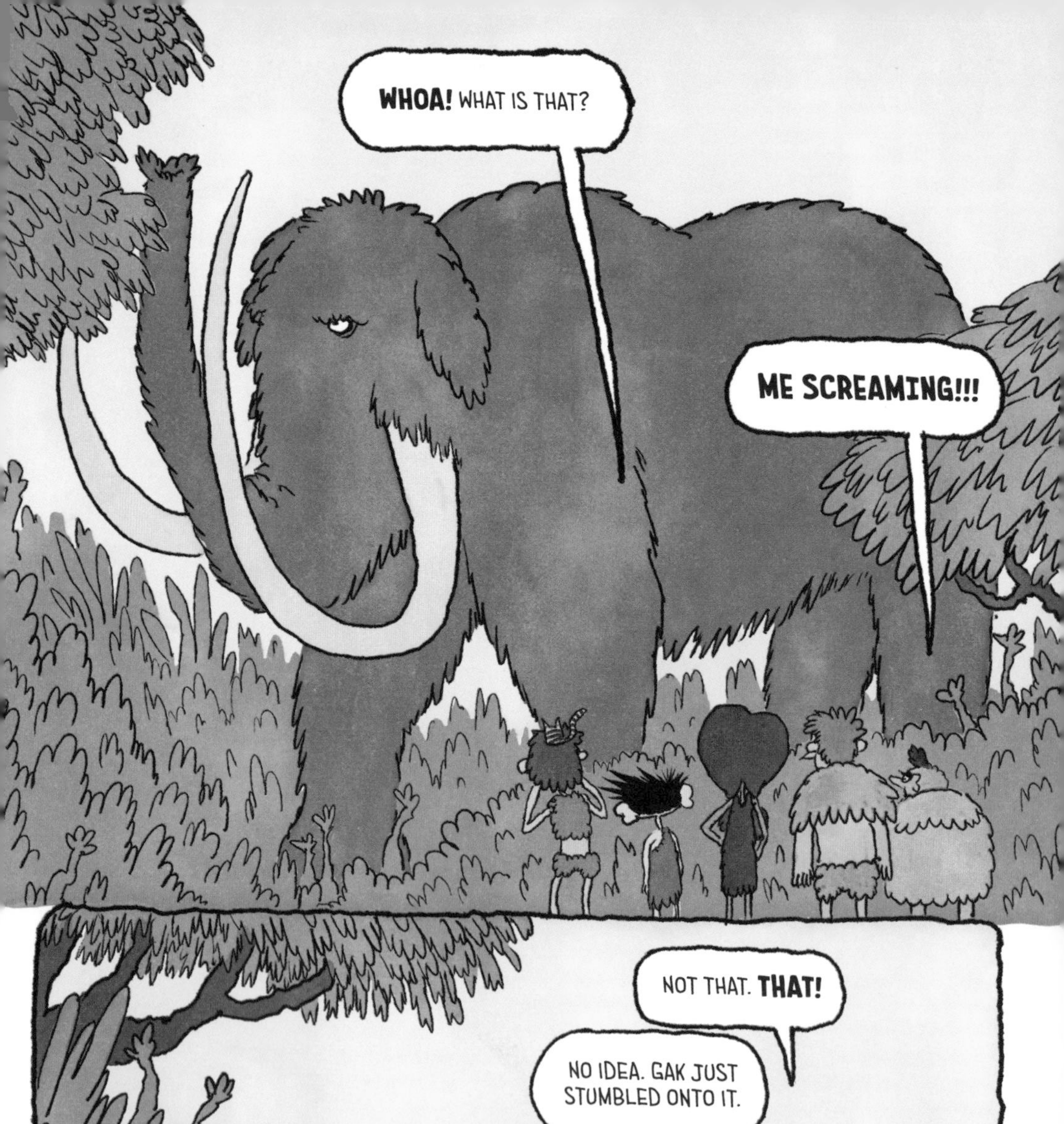
WHOA! WHAT IS THAT?
ME SCREAMING!!!

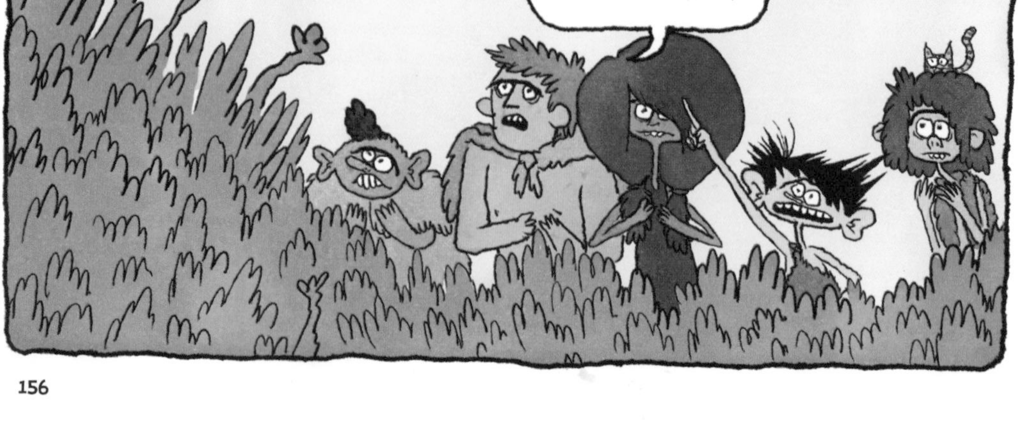
NOT THAT. THAT!
NO IDEA. GAK JUST STUMBLED ONTO IT.

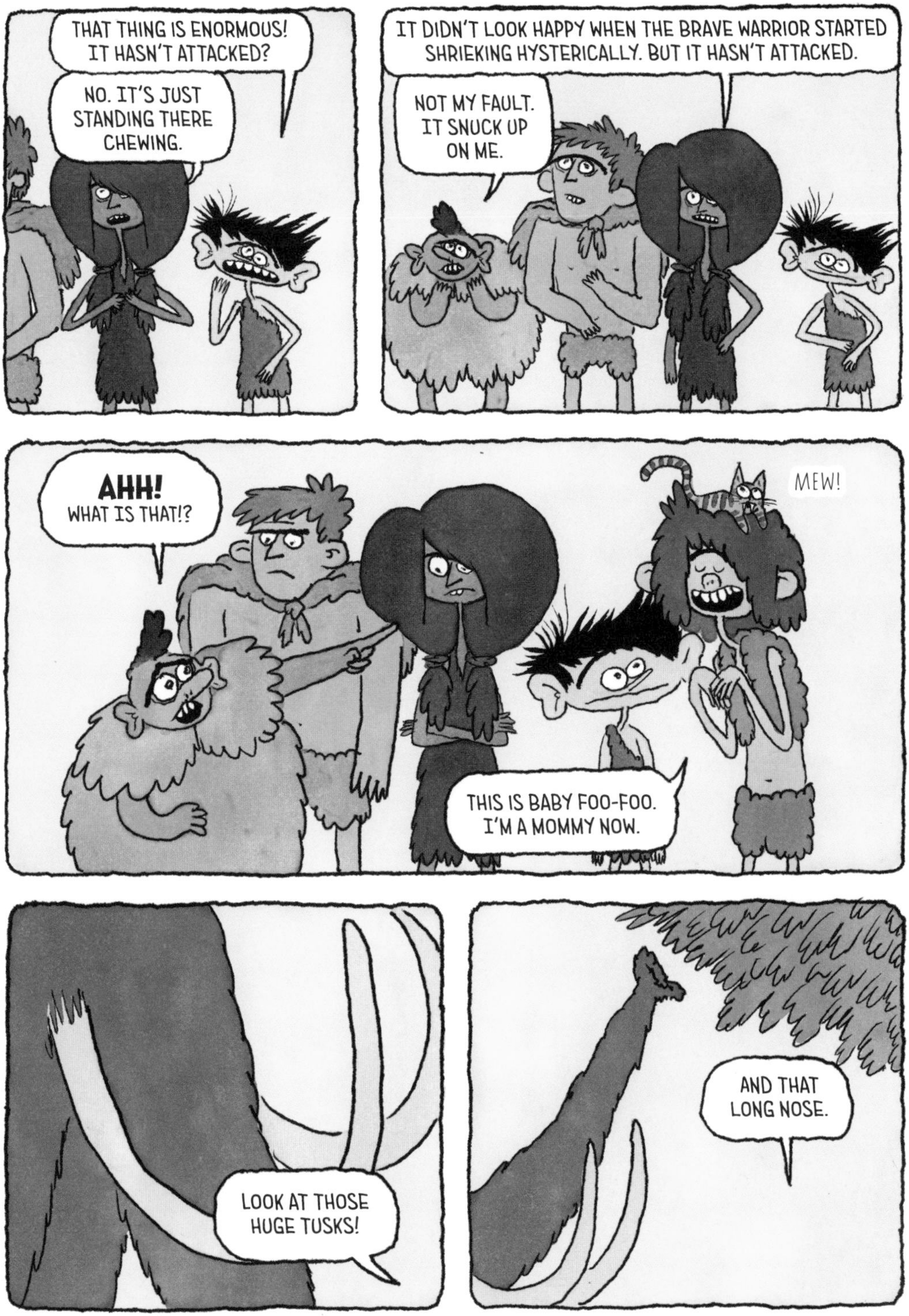
THAT THING IS ENORMOUS! IT HASN'T ATTACKED?
NO. IT'S JUST STANDING THERE CHEWING.
IT DIDN'T LOOK HAPPY WHEN THE BRAVE WARRIOR STARTED SHRIEKING HYSTERICALLY. BUT IT HASN'T ATTACKED.
NOT MY FAULT. IT SNUCK UP ON ME.
AHH! WHAT IS THAT!?
MEW!
THIS IS BABY FOO-FOO. I'M A MOMMY NOW.
LOOK AT THOSE HUGE TUSKS!
AND THAT LONG NOSE.

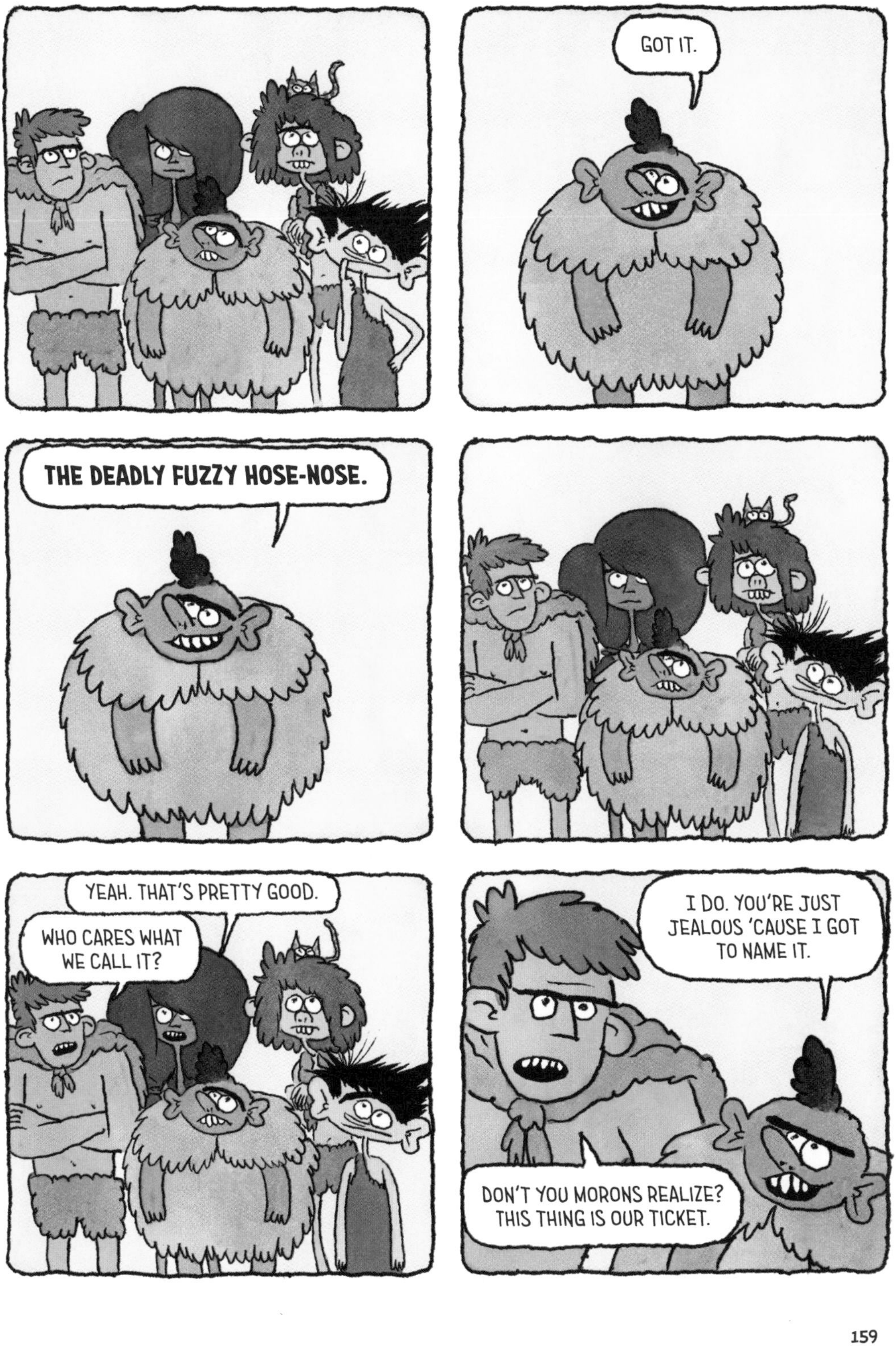
GOT IT.
THE DEADLY FUZZY HOSE-NOSE.
YEAH. THAT'S PRETTY GOOD.
WHO CARES WHAT WE CALL IT?
I DO. YOU'RE JUST JEALOUS 'CAUSE I GOT TO NAME IT.
DON'T YOU MORONS REALIZE? THIS THING IS OUR TICKET.

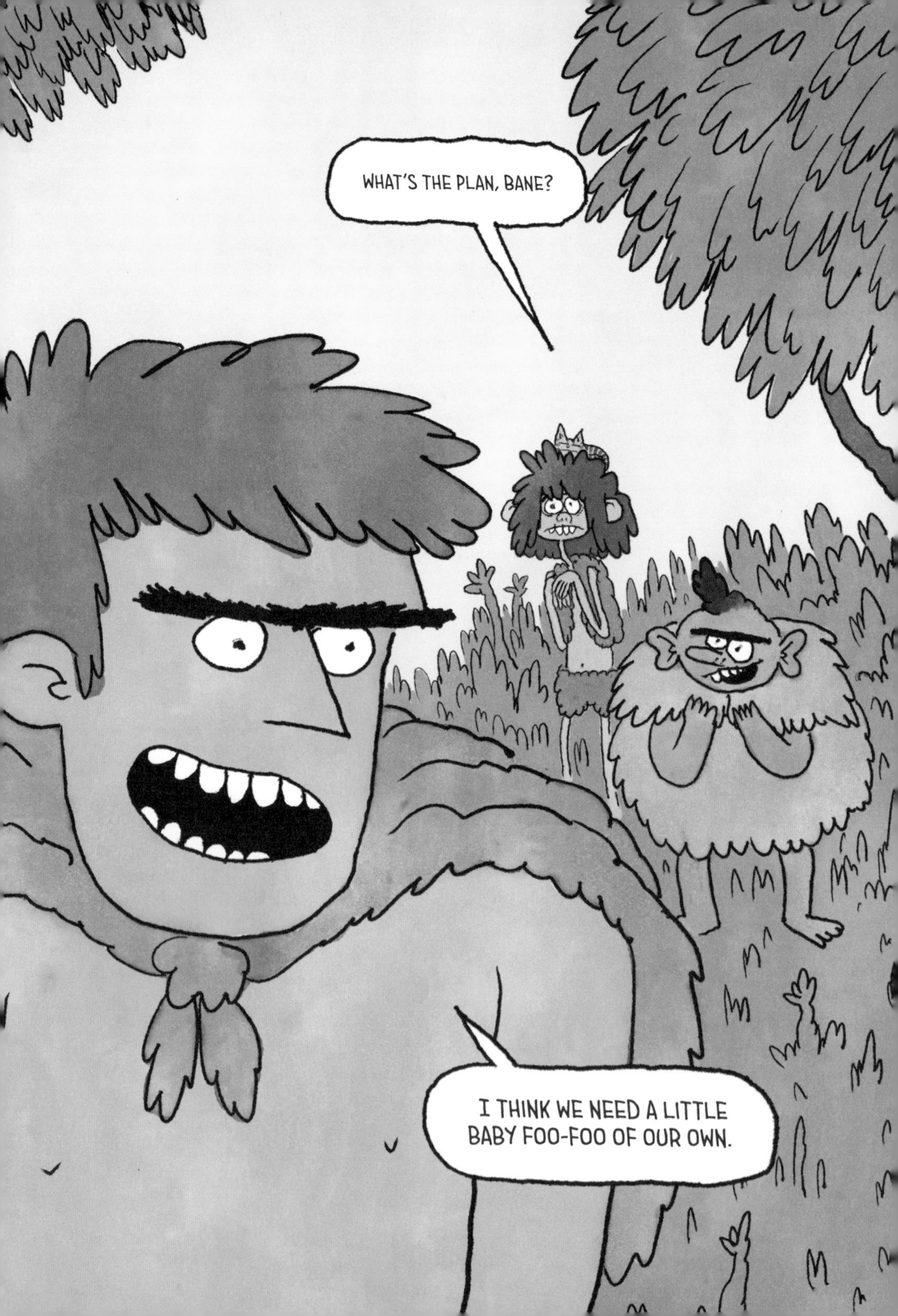
WHAT'S THE PLAN, BANE?
I THINK WE NEED A LITTLE BABY FOO-FOO OF OUR OWN.

168

171

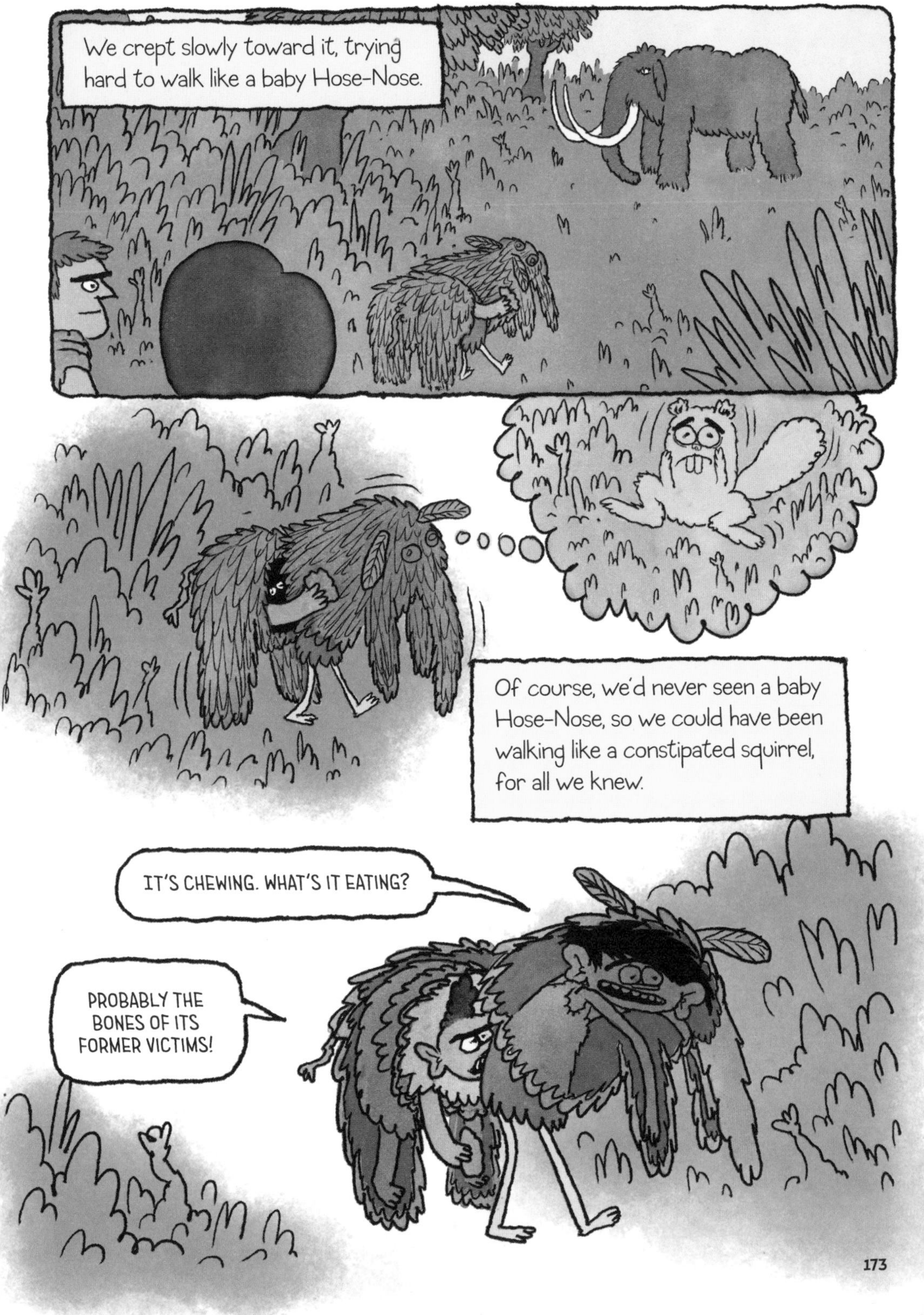
We crept slowly toward it, trying hard to walk like a baby Hose-Nose.
Of course, we'd never seen a baby Hose-Nose, so we could have been walking like a constipated squirrel, for all we knew.
IT'S CHEWING. WHAT'S IT EATING?
PROBABLY THE BONES OF ITS FORMER VICTIMS!

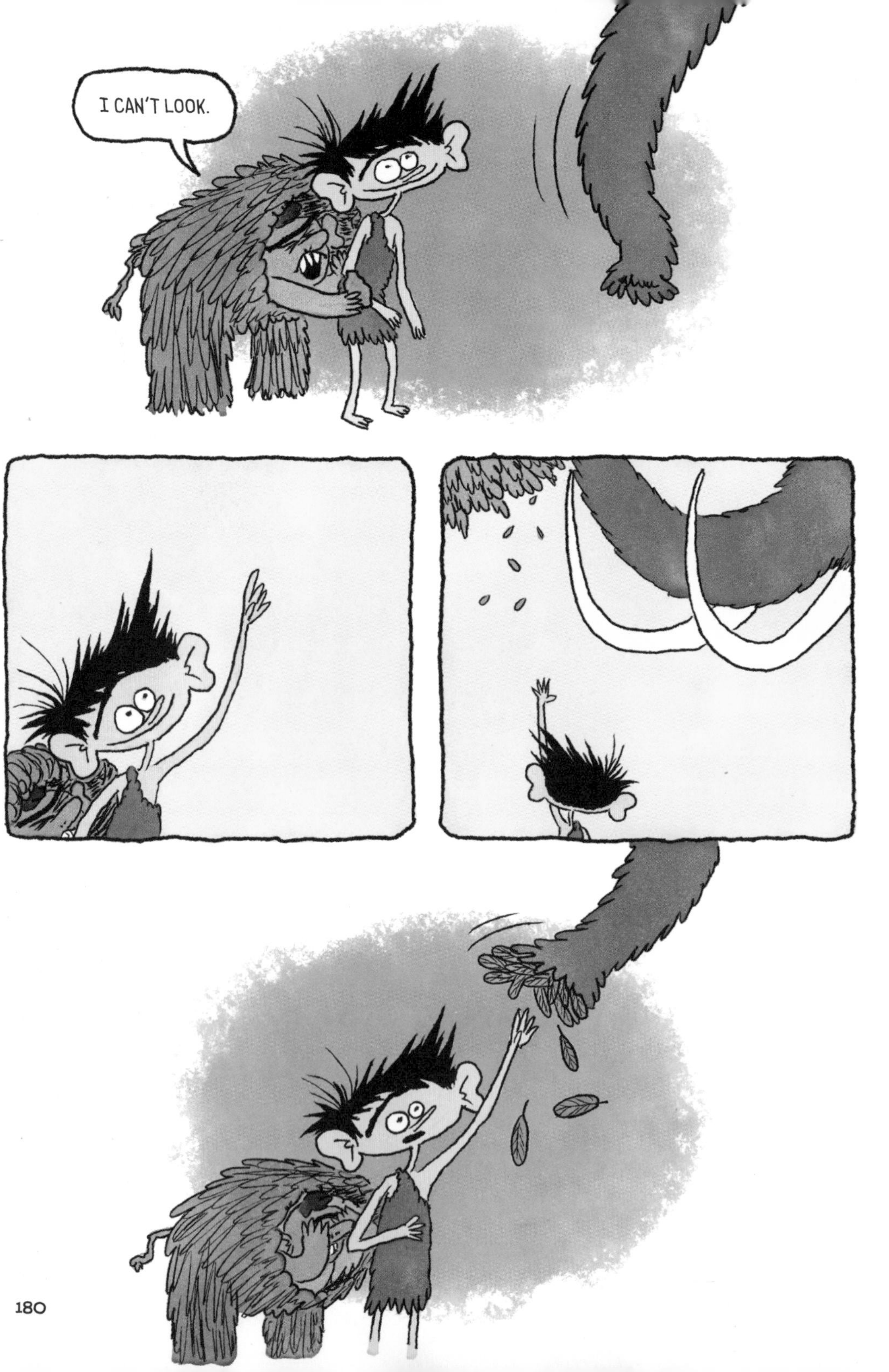
I CAN'T LOOK.

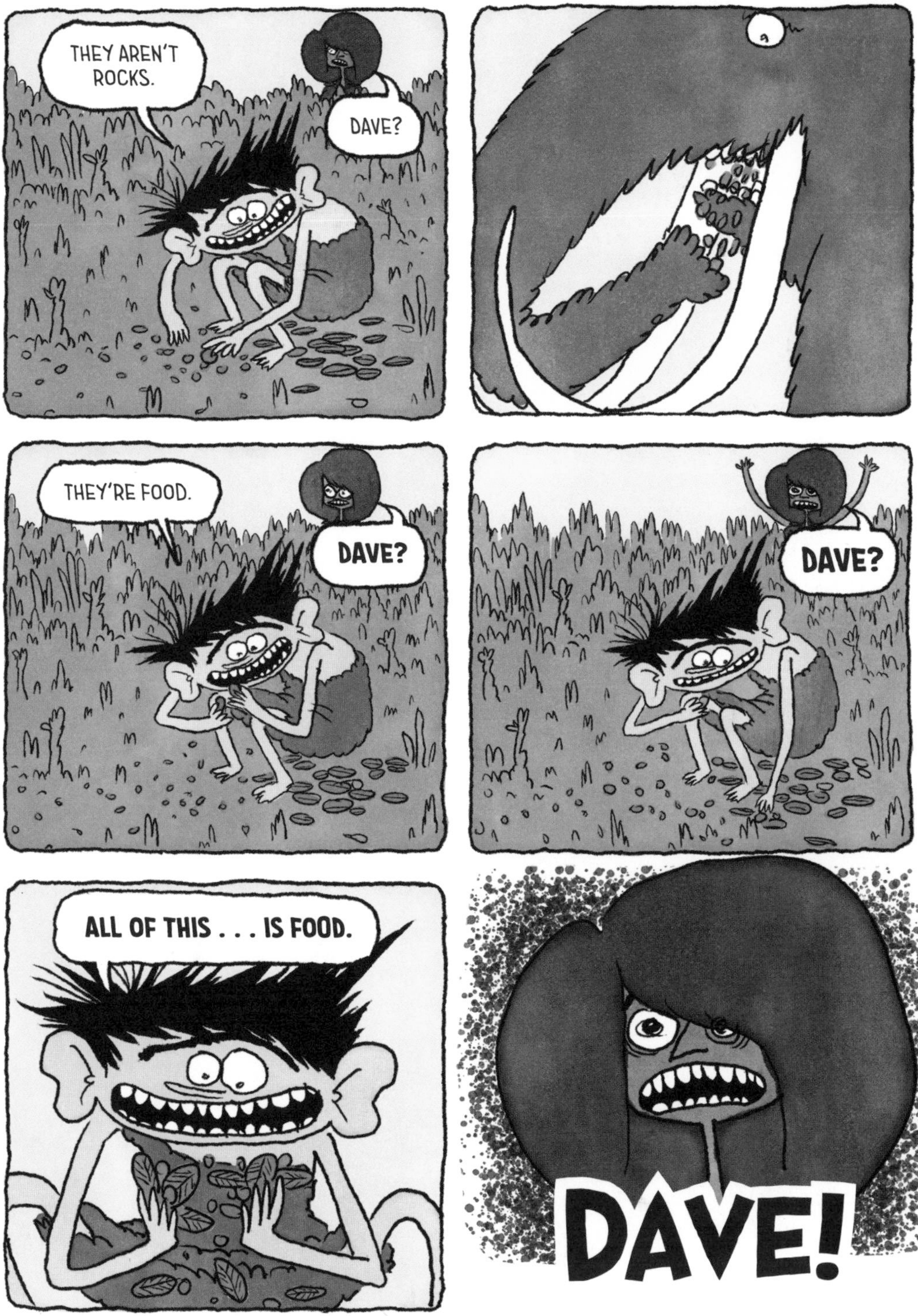
THEY AREN'T ROCKS.
DAVE?
THEY'RE FOOD.
DAVE?
DAVE?
ALL OF THIS . . . IS FOOD.
DAVE!

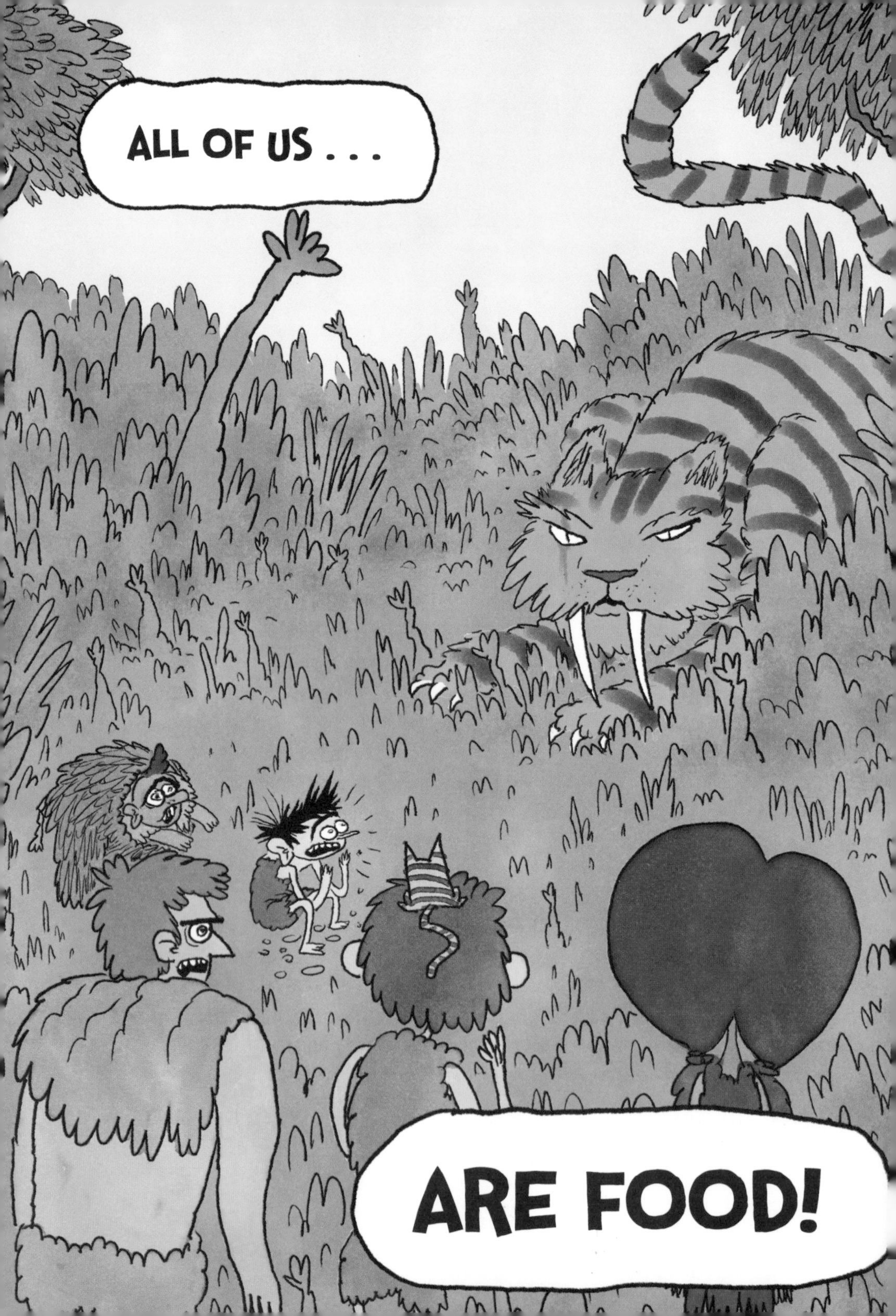
ALL OF US . . .
ARE FOOD!

191

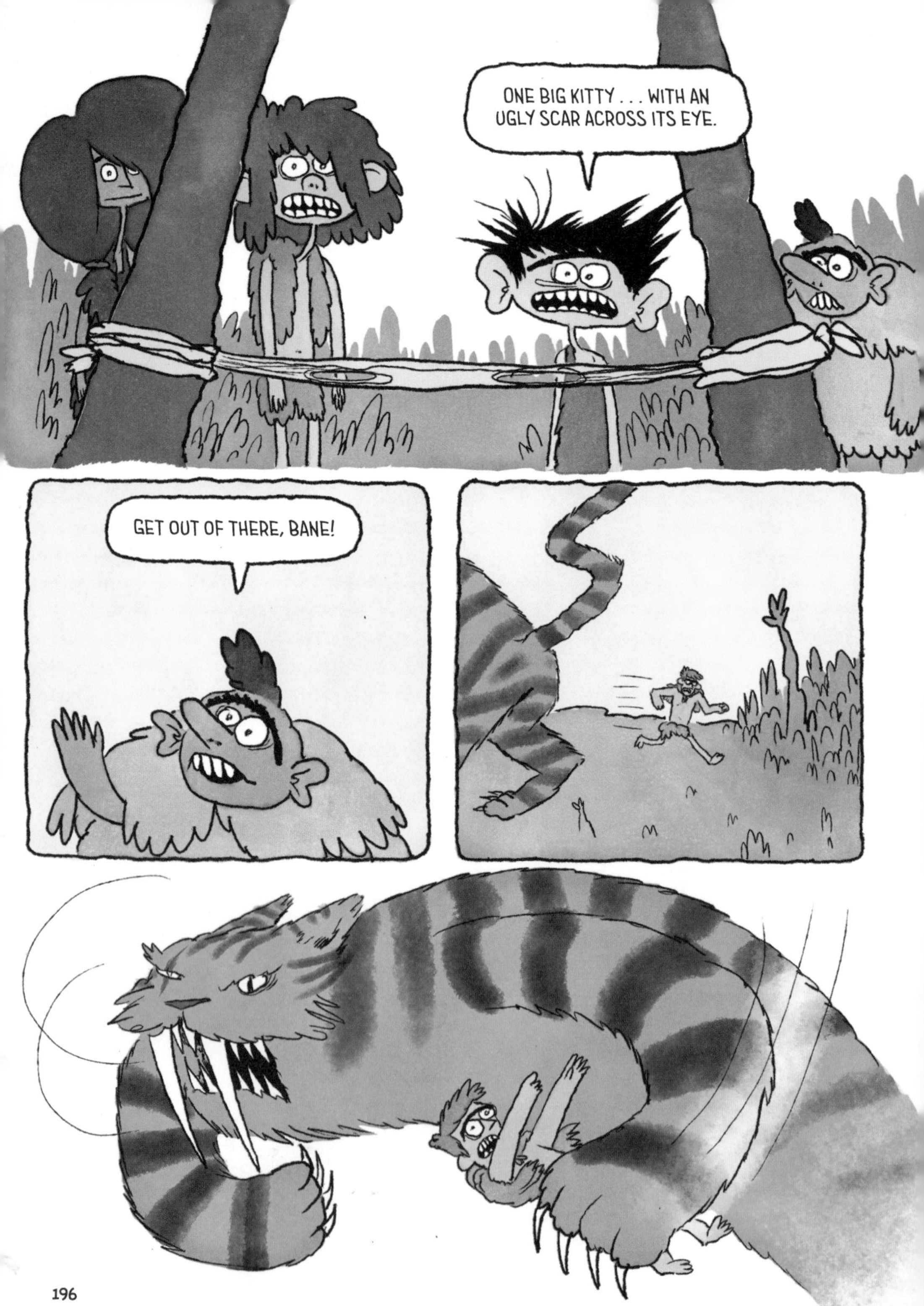
ONE BIG KITTY . . . WITH AN UGLY SCAR ACROSS ITS EYE.
GET OUT OF THERE, BANE!

197

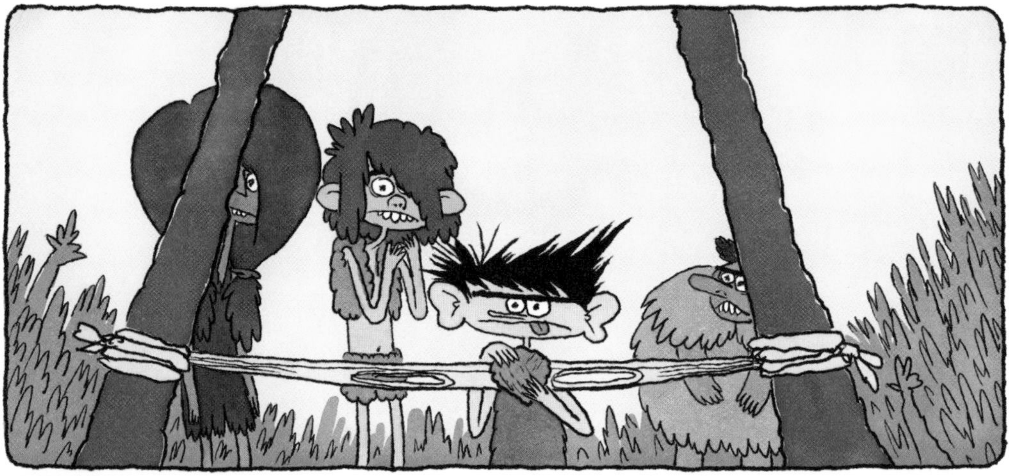

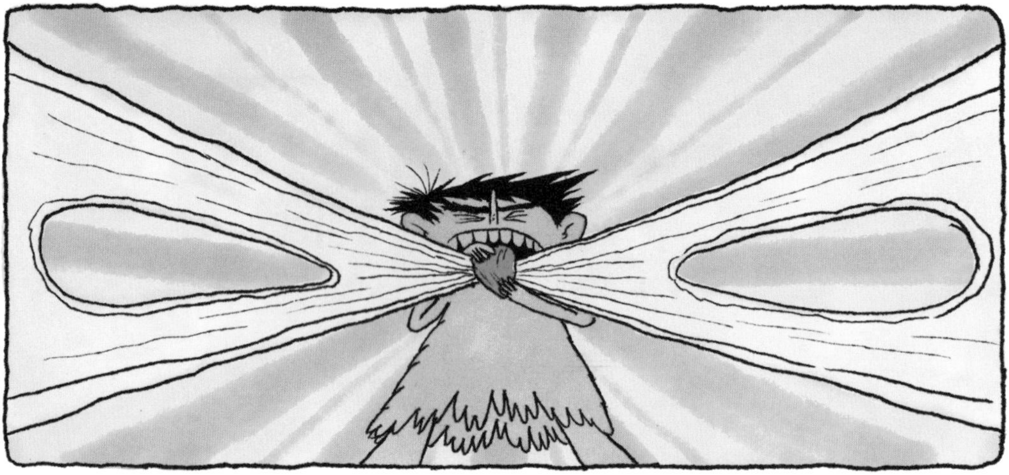

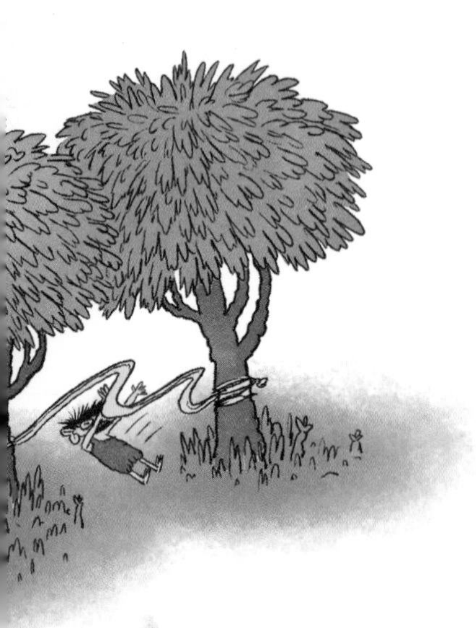

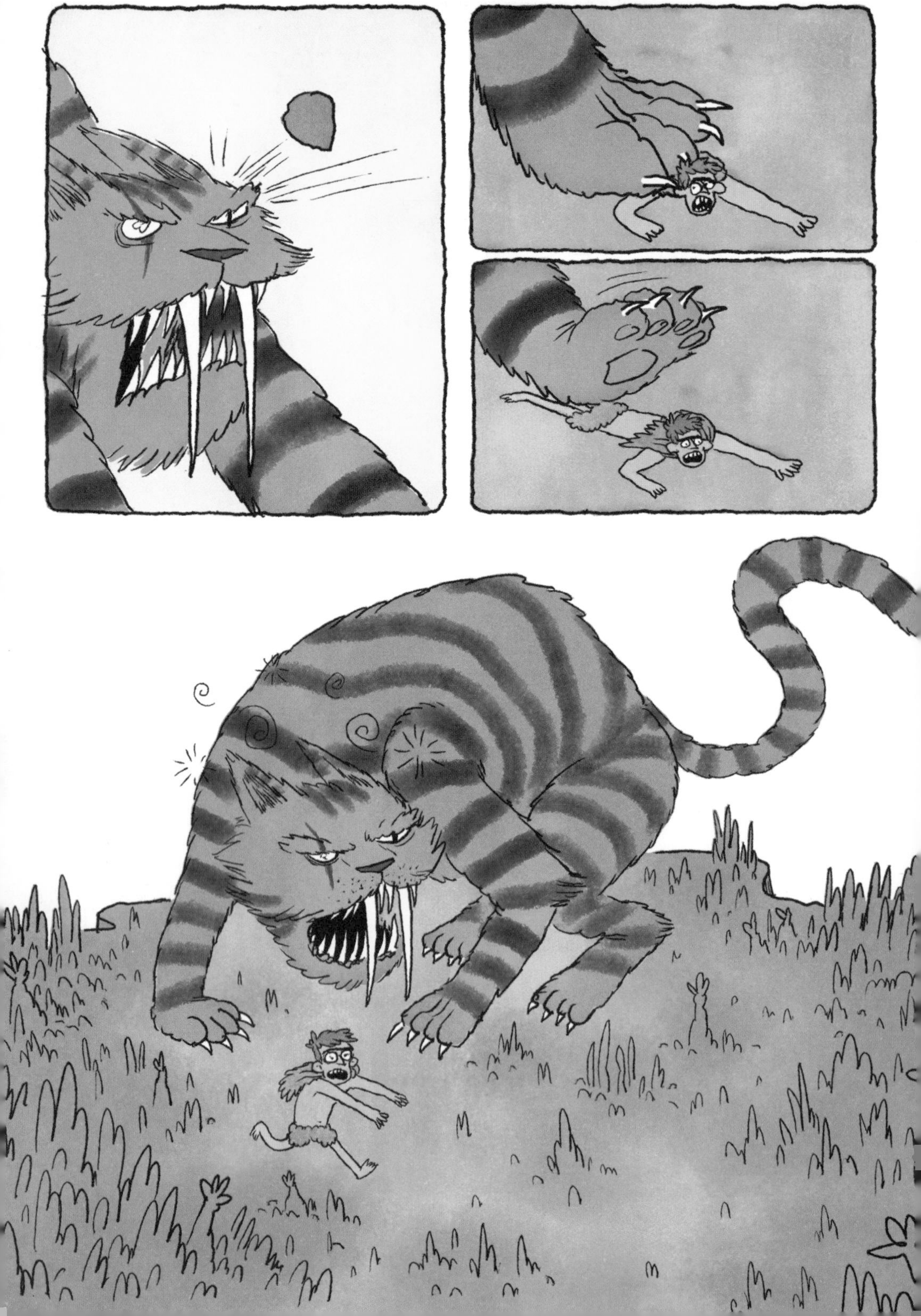

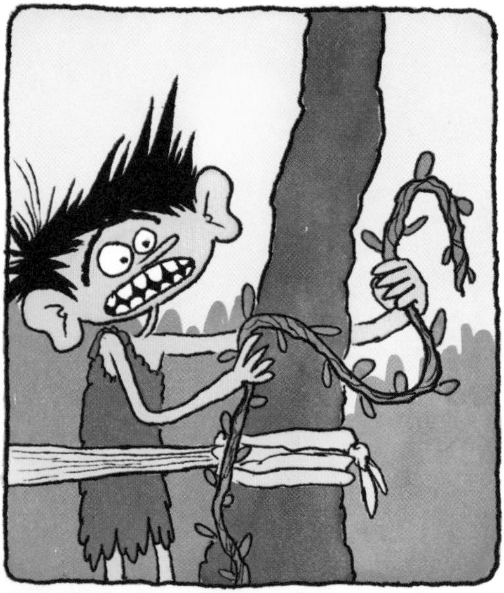

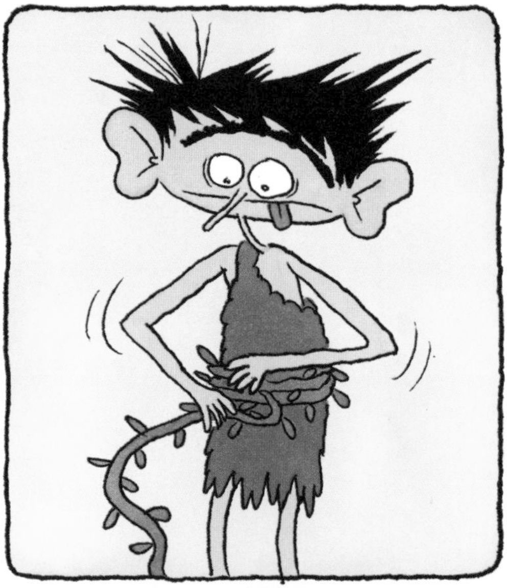

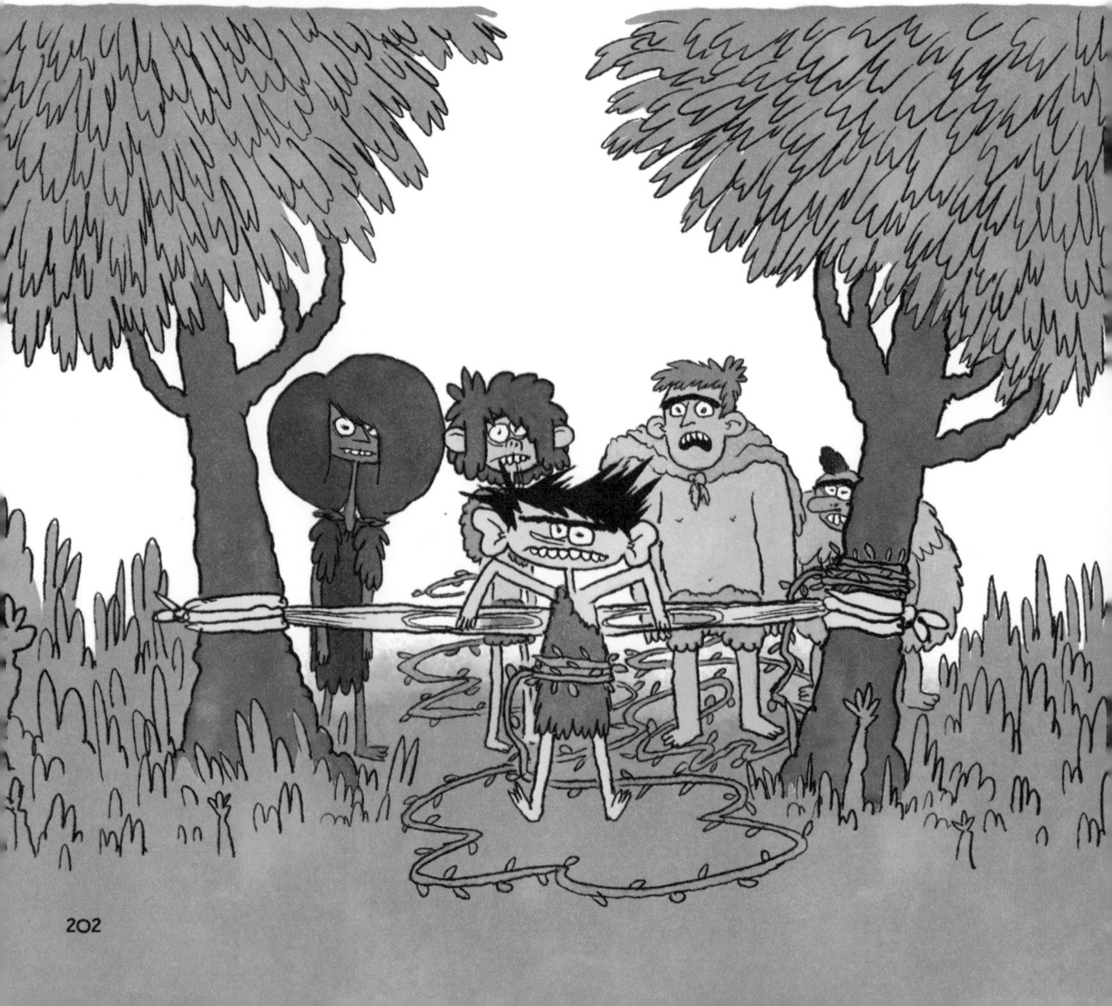

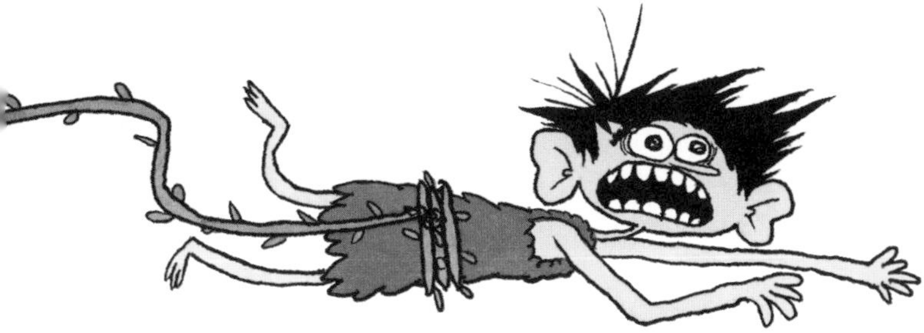

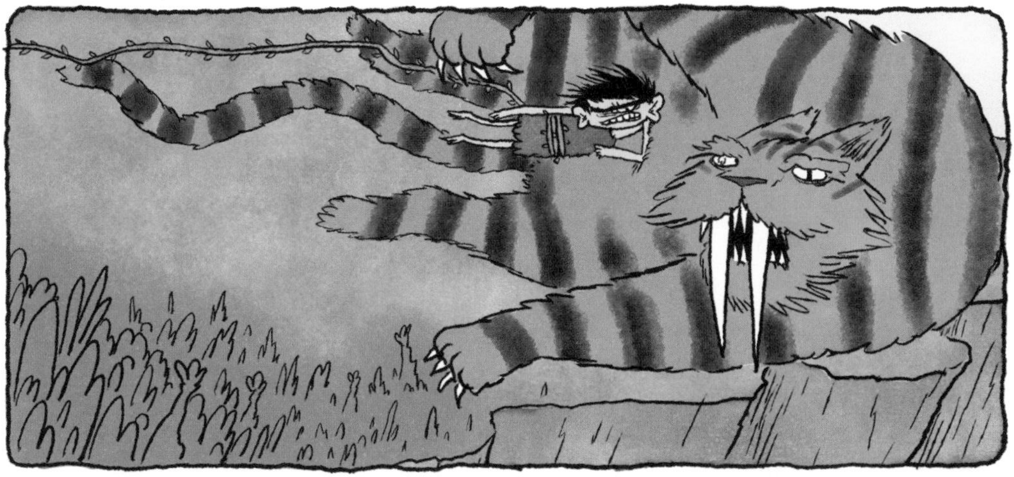

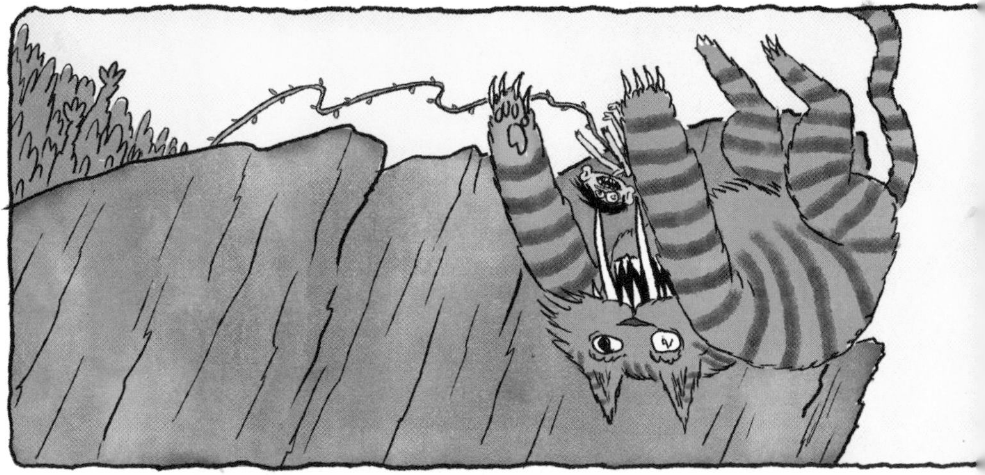

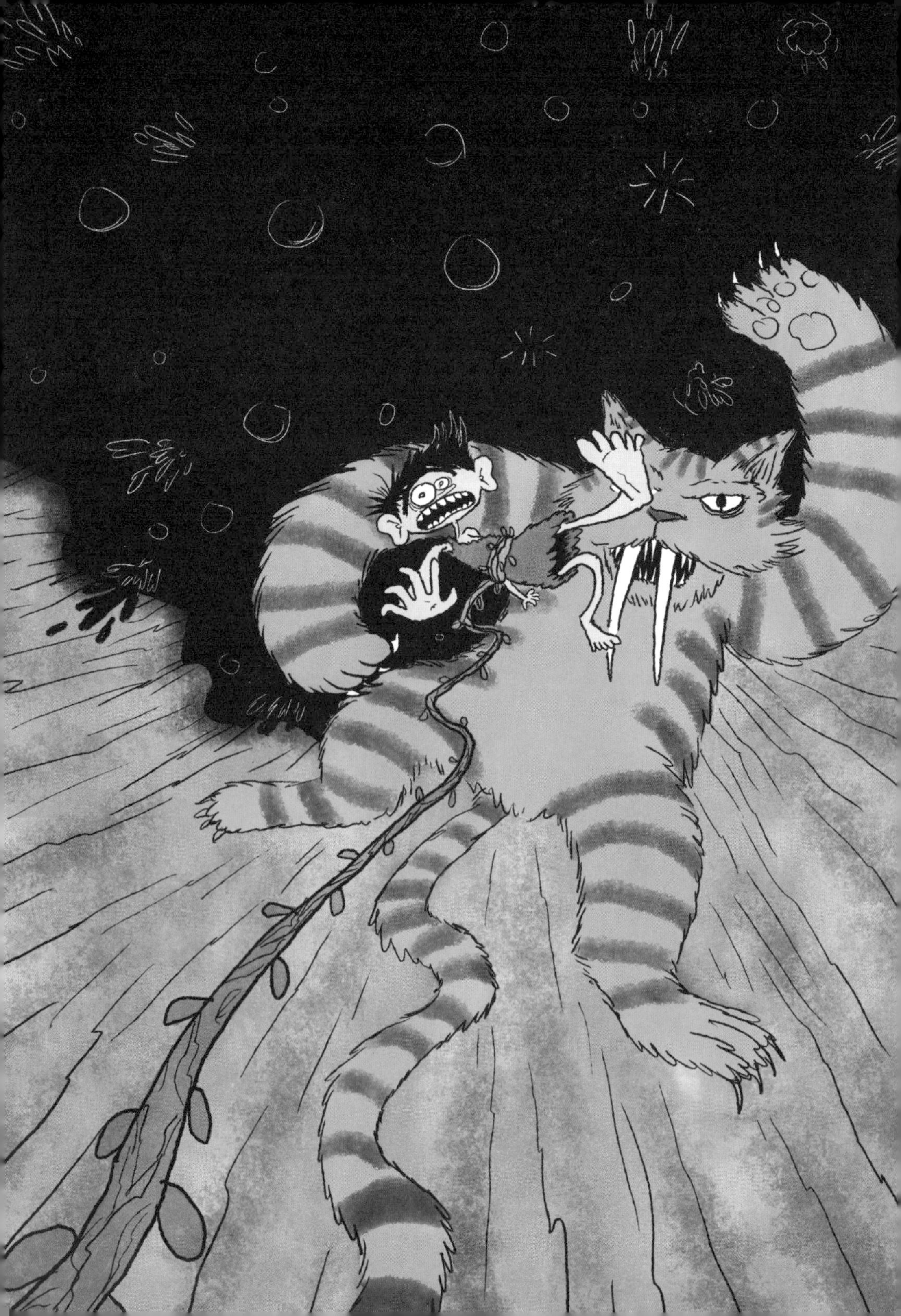

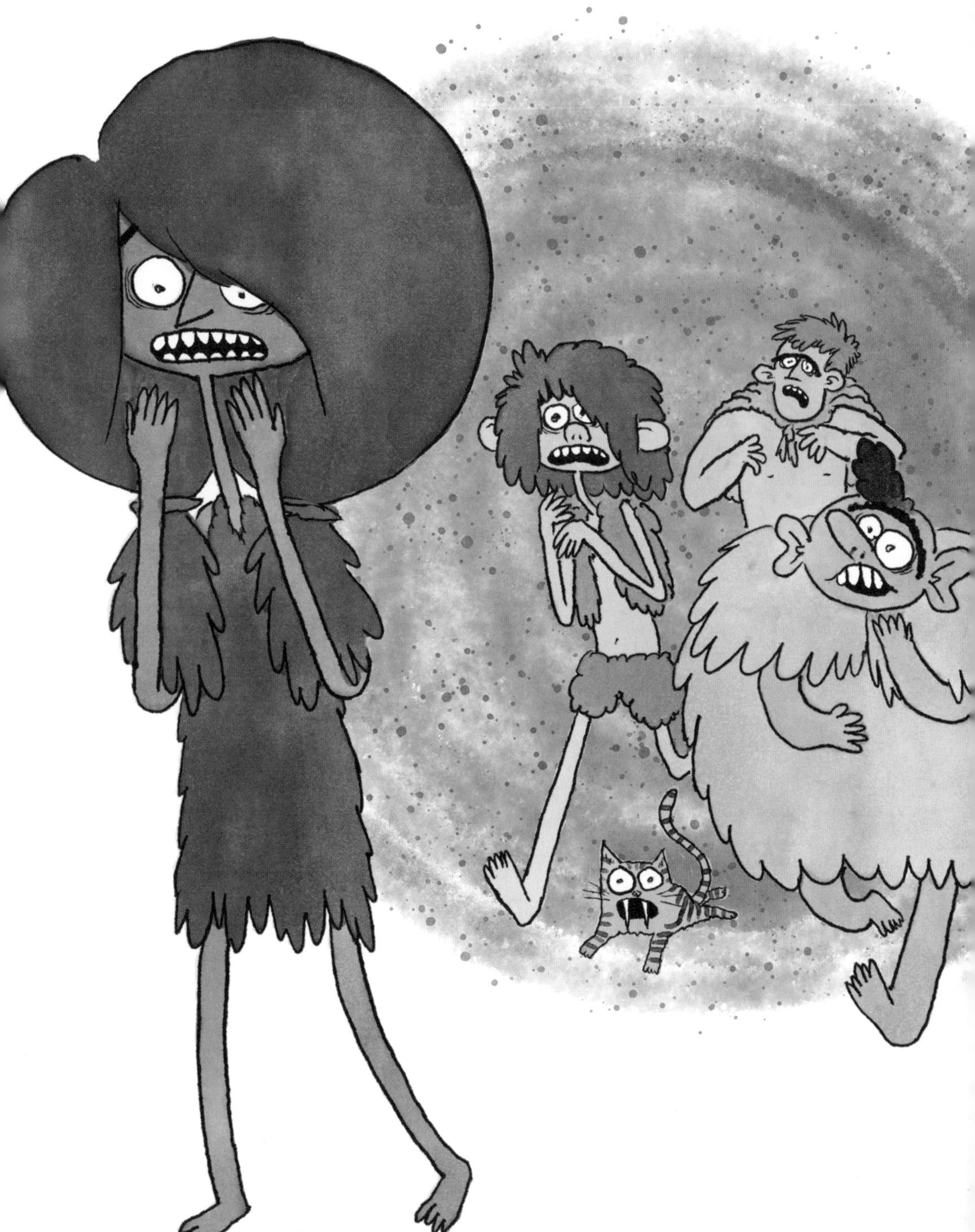

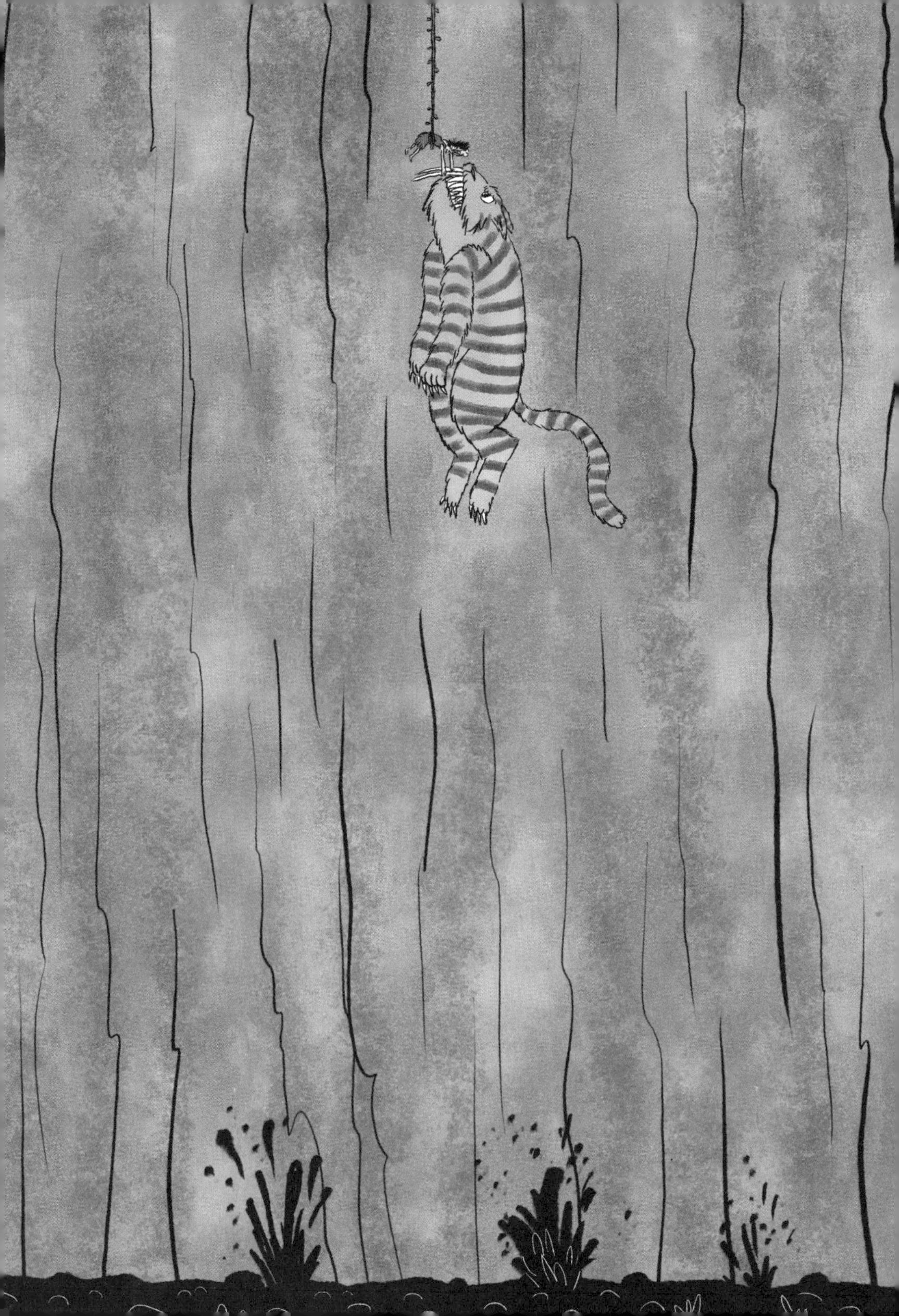

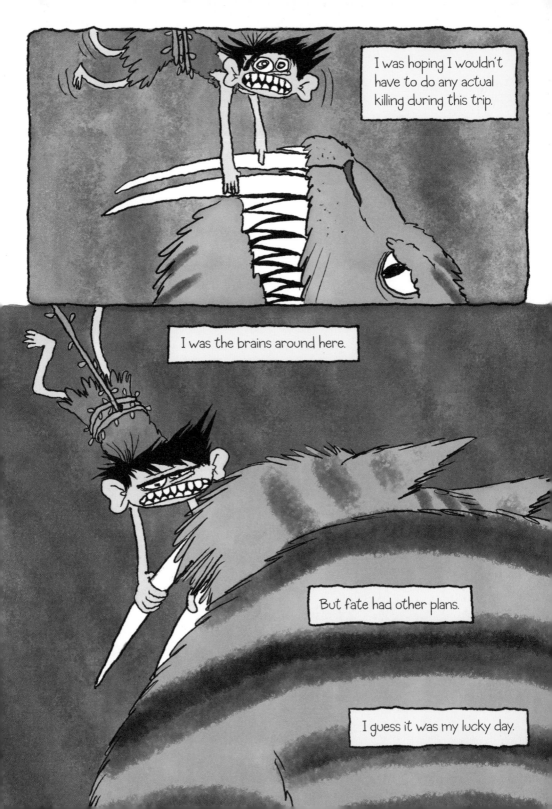

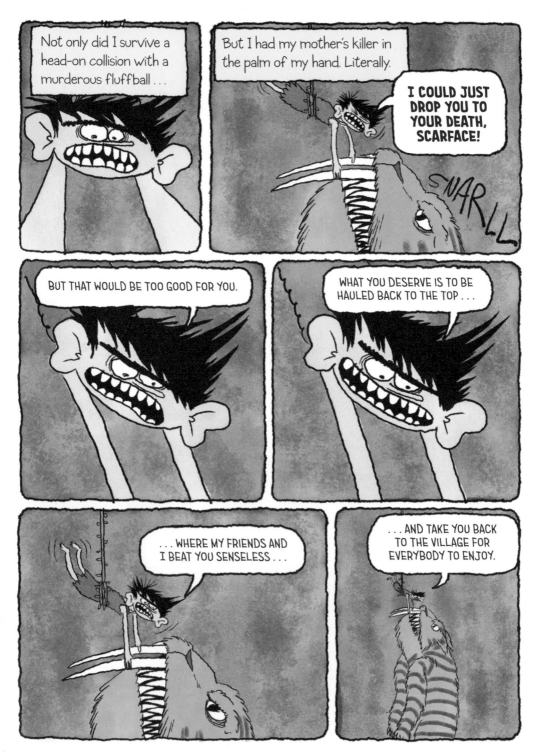

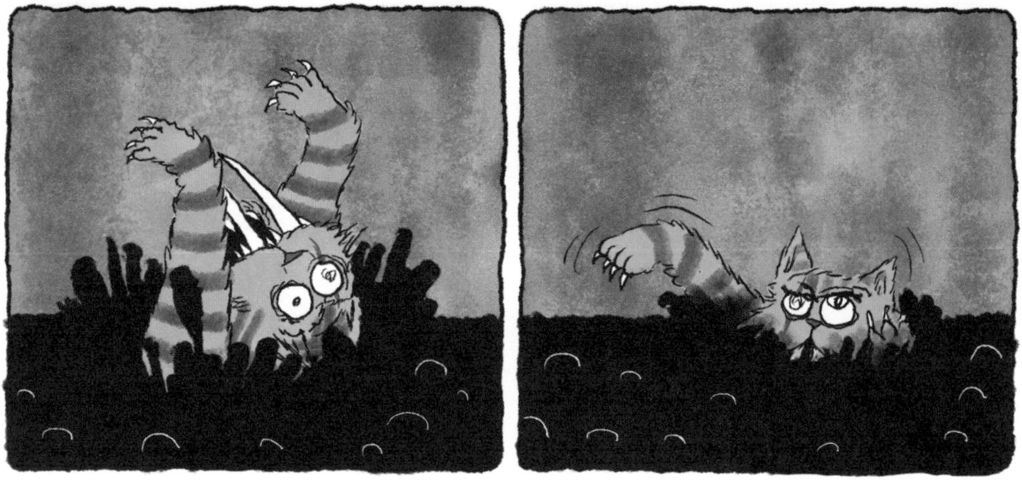

I guess I could.

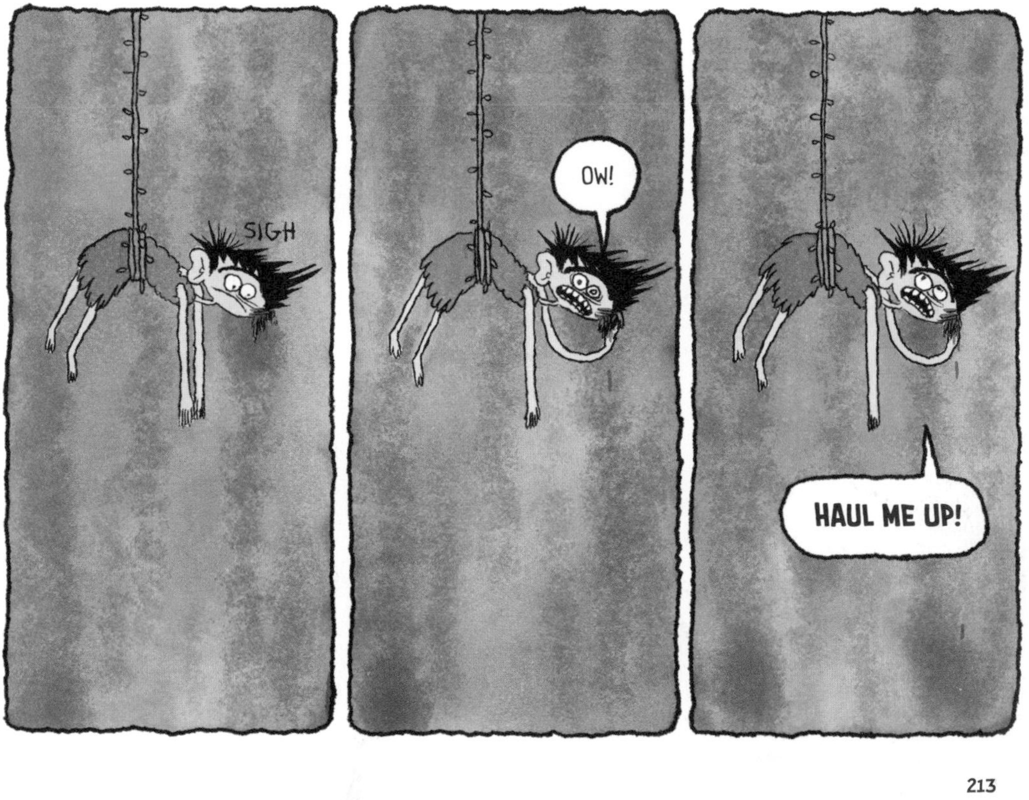
SIGH
OW!
HAUL ME UP!

216

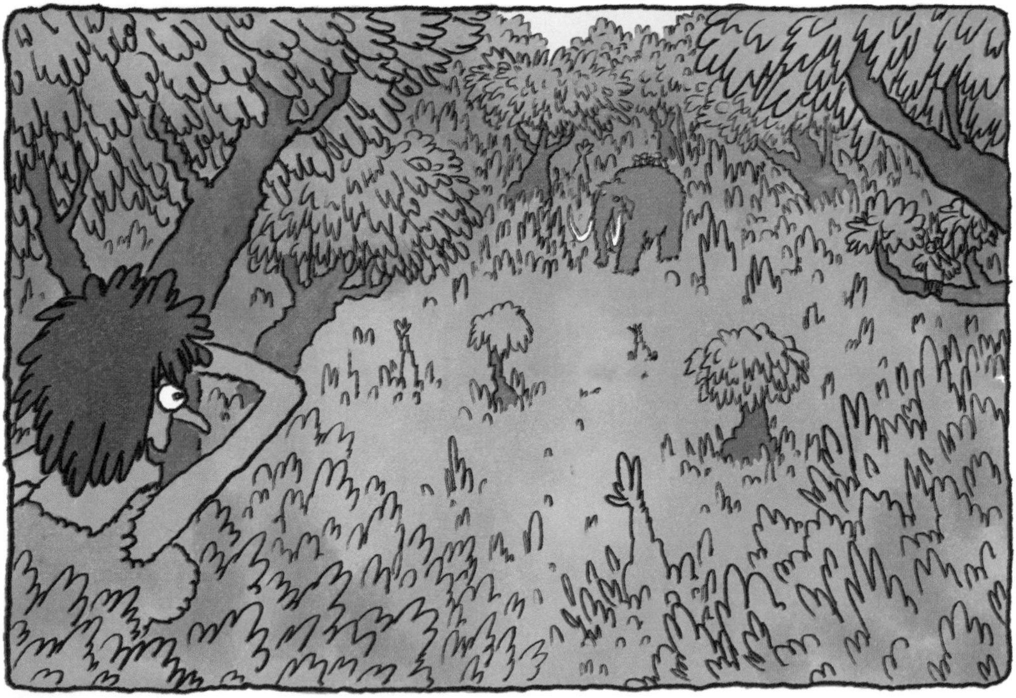

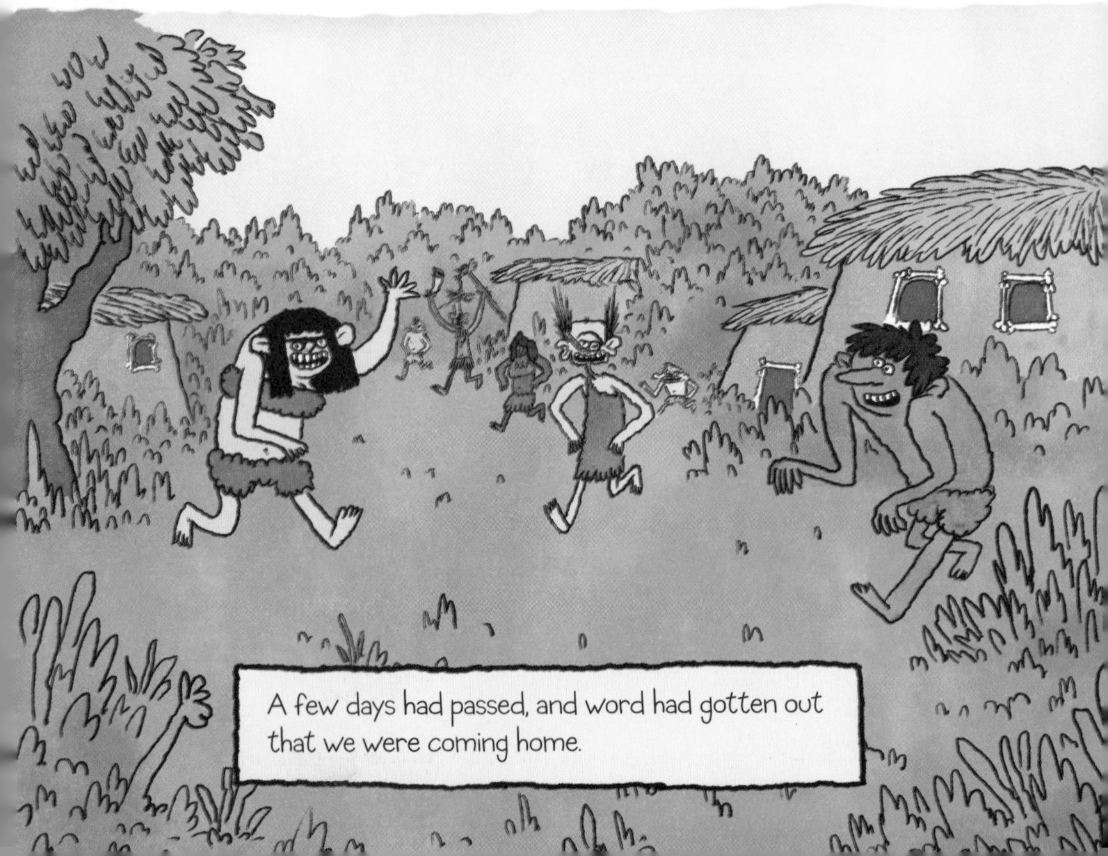
A few days had passed, and word had gotten out that we were coming home.

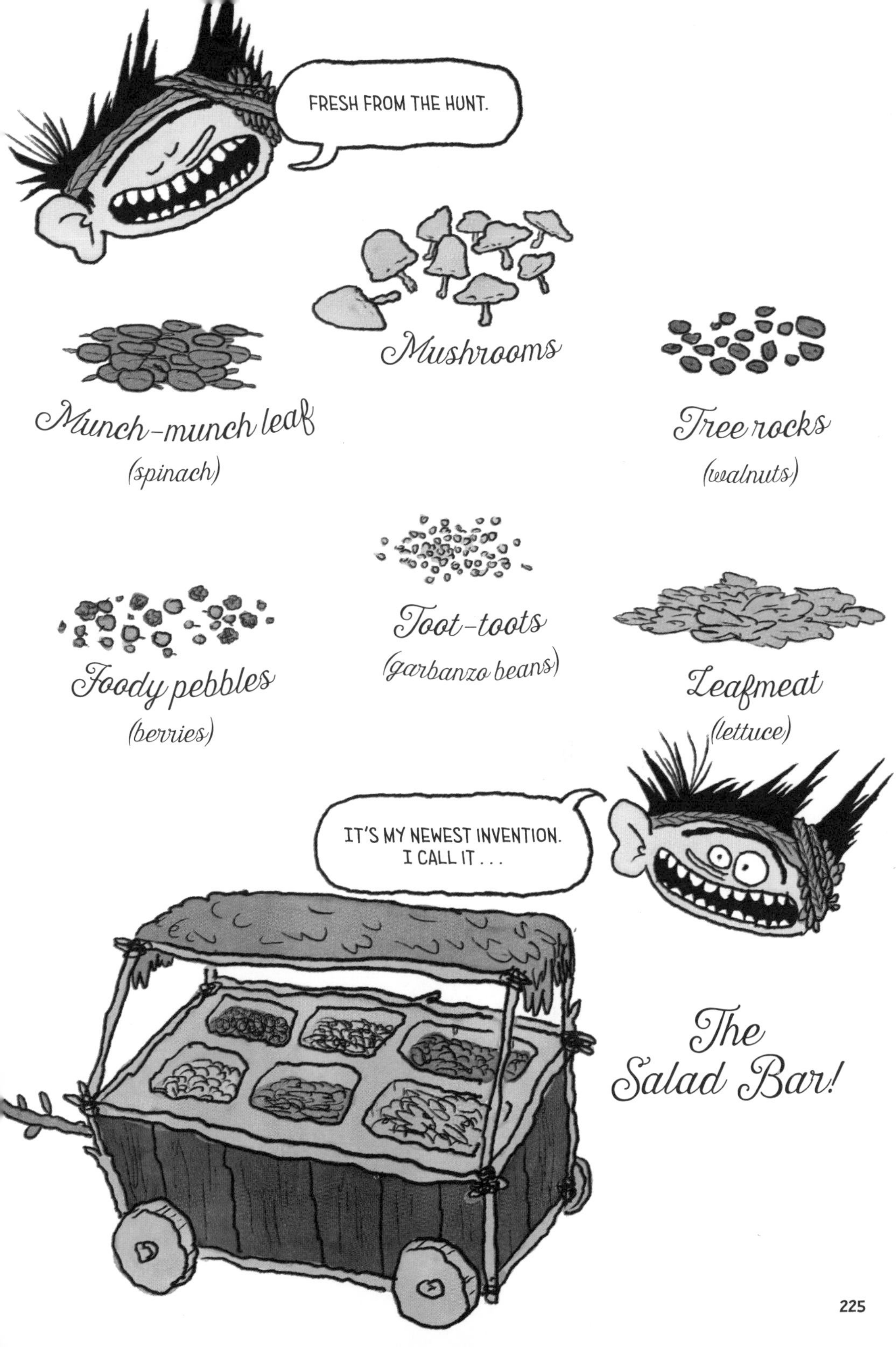
FRESH FROM THE HUNT.
Mushrooms
Munch-munch leaf
(spinach)
Tree rocks
(walnuts)
Toot-toots
(garbanzo beans)
Foody pebbles
(berries)
Leafmeat
(lettuce)
IT'S MY NEWEST INVENTION.
I CALL IT . . .
The Salad Bar!

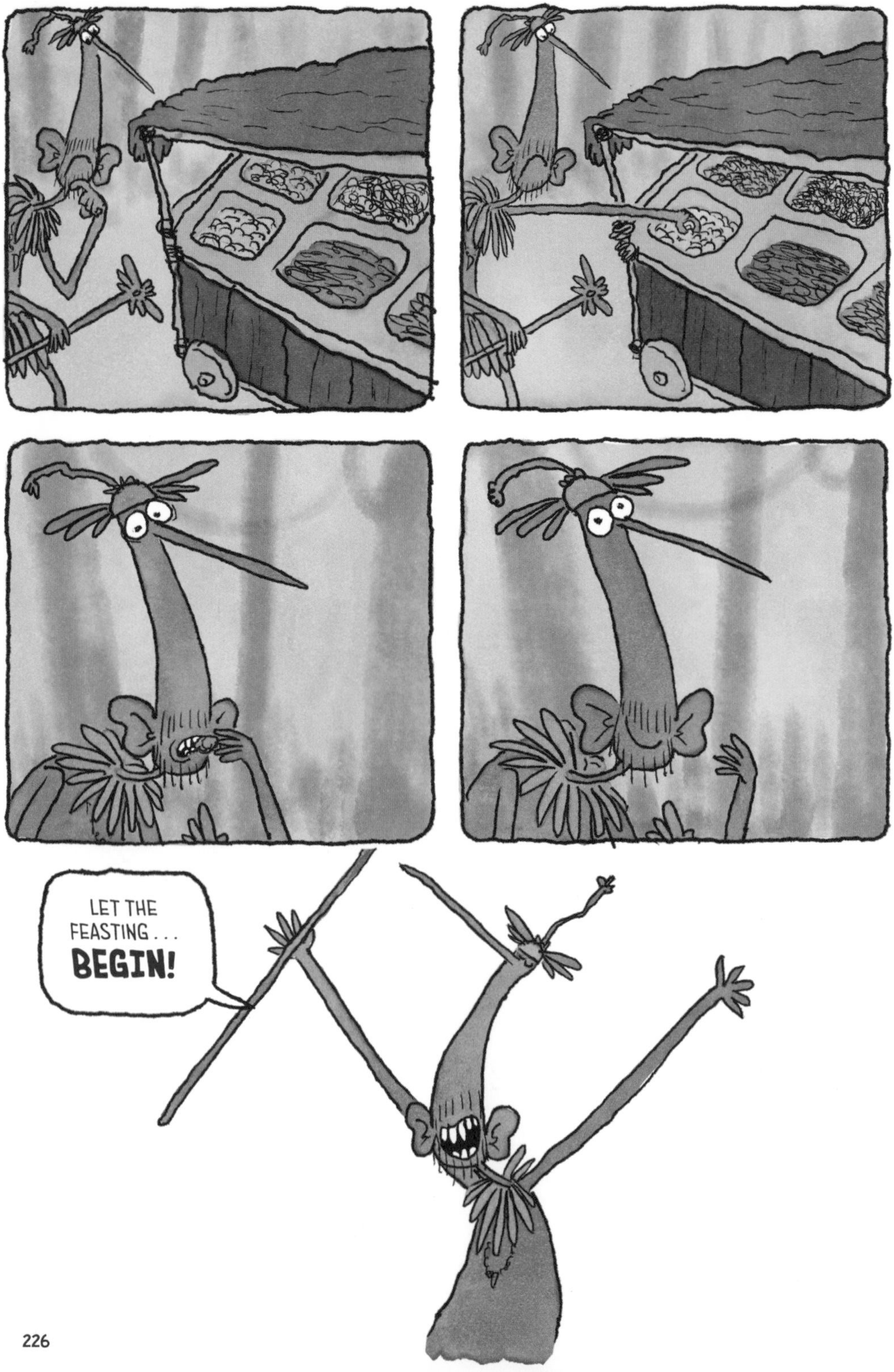
LET THE FEASTING . . . BEGIN!

227

229

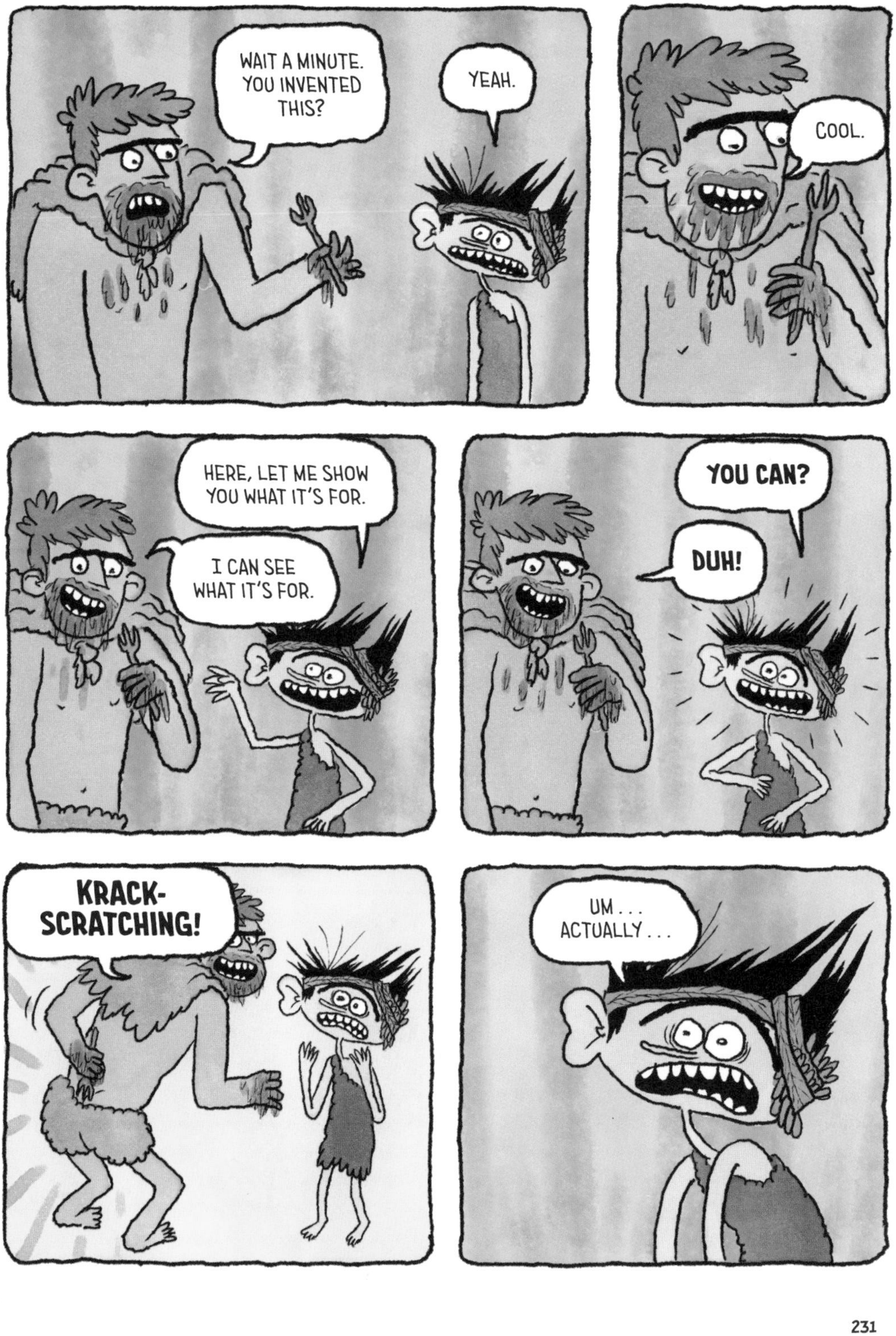
WAIT A MINUTE. YOU INVENTED THIS?
YEAH.
COOL.
HERE, LET ME SHOW YOU WHAT IT'S FOR.
I CAN SEE WHAT IT'S FOR.
YOU CAN?
DUH!
KRACK-SCRATCHING!
UM . . . ACTUALLY . . .

232

233

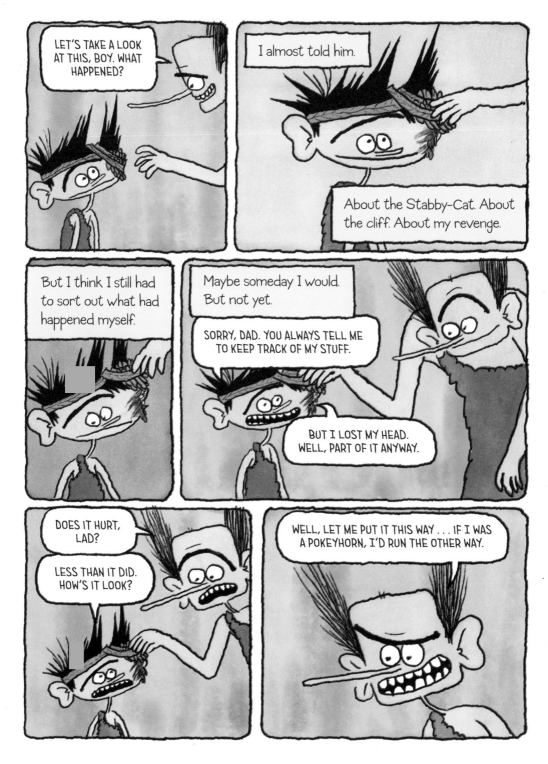

236

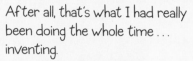

After all, that's what I had really been doing the whole time... inventing.

Not just slingshots.

And krack-scratchers.

And salad bars.

STARRING...

DAVE UNGA-BUNGA (Me!)

MR. UNGA-BUNGA

(My dad.)

BLA UNGA-BUNGA

(My sister.)

UG SMITH

(He's 100% Ug...)

ROCKIE FIREGOOD

(She keeps me on my toes.)

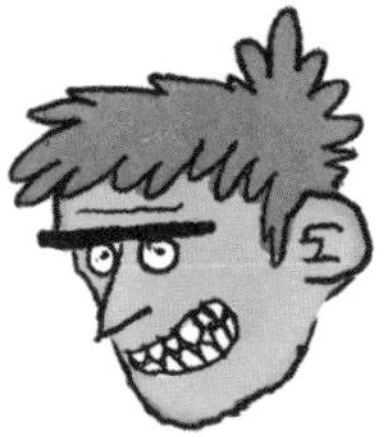

BANE BONESNAP
(Our best hunter . . .
and boy does he know it.)

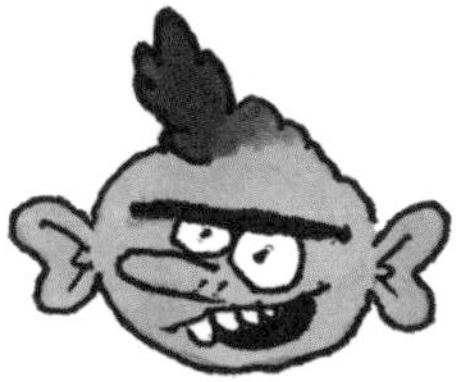

GAK CLUBBERSON
(Class clown.)

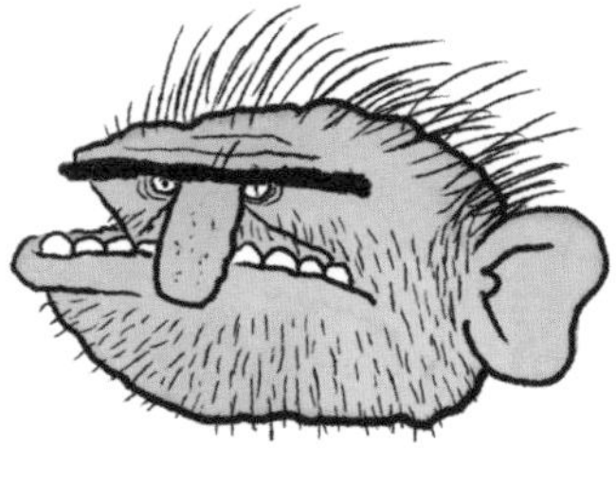

MR. GRONK
(Gym teacher
and soul crusher.)

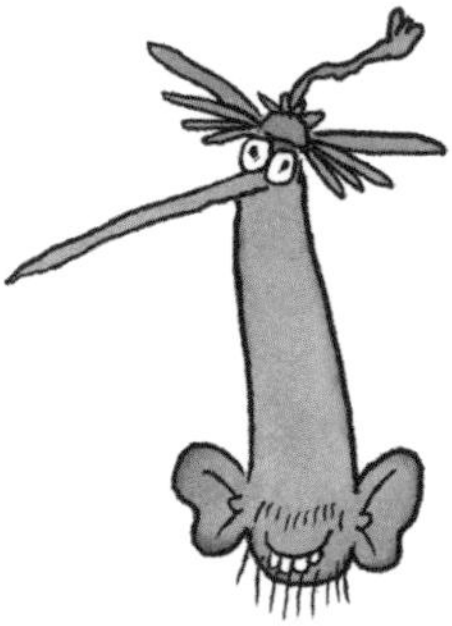

SHAMAN FABOO
(Our flashy and
fearless leader.)

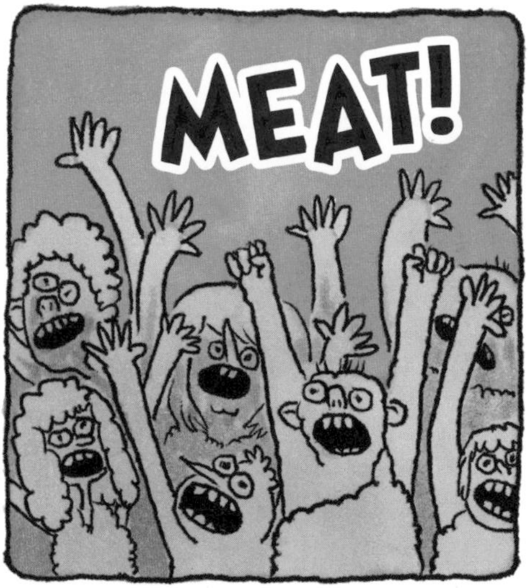
MEAT!

THE VILLAGE
(They like meat.)

Want more Caveboy Dave?

CAVEBOY DAVE
NOT SO FABOO

Coming soon!

When Dave Unga-Bunga discovers a column of smoke rising from the forest, he rushes to tell Shaman Faboo. Could this mean there's another village nearby? And are they *friendly* villagers or *evil* villagers?

The situation goes from curious to ominous when Shaman Faboo is nowhere to be found. Word gets out and panic floods the village. SHAMAN FABOO . . . HAS DISAPPEARED!

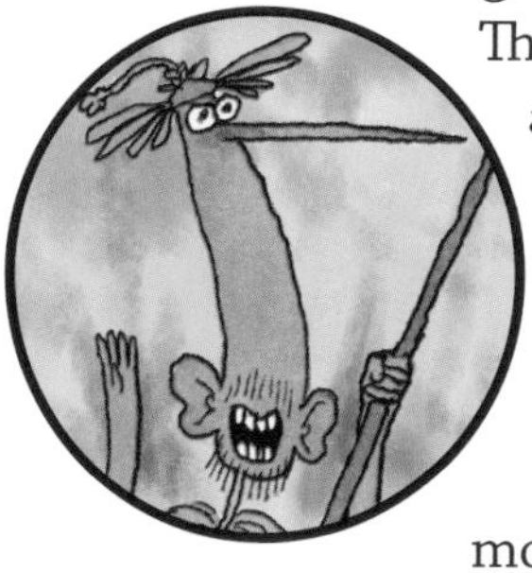

The villagers immediately look for somebody—anybody!—to tell them what to do. Dave's cool, rational thinking calms the crowd, and it becomes clear to the frightened villagers that Dave must lead . . . alongside two advisors, one of whom is Dave's dad.

Dave thinks this plan stinks worse than a month-old loincloth. He can't lead a village—he's only twelve! Will he successfully protect the village or inadvertently burn it to the ground? Will he ever find Faboo or is he stuck being the shaman forever? Is it possible to peacefully work with his dad or will they end up at each other's throats? And what about those other—most certainly sinister—villagers?

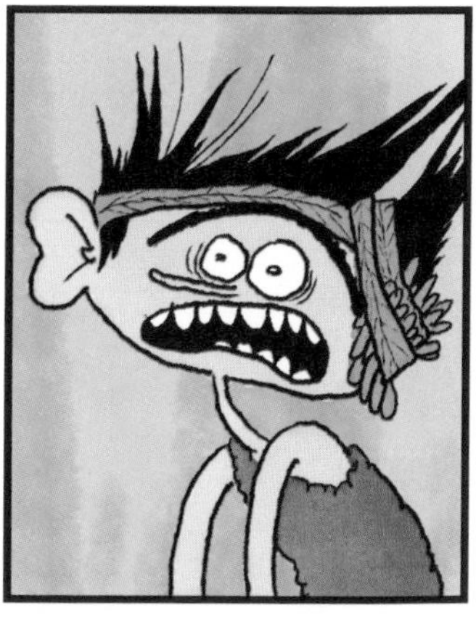

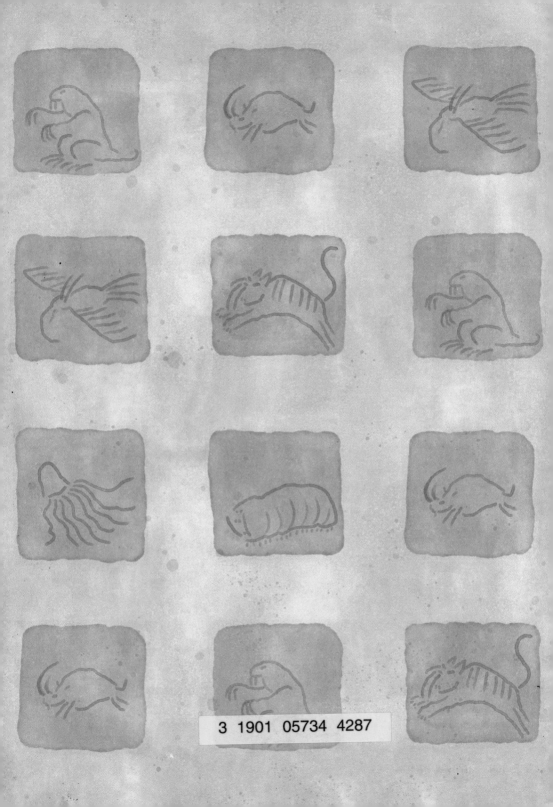